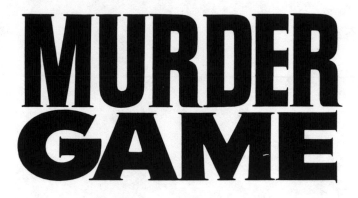

MURDER
GAME

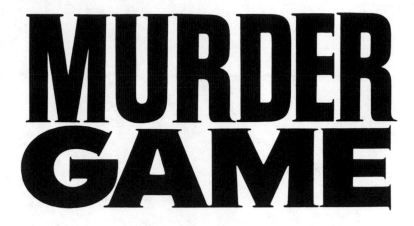

MURDER GAME

THERE'S A
$10,000
REWARD
FOR SOLVING
THE CRIME.
IT COULD BE
YOURS!

A NOVEL CREATED BY BILL ADLER
WRITTEN BY BRUCE CASSIDAY

Carroll & Graf Publishers, Inc.
New York

Copyright © 1991 by Bill Adler Books, Inc.

All rights reserved.

First Carroll & Graf edition 1991

Second printing 1991

Carroll & Graf Publishers, Inc.
260 Fifth Avenue
New York, NY 10001

Library of Congress-Cataloging-in-Publication Data

Cassiday, Bruce.
  Murder game / created by Bill Adler ; written by Bruce
Cassiday.
     p.   cm.
  ISBN 0-88184-696-1 : $18.95
  I. Adler, Bill. II. Title.
PS3553.A7955M87 1991
813'.54—dc20   91-13490
                                                  CIP

Manufactured in the United States of America

OFFICIAL CONTEST RULES

1) *HOW TO ENTER:* Complete the Official Entry Form on page 8, and answer all questions 1 through 20 (see Contest Questions). In addition, you must answer question 21, and your answer to question 21 must be *legibly printed or typed* on any 8½" by 11" paper(s) and attached to your entry form.

Clearly print or type your name, address and telephone number in the upper left corner of each sheet and mail completed entry to:

"MURDER GAME" CONTEST
P.O. Box 197
Chappaqua, NY 10514-0197

You may enter more than once, but each entry must be accompanied by an Official Entry Form plus a $1.50 non-refundable processing fee (check or money order only, payable to Carroll & Graf Publishers, Inc.). *Canadian residents only* do not require processing fee. Official Entry Forms may not be copied or mechanically reproduced. Entries must be completed in English, *legibly printed or typed only,* and must be received by November 30, 1991.

2) *JUDGING:* All questions in this contest were prepared by the author. The correct answers to all questions have also been determined by the author and have been sealed in a bank vault. The answers for questions 1 through 20 on all entries will be reviewed under the supervision of Shambroom & Hepner, Inc., an independent judging organization, whose decisions on all matters relating to this contest will be final.

All entries having correct answers to each of questions 1 through 20 will then be reviewed for the answer to question 21. The contest winner will be the one entrant who in the sole opinion of the author has best expressed the correct answer to question 21, *using 325 words or less.* The best answer will be the one judged to be the closest in meaning, logic and style of expression to the actual words the author has used in his answer. Author's answer was written in advance of contest and stored in bank vault.

If no entry has all 20 correct answers to questions 1 through 20, then contestants with the greatest number of correct answers will be judged on question 21 and will be eligible to win the contest prize. The author will not have access to the names of contestants whose entries are being judged until after the contest winner has been selected. The author's decisions on question 21 will be final.

3) *CONTEST PRIZE:* A single prize of $10,000 will be awarded. Contest winner will be notified by mail on or before March 15, 1992, and upon verification, will be awarded $10,000. Winner (parent or legal guardian if a minor) will be required to sign and return an Affidavit of Eligibility and Release form, within 15 days of receipt. Winner's name and likeness may be used for advertising or publicity purposes without additional compensation. Taxes on prize are winner's responsibility. For name of winner, send a stamped, self-addressed envelope to: "MURDER GAME" CONTEST WINNER, P.O. Box 197, Chappaqua, NY 10514-0197. To be fulfilled, all requests must be received before November 30, 1991.

4) *AUTHOR'S CONTEST ANSWERS:* For a copy of the author's solution, check the appropriate box on Entry Form and send $1.00 *(check or money order only,* payable to S&H, Inc.) to: CONTEST ANSWERS, P.O. Box 197, Chappaqua, NY 10514-0197. Requests for author's solution will be fulfilled after November 30, 1991, but not later than March 15, 1992. Requests must be received no later than November 30, 1991.

5) *ELIGIBILITY:* Contest open only to residents of U.S. and Canada, except the author, author's family, employees and their immediate families of Carroll & Graf Publishers, Inc., its subsidiaries, advertising agencies and the judging organization. Contest

is void in Arizona, Maryland, Vermont and the Province of Quebec, Canada, and wherever prohibited or restricted by law. Subject to all federal, state, provincial and local regulations. If winner is a minor, prize awarded to parent or legal guardian.

Entries or requests will not be honored unless legible and accompanied by processing fee and/or correct postage and handling fee. No responsibility will be assumed for any late, lost or misdirected mail. Entries become the property of Carroll & Graf Publishers, Inc., and will not be acknowledged or returned. No correspondence regarding this contest will be answered, acknowledged or returned.

OFFICIAL ENTRY FORM

This original form must be used to enter the contest and/or to request the author's solution insert. All answers and solutions requested must be *printed or typed,* and received no later than November 30, 1991. Check the appropriate box(es) below:

1. [   ] *Please enter me in the contest. I have:*
    a) answered questions 1 through 20 which begin on the following page;
    b) answered question 21, in 325 words or less, on an attached 8½" x 11" paper;
    c) enclosed a check or money order for the $1.50 processing fee made payable to "Carroll & Graf Publishers, Inc." (No fee required for Canadian residents only.)

    Mail Entries to: MURDER GAME CONTEST
    P.O. BOX 197
    CHAPPAQUA, NY 10514-0197

2. [   ] *Please send me the author's solution insert:*
    a) I have enclosed a check or money order for $1.00 postage & handling made payable to S&H, Inc.
    b) I understand that the solution inserts will be fulfilled after the contest closes November 30, 1991.

    Mail solution requests to: CONTEST ANSWERS
    P.O. BOX 197
    CHAPPAQUA, NY 10514-0197

Name of Entrant_____Age_____

(please print or type)

Address_____Apt_____

City_____State_____Zip_____

Telephone_(____)_____

CONTEST QUESTIONS

To be eligible for the $10,000 contest prize, print or type your answers to questions 1 through 20 below. In addition, attach your complete answer to question 21 to this form. Be sure to print or type your complete name, address, and telephone number at the top of each sheet you attach.

I) Using your powers of deduction, thinking like Inspector Birkby, write the letter that corresponds to the character's name which correctly answers each of questions 1 through 10. The same character(s) may be the correct answer to more than one question. Use only names listed below:

(A) Brett Allenby   (E) Abner Featherstone   (I) Irene Manners
(B) L. Clifford Boone (F) Mitchell Fixx   (J) Abigail McGuin
(C) William Bonney (G) Lotte Loomis   (K) Raymond McGuin
(D) Saul Brody   (H) Yves DuBois-Maison   (L) Dusty Scanlon

Q.1   Who was primarily responsible for
       kidnapping Ray McGuin?   A.1 _____

Q.2   Who assisted the kidnapper of Ray
       McGuin?   A.2 _____

Q.3   Who killed the victims of the Jimson City
       massacre?   A.3 _____

Q.4   What were the identities of the Jimson
       City victims?   A.4 _____

Q.5   Whom did Det. Giardino arrest in the bus
       terminal?   A.5 _____

Q.6   Who killed the homeless man behind
       Wendy's?   A.6 _____

Q.7   Who bugged the Raymond McGuin
       mansion?   A.7 _____

Q.8   Who blackmailed Raymond McGuin?   A.8 _____

Q.9   Who actually killed Dusty Scanlon?   A.9 _____

Q.10 Who took the million dollars ransom
       money out of the packet?   A.10 _____

II) For each of questions 11 to 20, indicate whether the points described are *"real clues"* or *"red herrings"* according to Justin

Birkby in his attempt to solve the murder mystery. Check the appropriate box for each question:

	Real Clue	Red Herring
Q.11 The postcard code	[ ]	[ ]
Q.12 The splinter of glass	[ ]	[ ]
Q.13 The written figures 3 and 4	[ ]	[ ]
Q.14 The airlines boarding pass	[ ]	[ ]
Q.15 The film *Strangers on a Train*	[ ]	[ ]
Q.16 The film *Rear Window*	[ ]	[ ]
Q.17 The spelling of "pfui"	[ ]	[ ]
Q.18 The son of Ray McGuin	[ ]	[ ]
Q.19 The crumpled $5 bill	[ ]	[ ]
Q.20 Raymond McGuin's affair	[ ]	[ ]

III) Answer question 21 on a separate 8½" × 11" paper in 325 words or less. Entries will be judged by author based on these criteria: closeness in meaning, logic and style of expression to the actual words the author has used. The author's solution to the following question was written prior to this contest and is stored in a bank vault.

Q.21   Describe how Raymond McGuin's kidnapping was executed, what the kidnapping was meant to accomplish, and how Birkby was able to solve the kidnapping mystery by using the clues at hand.

IMPORTANT: See official rules for judging criteria and procedures (rule #2). This Official Entry Form may not be mechanically reproduced and must accompany all entries and/or requests. Be sure to enclose appropriate processing fee and/or postage & handling fee. Residents of Arizona, Maryland, Vermont and the Province of Quebec, Canada, are not eligible. This form must be received by November 30, 1991.

Contents

Death in the Med

1.

Justin Birkby awoke from deep sleep—the kind of torpor you sink into when you first fall off after an exhausting day.

Someone was pounding on the stateroom door. Hard. "Mr. Birkby! Mr. Birkby! Please—"

As rapidly as he could, Justin oriented himself. Except for the suppressed panic in the voice outside, everything was as it should be. They continued churning through the Mediterranean Sea, heading south toward Malta on a special three-day luxury cruise to celebrate the Loren Hartts' first anniversary of their ownership of the yacht *Shangri-la*. The gentle tremor of the twin screws resonated in the metal decking and bulkheads. Irene Manners lay beside him, stirring irritably now out of her own cocoon of sleep. Justin's wristwatch on the night table said twelve forty-five.

He clambered out of bed, flipped on the light, and opened the door.

It was Angelica Farr. She was wide-eyed, distraught, her face flushed. Her hair was loose and disorganized. What startled Justin the most was the fact that she was cold sober. It was the first time he had seen her so since the "Malta Interlude" cruise began in Nice harbor the night before.

"What's the matter?"

"It's Scotty," Angelica said breathlessly. She meant Tammy Scott, the cosmetics queen. "I'm supposed to be meeting with her at midnight. I called and called on the phone. Then I banged on her door. I can't rouse her."

"I'm sorry, I don't quite know—"

"I have her key, of course. She gave me a duplicate when we boarded the yacht. She's always meticulous about that. She likes her privacy, but at the same time she likes punctuality. The horrible thing is I've mislaid her key."

"Come in, come in," Justin said, pulling Angelica Farr in from the corridor and closing the door. He was trying to sort out the clutter of details she had given him. He could hear Irene putting on her robe behind him. "You were to meet her in her cabin?" he asked slowly.

"Yes!" Angelica kept blinking.

"Perhaps she changed her plans and is visiting with someone."

"But I've gone all over the yacht. Top to bottom. I've checked with everyone I could."

"And you can't locate her?"

"She's in that suite. She *must* be."

Or she's overboard, thought Justin with a shudder. "Maybe she fell asleep—earplugs, that kind of thing," he said somewhat desperately.

"She doesn't *do* that!" snapped Angelica. "It's *unusual* for her to be unavailable. I'm—I'm afraid something—has happened to her!"

"Why come to me?" he asked.

Angelica stared at him. "I may act dumb, but I'm not. I think the Hartts invited you here to keep a lid on things. Just in case."

Justin was stunned. True, he *was* a retired chief inspector of Interpol. True, he had helped solve many criminal cases of international note. True, he did take on contract cases every now and then. But on this cruise he was along strictly for the fun of it. Fun? With a guest list calculated to make an East-West summit meeting look like a tea party by contrast?

Meanwhile, his inquisitive mind was beginning to function in a normal fashion. Angelica Farr was no fool. She would not have panicked unless there was good reason to. It was becoming evident to Justin that something indeed *was* wrong in that suite. Justin's experience in cases of trouble like this was to take care of his own defenses before proceeding.

His natural instinct—an instinct honed by years of police work —was to go to the top for help. "The captain," he said to Angelica. "He is in charge, according to the law of the high seas. At the owner's pleasure. He should have access to any area of the yacht."

"That's why I came to you. I need your authority to get in there. I —I don't know what we'll find, either. I'm—I'm frankly frightened."

"Darling," said Irene Manners, interrupting in her usual take-charge manner, "you two get the captain. I'll tell Mr. Hartt there's something wrong."

Within minutes Justin Birkby and Angelica Farr were standing outside the door to Tammy Scott's suite. A burly man in a thick Irish-knit fisherman's sweater hastened toward them. He was blue-eyed, round-faced, and gray-haired—the image of the seagoing skipper.

"I'm Captain Van Meter," he told them in a deep, guttural, slightly accented voice. "I'm told you've locked yourself out." This to Angelica Farr.

She shook her head briefly. "No, sir. I'm to meet with Mrs. Scott. She's inside. I can't raise her."

"I see." The big man fumbled with a cluster of keys on the end of a link chain. He selected one carefully, inserted it in the lock, and turned it. "Mrs. Scott," he called out loudly in warning. "Mrs. Scott!"

There was no answer.

The door opened smoothly inward. A nightlight glowed in the main cabin. The bed was empty, unslept in. It had not even been turned down yet and the chocolate wafer was on the pillow. Justin noted over Van Meter's shoulder that the bathroom door was ajar and the light on. He could see through the opening to the bathing area.

"My God!" gasped Angelica. She swayed momentarily, then righted herself.

"You wait outside," Justin ordered her. "The captain and I—"

She thrust him roughly aside. "I'm coming in with you!"

The three of them soon stood inside the spacious bathroom over a sunken bathtub shaped like a huge scallop. It was inlaid in black onyx, with a gold border around the edge. What was left of a foamy blanket of soap bubbles floated in a lackluster manner on the surface of a tubful of water.

Just barely visible under this uneven nimbus of foam was the dim outline of a woman's naked body. Soon Justin could discern the familiar lines of Tammy Scott's visage. Her face was half in a cloud of wasting bubbles, her eyes staring into space.

Van Meter glanced at Angelica, then knelt by the tub and reached into the water for the pulse in Tammy Scott's throat. Without a word he rose and faced Justin. "Nothing."

Bemused, Justin murmured, " 'A tale of a tub, my words are idle.' "

Angelica stared at him blankly. Justin was immediately apologetic. "Sorry. That was quite out of line. The 'tub' in Webster's words was something else entirely." Irene would have kicked him hard if she had been there. He was a showoff—an unmitigated intellectual snob. If a quotation from the Elizabethan stage surfaced during an investigation, he was sure to give it voice. Now he vowed to remain silent for the duration of this painful scene.

Angelica had finally gotten control of her tongue again. "Tammy!" she cried out in disbelief. Her eyes traveled from the tub to a shelf on the nearby wall opposite. There, plugged into an electric outlet, stood a small television set. It was turned off.

"The commercial," said Angelica, with a catch in her voice. "She had that in here to watch her commercial."

Justin and Van Meter turned toward her, frowning.

"It was a thing she did," Angelica explained apologetically. "Every night. She'd soak in a bubble bath and watch herself doing the Scott commercials. She was in them all."

"I see," said Van Meter diffidently. He may have *seen*, but he did not *understand*.

Justin glanced at Van Meter. "Do you have someone qualified to sign a death certificate, Captain?"

"Ship's doctor," said Van Meter. "I'll get him."

Justin turned to Angelica. "Did she have a heart condition?"

"No."

"Was she on drugs?" Justin persisted.

"Certainly not!"

Justin stared down at the scented bubbles that were still in the process of self-destruction. "Could she have fallen asleep and drowned?"

Loren Hartt, the owner of the yacht *Shangri-la,* appeared in the doorway, Irene Manners directly behind him. He peered over Justin's shoulder, took one hard look at the tub and what lay in it and lurched into the corner of the bathroom and threw up.

A moment or so later the yacht's millionaire owner was wiping his face off with a towel and murmuring abject apologies for his gaffe as he gazed once again on the onyx bathtub and what lay in it.

Irene was standing near Angelica, studying the room with the concentrated attention of an artist. In a moment she had a small sketch pad out of her robe, and was making a quick line drawing of the scene—a thing she was trained to do and that had made her one of the best-known sketch artists on the Continent.

Justin was paying only token attention. His mind was moving about in its own eccentric patterns. His eye moved past the tub to the television set on the shelf. In a moment he was at the shelf and holding the television set in his hand. "It's dry," he noted absently.

Van Meter had apparently picked up Justin's train of thought. "It's had an hour and a quarter to dry off. The outage occurred at eleven-thirty or thereabouts."

Justin nodded. He examined the set further and pulled at the cord attached to it. About one inch from the grommet that secured it to the set there was a freshly made knife cut—on the underside of the cord, out of sight. There, bare wires glinted in the bright bathroom light. Justin pinched the cord to bend it, exposing the wires more fully. Now he could see that the inner insulation was still damp.

"What's going on here?" Loren Hartt growled. "What's that set got to do—?" He grimaced toward the tub.

Van Meter straightened. "Mr. Birkby is pointing out that the short circuit and subsequent outage the ship experienced at eleven thirty last night might have been caused by those live wires in the tub of water." He pointed to the sunken bathtub with the body of Tammy Scott in it.

"Electrocution!" gasped Loren Hartt.

Justin nodded. "Live wires in water."

Loren Hartt frowned. "Suicide? Did she do it?"

"Scotty? Suicide?" Angelica Farr snorted. "Don't be silly!" Her eyes widened at the direction the discussion was taking.

Irene was not speaking, but she was following the conversation closely. Even now she was making a drawing of the television set in place on the shelf. Her eyes were moving about the room for other details she might like to picture.

"Whoever dropped the set into the tub pulled the plug out immediately afterward—once the current had done its job. If the cord was still attached to the outlet, the short would have continued."

"What you're saying is that somebody dropped that set into the tub *deliberately* to kill her!" Angelica said.

Justin nodded. "It certainly was no accident. If the set had fallen off the shelf, it would have landed on the floor." He turned to Van Meter apologetically. "I don't *know,* of course, but it seems a logical deduction."

"If she was electrocuted," Angelica asked, shuddering, "why can't we see any burns on her body?"

"Her appearance is compatible with cases of electrocution of a body submerged in water," Justin explained. "No one is really sure *how* death occurs. One theory is that the current of electricity causes immediate death by ventricular fibrillation of the heart. Another hypothesizes that death results from the paralyzing action of the current on the respiratory centers of the medulla oblongata. Whatever causes it, the body appears the same as it might if a heart attack or a drug overdose had occurred."

"You've *seen* this kind of death before?" Loren Hartt asked incredulously.

Justin nodded briefly. Irene hid a smile, and she began a rough draft of Loren Hartt's expression.

Loren grimaced. "We need your help, Mr. Birkby."

"In what way?" Justin wondered.

"We've got to do something immediately about finding out who's responsible for this outrage. Before we dock tomorrow in Malta." He turned to Van Meter. "Captain, you're in full charge. Might I suggest that we delegate Justin Birkby to conduct an investigation into this matter? He has been an authorized agent of the law—a chief inspector of Interpol and a one-time member of Britain's Scotland Yard. Isn't that correct, Mr. Birkby?"

Irene paused in her work. "That is correct, Mr. Hartt."

"Certainly," said Van Meter, gazing at Justin with new respect.

"I'll alert the guests to this development," Loren Hartt said. "Perhaps you'd like to see each guest individually as soon as possible?"

Justin sighed. "I haven't really said yes," he protested. The protest was a feeble one. So feeble that Irene Manners smiled again, turning to Angelica for a profile.

"You must!" snapped Angelica, her eyes glinting in anger over the death of her employer.

"I agree," Justin said. "But you must allow me to conduct my investigation in my own manner." He eyed Loren Hartt. "I hope I'll have everyone's cooperation."

"I'll see to that," Loren said.

There goes my vacation, thought Justin with a philosophical shrug. His mind was occupied with other things. He was looking back into the immediate past, at events and incidents that had occupied him since he and Irene had left Nice airport for the *Shangri-la.*

" 'There are a thousand doors to let out life,' " he said absently.

Irene inclined her head toward him. "Philip Massinger. I remember that one. You're beginning to repeat yourself, dear."

Justin ignored her, not actually realizing she was drawing a front view of him, now. He was thinking that perhaps somewhere along the line of his review of the past thirty hours he could uncover some important clue as to who had chosen to open one of those thousand doors that had let out the life of Tammy Scott.

2.

At 6 p.m. on a balmy June day on the French Riviera, Justin Birkby and Irene Manners boarded a trim little eight-passenger Sikorsky helicopter at the Nice airport and took their seats behind a fortyish man who had preceded them aboard. The pilot followed Justin and Irene into the cabin, slammed the hatch closed in a businesslike manner, and moved forward into the cockpit.

There was a murmur as the pilot exchanged data with the tower and then toggle switches were flipped and the four big propellers began fanning the air above the ship.

The lone passenger in front of Justin turned around and smiled engagingly at him. He had a gangling, loose-jointed, Jimmy Stewart look about him. His voice, too, was like the actor's.

"I'm Ray McGuin," he said in a broad midwestern drawl.

His eyes darted back and forth between Justin and Irene, and then he grinned again, his own patented introduction to a joke.

"And I guess you know who you are."

He turned around in his seat, waiting for the plane to lift off.

Justin raised an eyebrow. Irene stifled a comment. Then Justin leaned forward and touched McGuin on the shoulder. The lean man turned slightly.

"Justin Birkby. And this is Irene Manners."

McGuin turned fully around, gazed at Justin and then at Irene. His eyes flicked back to Justin. A slight smile, another hesitation: "I'd have guessed Mr. and Mrs."

Irene was about to say something in response when abruptly the open cockpit door was filled with the hulking, irritated figure of the pilot.

"Just got word two more passengers are on their way." There was a pause. "With a Riviera police escort! We wait." With that he stomped over to the hatch and cracked it open. The hatch folded out and the aluminum steps somersaulted over to touch the tarmac.

By habit, Justin Birkby had been turning the name Raymond McGuin over in his mind. As often was the case with Justin, the name suddenly took on a great deal more meaning than the group of phonemes and nephomes that composed it. Ray McGuin. Raymond Standish McGuin. Of course, he *would* be a guest aboard the Hartts' enormous yacht. The host and hostess —Loren and Steffi Hartt—were probably the richest couple in New York City. Real estate. Construction. Small airlines. Atlantic City hotels. All sorts of goodies.

Certainly they would know Ray McGuin—numero uno on the charity circuit—a rich philanthropist who put his money where his mouth was, who helped run some of the country's most prestigious charities. Although he managed a fund-raising organization, he lent his name to dozens of the country's worthiest charities. His name on a fund-raising letterhead was tantamount to opening up the coffers of Fort Knox by stimulating the well-to-do to pledge obscenely large contributions.

An anomaly, thought Justin—a personality out of another era. They came more whippet-lean now, more yuppie sleek, more honed and burnished. It just wasn't the style now to *be* a low-key type like Ray McGuin. Justin was making no rational effort to assess the man, but was simply indulging in his usual quota of curiosity about people. After all, what could be more interesting than to wonder about people and try to ascertain what made them tick?

But this wasn't work; this was play. The Nice interlude was in no way an assignment for Justin. If he had been on special duty for Interpol, for example, he would not only have pulled McGuin's package long ago from his contacts in Washington through Scotland Yard, but he would also have called up at least a half dozen terrorist dossiers from the Interpol reserve itself. Those were the best in the world for conciseness, accuracy, and completeness. They had to be. After all, Justin had helped establish their format. Some of the classic profiles in the recesses of Lyons's basement were in his own words.

McGuin was no criminal. But Justin could always tap Interpol's special file on the world's richest families. In the international world of terrorism and kidnapping, oftentimes the habits of the *victims* were as important as the habits of the terrorists. And that was the area in which Justin's expertise was second to none.

Irene's hand tightened on his wrist. "Listen!"

He heard it—the wailing, skirling, banshee squeal of a siren in the night—distant at first but rapidly approaching from the direction of Nice proper. He peered out through the helicopter window toward Nice harbor, where he knew the *Shangri-la* lay at anchor, a shining, glittering opalescence of brilliance and glistening jewels in the night, just where she had been all afternoon and evening, waiting—waiting and causing Riviera sunbathers to salivate with envy at the sight of all that glamour and *money* so close by, and yet so . . . untouchable.

Most partygoers boarded yachts in sleek, showy tenders. The chopper was apparently the Hartts' tiny extravagance—their idea of showy opulence. Justin realized he was making an entirely unwonted and unfair character appraisal of them. They deserved better. After all, they were not *his* acquaintances. It was Irene's expertise and fame that had merited this coveted invitation to the Hartts' "Malta Interlude" party. After all, a retired Interpol chief inspector had no reason to be part of this celebration of conspicuous consumption. For that matter, it was doubtful that even the best sketch artist on the Continent did, either. But Irene was always getting—well—the "Irene" treatment.

"*Your* people, darling," Irene said with just a touch of ironic amusement.

"Indeed," murmured Justin distantly. It was so like her to tease him about his connections with law and order and the hateful gendarmerie—in the snide, underplayed manner of the superior liberal.

"Those guests must be connected to deserve that kind of reception!" Irene mused.

"They are. Or, *she* is. It's Tammy Scott." The man named McGuin had turned his open, prairie-seasoned face toward Irene with an easy smile. "I saw her in Nice today. Reducing a terrified clerk to quivering jelly. You can bet she's the only one with the gall to order a police escort—and get it."

Irene gripped Justin's arm hard. "Tammy Scott!"

McGuin had faced front again, folding his arms over his chest, purposefully letting it be inferred that he was bored with celebrities of dubious social status.

The sirens screamed and the air was soon vibrating with their undulating wails. There was a screech of brakes, a splatter of gravel spewed up from the tarmac, and the tearing of rubber against the pavement. Abruptly and happily, all sound ceased. Car doors slammed. Spike heels clattered over the tarmac. The three passengers in the helicopter could hear the murmur of angry voices, the hard sharp snap of steps on the aluminum treads, and quite suddenly and marvelously there she was, limned in the hatchway, the soft backglow of Nice's foothills acting as a most unsuitable backdrop to showcase this figure of twentieth-century royalty.

Tammy Scott.

Even Justin recognized the face that was on almost every package of Scott Fragrance, Scott Powder, Scott Eyeliner, Scott

Lipstick, Scott Firming Cream. Tammy Scott was the icon of the cosmetics world. Tammy Scott. The Woman of a Thousand Faces—Every One of Them Beautiful.

She was an ad man's dream, Justin realized.

She was glaring at him. Well, not at Justin Birkby alone. She was able to glare simultaneously at Justin, at Irene, at McGuin, and even at the pilot, who was almost behind her, leaning over to slap the hatch closed again.

Without a word Tammy Scott turned to the woman who had come in with her, waved her hand at the three passengers, and cooed in an imitation finishing-school bray: *"La bonne blaque!"*

Justin shuddered at the woman's fraudulent accent. It was one thing to try to pronounce French words; it was still another to *pretend* sophistication and betray such a lack of familiarity with the real thing. There was also the woman's utter churlishness. What a joke, indeed. What right had she to put the three of them down before she even tried to find out who they were?

As the hatch slammed shut the pilot stood erect and stared at Tammy Scott. She was tall and trim and firm, a statuesque figure of heroic proportions. She had big bones and a superb skeletal structure that revealed a power paralleling her psychological profile. A dangerous woman, thought Justin instinctively. Yet the total effect was one of effulgent glamour. She was dressed in a stratospherically expensive party gown, and there was something in her eyes that showed she had the ability to dominate everyone and everything in her line of vision.

"Ladies," bawled out the pilot in his controlled tall-Texan drawl, "you'll find two seats at the rear. Now, if you'll just settle down," he continued, turning toward the cockpit, "I'll get this show on the road." And he disappeared.

Tammy Scott glowered at the after-image of him. But it was her companion who responded. There was no better way to describe her than with the time-worn word *plain*—plain features, plain hair, plain clothes, plain makeup. A strange persona for an associate of the world's most visible beauty. But of course! Justin thought. Beauty and the Beast.

The plain one was obviously unsteady on her feet. It certainly was not the unsteadiness of the helicopter. The aircraft was as steady as a rock. Yet Tammy's companion was teetering on her sensible shoes as if they might be unfamiliar spike heels six inches high.

Now she curled her lip and spoke in sardonic caricature of the pilot's words—although she was unable to reproduce his tall-Texan accent. Her words, in fact, seemed to be very much slurred and uncertain, but what she said was quite clear.

"Ladies and gentlemen, this woman with me is Tammy Scott, the great cosmetologist. I'm Angelica Farr, and don't let this face fool you. It's an incredibly cunning disguise. Beneath this mask lies one of history's great beauties!"

"Shut up and sit," snarled Tammy Scott. There was anger and spite in the voice.

Angelica seemed frozen to the spot. She wove about there like a reed in a wind, unable to free her feet. Tammy Scott quite suddenly unleashed herself from her indolent stance and aimed a powerful roundhouse blow at her assistant's shoulder. Angelica, startled and unable to cope with the strength of the blow, staggered backward, trying vainly to keep her balance. Instead she fell limply into Irene Manners's unprepared lap.

Justin's blood boiled. He rose and made a move toward Angelica Farr. However, realizing that the woman was most certainly drunk, he caught himself in frustration and sat down again. He glowered at the cosmetics queen, studying her face with new insight. The woman was unpredictable, unstable—and extremely ruthless. She was someone who should be watched carefully. The rage that he had seen in her face had vanished now. She slid silently into the rear seat of the helicopter and demurely fastened her seat belt.

Angelica Farr, completely chastened and pink in the face, picked herself up off Irene Manners, apologized in a slurred, once-over-numbly voice, and crept to the back row to follow suit.

In a moment the aircraft slowly lifted and they were airborne. The cosmetics queen caught Irene Manners's eye and winked broadly. "She's my gofer. Isn't it a shame? All that beauty and no talent."

Angelica Farr choked at the insult, reddening and holding her temper with difficulty. Sometime, sometime, her manner indicated, she would be able to respond to her tormenter. And when she did . . .

" 'You must be proud, bold, pleasant, resolute,' " Justin quoted, " 'and now and then stab, as occasion serves.' "

Irene heard him. "Really, Justin!" she snapped.

"Apologies!" Justin raised his hands in surrender. "To Christopher Marlowe."

McGuin turned half around in his seat and nodded affably at Tammy Scott. "Hello, Mrs. Scott."

"Really!" Tammy Scott groaned as she took a harder look and recognized him. "I gave at the office. I simply don't *have* another million and a half for you tonight."

Ray McGuin chuckled, playing the good sport. Justin saw the line of crimson creeping above his collar and into his light blond stringy hair. What an abrasive personality the rich cosmetics millionaire was, Justin thought.

Next to him he could see Irene with her sketch book out, casting Tammy Scott's head and shoulders into lines and shadows. She had caught the woman's obvious glamour along with her interesting undercurrent of malicious evil.

Justin's mind, operating on its own, had by now sorted out the details of Tammy Scott's tangled relationships. Sam Scott was her fourth husband. She had dumped two, or they had walked out on her—the evidence was unclear—and she had buried the third. It was Sam Scott who had raised her from rags to riches. *He* had a thriving cosmetics business that she inherited, lock, stock, and barrel, when he blew his brains out on the living-room floor one evening as he sat watching "The McNeil/Lehrer Report" on public television.

And then Justin had the last detail that filled in the big picture. Tammy's husband number 2 had been Loren Hartt. Long before Loren married Steffi, his current spouse. Justin remembered a rancorous trial at which Tammy Hartt had tried to walk off with the major portion of Loren's fortune. She'd lost the case, but she'd made him look like a prize jackass—a rich, silly, wimpish nerd, Loser of the Year.

Odd were the ways of the very, very rich, Justin mused, to invite someone despised and detested to their opulent yacht for a three-day cruise to Malta. Odd indeed.

3.

From the deck of the *Shangri-la* Steffi Hartt watched as the helicopter lowered toward the landing pad in the stern. Squinting against the glaring reflection of the lights focused on the ship and the pad, she could see the pilot's face through the rounded strip of glass windshield as he maneuvered the aircraft carefully to touchdown.

She removed the crumpled fax from the pocket of her windbreaker and read the names on it. Tammy Scott and Angelica Farr. Who Angelica Farr was made no matter. It was Tammy Scott in whom Steffi was most interested. Even now that name could provoke her generally unflappable husband Loren Hartt into a towering rage that was as magnificent as it was semifraudulent.

Steffi was quite aware that the love-hate relationship that had always existed between Tammy and Loren tended to shift gears from forward to reverse and vice versa at the drop of some invisible hat. Even now Steffi could feel the rage surge within her at the memory of such a scene on the day of her wedding to Loren.

With nothing but vitriol on Loren's tongue concerning Tammy Scott, he had been spotted by Steffi's own sister in a rather secluded part of the garden at the family's Palo Alto home raptly engaged in whispered conversation with the hated Tammy, one arm half around her waist and gently encircling and stroking her rounded bottom.

Steffi Hartt—not even Steffi Hartt then, but Stephanie Johnson—had confronted the two lovebirds, spoken her piece to the craven Loren, and informed the grinning Tammy that she had better be out of his reach within ten minutes or Steffi would run the spikes of her heels through Tammy's skull preparatory to stuffing the rest of her down the garbage disposal.

But that was long ago. Steffi's one shortcoming—her firecracker temper—had since been placed firmly under the control of its owner. She was now a lady. At least on the surface. Just let Tammy fire up her incipient rage again, however, and . . .

Now, with the roaring of the engines, the Sikorsky settled uneasily onto the yacht's pad and the grinding roar of the motor faded as the pilot shut it down. The propellers continued their rotations above the fuselage, gradually coasting to a stop.

The hatch opened, the steps came down, and the pilot waved and stood aside. First out was Tammy Scott, of course, as Steffi had guessed. Steffi lifted her hand to wave, painting a smile on her face, but quite suddenly Loren was in front of her—from where he had appeared she had not the slightest notion—running up to the chopper, with a big broad grin on his face.

"Tammy!"

"Darling!" cried Tammy in that totally false sincerity cultivated by the rich and famous, waving her Mandarin fingernails at him. The searchlight that could be so cruel on others made her outsize perfection of form suddenly luminescent and unforgettably gorgeous. Steffi's heart sank.

And then, to her wretched disgust, the two did a Hollywood kiss and Steffi was frozen in absolute disbelief as Loren helped his first wife down the steps to the deck of the *Shangri-la.* In a moment they were face to face with Steffi.

"It's Tammy, love!" said Loren as if he had just discovered the secret of water displacement.

"So it is," Steffi whispered, smiling brightly nevertheless, holding out her hand.

It was duly taken in Tammy's cool dry one. They engaged in a struggle not to touch one another as they nuzzled cheeks, then rapidly separated.

"Angelica!" shouted Tammy, turning away from Steffi.

Perhaps the plainest woman Steffi had ever seen appeared behind the gorgeous Tammy Scott, her eyes slightly glazed, her mouth turned up in a grimace of distaste as she tried to negotiate the steps down. She was tipsy, Steffi realized with amusement. Who would not be, working for Tammy Scott?

"Oh, there you are, you gorgeous hunk." Tammy beamed. She turned to Loren. "Isn't she just lovely? It keeps me concerned about my own beauty, you know. Such competition!"

Steffi could see Loren wince, but pretend amusement. If looks could kill, thought Steffi, watching the young woman drag down the heavy carry-on bag and set it at Tammy's feet. *Bitch,* the young woman mouthed cheerfully out of sight of Tammy's watchful eyes.

"Well, don't just deliver that luggage to me as if it's a prize pheasant I've just shot! Move it to my suite!" snarled Tammy. "Can you help us, Steffi?" she purred, turning to Steffi and putting on that phony smile. "Have you got a crewman or some urchin to direct my beautiful one to my hutch?"

Hutch, thought Steffi. Wherever did she dig up that term? Anything for a putdown. Smiling gently, she turned and signaled the nearest crewman in sight, who came hopping.

In a low voice she instructed him to offload the Scott luggage from the chopper, and to lead Tammy Scott's private secretary to the Gold Suite.

"Yes, ma'am," said the crewman, and he approached Angelica Farr. He picked up the luggage, snapped to attention, and waved her to follow him. With that the two of them trooped off and Tammy turned to Loren, who had been watching the byplay with muted interest.

"Oh, here's my fabulous charity circuit leader," Tammy sang out, waving to Ray McGuin, who was just descending from the aircraft with his carry-on. "Do you know the Hartts?" And she began the introductions.

Steffi was more interested in the man and woman who followed McGuin out of the plane. Something about the man intrigued her. He was not particularly attractive, but he had a cool, reserved, unpretentious way about him that put her at instant ease. The young woman he was with was strikingly beautiful in an underplayed but stylish fashion. She had a round face, with bright, humorous brown eyes, and thick brown hair. There was something fanciful and exotic about the way she was put together.

She moved over to the man. "You're Mrs. Hartt," said the man, executing a slight bow without seeming to do anything out of the ordinary. "I'm Justin Birkby, and this is Irene Manners."

Oh, yes, thought Steffi. They went together, like cake and frosting. No one knew whether or not they were man and wife or singles working the doubles game. It was the attitude of the woman, mostly, that spelled out the attachment; no one was going to get him away from her. Yet withal the woman was gentle, calm, and self-assured.

As for the man, he was in total control. His game was simply to play it as cool and calm as he could—until something occurred to disrupt his routine. Steffi knew the type well.

Justin Birkby. Very well. And Irene Manners.

"It's Irene who's on your guest list," Justin confessed with a smile. "Sketch artist for *Le Figaro.*"

Of course! thought Steffi. Irene's sketches of celebrities, noncelebrities, animals, politicians, actors, clowns, children— they were world-famous. How several lines of ink could bring to life so many different kinds of people and things was not within Steffi's understanding. But Irene Manners had the knack.

"I'm Steffi Hartt."

"Of course."

"Your wife sketches," Steffi ventured diffidently to the man, "whereas you—?"

"—am a victim of early retirement," chuckled Justin.

"Stockbroker? Arbitrager? No? Politician! No? Chief executive officer of whatever? No? Dear me—"

"Chief inspector of Interpol," Irene broke in, smiling in delight at Steffi. She put out her hand. "You're every bit as interesting as your pictures," she told Steffi, a kind of pixyish interest shining through her expression.

"Until I've been sketched by Irene Manners, I feel I simply haven't been noticed."

Irene had the grace to blush.

"You cheap dirt bag!" screamed a voice nearby.

Everyone turned.

Of course, the crier was Tammy Scott. She had been standing chatting with Loren Hartt, but now she had turned from Loren and was facing another woman wearing a night jacket partly covered by a lime-green shawl.

Steffi recognized Dara Lukas. Dara was no longer young. But she had retained much of her early vaunted beauty. For a journalist, beauty was one of those extras that few of the tribe ever managed. But then, Dara Lukas—"Brown" was her working name—had never been ordinary.

Brilliant, scholarly, politically astute, she had managed to become in the several decades she had worked for the *Los Angeles Times* one of the top names in world journalism. She had covered Korea toward the end, and Vietnam toward the beginning, and had traveled all over the world interviewing heads of state and writing about them and their opinions of geopolitics.

Two years before, she had written a casual biography of the female prime minister of an Asian state. There was a good deal of sexual revelation in the book; the woman was attractive and active. The publication of the book was an event. It became an instant best-seller and went into edition after edition; it was translated into most of the languages of the world.

Dara continued to do her weekly columns on politicians and geopolitics, but of course her publisher wanted another block-buster exposé from her.

"I heard you were sending people into my files!" Tammy was screaming. "If you don't back off, I'll tear your eyes out!"

Dara Lukas, maintaining an icy silence, simply wrapped her arms in the shawl around her shoulders and stared at the cosmet-ics queen. "I have no idea what you're talking about."

"Come on, Dara! This is me—Tammy Scott! You and I played around in high school—trying on all the jocks on the football team for size, and half the scholars as well! You don't fool me one bit. You're putting together another of those monstrosities you call books—and this one on me!"

Dara's smile was cool and crooked, her gray eyes glinting like glacier ice. "Who would be the slightest bit interested in finding out about your secret life, my dear?"

"Get off my case, you blackmailer. I said *blackmailer!* I'll sue the shit out of you if I catch one of your sleaze bags on my property again. Investigative reporter. Bullshit! You're a peeping Thomasina. That's what. But you're not going to peep on me!"

Dara's lips curled, and she drew herself up to turn away from Tammy Scott, but Tammy was too quick for her. Bunching up her fist in a fury, she swung from as far down as she could reach, clouting Dara on the cheekbone with the return blow.

Stunned, Dara fell backward, stepping quickly to keep her bal-ance. Unfortunately, the punch had loosened whatever of her wigs she was wearing. It fell askew and then slid to the decking. The brilliant spotlight, still illuminating the area around the cool-ing helicopter, shone brightly on her hair—which was combed tightly to her skull, quite gray, streaked with white, and thinning visibly.

Justin was reminded of the scene at the beheading of Mary, Queen of Scots, that glamorous redhead, whose head had dropped into the basket separated from a bright flaming wig, the skull's gray hairs combed close, revealing to the world the former queen in her most unbecoming and revealing light.

No one said a word.

Dara's eyes were unreadable. She leaned over and picked up the wig carefully, brushed it off, adjusted it to her head, stretched it into place, and once again pulled her shawl tightly around her shoulders.

"You always were a peasant, weren't you?"

For once, the unflappable Tammy Scott was unhinged. The shock of her own action, the embarrassing revelation of Dara's graying hair, the ensuing look of pure hatred in the journalist's eyes—Tammy could hardly believe what she had done.

"Really, Dara—"

"You haven't seen the last of me, Tammy." Dara glowered a moment, turned stiffly, and vanished through a door into a nearby corridor.

Steffi watched the journalist beat a retreat from Tammy Scott, almost able to *feel* the animosity smoldering in the air.

Tammy shook herself free from whatever trance held her. "Where's that drunken Sherpa of mine?" she howled, and she strode off down the deck.

Steffi looked up and saw Loren eying her.

"What was *that* all about?" Loren wondered.

"I don't know," Steffi admitted, "but I can sure guess."

4.

Much had been written about the *Shangri-la* and its amenities. Yet to call golden faucets and richly embroidered duvets "amenities" was to make a mockery of the English language. The yacht had originally been built for an Iranian sheik, but had been sold during one of the stock market's volatile dives in the late eighties. The buyer was a rich Japanese businessman, who had then sold it to the Hartts.

It resembled most of all a floating palace—192 feet long, two-thirds as long as Donald Trump's famous *Trump Princess*. It was designed like a cruise ship, but decorated like an Eastern potentate's harem. While Donald Trump's enormous yacht was able to accommodate twenty-two guests, the *Shangri-la* was only able to take twelve, plus the two owners. It took a support crew of thirty-five to service the craft, however!

Each suite was designed in a different manner, and named for and decorated with a precious metal or stone: the Gold Suite; the Emerald Suite; the Lapis Lazuli Suite; the Opal Suite. Bathrooms were designed with saunas in some, Jacuzzis in others, fantastically shaped tubs in still others.

When Justin Birkby and Irene Manners were ushered into their suite, they could immediately see the gem-coding to which they had been assigned.

"Oh, it's opal!" gasped Irene Manners.

Justin nodded. There *was* an opalescent color to the décor. The bathroom fixtures were set with opals, and so were the fittings in the small bar built into the corner of the cabin.

Eyes alight, Irene could not stifle her delight. Nor could she restrain herself from moving through the suite and touching everything that glittered and shone—quite like a small child at Christmastime, even though such a role was out of character for the sophisticated boulevardière that Irene Manners was.

"I'll never be able to face our apartment in Lyons after this!" she sighed, flopping down on the comfortable opalescent bed.

Justin was peering about. "It's all a tasteless joke, darling," he murmured, shuddering at the glitz and the artificial glamour of the Hartts' famous logo on the headboard of the bed: a pink heart pierced by an arrow.

"Don't be so grumpy! This is *living.*"

"Is *this* the kind of thing that makes Tammy Scott the impossible bitch she is?"

"Spoilsport."

Justin continued his study of the interior of their suite and sank down on the bed by Irene. "What's the dress code for tonight?"

"Come as you are!" Irene informed him. "Eight o'clock on deck, bon voyage party as we weigh anchor! So the room steward said."

"I think I'll take a turn around the deck. You interested?"

"I'm interested, but I'm not ready yet. I think I'll stay here and take a shower. I'm all grungy from the flight down from Lyons. You go. I'll be out in half an hour."

She bounced up off the bed and headed for the bathroom door, making a fast grab for her carry-on as she did so.

Justin leaned back on the bed and found himself wondering what on earth had prompted Loren and Steffi Hartt to invite Tammy Scott along on this three-day cruise. If anyone should *not* be welcome, it would be Tammy Scott. After what she had done to Loren Hartt, you would think Loren would invite her only to her own execution. And yet, all the affability in the world had spread like treacle on the deck when he had greeted her aboard tonight.

"What was that?" Justin asked aloud.

"What was what, dear?" Irene asked through the bathroom door.

"Someone rapped."

"You're just imagining things."

Justin hesitated, about to step across the cabin to open the door. At that moment he could hear a key being inserted outside in the lock. He moved quickly, calling out: "One moment."

He opened the door. A young woman of about twenty-five, loaded down with a pile of freshly laundered towels, stood there, smiling up at him. She had removed the key and put it back in the pocket of her skirt.

"Towels?" she asked softly, the accent in her voice unfamiliar.

"I'll see." Justin knocked on the bathroom door. "Towels, dear? Do we need towels?"

"We're full up," Irene called out.

"We seem to have ours," Justin told the young woman.

"Merci!" said the young woman, ducking her head in a kind of curtsy, and moved quickly out into the corridor.

Justin was puzzled. She had not *seemed* French at first. But then—

"Elena," said Justin aloud.

"What's that, dear?"

"Elena. She had a pin on her blouse. Elena."

"Oh." Irene turned on the shower, putting an end to the exchange.

Soon afterward he went out, closing the door and trying the knob to make sure it was locked. The promenade deck was on the same level as their suite. So was a lounge that seemed to be deserted and waiting for evening custom. A vacant-faced bartender was doing the usual thing: absently polishing glasses.

"Sir?" He was an American.

"Scotch and soda on the rocks," Justin said carefully, avoiding the ambiguous "whiskey and soda."

The American quickly selected a bottle of Glenlivet and dumped in the ice, pouring out a brief dose of soda, which Justin indicated should be stretched, which it was.

"English?" the bartender asked.

"Mostly," said Justin with a vague smile. It was always easier to put it that way. Actually, he had been born in Massachusetts, which made him a Yank. But he had moved to Toronto when he was very small, and had then gone on to London as his father, a low-grade civil servant in the British diplomatic service, was returned to England. After graduating from Cambridge, Justin had served as a diplomatic clerk during the most stressful years of the cold war, had joined Scotland Yard, and had been assigned to Interpol in Paris as chief inspector, moving to Lyons when headquarters had changed its locale. "Mostly" English, because his Quebeçois mother spoke fluent French. He had always been bilingual—hence his easy way with Irene, who was also Franco-Anglican with just a touch of St. Lawrence Indian thrown in.

"Not stuck up like most limeys," noted the bartender.

Justin nodded. "So I'm told."

"What's wrong with your upper-class types?"

"Inbreeding, possibly."

The American laughed. "There's a lot of that going around."

Justin was puzzled as to exactly what the man meant, but he did not question him. Instead, he had turned and was studying a young man who had just entered the lounge and was looking over the bottles standing in front of the bar mirror.

"Very dry martini, with just a twist of lemon," said the young man. He, too, was American, to judge from the accent.

Justin studied him in the bar mirror: one of those big, soft-spoken jocks, with an easy carriage that bespoke lots of weight lifting and muscle building on complex gym machines. He was handsome in a regular-featured way—good cheekbones, good jaw line, good strong nose. His hazel eyes looked directly at one, Justin noted. But somehow there didn't seem to be a great deal of—well—weight, upstairs. The total effect of the face was one of penetrating blankness. An unsigned check. A *tabula rasa*.

"Evening," said the young man, sizing up Justin briefly. He was polite enough. But it was obvious what he thought from the expression on his face. He had Justin tabbed as middle-aged, in his late forties or early fifties, an unimaginative dresser, in no way dangerous, probably a stockbroker or trader of some kind.

"A friend of the Hartts?" Justin wondered aloud.

"Of all the people, rich *or* famous," the American responded, with a fairly vacant grin spreading over his face. He seemed to be bent on playing the humility role, but he had no humility to dispense. He was playing a part for which he was totally un-suited.

"My name is Birkby. Justin Birkby."

"Hello, Justin," said the young man. "What line of business you in?"

"I'm retired. Newly retired."

The lips puckered outward and whistled. Somehow it seemed to be an artificial, possibly a practiced, gesture. "Aren't you young for a pensioner? I mean, most retirees are over the hill, you know?"

Justin nodded. "My line of business, as you put it, was mostly paperwork."

"Clerk." A knowing nod. "Understood. You're well out of it." There was a momentary pause. "You marry rich or something?"

"Or something," Justin said.

A puzzled frown.

"And you?"

There was another assessing stare, with a shade of annoyance in the greenish eyes. "I'm an actor."

"Stage or screen?" Justin asked.

"Film and television," the American snorted. "You're English?"

Justin nodded.

"That accounts for it. I'm big in the States. But not big over here. In Europe."

"I see." Damn! thought Justin. If only Irene were here. Then he could get a proper line on this young man. She would know him, probably by sight.

Suddenly the young man's face flushed. He ground his glass on the bar and sloshed some of the drink out over the brim. "Not big any longer at home, either. Thanks to Herself."

The barkeep was listening now. Justin saw a flicker of amusement on his face. *He* knew what the young man was talking about.

"Steffi invited me. *She* doesn't think much of her, either."

Her? wondered Justin. Then he tumbled. Of course. Whom was everybody talking about? Tammy Scott!

"Loren, too, for that matter. Hell, she cut *him* up into mincemeat! It's a wonder the Hartts had the chutzpah to invite her aboard." He burst into laughter. It had a nasty sound. He finished his glass and pushed it over to the bartender for a refill. "If you're in their tax bracket, you've got to put up with women like that." He lifted the fresh glass. "Cheers!"

And with that he chugalugged the entire glass and sat there staring into the bar mirror.

"'Admired I am of those that hate me most,'" murmured Justin.

"Huh? Oh, yeah! I see what you mean." The American grinned hugely, enjoying his unexpected renown. Then, making up his mind, he slid off the stool, patted Justin on the shoulder, and said: "See you, Pops."

And off he went, moving quite steadily for the quick double he had just finished off.

Justin flushed. The idea of being called "Pops" did not appeal to him. Yet it was nothing *bad* really. Just poor breeding. Americans, Americans.

He was curious what the young man would think if he knew the words he fancied had been written by Christopher Marlowe about Nicolo Machiavelli. Probably never had heard of either one of them.

"Big star two years ago," the bartender said softly.

"The young man?"

The bartender nodded.

"What's his name? He never told me."

"That's Arn Thorn," the barkeep said, with one of those looks at Justin: What planet you come from, buddy? "Got a lucky break in a prime-time soap. Tammy Scott found him there. He was beautiful and in no time she was humping him regular. Kid began believing the notices she arranged for the show and thought he could act. Also, he got the impression he was the Errol Flynn of the eighties. She hired a private eye to get the goods on him."

The bartender picked up a glass and began drying it mechanically.

"He caught the kid with one of those big-busted starlets. Pictures. The works. The two of them didn't even *know!* And Herself maneuvered him into one of those interview shows—with her as his mentor. It wasn't Barbara Walters, but somebody big like that. This was network—all over America. Right in the middle of the double interview—about how great the kid was with women—she turns on him. She tells the world how inept he is in bed. Can't get it up. She tells them how he's a closet alcoholic, a druggie. The works."

Justin sipped at his drink. "They believed her?"

"Fell for it, hook, line, and sinker. Look, I'm not standing up for the kid. But she's a real castrater. A ballbreaker."

Justin nodded. "What happened?"

"She had her commercials on the kid's show, and she moved in on the production company, had the kid written out of the story line, fired him from the cast, badmouthed him all over town, painted him persona non grata at central casting. He was done." The bartender shook his head, bemused. "And all because the kid couldn't resist a little second-rate poon."

"What's he doing now?"

"I don't know. I was surprised to see him walk in here tonight. Maybe he's got something on with the Hartts. I just couldn't guess." His eyes glittered suddenly. "But I'd sure like to be there when he runs into Tammy Scott! That'll be something to watch! The kid once said he'd kill her if he ever saw her again."

Justin shrugged. "Just talk."

"I suppose so," mused the barkeeper. "But coming from Arn Thorn—I don't know."

Justin finished his drink and slid off the bar stool. "Later," he said, trying out his American idiom.

"Later," nodded the American, polishing, polishing.

5.

On deck members of the crew had set up a long serving table loaded with glasses and bottles of champagne—French, Italian, Spanish, German, Californian, and New York State. At about quarter to eight a trio of musicians—an accordion, an amplified keyboard, and a slightly off-key trumpet—began thumping out songs from the golden age of musical comedy. The numbers were distinguished, Justin felt, by a slight Mediterranean accent, but they were recognizable. Irene, in a low-cut, stunningly fitted cocktail dress, had joined him on the deck.

With great care Justin selected a Dom Perignon 1945—the year of his birth—and sipped it with satisfaction. Irene chose a blend from New York State, just to be different. The guests were all milling about on the deck now, with a silken night breeze skimming the harbor. Justin and Irene stood by the rail of the yacht, staring off into the distance where the lights of the French Riviera produced a dazzling display against the blackness of the night and the silhouette of the Alpes Maritimes rising behind the jeweled setting of Nice.

Suddenly the three-piece group broke out into a rollicking, almost-recognizable rendition of "Anchors Aweigh," and a voice came over the speakers:

"This is your host, Loren Hartt! Greetings, and welcome aboard! We're leaving Nice harbor, ladies and gentlemen! Welcome to the 'Malta Interlude.' "

There was a click and the speaker cut out.

"Strange man," Justin commented after the guests had all broken out into a cheer and joined in a spirited round of "Anchors Aweigh."

"Oh?"

"Strange guest list," Justin said by way of explanation. "I wonder what he's up to."

"A three-day cruise," said Irene. "That's all. You shouldn't always be so suspicious."

The *Shangri-la* was now circling about the harbor and turning to point its way to sea. Most of the guests were strolling the promenade deck or leaning against the railing as Justin and Irene were, watching the water and the sparkling lights of the Riviera beyond it. A million stars blinked in the night above.

"I'm Rosalyn Acres," said a young woman at Justin's left. She was standing beside him, peering out into the night and sipping champagne from the glass in her hand.

"Justin Birkby," said Justin politely. "It's Irene Manners who is the guest here, not I." Irene and Rosalyn nodded to one another. Rosalyn was about thirty, Justin guessed. He could tell from her voice that she had probably grown up in New York City, although she might have picked up the accent after coming from somewhere else.

She was brunette—brown eyes and black hair—and trim in figure. She had that almost jarring cosmopolitan aggressiveness that leaped out at one. But she was well groomed and certainly seemed able to keep her energies in control.

"I once worked for Tammy Scott," she said with a reminiscent smile. "I say that because this entire party seems to have been put together out of Tammy Scott's—well—past."

"Ah," said Justin, thinking that he might now begin to understand the peculiar cross-pollination of the guest list. "And whom *else* do you recognize?"

Rosalyn turned and gestured to her own left. A rather thick-waisted and big-boned man was leaning with his back to the railing, drinking and watching the three-piece band serenading the guests. He seemed mildly amused at their antics, and even more than bemused by the sounds they were creating.

The man resembled nothing so much as an assistant wrestling coach at a second-rate American cow-town college, Justin thought. His hair was black and slicked down to his round head. It had the appearance of being tinted, and done with not much attention to detail.

His eyes were black and heavy-lidded, giving him a slumbering, rather reptilian look. His mouth was composed of cherry-red lips, the kind that were frozen in a continual pout. He was going to fat already, even though he was only somewhere in his thirties. The jowls were beginning to sag. Yet he carried himself in a way that reassured one he had enough muscle to sustain the flab.

Occasionally a drop of perspiration would roll down his cheeks and slide off his chin, even in the relative coolness of the late spring evening. The sweat was undoubtedly caused by the man's natural hypertuned metabolism, Justin reasoned.

"That man was my boss," Rosalyn continued smoothly. "Clifford Boone."

"And Mr. Boone was—?"

"He *is* Tammy Scott's treasurer—the company's financial manager."

Justin smiled. "And you?"

"I *was* in the finance section." She spoke softly. "It was through Scott Cosmetics that I met Arn, you know."

"Arn being the actor, Arn Thorn?" Justin asked, stifling his pride in having remembered the name of the man he had met in the bar that evening. "I didn't realize you had met him through Scott Enterprises."

"Scott Cosmetics sponsored the television show Arn was in. It was a prime-time soap." Rosalyn was swelling proudly. "Almost as big as 'Twin Peaks.' "

Justin nodded blankly. "What show is Arn in now?"

"He's resting," said Rosalyn bitterly.

Irene had been listening to the conversation. "You know Arn Thorn well?" she asked with characteristic insouciance.

Rosalyn's face lit up. "I'm his—" She hesitated. "Yes. Very well." A flush was spreading up from her sternum into her face.

Irene was getting up a full head of steam. "Isn't Arn Thorn's agent on board ship? Didn't I see Reginald Dunwoodie a moment ago?" Irene searched around, but could not point out the man she meant.

Justin felt hopelessly out of his depth. Irene read all the gossip columns, French *and* English.

"Yes!" said Rosalyn. "He's Arn's business manager. Big actors don't have *agents* anymore. They have *managers.*"

"Like a boxer," Justin said brightly.

Rosalyn froze him with a look.

"I think Arn is with Reggie," said Rosalyn with a smile. "No," she corrected herself as she spotted someone in the semidarkness of the deck. "There's Reggie now."

Justin turned with Irene to study the man Rosalyn was pointing out. He was a large, slovenly individual in his late fifties, with an almost egg-bald head, gray tufts of wispy hair hanging down around his ears and in a fringe across the back of his skull, with gray sprouting out of his huge ears, a hangdog look to his eyes and cheeks, and a winsome tenderness in his brown eyes.

He was an obvious, flaming homosexual, Justin could see, one who had never been in a closet to come out of. He was talking to a much smaller man—a young and tender male who resembled a green shoot reaching out into the sky in early spring. He was red-haired, tall, and slender.

"That's Henry the Eighth," said Rosalyn, in a cutting tone, indicating the young man.

Irene frowned. "Henry the Eighth? Because his name is Tudor?"

"No," laughed Rosalyn, who had apparently absorbed *some* history. "His name is really Henry Haight. But *hate* is a bad word. He likes to be called Henry the Eighth."

Justin thought Dunwoodie would be better served by such a nickname than would Haight, if only for his resemblance to the role played with such consummate artistry by Charles Laughton in the black-and-white cinema classic.

"He plays a smashing game of tennis," Rosalyn added.

"What else does he do?" Irene asked absently, then corrected herself. "I mean, besides being Reggie's 'significant other'?"

"Not much. All his living hours are spent closeted with his—"

"—friend," supplied Irene.

Rosalyn giggled. "They're both very nice."

"How could they be otherwise?" Irene asked dryly.

"What do you do now?" Justin asked as the conversation seemed to pause for a new direction.

"I prepare IRS forms for clients at tax time," Rosalyn said. "In Hollywood." She looked at Justin carefully. "I haven't seen Mr. Boone for ages."

"I see," said Justin, who did not see all the nuances, but who could be counted on to search them out.

Rosalyn turned from Justin and moved down the railing to where Cliff Boone was now watching some of the guests getting champagne at the on-deck bar. She edged toward him. He glanced at her and almost did not recognize her. Then: "Hello, Rosalyn," he murmured in a low voice.

"Hello, bastard!" she snapped and emptied her champagne glass in his face.

Then she moved quickly along the deck and was gone.

Justin turned away in embarrassment, and then he cursed himself for his immediate instinct to detach himself from any contretemps. He moved toward Boone as the big man got out his handkerchief and tried to dry off his shirt and jacket.

"'Tis no shame to be bad, because 'tis common,'" he quoted, by way of explaining away Rosalyn's action.

The corner of Boone's mouth lifted sardonically. "A scholar.

It's always easier to hide behind a literary quotation than to speak the unvarnished truth."

"An Elizabethan drama freak," Justin countered, realizing that Boone was not the lout his exterior proclaimed him to be.

The big man continued to dab at his shirtfront with an air of injured dignity.

"What was *that* all about?" Irene asked when Justin rejoined her.

Justin shrugged with Gallic aplomb. He was amused. Irene had her small sketch pad out and was whipping off a drawing of Clifford Boone drying off his shirtfront. He saw that she had already drawn a picture of the three-piece band that was still playing—now a melancholy Cole Porter tune from the master's vintage years.

"You stupid bitch!" screeched Tammy Scott.

Everyone turned toward her. She was glowering at Angelica Farr, who was engaged in a quiet conversation by the rail with Ray McGuin.

Finally Angelica turned toward her tormentor. "What is it, Tammy?"

"It's eight goddamned thirty-five o'clock, that's what!"

"I salute you for your acumen," responded Angelica, her tongue only slightly slip-sliding over the consonants. "In fact, it is eight thirty-seven o'clock, Ms. Scott."

"Eight o'clock sharp! I told you to warn me when eight thirty was going to occur so I could check out my commercial!" Tammy was now accompanying her voice with the raucous pounding of her clenched fist on the table at which the champagne was being served. Wineglasses bounced, silver trembled, and coffee cups chattered in saucers.

A sudden silence ensued. Angelica was fumbling in her saddlebag, which she carried on her hip. She extracted, after some difficulty, a slip of paper, and held it up to the light to see what was written on it. She had trouble focusing her eyes.

"Nope!" she snapped triumphantly, waving the slip in the air. "You didn't goddamned remind me of it at all!"

"I told you last week before we flew to France that I wanted to view that commercial! Eight thirty! Tonight! French TV!"

"Tough tiddy," snapped Angelica, her face reddening. *"This* is the list of my instructions! I follow *this* list—not something you make up all on your own!"

But Tammy Scott was not to be denied her moment of vindictiveness. "You haven't heard the last of this dereliction of duty!" she yelled. "You're incorrigible! One more missed assignment and you're history!"

Angelica stared glassily at her employer. Then, to the surprise of everyone, she started to giggle, and finally she was letting it all out in obscene guffaws that lurched up from her inner self like the eruption of a volcano.

Tammy's face was crimson. She pounded on the serving table again. "Bring out my TV! I'll have to monitor the nine o'clock break instead! You hear me?"

Angelica raised her hands palms forward. "Yes, O Queen of the Cosmos! I go!"

She whirled around, something like a dancer executing a step in a comic ballet, stumbled, and fell flat on her face on the deck. Where she lay, stoned out of her mind.

Tammy was roaring with rage. "Pick up that slut and haul her back to her cabin!"

"Yes, sir," said a crewman, appearing as if by magic, and hastened forward with two of his assistants to take care of Angelica.

When Tammy left, there was a sudden release of tension. Someone began tittering. Finally there was a heartfelt burst of laughter, and soon several were holding their sides.

The relief was not to last.

Tammy Scott stomped back onto the deck carrying a small TV set, and she began searching along the bulkhead for an electric outlet. A crewman found one and plugged in the electric cord. Tammy snapped on the knob, turned to a channel, and set the television on a chair standing near the serving table.

"There!" she said. A drama was coming to an end, the crawls moving down over the freeze frame, and quite suddenly there was Tammy Scott, herself, smiling into the night, and turning her face from side to side as a French voice-over extolled the virtues of Scott Eyeshadow—all in marvelously intoned *français.*

When it was over, Tammy unplugged the set and turned to the guests on the deck. "I apologize for Angelica's behavior," she said softly. "Can you forgive her?"

Someone had the discourtesy to wonder: "Who's going to forgive you?"

Tammy's mind was on herself and she did not hear.

The answer came from John Webster, through the mind of Justin Birkby:

" 'They that sleep with dogs shall rise with fleas.' "

6.

When Justin Birkby and Irene Manners rose in the morning to take their early stroll around the deck they found they were charging southward through the gentle swells of the Mediterranean on an absolutely superb June day. The sky was clear of clouds, except for a tiny puff of cumulonimbus in the distance almost on the horizon—in the direction of North Africa—and the sun was bright over the land mass of Italy to the east.

"I haven't figured it out yet, have you?" Justin murmured as they made their third turn and headed back forward on the port side of the ship.

"Figured out what, dear?" Irene was relaxed and all smiles, her jogging togs clinging to her body like fine wisps of ocean spray.

"What's the purpose of this cruise?"

" 'Malta Interlude.' *Malta:* Republic in the Mediterranean Sea south of Sicily, comprising the islands of Malta, Gozo, and Comino. Fully independent since 1964, with last British forces withdrawn in 1979. *Interlude:* from Latin *inter*—between—and *lude*

—game. An interval between, during which games are enjoyed. I *certainly* don't have to tell you that, Justin!"

"You know what I mean," grumbled Justin.

Irene laughed. "You're always so ridiculously logical. There always has to be a reason—for you. Relax and enjoy, darling."

What was the sense of arguing? He knew there *was* some reason behind this conglomeration of guests, but he had no idea what it was. Of course it had something to do with Tammy Scott and Scott Cosmetics—he'd bet on that—but exactly *what* he could not guess.

"I tell you one thing," Justin said. "If I were that Scott woman, I don't think I'd push any harder on Angelica Farr. I think she's reached the point of combustion."

"Agree. That Boone person—the fat one with the overactive *glandulae sudorificae*—he's worried about something, too, you know."

"If I were that man, I'd be up here jogging. He's far overweight."

"I don't mean that, you idiot. He's the treasurer of Scott Cosmetics, you know."

"You mean he's got his fingers in the till?" Justin leered with vaudevillian exaggeration.

"Don't be so all-mighty sophisticated!" snapped Irene. "He could be draining off the profits, you know."

"That kid actor doesn't like Mrs. Scott much either," Justin said, changing the subject just to irritate Irene.

"Oh, yes. Arnold. No. Not after what she did to him!"

Justin turned to Irene in astonishment. "You know already? I was going to make points telling you about it!"

"Everybody knows what she did to him—on that TV interview. Justin. Sometimes you make me wonder about your competence in the field of general knowledge."

"Thanks veddy much."

"Whew!" sighed Irene. "Let's sit. Here's a couple of nice deck chairs. I'm exhausted."

They sat down and leaned back, stretching out to relax.

All was silent. The yacht continued plowing through the mild combers and the sun rose higher and higher in the sky.

A woman dressed in white slacks, windbreaker, and cap sank into a chair next to them. "May I join you?"

Justin introduced himself and Irene.

"I'm Madge Overstreet," said the woman. She was a New Yorker, originally from Sioux City, Iowa, via Chicago, Illinois. Justin doubted that Overstreet was her real name. It seemed manufactured.

The woman grinned. "I'm a designer. I plan to be the next arbiter of the fashion world."

"Lots of luck," said Irene with a smile to take the sting out of the sarcasm.

Madge caught the intent. "Touché. Anyway, just to put you in the picture"—she turned to Justin—"isn't that what you Brits say?"

"We say it," Justin nodded. "I'm actually French."

"Oh?"

"He's as British as Earl Grey Tea!" snapped Irene. "Technically he is a French citizen. But the long way round."

"I'm part of Scott Cosmetics," Madge informed them.

"But you said you were a designer," Irene interrupted.

"Just to put you in the picture, I'm part of the Scott package now," she said ruefully. "She took me over six months ago. I almost went belly up. She bailed me out, took me on, and now she owns me."

"You don't particularly like it?"

"I hate it!" said the woman in a low, vibrant tone. The silence lengthened.

"It's odd," Justin said thoughtfully, "but almost everybody on this yacht has some kind of grudge against Tammy Scott. And yet she's the one everybody's celebrating and talking about. I'm afraid I simply don't understand the ambiguity of it."

Madge Overstreet stretched and closed her eyes. "That assistant of Tammy's is really something, isn't she?"

"Something else," agreed Justin.

"Didn't you just howl when the great Ms. Scott brought out that wretched Japanese TV and plugged it in to watch herself on that terrible commercial last night?"

Irene laughed. "Is she in the habit of doing things like that?"

"Absolutely!" said Madge. "I've seen her in action at a reception in the Plaza Hotel in New York. On the dot of the hour, she was out there and into the checkroom, back again, plugging that damned set into the wall to watch herself."

Justin laughed. "For someone who isn't gauche, she tends to be just a bit—gauche."

"Well, she certainly isn't droit," Irene said, to more laughter.

Madge Overstreet finally got up and wandered off. Justin and Irene remained, watching the people on deck.

"Nice person," said Irene.

"Somebody else in Tammy's shadow," murmured Justin. "That Scott person must own half the world."

"I wonder what Steffi thinks about all this?"

Reggie Dunwoodie, accompanied by Henry Haight, strolled by, both protected by strip sunshades and huge sun caps. Dunwoodie's fat legs looked gross pumping along in his Bermuda shorts. Henry was wearing tapered slacks that clung to the curves of his backside.

"Doesn't he look gorgeous?" Irene whispered.

"Reggie?" Justin was shocked.

"No, no! Henry the Eighth!" Irene was still following his languid graceful stride with her eyes.

"Irene! For God's sake. Please!"

Arn Thorn and Rosalyn Acres appeared, waved to the two of them, and continued on down the deck, followed by Cliff Boone. Justin was watching carefully.

"I'll be damned," he said softly.

"At what?" Irene wondered.

"The Scott Cosmetics treasurer. He's been in the service. I wouldn't have guessed."

"How do you know?" Irene asked.

"He's wearing a service medal. For sharpshooting. Didn't you see it?"

"No. I was looking down the deck at Henry the Eighth's leg muscles. He keeps in good shape."

"Unbelievable," Justin sighed.

"Go ahead, say it! Just like a woman!"

"You didn't hear *me* say that."

Justin closed his eyes and silence ensued. The sea and the sky rushed by.

7.

Tammy Scott stretched luxuriously in the scallop-shaped tub in her suite's bathing area and gazed around at the fittings and the furnishings of the room in total disbelief. Who but a sheik with oil rights of one-third of the petroleum in the world could ever afford to furnish a place this way?

She was in the famed Gold Suite. All the fittings in the bathroom were gold—plated gold, probably, not solid, but what the hell! The fan-shaped bathtub—tiled in deep black onyx!—had a Jacuzzi attached; Tammy had enjoyed a Jacuzzi massage just before going to bed the night before during her usual eleven-thirty soak. She had even watched the French version of her commercial again. And enjoyed it!

In such surroundings, even her own Scott Bubble Bath seemed adequate. Actually, she despised it; it was a legacy of her husband, Sam Scott. Yet the stuff sold well, and she kept the product on more or less as a concession to his bad taste and the bad taste of many of her customers.

Tonight she had promised herself a go at a new product the

French had come up with. L'Etoile was Scott's biggest and most successful competitor on the Continent. Maybe she could learn the secret of L'Etoile's Plain de Bulles. And maybe not. The trouble with business was that you always had to keep ahead of the competition. Some sports figure had once said: "Never look back. They may be gaining on you." That was her philosophy, too.

Rising from the tub, she stepped over the border that surrounded it and stood on the mat placed on the tile to minimize slipping. She reached for the towel hanging from a rack bolted to the bulkhead at the side of the tub, the Hartt logo pink, Disney-like in its dopey simplicity and pseudocharm.

Toweling herself rapidly, she shook out her hair, towel-dried it twice, and then peered at herself in the mirror over the basin. Not too bad for a fifty-five-year-old relic, she thought critically. She turned her profile and surveyed herself. She was putting on a little weight. That was a no-no in her business. She'd have to watch what she ate. And drank.

The implants in her breasts were holding up. So were the tucks that Rodeo Drive supersurgeon had taken six months ago. You could hardly see the scar under the jaw. She had a good ten years more before the wear and tear would begin to show.

She plugged her shaver into the socket and gave her underarms and legs a quick runover. The voltage was American—120 volts, 60-cycle—you could count on Loren Hartt to have taken care of that. He knew exactly what he was doing when he set up cruises like this one. She might have been unable to get along with him as a wife, but she knew he had some good points. Business and the way of doing it was one of them. Entertaining and keeping his guests satisfied was another. *Satisfied* in its broader sense, of course.

She unplugged the razor, packed it away, and reached up to take her clothes off the hanger. As she put the finishing touches to her lipstick and eyeshadow, she wondered how Angelica was faring. Ha ha! Good joke, she thought. How Angelica was *Farr-*

ing. Get it? The poor dear had certainly been loaded the night before.

Fully dressed and made up, she grabbed her key, touched her hair in place, and stepped out into the corridor, turning to check that her door was locked. It was Angelica who had chosen to bunk separately. Tammy had expected her to revel in the luxury suite with her. An odd person, Angelica—but brilliant in what she could do with numbers.

The yacht's dining room was set up for breakfast. A long table was placed against one bulkhead, with numerous serving dishes arranged for easy access. Tammy strolled along carefully looking over the selection of foodstuffs, and finally took her loaded tray over to one of the smaller tables that had been set up in the middle of the room. At it sat Clifford Boone.

With cool deliberation, Tammy took a place directly opposite him. Boone had been watching her, and he now smiled tentatively and began playing with the bacon and eggs left on his plate.

"Hello, Cliff," said Tammy brightly.

Boone smiled with some difficulty and cleared his throat. He looked uncomfortable. "Hello, Mrs. Scott."

"Is there something troubling you, Mr. Boone?"

He picked up a napkin and dabbed at his full rosebud lips. A drop of perspiration had started at his forehead and was now rolling down his cheek. He looked around the dining room furtively. Not far away sat Irene Manners. Boone had seen her companion, that Interpol man Justin Birkby leave some five minutes before. Irene had said something about wanting another cup of coffee before joining him on deck.

Boone leaned toward Tammy Scott. "I've been told the auditors have been looking at my books."

"A normal process, Mr. Boone." Tammy Scott was direct and open and outspoken. Her voice carried.

Boone bit his lip. "Yes, but *this* audit seems a bit more extensive than usual."

"Perhaps there is some reason for that," suggested Tammy Scott, barely able to keep her smile concealed.

"Since I've worked for you, Mrs. Scott, I've never had an audit quite so in-depth as this one." He looked her in the eye. "Is there something *wrong?*"

Tammy Scott returned his gaze. "It would be ridiculous, Mr. Boone, to pretend that there is nothing wrong. I have a feeling you are quite well aware of what the problem is."

Boone's face was pale. He was trembling. "I have absolutely no idea what you are talking about." His voice was as soft as a distant whisper in a cave.

"It's the Deseret Chemical Company, Mr. Boone." Tammy's voice was as loud and as full as it always was. Boone seemed to be shrinking away from it and from her.

"What about it?"

"Well, the fact is, it's a chemical supply house."

"I'm not quite sure I've ever heard of it."

"That's the first honest thing you've said, Mr. Boone." Tammy cut into her cantaloupe. She smiled. "Because, of course, there *is* no such company."

Boone grimaced. "I don't—"

"I think you *do,* Mr. Boone. It's a dummy. The payments for supplies are fake. They go to a mailing address, the checks are endorsed, and they are received into an account set up by a dummy name." There was a pause. "I have sufficient reason to believe that you are the person who eventually draws from that dummy account."

Boone was dabbing at his lips again. "Is this an accusation, Mrs. Scott?"

"If it was, what would you say to it, Mr. Boone?" Tammy was playing with him now. He knew it and he knew that she knew he knew it.

"It's a malicious lie. If you make it official, I'll sue you." Boone stared at her with smoldering malevolence.

"I have all the facts in my papers," Tammy intoned. "Perhaps you'd like to see them?" She reached for the attaché case she carried with her everywhere and opened it. Inside lay a series of manila folders, all colored hot pink. Quickly Tammy removed one folder, glanced at its label, and opened it. She drew out a set of papers clipped together with a colored paper clip matching the hot pink of the manila folder. She thrust the papers into his hands.

Boone started to read, his face contorting. He slapped the papers down on the table and crushed his napkin on top of them —twin gauntlets thrown down as by a rebuffed cavalier—and leaned forward toward Tammy Scott. "I don't believe in looking at books that have obviously been cooked," he snapped.

"I'll see you in court, Mr. Boone," Tammy said airily, matching him stare for stare.

Boone reconsidered. There was a thin film of perspiration on his forehead, running down into his eyes. His eyes were glittering behind his pudgy flesh. "We should be able to work out some kind of rapprochement, Mrs. Scott," he said in a buttery tone.

Tammy moved her cantaloupe rind away and began on her bacon and eggs. She glanced up at him as if she might have just noticed him standing there.

"If you returned every cent you stole from me over the years, Mr. Boone, there is no *possible* way you could keep me from prosecuting you to the fullest extent of the law." There was a pause. "Is that understood?"

Boone drew himself up. "Yes, Mrs. Scott." With that he stalked out of the dining room.

Irene Manners watched him go. She then took out her sketch book and drew a profile of Cliff Boone. She began a sketch of Tammy Scott. Then she drew the two of them leaning toward one another, like animals ready to strike. Two dangerous people, she decided as she flipped the page over and began a scene of the ocean through the open door to the deck.

The brilliant sunshine beat down on the waters of the Mediterranean Sea, reflecting a brilliant coruscating light onto the ceiling of the dining room, which flooded the eye like some kind of mad stroboscope in a 1960s discotheque. Irene tried various angles to bring out the play of the sun on the ceiling, and then she abandoned the drawing.

Tammy Scott was not even aware of Irene's presence. But quite suddenly she knew someone was standing close by. To her surprise she saw it was Steffi Hartt. Steffi was holding an envelope in her hand, tapping it on the edge of the table. Tammy watched her for a moment, and then went back to her food.

"Excellent cuisine," she said with a smile.

Steffi nodded. "Loren has done a superlative job in preparing the *Shangri-la* for entertainment. Sven Norquist is the best."

Tammy nodded. "The Continent's top chef. And he's working for you full time? I'm impressed."

"On a contract basis," Steffi said. She held the envelope out. "Loren wanted me to give you this."

Tammy quirked an eyebrow. "Oh? And what does my ex want?"

"He doesn't tell me *everything.*"

Tammy laughed. "He never did me, either." The laughter came out forced. She took the envelope and studied it. It was unsealed. She flipped it open and removed a simple card with handwriting on it. It was in Loren's familiar scrawl.

Five o'clock. Forward lounge. Let's talk.

And that was it.

"Sure," said Tammy. "Tell your lord and master that his servant awaits. Ta-dah!"

"Awaits?"

Tammy extended the card, which Steffi read quickly.

"He hasn't let me in on it," Steffi said.

Tammy poured cream into her coffee. "Didn't I see you last night with Dara Lukas?"

Steffi nodded. "I've always been fascinated by her reports from Europe."

"She's using you." Tammy looked Steffi in the eye.

"Oh?"

"She's doing a hatchet job on me."

Steffi shrugged. "Perhaps."

"I think you're leaking data about my earlier days with Loren, Steffi."

Steffi's eyes narrowed. "You can think what you want, dear. That doesn't make it true."

"There were so many lies about me in those days," Tammy mused.

"Many of the so-called lies were true." Steffi watched Tammy carefully.

"I know what's true and what's made up," Tammy snapped. "I can sue."

"Not if what I say is the truth."

"Watch your step," Tammy said in a husky, lowered voice.

"I always have."

"Not necessarily," Tammy observed challengingly.

Now Steffi's face was hard. "You're threatening me!"

"Am I?"

Immediately Tammy rose and sailed out of the dining room, waving the envelope and the card in it in the air, trailing that delicious perfume she had created for herself.

Steffi Hartt watched her as she left, a troubled expression on her face.

In a moment Irene was adding Steffi's face to her collection of sketches.

8.

In the afternoon Justin Birkby moved a deck chair next to one of the lifeboats, where he could relax in the sunshine without interruption from promenaders and joggers. He put on a pair of wraparound sunglasses to protect his eyes. On his head, to shade his scalp, always vulnerable to bad sunburn because of his blond hair, he wore a floppy cap with a front brim folded out for maximum screening.

He came awake quite suddenly, aware that he had dozed off for some minutes, but not completely cognizant of the amount of time he had been asleep. He could hear footsteps near the lifeboat. Was that the reason he had awakened? He frowned and opened his eyes, but could make out no one in his line of vision.

The footsteps halted.

"Hello, Arn," said a familiar voice quite near him. Justin realized that someone—perhaps two people—had taken up position on the opposite side of the lifeboat, within its shadow, apparently to stand or rest for a while. The speaker was Tammy Scott. He could recognize her voice anywhere.

And he could hear how charged with sexual interest that voice was now. Justin could not see either of the two people, but he could imagine how Tammy Scott's eyes were glowing. Aroused sexual attraction informed her voice.

"Hello, Tammy," said Arn Thorn. Justin recalled the studied manner in which the young actor spoke. Now, he could not quite determine exactly what emotional content the actor wanted his voice to convey. Justin wondered why it was so flat, so shorn of any kind of expression.

"You're looking well," Tammy went on, her voice carrying the continued attitude of sexual arousal. Justin imagined her eyes traveling up and down Arn Thorn's body. She was that kind of woman—not one to conceal her emotional thralldom in any way.

"Thank you," Arn Thorn said. He was obviously making a great effort to conceal his hostility. Was this the first time Tammy and he had met face to face since the cruise began? Justin wondered. Obviously yes, he assured himself. Most interesting. He removed his sunglasses, but could not see anything but two pairs of feet below the lifeboat. One in sensible heels (feminine); the other in ugly but utilitarian deck shoes (masculine).

"I see you're with *her,*" Tammy said slowly, her voice edged with maliciousness.

"Let's not get into personalities," Arn retorted.

" 'Personalities!' " snorted Tammy. "She stole money from me!"

"So your treasurer would have you believe."

"I fired her because she deserved it," Tammy said stoutly. "If she's to your taste, the more I pity you."

Arn Thorn growled in his throat. "I'm not here to plead her case."

"Good. Whose case *are* you here to plead?" Tammy sounded amused now. Her voice was more relaxed. And more frightening.

"Mine," said Arn. "I want to make a deal."

"A deal?" Tammy's voice rose slightly. "Like the deal you pulled on me with that stupid starlet?" Her voice dripped venom.

"Haven't you ever made a mistake?" the actor asked with an only half-successful attempt at banter.

"Not like *that,* I haven't!" snarled Tammy Scott. "Besides, who ever said it was a mistake? You told me it was the *real thing.*"

"Talk is cheap," Arn said softly. He seemed to be backing away from the argument.

"You also said that we—that is, you and I—didn't get it on together the way you and she got it on together."

Arn sighed. "I always did talk too much."

"And now you want to make a deal." The scorn was so thick it could have been cut with a knife. "A deal!" she repeated.

"What happened is all in the past," Arn said pleadingly. Justin thought that he was not really giving his plea much of a reading. It sounded more like the rote stuff a third-rate actor would give to a boring role—a role he did not believe in. "I want to get back to work."

Tammy laughed harshly. Justin was watching the footwork with fascination. Arn had begun to move toward her, and she had stood her ground. Now she was beginning to move toward him, and he was backing off.

" 'Work'?" Her intonation was almost a whack in the flesh. "Play!" she snapped in contrast. "You want to get back into the acting business." Dripping with scorn.

"I'm a good actor, Tammy, love."

"So now it's 'love,' is it?"

"Come on," Arn wheedled. "Give me a break!"

"To you, Arnold Thorn, even if you are a good-looking stud—a nice hunk of meat, as we liberated women have it—I'm giving nothing! Acting to you means rutting around Hollywood with cheap little upwardly mobile bimbos. Eh?"

"Tammy, Tammy!" whispered Arn.

"That's the *deal,* isn't it? You do the playing. I do the paying." Tammy's voice was rising. "No, punk! I'm through dealing with you. You can find some other line of country to get along in."

"Come on, Tammy!" Arn's voice was quivering.

"Go back to your light-fingered live-in, Arn. I'm sure you can make out with her. She's had plenty of practice."

"Please, Tammy—" If Justin had not seen his feet he could have sworn the actor was down on his knees to her. Perhaps he *was* reading the lines with just a little more sincerity now. He was desperate, and desperation could sometimes breed conviction.

"It's 'Mrs. Scott,' you cheap jock! Mrs. Scott!"

"What is it with you, anyway?" he whispered.

"You're finished, Arn! Through! You hear me? You thought you could go to Dunwoodie and have him fix you up with a new career. Now you know the truth. I bought Dunwoodie out and I've got you by the balls. You're going exactly—nowhere!"

Justin rose from his deck chair. He was watching Arn's feet. The actor was retreating from the inexorably advancing Tammy Scott; stumbling backward in his haste.

"No deal, cockhound! No deal at all. You hear me?"

Justin could see Arn Thorn now, having trouble maintaining his balance on the slippery decking.

"Look out!" cried Justin in warning.

Arn Thorn suddenly realized his danger, and he turned quickly. But at the same moment, Tammy Scott was reaching to belt him one in the face. Her blow grazed his cheek, and he spun to avoid a follow-up. Justin was amazed at the woman's strength, and at her implacability. She continued to move toward him, lashing out again.

Justin reached for Arn Thorn to keep him from falling backward off the deck and into the sea, and for a moment he had a grip on him. But Tammy Scott, her face inflamed with rage, hurled herself at him, and Justin's grip was broken.

"Arn!" cried Justin.

"Bum!" yelled Tammy.

Arn Thorn's cry was simply an exhalation of breath and a despairing shriek as over he went, backward and down into the water below.

"My God!" gasped Tammy Scott. "My God!" Realizing now

what she had done, she covered her face with her hands and shrank into herself.

Justin ran to the edge of the deck and looked down. He could see the yacht sliding past the flailing arms of Arn Thorn in the blue water.

"Man overboard!" came the yell of a crewman who had, luckily, witnessed the fall. Almost instantly there were three blasts on the whistle and the yacht's twin screws reversed themselves to bring the craft to an agonizingly slow, sliding halt.

The next moments were a vast confusion of sounds, cries, trampling feet, the tossing overboard of life preservers, the inflation of a rubber dinghy, and a great deal of running about. Tammy Scott collapsed against Justin Birkby, holding her palms against her face tightly, and sobbing. "I'm sorry! I'm so sorry!"

The barkeep, Justin thought, had been wrong. It wasn't that Arn Thorn might kill Tammy Scott if the two met, but that Tammy Scott might kill Arn Thorn!

Eventually the dripping-wet actor was delivered to the deck, with a concerned Loren Hartt standing there with words of consolation to greet him. He was taken to the infirmary, fed hot tea, and given an aspirin or two. An almost despondent Rosalyn Acres was there to kiss and fondle him.

Justin escorted Tammy Scott to her cabin suite and advised her to rest. By now Tammy's tears were dry, and she was smiling gratefully under Justin's ministrations. When he closed the door on her, she seemed almost radiant with a kind of recalled excitement.

" 'There's nothing sooner dry than women's tears,' " Justin quoted, shaking his head. Good thing Irene had not been there to hear those words of John Webster. She would have excoriated them as a chauvinist example of male arrogance.

9.

The forward lounge was very quiet. Most of the passengers were either sunning themselves on deck, napping in their suites, or maybe reading somewhere in the quiet shade. Things had calmed down a great deal after the extreme excitement of Arn Thorn's inadvertent immersion in the Med. It had taken all of Loren Hartt's powers of persuasion to calm him down and pack him off to a bar where he could find solace in a few recreational pints.

The young actor had finally resumed his basic blank look and seemed normal again. Loren Hartt now sat quietly gazing at the not unwelcome sight of Tammy Scott. It was five o'clock, and the rendezvous for which he had planned the entire "Malta Interlude" was about to take place.

She was still beautiful, he thought, and almost as sexy as beautiful. It was the attraction of her flesh that had drawn him to her in the first place. Even after they had parted upon discovery that they were causing each other more misery than pleasure—and that their marriage never should have been—he had missed her presence for months on end.

He realized that the part of him he could not control was still attracted to her, still wanted her, still *fancied* her. At the same time, that other part of him that he could control, and that he used to determine what course of action to take—his intellect and not his psyche—hated her. *Needed* to destroy her.

"Sorry about the wording of the note," said Loren casually.

"It had a touch of the lord of the manor about it." Her upper lip curled suitably.

"I did want to see you and I knew you'd come because you'd be too curious to pass up a rendezvous—especially with me."

"Go ahead, Loren. I read you like a book. Turn the page."

Loren smiled faintly. "And I, my dear, read *you* like a book. That is the advantage we have—*and* the disadvantage."

"Enough talk. Let's get down to it. What is it?"

Loren played with the manila folders he had in his hand and finally laid them out on the couch next to him. He was sitting on stuffed and bloated cushions that were so comfortable he sank almost to the floor. She was seated in a similar chair opposite him. They seemed to be floating in a puffy cloud.

"It's the biggest story of the year."

"I like stories, Loren," Tammy said sardonically. "Once upon a time . . ." she prompted him.

He gave her a look. Then he plunged into his folders. "I did want you to know all about this before the press got hold of it. In fact, that's the purpose of this cruise—to pique public interest in the people who are on the *Shangri-la,* and to afford a springboard to the story of the year."

"I'm still guessing," said Tammy. "Go on."

"It's Scott Cosmetics, my dear," Loren said with a smile. "You've always been ripe for a leveraged buyout."

"But we've always managed to fight off all offers with one technique or another," Tammy replied with a cunning smile. "I do hope you're not thinking about trying to take us over."

"Not thinking, love. I have taken you over. I own you,

Tammy. From head to toe. Every bit of that beautiful, impressive, heroic bod." Loren Hartt could barely contain his excitement.

Tammy Scott's face hardened. "I haven't the time to waste with idle speculation. *I'd* know, if what you say had *really* happened."

"As I said, you're being told now."

Tammy stood up, her face harsh and red. "If you're diddling me, Loren, I'm out of here!"

"Sit down!" snapped Loren. "And listen." His voice was suddenly different. The wimpishness was gone; steel had replaced it. Tammy sat, surprising even herself.

Loren spoke. It had to do with Scott Cosmetics stock. By purchasing portions through associates, Loren could now control the actions of each company that made up Scott Enterprises. And thus, control Tammy Scott.

"I haven't told my people to make their moves known yet," he said. "I wanted to savor your reaction to this monumental truth first!" Loren smiled. "Just as a matter of satisfaction on my part."

Tammy smiled faintly. Her flesh was pulled taut. "You're such a shit, Loren!" she snapped, her eyes flashing.

"Coming from you," Loren retorted, "that's high praise indeed!"

"Actually, I misspoke myself. You're a *simple* shit! Because owning me won't do you any good at all!"

"No?" Loren could hardly believe that. "Just having somebody looking over your shoulder brings you to cardiac arrest!" he chortled. "Admit it! You're dying now! Dying!"

"Do you think I'd sit still and let you take me over?" Tammy asked with a slowly widening smile.

"I'll admit it surprised me how easy it was to do it," Loren said softly. "But that's beside the point. I've got you, and I'm going to shake you till you rattle."

Tammy was beginning to laugh. The laugh was flat and rau-

cous. Loren could feel a frisson of fear skittering up his backbone.

"I succeeded," Loren went on doggedly, "because of that
huge hole in the middle of your financial setup. Your man Boone
has been robbing you blind for five years."

Tammy choked on her laughter. "I'm quite aware of that."

"It was easy to buy up stocks from disgruntled owners who
were counting on big dividends and who got nothing year after
year. Boone did you in. Not me."

"It still won't work, Loren!" she crowed.

Loren's anger was growing. "I've got the facts and figures in
these folders, if you'd care to look," he said belligerently.
"Here!"

She held up her hand. "You always did your homework. That
was one of the things about you that I always approved of. I
believe you."

Loren was annoyed. He leaned toward this woman he hated so
and said: "You're so goddamn cool about it, Tammy. Don't you
understand? You're finished! You're through! I'm in charge! Me,
the wimp. The nerd. The yuppie."

Tammy stifled her laughter and gazed at him crookedly. "No.
You're not in charge. I am. Still. I have a few folders myself." She
opened the big attaché case she carried and removed a handful of
the hot-pink manila folders in her own distinctive color.

Loren stared at them. He could feel his stomach turning over.
What in hell were the papers in that folder? Somehow he knew
they were important. Important to his future. Important—and
fateful to him.

"Affidavits and statements of one kind or another." Tammy
smiled.

"About what?"

"About some of your early dealings in Manhattan. When you
first began to build the Hartt empire."

Loren frowned. He was shaken inwardly. This woman always
managed to scare the living shit out of him. "So?"

"You release your story, and I'll release mine."

"Your story?" Loren laughed brashly. " 'How I Lost a Fortune to Loren Hartt'?"

"My story. A story about a neophyte developer who got his start by bribing politicians and Mafia goombas. It's a story of networking in intrigue, Loren."

Loren snorted. "Bribery is a way of life in the big city."

"Sure it is. Normally it wouldn't hurt you a bit, would it?"

Loren's face was suddenly hard. Now he knew he had stepped into quicksand. He could feel it sucking him down and down.

"The Las Vegas gambling permits!" snapped Tammy, gleeful now, her face alive, her eyes sparkling. "What a bad time to have that news—news of bribes and shenanigans and deals with the mob—to be published everywhere! You'd lose your permit, wouldn't you? I mean, they'd deny it. You couldn't open up that huge pleasure dome you've been building in Vegas, could you?"

Silently Loren reached out and took one of the folders from his ex-wife. He removed the hot-pink paperclip and leafed through the pages for a moment in total silence. As he did so, his face drained of color. Then, slowly, he handed it back to her.

"And if you can't open your gambling palace, you can't pay off all those loans you took out to pay for construction costs, can you? The days of junk bonds are over, Loren! It's tough out there in the real world to keep a steady flow of cash coming in."

Loren Hartt said nothing, simply stared at her.

"I think I've made my point." Tammy rose, her face regaining its lost animation. "If I have your word you won't release my story, you have my word I won't release yours."

Loren rose and faced her. For a long time he studied her.

She turned on her heel and floated out of the lounge to vanish in the corridor. Loren Hartt's hands were clenched into fists. The jaw muscles rippled at the sides of his face.

He was watching in his mind's eye the sight that had greeted him that afternoon—Arn Thorn helplessly flailing his arms in the angry sea around him, trying vainly to keep from sinking to certain death. Now he saw Tammy Scott's image there, not Arn Thorn's. He felt a surge of excitement course through him.

Death in the water!

"Bitch!" he said. "Bitch!"

10.

There had been a wonderful dinner—topped with a flaming baked Alaska that would have done any world-class chef proud—and now Irene Manners was luxuriating in the warm night air on the darkened deck of the *Shangri-la*. She was drowsy, sated with the best food there was to eat, and was absolutely reveling in the fluid motion of the ship as it continued to ply its way southward toward Malta.

Justin had opted to view the latest film thriller in the "theater" —a screening room in the most sybaritic Hollywood tradition, complete with Dolby sound and all the accoutrements of luxury viewing. Irene had seen the picture in Paris on one of her weekly trips to deliver her quota of drawings to *Le Figaro* and had recommended it to Justin. He would obviously have figured it all out by now and probably would have the denouement in mind—but she knew he would like the casting and the acting nevertheless. For a thriller, it was a superior effort.

Her eyes had been closed for several minutes when suddenly she heard a sound and opened them. Someone was leaning over the rail looking out into the blackened night. They had passed by the tip of Sardinia during the early evening. Now there was nothing out there ahead. Whoever it was had obviously not noticed Irene in her deck chair—or perhaps he or she had simply opted not to speak to her.

Then a splash of light from an open porthole fell across the face and she recognized the pouchy, obscene presence of Reggie Dunwoodie. At the moment she recognized him he turned to look directly at her, squinting against the shaft of light that fell across his eyes.

"Ah! Miss Manners!"

"Hello, Mr. Dunwoodie."

"Reggie, please!" sighed the big man, coming over and settling next to her in the adjoining deck chair. "Blackjack can be such a bore! Besides, I needed a breath of fresh air."

Irene and he had talked a bit during lunch. He was making out better with the women than with the men, she could see. There was nothing unusual about that. He did put a man on his mettle; she could tell that just by Justin's bridling reaction to his overbearing homosexuality.

"Who's playing blackjack?" she asked.

"That Boone person. Is he banking? I don't know. My Henry. But he got bored about five minutes ago and split. And that McGuin person. Philanthropy, you know."

"Clifford Boone is one of Tammy Scott's executives."

"Yes, I do believe he is," said Dunwoodie.

Suddenly Irene sensed that Dunwoodie was looking past her into the darkness. She turned but could see nothing there. Apparently Dunwoodie had seen something. He tensed, gathered himself together, and rose. "I do have to scoot!" He moved quickly along the deck toward the bow of the yacht.

She lay there drowsing for some minutes. Then, abruptly, there was a flicker of darkness where there had been light before. She opened her eyes, but at that moment the lights that were in the distance to her left seemed to come on again.

Or had they really been off? What—?

There was nothing amiss. The yacht continued to ply the Mediterranean combers. The rolling continued in its easily anticipated rhythm.

Nothing. Nothing. Nothing.

Irene drifted off again.

At about the time Irene Manners was trying to figure out who was leaning on the rail of the *Shangri-la* in front of her, Justin Birkby was sitting in the gloom of the screening room trying to figure out what was going on in the inevitable mixup of characters in the international potpourri of intrigue that served as plot for the film he was watching.

The British agent was obviously a mole—or perhaps it was *too* obvious that he was a mole. Perhaps he was a double agent, a mole for the Russians, but actually working for the Brits on the ultimate level. There was an Iranian terrorist, or at least someone who looked like a terrorist, but Justin thought he was probably a CIA agent in disguise. And there was the inevitable drug overlord, right out of central casting, resembling Juan Valdez, chief of the Colombian Coffee Investigative Division.

Right now the screen was overflowing with lush silken flesh. The obligatory sex scene was under way, with the muscled hero squirming and bouncing in the bed in the grips of a somewhat bloated sex object of the opposite gender. Justin found his mind wandering. Someone in front of him, apparently suffering from the same lack of interest as he, stood up and edged toward the exit—a door that opened out into the night.

Justin found himself trying to reason out who it was. He had come into the screening room just as the opening titles were showing. He could see three or four dim shapes already seated, but—

No. He corrected himself. There were only *two* shapes there. One in front of him to the right and one to the left. He tried to backtrack in his mind as to who each might be. The one on the left was a woman. And then he had it. Of course. It was Steffi

Hartt. But the one on the right—the one who had just left the theater. Who could *that* be?

He refocused his mind on the shadowy departure and—

Yes. Of course. It was the way she walked. She was tall, erect, but slightly hunched forward. He remembered clearly now. He had noticed her posture the first night—the erect stance that was not actually quite so erect as one would imagine. The tallness, and the deliberate hunching to *seem* smaller. Irene had caught it nicely in one of her sketches.

It was Angelica Farr. Probably headed for the lounge for a pick-me-up, Justin thought with a faint smile. Then he immediately stifled his amusement. That was his trouble, as Irene constantly reminded him. He was policeman enough always to pick on a person's weakest character point or points and make the most of it or of them—rather than the strong points.

Yes, indeed.

As he sat there, thinking about Irene and Angelica, the lights blinked out. Instant and complete darkness engulfed him. Then, rapidly, the house lights came on, but the picture did not. There was a startled second while he tried to imagine what had happened, and it was at that moment that he realized he was alone in the theater. Steffi Hartt had also left—and he had never noticed her go. Probably during one of the more exciting action sequences of the film.

The house lights went off and the movie continued.

What had happened? Justin wondered.

Then, as the sex scene faded and the screen showed a sports car speeding down a twisting road against a background of snowcapped peaks, he found himself riveted to the screen once again and all thought of Steffi Hartt vanished from his mind.

Odd, thought Reggie Dunwoodie as he leaned over the railing looking down into the dark Mediterranean waters as the yacht's prow cleaved through them. Arn Thorn was nowhere in sight. Had he imagined seeing him? Or had he mistaken someone else for him? Perhaps his subconscious was playing tricks on him. He *had* wanted to talk to his client privately. This would be the best opportunity he had yet had. Perhaps his will had induced his eyes to formulate an image that wasn't there.

No Arn Thorn stood up here at the yacht's bow. Puzzled, Reggie turned and peered up at the bridge of the yacht. He could see vague shapes up there—two shapes, actually. Whoever had the night con and whoever was on the wheel. Interesting. He had thought all modern shipping was electronically mandated by computer. Yet here were two live *people.* Impressive! The human race might survive in spite of the incursion of the robots.

His eyes moved down to the main corridor that split the yacht in two. He could see the dim shape of someone standing halfway down to the end. It was a woman, he could swear to that. What cabin? Perhaps Tammy Scott's. The bitch. The goddamn bitch! To take him over—and then tell him what he could and what he couldn't do with Arn Thorn. The kid had *something.* Just because he'd buggered her with that starlet.

The woman wasn't Tammy. Tammy was bigger. It wasn't Angelica—the beast of Beauty and the Beast. She, too, was bigger. A small woman—

He heard steps. Someone was coming toward him in the darkness of the deck.

The spirited bidding continued and, quite suddenly, Dara Lukas found herself dummy once again.

"Sorry, Dara," said Loren Hartt, who was her partner.

Dara smiled. "I suppose there's a rather obvious message there somewhere."

Madge Overstreet giggled. Arn Thorn smiled winningly.

The four of them had been playing ever since about ten thirty, just after dinner. Dara was not the ultimate bridge player, nor was Loren Hartt, but they were good enough. It was Madge Overstreet who had suggested the game, and the three of them had recruited Arn Thorn, who was rooting about for something to do. Rosalyn and he had been in the forward lounge drinking, but Arn had decided he was getting too accustomed to drinking and had left the lounge "for greener pastures," as he had put it. Rosalyn had stayed to drink.

Arn Thorn was not a great player—not even a very good one. But he had learned the game for a role he was playing, and the rudiments were not too complicated for him. It was a good way not to think about the things that were really worrying him. Like his damned career. And like Reggie Dunwoodie, whom he had thought would be his savior. Savior, hell! The old queen kept eying him as if he might come on to him. Arn shuddered. What a turn!

Dara rose. "Excuse me. I think I'll get a breath of fresh air."

It was cool on the deck. Dara drew her scarf around her shoulders and looked forward and aft. There didn't seem to be anybody around. It was pitch dark out. The moon was definitely not up yet. The sky was glistening with the tiny points of a million stars.

She strolled over to the railing and looked out at the water. Time to examine her thoughts a bit; probe, as it were, into her psyche. Was this book she was doing on Tammy Scott a *professional* job? Or was it a *personal* one? Difficult to separate the two concepts in her mind.

She had to admit it: she *hated* Tammy Scott. Hated her to the ends of her being. Tammy had done everything she could but outright destroy Dara in high school. Every boyfriend she had managed, Tammy had stolen. Every honor she had tried to win, Tammy had beaten her to it. Steve, Dara's estranged husband, had ground it in even more harshly: "You should be more like Tammy, Dara. *Can't* you be more like her?"

This hatchet job on Tammy Scott might be nothing more than her nasty way of getting even for all those tiny hurts that were long gone from everybody else's memory—everybody's but Dara's. Dara's psyche revolted against the idea that she was doing this just for spite. And yet . . .

She sighed softly, wrapped the shawl more tightly around her shoulders—it was colder than she had anticipated!—and turned to walk along the deck toward the bow of the yacht. A slight breeze had come up, but it was a gentle, friendly breeze, one that caressed her cheeks and ruffled her hair.

A shadow loomed out of the darkness.

"You frightened me!" Dara gasped.

Reggie Dunwoodie chuckled. Dara shuddered at the unctuousness of the tone. She struggled against her atavistic dislike of deviants and smiled.

"How nice to see you, Mr. Dunwoodie."

"It's a pleasure to share a cruise with someone of your intellectual stature, Ms. Brown. Or do you prefer Lukas?"

"Thank you. Lukas, if you don't mind." Suddenly Dara remembered—or *pretended* she remembered. Dara could not be sure where her pysche ended and her willpower began. "Goodness! You know, I'm supposed to be playing cards! I'm dummy—"

"Never, Ms. Lukas! Never dummy!" Dunwoodie chuckled.

Dara flushed. "I must be returning to the main lounge."

She hurried off as Dunwoodie stared after her. She wondered why he was so interested in watching where she went. She hastened along the main corridor, still wondering. Then, abruptly remembering the unexpected coolness of the night air, she turned off the main corridor toward her cabin.

It was while she was in her cabin, hanging up her scarf and putting on a sweater, that the lights suddenly went very low, vanished, and then came on once again.

The woman was a slim, slick, glossy twenty-five. She had skin as white as milk. But it was the fluidity of her movements that enthralled Cliff Boone. Her face was smooth and pale. She seemed to be a person who was born for the night.

He stared at the flow of her movements as she slipped the card out of the glistening black shoe. A queen. A five. Pause. "Hit me." A seven. And then the silken gathering up of his chips and his cards into the slim, silken, lovely hands.

Dunwoodie had left ten minutes ago, just after Henry Haight had forsaken the card room himself. Ray McGuin was standing behind Boone, as he had been most of the evening, watching with amusement. Boone looked at the dealer. She looked at him.

"Again?"

"Again."

And he watched her hands, slim, slick, gentle.

He and she were alone in the world.

Alone. And broken-hearted.

It must have been five hands later that the lights went out momentarily. After a short sharp shock, they went right on again.

"Oh," said the dealer. She smiled at Boone. She smiled at McGuin.

Boone smiled back at her. "I wonder what that was?"

"Somebody blew a fuse," said the dealer.

McGuin smiled.

She continued to extract the cards slickly from the shoe. One, two, three . . .

11.

By one o'clock the news of Tammy Scott's death by electrocution had spread rapidly throughout the pleasure yacht *Shangri-la,* rousing all those asleep from bed and drawing all those awake out of bars and lounges to congregate excitedly in the forward lounge. There everyone seemed suddenly to find the need to examine one another's degree of shock, consternation, and/or relief.

The more important fact—namely, that the death of Tammy Scott was quite probably not an accident at all, but a carefully calculated act of murder—caused an even deeper sensation to reverberate through the *Shangri-la.*

Justin Birkby added to the impression of alarums and excursions by informing the guests assembled that they would be informally questioned by him one by one, at which indignant cries of "police state," "inquisition," and other epithets clinging to life from the 1960s surfaced, only to die away into eventual silence as the seriousness of the situation became evident.

"Tammy Scott died, so far as we can determine, at eleven

thirty-five," he told them with characteristic restraint. "I am distributing five-by-eight cards on which I would like you to outline the facts of your life in profile, and then in as few words as possible explain exactly what you were doing at that time, with whom you were doing it, and where aboard ship you did it. This will give me salient background data and allow the questioning to proceed with maximum expedience."

"Where will we be interrogated?" Loren Hartt asked.

Justin smiled indulgently. "We call it 'Q & A,' not 'interrogation,'" he said. "Could we have a table set up in the dining room?" Loren signaled a crew member on the outskirts of the assembled guests and the designated seaman hurried off to carry out the order.

Justin turned to Irene, who was in the act of sketching an artistic grouping of Reggie Dunwoodie, Arn Thorn, and Rosalyn Acres deep in conversation in a quiet corner of the lounge.

"You and I have a job to do," he told her in a low voice.

Irene Manners understood. She had heard Justin inform Van Meter that, with the captain's permission, he would organize a quick search through each suite on the yacht at the time the guests were all congregated in the forward lounge; simultaneously Van Meter would have the crew's quarters covered.

"Let's go," said Irene, closing her sketch pad.

Justin Birkby was as skilled at tossing a room as anyone in his chosen profession, and Irene was not only as good as he, but neater in replacing objects exactly where they should be after a quick examination.

"First, the victim's suite," Justin told her as they hurried down the corridor. She frowned slightly, but she followed him nevertheless. He saw her hesitation. "The papers," he explained as they opened the suite door with the master key Van Meter had supplied.

Tammy Scott's familiar attaché case was lying on the counter that stretched along one of the suite's bulkheads under a wide mirror. It was not locked, Justin noted with some surprise. He flipped it open as Irene watched, and found the series of "Scott hot-pink" manila folders lying inside. Each was labeled. Each dossier had the hot-pink paperclip attached to its upper left-hand corner.

" 'Loren Hartt,' " he read, flipping through the folders. " 'Rosalyn Acres.' 'Arn Thorn.' 'Madge Overstreet.' 'Reggie Dunwoodie.' 'Dara Lukas.' " He stopped, riffling back through them. "Did I miss something?" Finally he shook his head. "No. You see the significance?"

Irene was puzzled. "Not quite."

"You heard Tammy Scott accuse Cliff Boone of embezzling from the firm. Where are the papers she spoke of?"

Irene stiffened. "I see. You mean that perhaps the killer—?"

"—stole the papers. Indeed I do. You try her closet. I'll try the luggage."

The two of them began moving about the spacious cabin, making a quick, probing search of the premises. The Clifford Boone folder did not surface.

"She could have been lying," Justin said. "A bluff."

"Yes. Or she could have done something with it."

"Or," Justin continued, "the killer could have *taken* it. In which case it will surface in one of the suites."

They locked up the suite and proceeded down the corridor. It was in Rosalyn Acres's suite—the one she shared with Arn Thorn—that Justin discovered what he described as an "interesting" object in the spacious bathing area adjoining the room. When Irene came in from the main cabin, he held out to her an old-fashioned and very worn-out hair dryer.

"What's so interesting about that old thing?" Irene wondered, taking it and looking it over dubiously. "If this was mine, I'd have scrapped it months ago. Years ago."

"Exactly," said Justin with satisfaction. He took the dryer and pointed to the cord near the blower motor. The plastic insulation was crumbling away. Some of it had chipped off. Two live wires were visible, almost touching one another.

"What do you mean, 'exactly'? I don't see what you're getting at."

"The *idea*," Justin explained. "Perhaps Arn Thorn was looking at that broken insulation and thinking. Thinking about live wires and electrocution. Thinking about water, perhaps, and live wires in water. Thinking about Tammy Scott's TV set. If *that* insulation was broken—or maybe even *cut*—he could plop it in her bath water and—"

"Oh, come on! Pure speculation. You can't call *that* a clue?"

Justin tapped his head lightly. "Nevertheless, I do."

Next it was Irene's turn. As soon as they entered Dara Lukas's suite, she went for the clothing closet. Reaching above on the shelf where the life jackets were stored, she encountered several hats and other—well—"interesting" objects. "Justin!"

He came in from the bathing area and watched as Irene lifted out a half dozen stretch wigs of varying colors from the closet shelf. "She can be a blonde, a redhead, a brunette, a light-brown, a basic black. It's amazing!"

Justin moved quickly toward her. He took one and held another in his other hand, comparing them. "They're different *styles* of coiffure!"

"That's the *point* of stretch wigs," sighed Irene. "It's to cut down on hairdressing. You buy a wig for style as well as for color."

"Did she do it for some sinister reason? Disguise? Or did she do it simply to cover her head?"

"I don't know," Irene said softly. Justin was writing a note on a card he carried.

It was he who came up with the next discovery. Someone had left a copy of a Nice newspaper in the wastebasket in Clifford Boone's suite. Justin took it out and glanced at it. He was about to discard it where he had found it when a random thought occurred and he began leafing through it. To simplify the process, he laid it on the duvet and turned the pages one by one. It was near the end that he noticed a section had been torn out of a sheet.

"Irene."

She joined him. "It's the television listings," she told him immediately.

"Yes. Mr. Boone doesn't speak French, does he?"

"I have no idea," said Irene.

"We'll find out."

"But he's interested in the ten, eleven, and twelve p.m. programs on French television."

"Does that spark any interest in your mind?" Justin asked.

"The eleven-thirty programming! He *knows* Tammy Scott watches her commercials. And he *knows* she relaxes in her bubble bath every night. A reminder?"

"I don't know," Justin said warily. "Still—"

Irene turned the torn sheet over. There were several filler news stories there in the area of the hole ripped out. "Unless he collects small news items."

Carefully Justin folded the newspaper and dropped it back in the wastebasket.

It was, however, Irene Manners who discovered the main object sought in their search of the yacht. As they were about to enter the door to the suite assigned to Reginald Dunwoodie and Henry Haight, Irene noted that the plastic laundry bag prepared for pickup by the laundry detail was hanging on the doorknob. Riffling through it rapidly, she felt rather than saw the cold metal of the key at the bottom of the bag.

"*Voilà!*" She held it up without comment to Justin's widening eyes. Within moments they had tried it in the door to Tammy Scott's suite. It worked. It was no doubt the copy Angelica Farr had been given.

"Two possibilities," said Justin. "One. It implicates Dunwoodie and Haight. Two. Someone else discarded it there to avoid detection. The killer?"

"Or three," Irene said with a smile. "Somebody found it and simply put it in the nearest receptacle without even wondering whose it was."

They found nothing else of consequence in their admittedly superficial search.

"You'll note the Cliff Boone papers did not appear," Justin told Irene as they hurried back to the forward lounge.

It was close to one thirty when Justin and Irene returned to the guests and announced that the Q & A session was about to begin. Then Justin collected the five-by-eight dossiers and proceeded to the dining room where he and Irene sat down at the table ready to begin.

NAME: STEPHANIE HARTT. AGE: 45. BORN: SAN JOSE, CALIFORNIA. EDUCATION: B.A., SAN JOSE STATE. BECAME MARKETING DIRECTOR FOR FABRICS FIRM IN LOS ANGELES. WHEN LOREN HARTT BOUGHT UP COMPANY, HE MET SUBJECT AT SALES CONVENTION, FELL IN LOVE WITH HER. SUBJECT AND LH MARRIED SIX MONTHS LATER. RELATIONSHIP WITH VICTIM: SUBJECT KNEW TAMMY SCOTT FROM HUSBAND'S INVOLVEMENT WITH HER IN LATE SIXTIES. SUBJECT AND VICTIM MET OCCASIONALLY, BUT ONLY TO OBSERVE ONE ANOTHER FROM A COOL DISTANCE.
SUBJECT'S WHEREABOUTS AT 11:35 P.M.: SUBJECT SAYS SCREENING ROOM. (SEEN BY JUSTIN BIRKBY AND ANGELICA FARR?)

EXCERPTS FROM Q & A TRANSCRIPT:

JUSTIN: Mrs. Hartt, I was in the screening room myself at eleven thirty-five. But you weren't there then.

STEFFI: I beg your pardon!

JUSTIN: The lights came on just after the power outage and before the film began again. You had been sitting in front of me to the left, and you weren't there when the lights came up.

STEFFI: Oh, dear. Well, I suppose you're right—if you say so.

JUSTIN: I am. I do.

STEFFI: Then I—That's odd. I *thought* I was there when the power failed. But if I wasn't . . .

JUSTIN: Shortly after or shortly before you went out, Angelica Farr went out also. Did you see her after you left the screening room?

STEFFI: Oddly enough, I did. We were hurrying in opposite directions and as she came around a corner, I ran into her. We both sprawled on the deck. It was not a pretty sight.

JUSTIN: Was Miss Farr intoxicated?

STEFFI: I believe she was—not! If that's a surprise.

JUSTIN: What did you talk about?

STEFFI: Nothing earthshaking. Just, sorry about that. I helped her pick up the things that spilled from that saddlebag she carries.

JUSTIN: A key, perhaps? To Tammy Scott's suite?

STEFFI: Actually, I don't *recall* it. But—

JUSTIN: Then where did you go, Mrs. Hartt?

STEFFI: I was thirsty. I went to the Coke machine aft.

JUSTIN: Where did Miss Farr go?

STEFFI: I'm sorry. I have no idea. It was an embarrassing encounter.

JUSTIN: Did anyone see you at the Coke machine?

STEFFI: I think no one saw me.

JUSTIN: The Coke machine aft, as I recall, is about ten feet from Tammy Scott's stateroom door, is it not?

STEFFI: It is.

ASSESSMENT OF Q & A:

Irene Manners put her long legs out, crossed them at the ankles, and stretched a moment. Justin thought of a cat, sleek, well-fed, purry.

She lifted a piece of paper and showed Justin a sketch she had made of Steffi Hartt. "She's a beautiful woman."

Justin fretted. "So was Lucretia Borgia. What do you think of her answers?"

Irene considered. "I believe her."

"That key! Look. She grabs up the key, palms it. Then she goes into Tammy Scott's suite and does her in. Don't you see how easy it would be?"

"I don't believe she did it. She's not right for the part of a murderer."

Justin rolled his eyes. "Irene! You *know* appearances don't count in a murder investigation."

"Motive? Why? Revenge for all the evil things Tammy Scott did to Loren Hartt?" Irene shook her head. "She's not vindictive. She's—well—wholesome. The other way around—Steffi the victim, Tammy the killer—yes! I don't believe she did it. Sorry."

"Write this down," snapped Justin. "Motive: revenge on a secondary level. Means: the television was there. All she had to do was drop it in. And I think quite possibly Tammy Scott might have stayed in that tub if Steffi walked in."

"Well—"

"Opportunity: all the opportunity in the world, if she picked up that key!"

"Yes, but—I just don't think she did it."

"But all three elements prove out—motive, means, and opportunity. And she doesn't have an alibi."

NAME: REGINALD DUNWOODIE. AGE: 51. BORN: SAN FRANCISCO, CALIFORNIA. TRIED STAGE IN SMALL PRODUCTIONS: PASADENA PLAYHOUSE, LA JOLLA, ETC. TELEVISION. DRIFTED INTO AGENTING. BECAME REMARKABLY SUCCESSFUL. FORMED OWN COMPANY, LATER PURCHASED BY TAMMY SCOTT.
RELATIONSHIP WITH VICTIM: THROUGH SUBJECT'S EXPERTISE, VICTIM ADVERTISED COSMETICS LINE ON TV, USING SOAP OPERA STARRING ARN THORN.
WHEREABOUTS OF SUBJECT AT 11:35. ON DECK.

HAD JUST LEFT CASINO AND WAS STROLLING ON DECK. WITNESSES: IRENE MANNERS AND DARA LUKAS.

EXCERPTS FROM Q & A TRANSCRIPT:

JUSTIN: I'm curious as to a possible reason why the key to Tammy Scott's cabin should have been found in the laundry bag you and Henry Haight left hanging on your doorknob.

DUNWOODIE: It's obvious to me, sir, that someone slipped that key into our laundry bag to make it *appear* that we were guilty of murder. I'd suggest you bend all your efforts to identifying *that* person, and you'll have your killer!

JUSTIN: Did you enter Tammy Scott's stateroom tonight at any time?

DUNWOODIE: No, sir, I did not. But I did see a woman just outside her cabin close to eleven thirty. I was a long way off, unfortunately.

JUSTIN: Did you recognize her?

DUNWOODIE: No, sir, I did not.

JUSTIN: Was she short or tall?

DUNWOODIE: Medium. I'm sorry—I've thought about it and thought about it. I have no idea who she was.

JUSTIN: Tammy Scott bought up your talent agency. Do you bear her any ill will?

DUNWOODIE: You're barking up the wrong tree, sir. She saved my skin. I was going broke.

JUSTIN: One of your clients is Arn Thorn.

DUNWOODIE: He'll be a hot prospect someday. You wait and see.

JUSTIN: Tammy Scott blackballed him all over town.

DUNWOODIE: Correct. But we'll make out yet.

JUSTIN: Now you will, with Tammy Scott out of the way.

DUNWOODIE: I didn't mean that, sir.

ASSESSMENT OF Q & A PRODUCED NO NEW DATA. [SIGNED: J. B.]

NAME: LOREN HARTT. AGE: 58. BORN: ALBUQUER-
QUE, NEW MEXICO. REAL ESTATE DEVELOPER,
CONSTRUCTION ENGINEER, FINANCIER, CEO, HO-
TEL OWNER, ETC. MULTIBILLIONAIRE.
RELATIONSHIP WITH VICTIM: SUBJECT MARRIED
VICTIM IN 1968. WAS BRUTALIZED DURING DI-
VORCE PROCEEDINGS BY VICTIM, WHO CHARAC-
TERIZED SUBJECT AS A "WIMP," A "YUPPIE ADO-
LESCENT," A "NERD," AND A "NAIF."
WHEREABOUTS OF SUBJECT AT 11:35 P.M.: PLAY-
ING BRIDGE IN THE MAIN LOUNGE. WITNESSES:
ARN THORN, MADGE OVERSTREET. DARA LUKAS
WAS OUT AT THE TIME.

**SUBJECT GAVE AN ALMOST VERBATIM
ACCOUNT OF HIS CONFRONTATION WITH
VICTIM. NO NEW DATA. [Signed: J. B.]**

NAME: ANGELICA FARR. AGE: 35. BORN: CHICAGO,
ILLINOIS. GRADUATE, UNIVERSITY OF CHICAGO.
FURTHER STUDIES AT MASSACHUSETTS INSTI-
TUTE OF TECHNOLOGY.
RELATIONSHIP WITH VICTIM: SUBJECT MET VIC-
TIM AFTER VICTIM HAD INHERITED SAM SCOTT'S
COSMETICS FIRM. SUBJECT BORED WITH ELEC-
TRONICS ENGINEERING, WANTED A MORE GLAM-
OROUS PROFESSION. OPTED TO BECOME VICTIM'S
NUMBER ONE GOFER.
WHEREABOUTS OF SUBJECT AT 11:35 P.M.: IN THE
SCREENING ROOM. WITNESSES: JUSTIN BIRKBY
AND STEFFI HARTT.

EXCERPT OF Q & A TRANSCRIPT:

JUSTIN: Sorry, Ms. Farr. You had just *left* the screening room when the lights went out.

ANGELICA: Had I, now?

JUSTIN: Very definitely.

ANGELICA: Then I must have been just outside the theater.

JUSTIN: Only if you did not move from the moment you left. I calculate there must have been between five and ten minutes between the time you left and the time the lights went. I was in there, and I saw you leave.

ANGELICA: It was dark. Maybe you really saw Steffi Hartt leave. She was there, too, you know.

JUSTIN: It was you, Angelica. I saw you picking your way through the seats against a panorama of lascivious living flesh on the screen.

ANGELICA: That *was* quite a handful up there, wasn't it?

JUSTIN: You have a memorable profile—tall, but slightly hunched over.

ANGELICA: You're very observant.

JUSTIN: It's my profession. Did you meet Steffi Hartt in the corridor?

ANGELICA: Funny you should mention that. We cannonballed into one another. Both of us went down. All knees and elbows. No bruises, though.

JUSTIN: Did Tammy Scott's key come out of your bag when you fell?

ANGELICA: Of course not. I would have noticed it. So would Steffi Hartt. I'm sure not.

JUSTIN: Perhaps you dropped it so Steffi Hartt could pick it up as if by accident. Well?

ANGELICA: I told you—it was stolen!

JUSTIN: Was it? For the moment let's forget about Mrs. Hartt. How about this scenario? You use your key, you enter Mrs. Scott's suite just after leaving the screening room, you kill her, you leave, and you hide the key in the laundry bag hanging outside the cabin of Dunwoodie and Haight.

ANGELICA: Why the hell would I kill Mrs. Scott? I was not unhappy to be her—her right hand.

JUSTIN: Her *handmaiden,* did I almost hear you say?

ANGELICA: You're much too literary, Mr. Birkby. Scotty was boorish, she was a bully, but she was amusing.

JUSTIN: How well did you know Loren Hartt?

ANGELICA: I've only met him once. On this cruise.

JUSTIN: I have another scenario. Loren Hartt has plans to buy out Scott Cosmetics. He learns a great deal about the people working for Tammy Scott. He gets help from you so he can move in for the takeover.

ANGELICA: Oh, come on now! Me? Help him ruin Scotty?

JUSTIN: He tells Tammy Scott he has succeeded. But Tammy has something on Hartt, something to do with his early years when they were married. And he decides to kill her. He blackmails you to help him, because he has had your cooperation in raiding Scott Cosmetics.

ANGELICA: Utterly absurd!

JUSTIN: You agree to help him by supplying the key to Tammy Scott's suite.

ANGELICA: But I thought Loren Hartt was playing cards—

JUSTIN: He was indeed. He gives Tammy's suite key to his wife, who then—

ANGELICA: Utter balderdash! You're unbelievable, Mr. Birkby!

JUSTIN: Who do you think killed Mrs. Scott, Angelica?

ANGELICA: I hadn't thought about it.

JUSTIN: Come now! I'm sure—
ANGELICA: Cliff Boone.
JUSTIN: What do you know about Boone?
ANGELICA: He's a turd. And bad people.
JUSTIN: I see.
ANGELICA: Can I have a second choice?
JUSTIN: Certainly.
ANGELICA: All right. Arn Thorn.
JUSTIN: Difficult. He's got a good alibi.
ANGELICA: How about Dara Lukas?
JUSTIN: You dislike her?
ANGELICA: She's doing a hatchet job on Scotty. Sorry.
   Was doing.
JUSTIN: Motive?
ANGELICA: They've hated each other since they were
   kids together. Ask her about that.

ASSESSMENT OF Q & A INCONCLUSIVE.
[Signed: J. B.]

NAME: L. CLIFFORD BOONE. AGE: 42. BORN: SEAT-
TLE, WASHINGTON. ATTENDED GONZAGA UNI-
VERSITY, ENGINEERING MAJOR, THEN CHANGED
TO BUSINESS ADMINISTRATION. BECAME AC-
COUNTANT IN SAN DIEGO. HIRED IN NEW YORK
BY SAM SCOTT BEFORE HE MARRIED TAMMY.
RELATIONSHIP WITH VICTIM: EXCELLENT RELA-
TIONSHIP (HE SAYS).
WHEREABOUTS OF SUBJECT AT 11:35 P.M.: IN THE
CASINO, PLAYING BLACKJACK. WITNESSES: RAY
McGUIN. ALSO REGGIE DUNWOODIE, FOR PARTIAL
ALIBI.

EXCERPT OF Q & A TRANSCRIPT:
JUSTIN: You like to play cards, Mr. Boone?
BOONE: Don't we all?

JUSTIN: Some more than others. Would you say you had a *thing* about gambling, Mr. Boone?

BOONE: Of course not. Gambling is relaxing, isn't it?

JUSTIN: I notice you answer each of my questions by asking another.

BOONE: Is this a psychological evaluation, or a police inquiry?

JUSTIN: Both, perhaps. Now. How do you get along with Tammy Scott? I mean, of course—how *did* you get along with Tammy Scott?

BOONE: Fine. We had a perfect business relationship.

JUSTIN: I see. There were no problems? I mean, like the affair some time ago with Rosalyn Acres?

BOONE: That is all water under the bridge.

JUSTIN: I see. And there has been no hint of—of conflict between you?

BOONE: None whatsoever.

JUSTIN: Good. Are you married, Mr. Boone?

BOONE: No, sir. Why do you ask?

JUSTIN: We had no record of it. I simply wanted confirmation.

BOONE: Does the fact I am not married bother you, Mr. Birkby?

JUSTIN: I'll handle the questions, if you don't mind.

BOONE: Of course.

JUSTIN: Do you watch a great deal of television, Mr. Boone?

BOONE: Hardly any at all.

JUSTIN: But you *do* occasionally switch on a channel for relaxation.

BOONE: Possibly.

JUSTIN: Do you speak French?

BOONE: Well, I did take a little in high school.

JUSTIN: *Un peu, peut-etre, n'est-ce pas? Jusque assez pour vous vous faire compris?*

BOONE: Huh?

JUSTIN: It piques my curiosity, Mr. Boone, why,

when you cannot understand spoken French, you chose to tear out a column listing the eleven-thirty programming of the Riviera TV channels. It's almost as if you wanted to remind yourself to tune in. To what? "Twenty Questions" in a foreign language?

BOONE: Let the record show I was playing blackjack at eleven thirty tonight.

JUSTIN: Why in heaven's name would you want to know what program was on?

BOONE: I don't know myself. Why do you ask?

JUSTIN: We know you tore out the programming from the newspaper in your stateroom, Mr. Boone.

BOONE: I see. I don't remember ever doing that. Someone else—

JUSTIN: Someone else is doing a number on you?

BOONE: Exactly.

JUSTIN: That's an interesting pin you're wearing.

BOONE: Oh. Yes.

JUSTIN: What exactly *is* it?

BOONE: A service medal.

JUSTIN: For what specifically?

BOONE: Sharpshooting.

JUSTIN: You were in the service as a sniper?

BOONE: One does what the brass tells one in the service, sir.

JUSTIN: Of course. You now have an expensive apartment on Central Park South. I presume you make a great deal of money.

BOONE: Mrs. Scott is very generous.

JUSTIN: Indeed. And so, I believe, are you.

BOONE: I beg your pardon?

JUSTIN: Generous. With your money. Playing the casinos. Especially those in Atlantic City.

BOONE: I do like to gamble on occasion. Within reason.

JUSTIN: Then there is no truth to the rumor that

auditors have been called in to go over your accounts at Scott Cosmetics?

BOONE: No truth whatsoever, sir.

JUSTIN: Are you overdressed, Mr. Boone?

BOONE: I beg your pardon?

JUSTIN: It isn't particularly hot in here, is it?

BOONE: No.

JUSTIN: Yet you seem to be dripping with perspiration.

BOONE: It's a metabolic thing, Mr. Birkby.

JUSTIN: I do hope so.

ASSESSMENT OF Q & A:

Justin lay back in his chair and breathed softly. "One. He's
definitely a gambler. And a gambler always runs the risk of getting in too deep. That could be the reason for embezzling money
from Tammy Scott."

"He's a *compulsive* gambler, too," Irene said, scribbling something in her notes.

"Two. He's lying completely about his situation at Scott Cosmetics. He thinks we don't know. Because, of course, now there
is no Tammy Scott to pass on the information."

"And three, he's as nervous as a cat."

Justin sighed. "The only problem is that he has an ironclad
alibi."

NAME: DARA LUKAS. AGE: 55. BORN: VIENNA, AUS-
TRIA. CAME TO NEW YORK AS CHILD, EDUCATED
THROUGH HIGH SCHOOL ON LONG ISLAND. COL-
LEGE AT HARVARD, THEN TO COLUMBIA SCHOOL
OF JOURNALISM. HIRED BY LOS ANGELES TIMES.
COVERED END OF KOREAN POLICE ACTION. TO
BERLIN WALL CRISIS IN 1961. THEN TO ORIENT
FOR VIETNAM WAR.
RELATIONSHIP WITH VICTIM: SUBJECT AND VIC-

TIM WENT TO HIGH SCHOOL TOGETHER. ALWAYS
AT SWORDS' POINTS. LOATHED ONE ANOTHER.
DRIFTED APART AFTER GRADUATION.
WHEREABOUTS OF SUBJECT AT 11:35 P.M.: WALK-
ING ABOUT ON DECK. HAD BEEN PLAYING CARDS.
WITNESSES: LOREN HARTT, ARN THORN, MADGE
OVERSTREET.

EXCERPT OF Q & A TRANSCRIPT:

JUSTIN: I've read that you're writing a book about
Tammy Scott's life.

DARA: I was. I suppose I'll chuck it now.

JUSTIN: Why? Because a dead person isn't as interesting as a live one?

DARA: Because the publisher may welch on the contract.

JUSTIN: I thought you had the goods on her, as you
Americans say.

DARA: This wasn't to be a hatchet job.

JUSTIN: No? A true appreciation?

DARA: You aren't asking questions, sir, you're mock-
ing me.

JUSTIN: But you two were close in high school—in
Hicksville, Long Island, I believe.

DARA: That's right.

JUSTIN: Friends?

DARA: I wouldn't say that.

JUSTIN: Enemies?

DARA: Now you're putting words in my mouth.

JUSTIN: I see you're wearing the light brown one
now.

DARA: My stretch wig? Yes. If that's any of your
business.

JUSTIN: My business at this point happens to be
murder, Miss Lukas. And anything that con-
cerns this murder.

DARA: Mrs. Lukas.

JUSTIN: And sensitive issues surface when one deals with personalities and personal relationships.

DARA: I wear stretch wigs because I am in the public eye a great deal. I simply don't have time to do my hair. I spend a lot of hours waiting for planes at airports and driving from airports to hotels. It's a matter of practicality.

JUSTIN: But the enormous variety—

DARA: I have a wardrobe of travel clothes. Some wigs go with certain outfits.

JUSTIN: She embarrassed you the night before last.

DARA: I don't pretend not to be vain. I was made to look a fool.

JUSTIN: You said she hadn't seen the last of you. I took that to mean you'd be back to set things right.

DARA: I simply spoke without thinking.

JUSTIN: Do you still hate Tammy Scott?

DARA: How can I? She's no longer here to hate.

JUSTIN: Touché, I suppose, Mrs. Lukas. When you were walking about the deck, did you see any-one who might have been involved in entering Tammy Scott's cabin?

DARA: No. At least, I don't think so.

JUSTIN: And you? Did you enter her cabin?

DARA: Never in a million years.

ASSESSMENT OF Q & A:

Justin shook his head. "She's far too intelligent to get mixed up in something as sleazy as murder. If she wanted to do in Tammy Scott, she would have done it with words—and a long time before this."

"What do you think about those wigs?"

"Very attractive," said Justin.

"I mean—isn't there something a little odd about her casual-ness? I would have spit nails if I'd been unfrocked that way!"

Justin smiled. "I see what you mean." Suddenly his face froze. "Hey! Here's something we haven't considered!"

Irene looked up, startled. She could tell by his voice that he had had another idea. "What?"

"It's not Dara I'm thinking about. It's someone else. Suppose that someone found out about Dara's warehouse of wigs and borrowed one of them!"

"And used it?" Irene frowned. "So?"

"Don't you get it?"

"What would be the point? What woman would want to put on a wig to—"

"No, no, no! What *man?* Don't you see?"

Irene's eyes widened. "You mean the perpetrator—a male— stole one of her wigs and put it on to pass for a woman? In that case, the person Dunwoodie saw was really a man dressed in a wig—"

Justin heaved a sigh. "Too big. Most of the men are too big."

"Henry Haight," said Irene, as she shuffled through her drawings. "You know, he's only five foot five. And he's slim."

"But why in the world would Haight want to kill Tammy Scott? And how could he get into her cabin?"

"He found Angelica's key. After all, the key was in his laundry bag!"

Justin sighed. " 'You have ravished justice; Forced him to do your pleasure.' "

"Pish, tush!" snapped Irene. "I call them the way I see them."

NAME: HENRY HAIGHT. AGE: 25. BORN: HART-FORD, CONNECTICUT. YALE GRADUATE. STAGE-CRAFT, DESIGNING SETS AND PAINTING FLATS. TO BROADWAY. ON TO HOLLYWOOD. THERE MET REGGIE DUNWOODIE.
RELATIONSHIP WITH VICTIM: THROUGH REGGIE.
WHEREABOUTS OF SUBJECT AT 11:35 P.M.: BLACK-JACK TABLE. WITNESSES: RAY McGUIN. CLIFF

BOONE. (HAIGHT WALKED AWAY SOME MINUTES
BEFORE LIGHTS WENT OUT.)

EXCERPT OF Q & A TRANSCRIPT:

JUSTIN: I'm a little vague about exactly where you
    were tonight at eleven thirty-five.

HAIGHT: I had left the casino and made for the deck.
    I settled down in a deck chair.

JUSTIN: Where exactly was this, Mr. Haight?

HAIGHT: At the back of the ship.

JUSTIN: Aft.

HAIGHT: Yes.

JUSTIN: *Then* where did you go?

HAIGHT: I went to the weight room.

JUSTIN: Ah! That's just above Tammy Scott's suite,
    isn't it?

HAIGHT: I suppose it is. Look. If you think I did this
    thing, you're wrong. I had no problem with
    Tammy Scott.

JUSTIN: But you do support your friend Reginald
    Dunwoodie.

HAIGHT: Yes, I do. I respect you for not having badg-
    ered me for the details.

JUSTIN: And Mr. Dunwoodie does not like what
    Tammy Scott has done to him.

HAIGHT: I was pumping iron, I think, when the
    power outage occurred.

JUSTIN: I see. But no one was in there with you.

HAIGHT: No.

JUSTIN: So you could have used Tammy Scott's key
    —the one that she gave to Angelica Farr—to
    enter her stateroom and—

HAIGHT: The key in our laundry was a plant.

JUSTIN: Was it?

HAIGHT: I didn't kill her, damn it!

ASSESSMENT OF Q & A:

Justin Birkby stood up and walked back and forth a moment before seating himself again. Irene Manners did not disturb him; it was obvious he was in deep thought.

"There's something missing here," he murmured. "I don't mean with Henry Haight. I mean with the whole list of suspects. The thing just doesn't seem to come together properly. And I can't quite figure out why it doesn't."

Irene was sorting out a sheaf of papers on the couch next to her. "Ray McGuin really does look like Jimmy Stewart, doesn't he?"

Justin snorted. "You haven't heard a word I've said!"

She looked up, startled. "I'm in total agreement with you. There *is* a great deal missing. There's no ingredient—no *active* ingredient—to make the formula work."

"Maybe she killed herself. You know, got tired of the executive shuffle, and simply did herself in."

"Come now!" snapped Irene. "You can say that, about Tammy Scott?"

Justin sighed. "All right—no more of that! Who's next?"

"Raymond McGuin."

NAME: RAY McGUIN. AGE: 58. BORN: KANSAS CITY, MISSOURI. INHERITED A BUNDLE. BECAME IN-TERESTED IN PHILANTHROPIES.
RELATIONSHIP WITH VICTIM: SUBJECT PER-SUADED VICTIM TO CHANNEL MONEY INTO VARI-OUS TAX-EXEMPT CHARITIES FOR TAX RELIEF. ON FRIENDLY TERMS.
WHEREABOUTS OF SUBJECT AT 11:35 P.M.: PLAY-ING BLACKJACK IN THE CASINO. WITNESSES: CLIFF BOONE. DEALER. (HARRY HAIGHT HAD LEFT EARLIER.)

EXCERPT OF Q & A TRANSCRIPT:

JUSTIN: Why do you think you were invited aboard this yacht, Mr. McGuin?

MCGUIN: I am friendly with Mr. and Mrs. Hartt and a number of others aboard. Is that so strange?

JUSTIN: Yes. Because you alone on board seem to bear no animosity toward Tammy Scott.

MCGUIN: Of course not! She was a lovely woman.

JUSTIN: By "lovely woman" I assume you refer to her interest in your philanthropic enterprises.

MCGUIN: In my line of business, Mr. Birkby, one meets many people. I certainly judged Tammy Scott to be in the top echelon of creative industrialists. Her death is a grievous loss to the business community.

JUSTIN: Do you gamble much, Mr. McGuin?

MCGUIN: Almost never.

JUSTIN: Yet tonight—

MCGUIN: I kibitzed.

JUSTIN: Isn't it true that you have been spending most of your time in the casino?

MCGUIN: Not at all. I was in the weight room for several hours in the afternoon.

JUSTIN: You do a great deal of aerobics?

MCGUIN: Aerobics and good health are linked, sir. In fact, exercise has allowed me to meet a lot of very interesting people.

JUSTIN: For your philanthropies, I assume.

MCGUIN: You assume correctly, sir.

ASSESSMENT OF Q & A:

Justin frowned at Irene after the philanthropist had left them. "Why did Raymond McGuin, with no interest in gambling, spend most of his evening in the casino?"

"Perhaps he was interested in the dealer."

Justin frowned.

"She's quite a *type seduisant, non?*"

"Perhaps. But McGuin does not strike me as a womanizer."

"Still waters run deep," said Irene.

"Hmm," said Justin.

NAME: ARN(OLD) THORN. AGE: 38. BORN: NEW YORK CITY. SUMMER STOCK AT LONG WHARF THEATER, NEW HAVEN. OFF-OFF BROADWAY. ON TO LOS ANGELES AND TELEVISION.
RELATIONSHIP WITH VICTIM: WHEN VICTIM MET SUBJECT AT A SCOTT COSMETICS PARTY, SHE IMMEDIATELY COVETED HIM AND HE BECAME HER PET PROJECT. SUBJECT LATER PICKED UP WITH A STARLET, AND VICTIM DROPPED HIM, DESTROYING BOTH HIM AND HIS CAREER.
WHEREABOUTS OF SUBJECT AT 11:35: IN THE MAIN LOUNGE, PLAYING CARDS. WITNESSES: LOREN HARTT. MADGE OVERSTREET. DARA LUKAS (ALTHOUGH D. L. WAS NOT THERE AT THE EXACT TIME OF THE OUTAGE).

EXCERPT OF Q & A TRANSCRIPT:

JUSTIN: I know briefly about your relationship with Tammy Scott. What actually attracted you to her?

ARN: You got it wrong, Mr. Birkby. She came on to me, not I on to her.

JUSTIN: Your relationship was a one-way street?

ARN: She was insatiable in bed. *If* that's what you're angling for.

JUSTIN: I'm angling only for the truth, Mr. Thorn.

ARN: She's a bloodsucker.

JUSTIN: But it was you, if I'm not mistaken, who made the first move to destroy the relationship.

ARN: We had an arrangement, Mr. Birkby. We could

each go our own way if we pleased. Whenever
we wanted. It was only by chance that I was the
first to tire of the game.

JUSTIN: But she seemed enraged that you might prefer someone else to her.

ARN: She always acted in character.

JUSTIN: And of course you've resented her ever
since.

ARN: She ruined my career. She blacklisted me.
She's kept me out of the business for three
years! How could I pretend I didn't hate her?
Anyway, everybody knows where I was when
she was supposedly killed.

JUSTIN: But you might have prepared the wire be-
forehand. She might conceivably have acciden-
tally tipped the set over into the water herself.
And that would make you an accessory, Mr.
Thorn.

ASSESSMENT OF Q & A:

Justin's eyes wandered to the collection of bagged materials
they had brought in from their search of the guest suites. He
studied the hair dryer for a long moment.

"Rosalyn Acres's hair dryer?" Irene wondered. "Is that what
you're wondering about?"

"No." He leaned back, letting his eyes drift to the ceiling of
the lounge. There lights were inlaid cleverly to cut off the glare
and to conceal their presence. The fact of their cunning conceal-
ment struck him forcefully and in a moment he had another idea.

"We've been missing a bet here, Irene," he said finally. "We
have not explored the possibility of an accomplice. That is, the
murderer is visible and alibied, but the accomplice is hidden,
doing the dirty job. In other words, we've ignored the fact that
two people working together might have accomplished the death
of Tammy Scott. For example, perhaps one of the suspects with
a perfect alibi worked with someone else without an alibi. To-

gether they both had motive, means, and opportunity. Singly, neither would qualify as a true suspect."

"You're referring to Rosalyn Acres?"

"Yes. Let's get her in here and see what she was doing during that blackout."

NAME: ROSALYN ACRES. AGE: 30. BORN: NEW YORK CITY. DIVORCED AFTER EARLY MARRIAGE. SECRETARY, BOOKKEEPER. THEN WORKED FOR CLIFF BOONE UNDER TAMMY SCOTT. WAS FIRED. WORKED PREPARING IRS FORMS FOR CLIENTS IN DENVER. TO HOLLYWOOD WHERE SHE MET ARN THORN.
RELATIONSHIP WITH VICTIM: HAD BLOWUP WITH VICTIM; SUBJECT WAS BLAMED FOR PILFERING FROM PETTY CASH. HAD TO MOVE FROM NEW YORK. HATES VICTIM. HAD GOOD REASON TO DETEST CLIFF BOONE, WHO DID NOT STAND UP FOR HER.
WHEREABOUTS OF SUBJECT AT 11:35: IN FORWARD LOUNGE. (BARKEEP CAN'T REMEMBER EXACTLY WHEN SHE WAS THERE.)

EXCERPT OF Q & A TRANSCRIPT:

JUSTIN: Where were you at eleven thirty-five, Mrs. Acres?

ROSALYN: That's *Ms.* Acres. Acres was my own name. I dumped Gregory Jessup and I dumped his name, too. We grew up next door to each other. It didn't work out.

JUSTIN: I see. You haven't had a happy life, have you, Ms. Acres?

ROSALYN: I was in the forward lounge when you all say she cooked, damn it! I was drinking. I've a right to drink, haven't I?

JUSTIN: If that's your pleasure, certainly. Ben Babcock, the crewman who tends bar in the forward lounge, can't seem to remember where you were at eleven thirty-five. He remembers you drinking, but thinks you left *before* that time.

ROSALYN: He's wrong.

JUSTIN: And there's a witness who says he saw a woman in the corridor outside Tammy Scott's cabin at about eleven thirty.

ROSALYN: He's lying! It wasn't me!

JUSTIN: I didn't say it was a man. I said "a witness."

ROSALYN: I don't know *why* I said "he"! You've got me confused!

JUSTIN: How do you get along with Clifford Boone, Rosalyn?

ROSALYN: So it *was* him! He's out to get me.

JUSTIN: No. He's not the witness. I'm simply asking how you get along with Mr. Boone.

ROSALYN: He and Tammy framed me. How do you think I got along with them? Both! She hated *me. I* didn't hate her.

JUSTIN: Certainly after what she did to you—chucking you out without proper procedure—you must have disliked her.

ROSALYN: Not enough to kill her.

JUSTIN: Well, actually, it's not the motive I'm particularly concerned with. Or even the means.

ROSALYN: Means?

JUSTIN: The means of murder. The *modus* of the death. The electric cord that slid into the bath and electrocuted Mrs. Scott.

ROSALYN: If it's neither, what is it, then?

JUSTIN: It's opportunity. No one seems to know where you were at the time Mrs. Scott was killed. At eleven thirty-five, as we have determined it might be.

ROSALYN: You can't pin this thing on me! I was drinking, damn it!

ASSESSMENT OF Q & A:

Both Irene and Justin were sitting up when Rosalyn Acres left.

"Now there's a real live one," said Irene.

"You think she did it?"

"She and that actor working together *could* have."

"But *did* they?"

Irene studied Justin. "You seem less than sanguine about this."

Justin closed his eyes. "Would Tammy Scott be satisfied to sit in the bubble bath and let Rosalyn Acres approach her without resistance?"

Irene shook her head. "The vibes between them would hardly have permitted it. Tammy knew how much Rosalyn hated her. She certainly would have suspected something."

Justin pondered. "Also you have to consider that in our scenario Rosalyn is taking all the chances. The actor is taking none. Would she be willing to help him out for another roll in the hay? No. I doubt she has the nerve to take such a chance. For revenge? No way."

"But she's definitely a possibility."

"Oh, certainly."

NAME: MADGE OVERSTREET. AGE: 35. BORN: SIOUX CITY, IOWA. MARRIED, DIVORCED AFTER FIVE YEARS. TO CHICAGO. BECAME FASHION DESIGNER. TO NEW YORK. OPENED SHOP THERE.
RELATIONSHIP WITH VICTIM: VICTIM BOUGHT SUBJECT OUT. RELATIONSHIP CURRENTLY VERY STRAINED BETWEEN THEM.
WHEREABOUTS OF SUBJECT AT 11:35 P.M.: PLAYING CARDS. WITNESSES: LOREN HARTT. ARN THORN. ALSO DARA LUKAS.

Q & A PRODUCED NOTHING NEW. [Signed: J. B.]

ASSESSMENT OF ALL Q & A'S:

Irene was going over her drawings as Justin leaned back thoughtfully in his chair. "There's no sign of any link between Madge Overstreet and Clifford Boone, is there?"

Irene shook her head.

"Or between her and Arn Thorn?"

"Nope."

"Or Loren Hartt? Or even Angelica?"

"She seems all alone out there, trying to get along the hard way."

"Read 'em and weep," Justin said, sitting up again. "We have four principal suspects—people who have strong motives for killing Tammy Scott. We have Cliff Boone—but he has a solid alibi that looks unbreakable to me. We have Arn Thorn—but he has an alibi as well. We have Loren Hartt—but he, too, is alibied. And we have Angelica Farr—who has no alibi at all, but somehow doesn't seem to be the killer."

Irene nodded. "Who do you guess did it?"

Justin Birkby was staring at that moment at the Hartts' insignia on the back of one of the chairs in the dining room. It was the rose-colored logotype of the Hartt family—the familiar heart-shaped object with the arrow through the middle. It appeared on drawer handles, blankets, duvets, towels, and linen of all kinds.

His mind was going through convolutions and inner quests over which he had little control.

Irene was watching him closely. She had seen him in trances of this kind many times before. She knew his subconscious was deeply at work, probing, twisting and turning, reprobing, putting elements together in new ways—

"I don't need to make any more rash guesses," he told Irene suddenly, turning to her and staring at her as if he had been away for a long time. "I *know* who killed Tammy Scott."

BECAUSE THE MURDERER OF TAMMY SCOTT WAS NEVER BROUGHT TO JUSTICE, THE FACTS IN THE CASE HAVE NEVER BEEN MADE PUBLIC. IN THE FOLLOWING CHAPTER, CHIEF INSPECTOR JUSTIN BIRKBY (RET) OF INTERPOL HAS WRITTEN A DETAILED SOLUTION OF THE MURDER, COMPLETE WITH IDENTITIES, NAMES, AND CLUES THAT LED TO THE SOLUTION—WHERE APPLICABLE.

Who Killed Tammy Scott?
Written by Justin Birkby

One of the most annoying elements of the Tammy Scott murder case was the clue of the missing suite key. From the beginning, it tended to tangle up logic rather than straighten it out. It
seemed obvious to me that whoever had stolen or appropriated
that key was the person who had entered the bathroom and
murdered Tammy Scott.

Where we found it added to the confusion. We had no idea who
had put the key in the laundry bag. Nor did we have any idea *why*
the key should have been placed in front of the Dunwoodie-
Haight suite, if indeed there was a reason.

It was not until some time after the case was closed that I
received a letter from Stephanie Hartt in which she wrote the
following interesting commentary:

> You'll have wondered quite probably who it was
> who placed the key to Tammy Scott's suite in the
> Dunwoodie-Haight laundry bag. It was I. A number
> of us on board the *Shangri-la* were angry enough at
> Tammy Scott to *do* something about her. I was one
> of them.
>
> When Angelica Farr and I collided in the corridor
> our things were scattered all about. I did not notice
> the key as we gathered our things up, but I saw it
> out of the corner of my eye as I left. When Angelica
> had gone, I grabbed it up and hastened toward
> Tammy Scott's suite.

I have a nasty temper. I was flaming mad. I knew that Loren's elaborate trap had not caught her clean; she had turned the tables on him. I hated her for humiliating me on my wedding day. I knew about her eleven thirty bubble baths. I would enter the suite, pretend friendship, and drown that dreadful woman in her sunken tub!

Suddenly, cold reason doused my temper. I was acting the fool. My God, I was endangering my own life! It was foolish—to ruin myself for the satisfaction of raw vengeance. I could *not* do it. I tried Angelica Farr's cabin to give Tammy's key back to her. She was not in. In the midst of my search for her, Loren found me. I could not admit to him the foolish thing I had planned. I had to get rid of the key!

We were passing Reginald Dunwoodie's suite at that moment, and I saw the laundry bag. I dropped the key in it as we passed. That was the last I saw of it.

So much for the matter of the appropriated key.

What had baffled me from the beginning was the simple fact that a woman in a bubble bath, no matter how much it covers her up, does not want to be *seen*—to be gazed at—by a stranger, even by an intimate associate of the same sex. In the case of Tammy Scott, it seemed to me her vanity would tolerate very few women in her naked presence. Certainly no one with whom she was on business terms.

I didn't know it at the time, but the missing key had absolutely *nothing* to do with the murder of Tammy Scott. Had I known the truth, I would still have been just as baffled as I was anyway. I finally saw the light while I was staring at the Hartts' logo on the back of a dining room chair. As I stared, my mind did a quantum leap. In my imagination I was sitting in my cabin the night before, hearing a rap on the door—or wondering if I *had* heard one. Quite distinctly, I then heard a key inserted into the lock, and saw the door begin to open. I jumped up and let in a woman delivering towels to the bathing areas.

It suddenly occurred to me—thinking back—that here was a person who, in her line of duty, had access to *any* cabin. And, of course, it also occurred to me that here was someone who had good reason to be in the same room with Tammy Scott—to supply her with a freshly cleaned towel! With no embarrassment on either side!

I remembered the name "Elena" on her blouse. Of course, I should have spotted the discrepancy: I mean the fact that "Elena" had spoken with an indeterminate accent. Though she had said *"merci"* she had not *sounded* French. American? "Elena" is not a common French name. It is Hélène in French.

I learned from Captain Van Meter that her full name was Elena Piccard. But her papers did not check out. Van Meter confirmed the fact that she was responsible for supplying Tammy Scott's suite. In a quick search of Elena's cabin, he found a collection of burnt ashes in her wastebasket, and an unburnt paperclip in the corner—a clip whose color matched exactly Tammy Scott's specially tinted decorator manila folders.

Even under the severest of questioning by Malta authorities, where Elena was taken into custody, she did not break, would not reveal her identity. She became "Jane Doe." I advised Interpol, which sent out a bulletin requesting identification of her fingerprints, but no record was found—in any country. She became the newest addition to Interpol's voluminous files, one more in a growing number of female terrorists and assassins for hire on the international murder market.

For months the case against our Jane Doe languished in Malta. Finally, when she was released from custody on parole, she vanished. Meanwhile, Loren Hartt had taken over Scott Cosmetics. Clifford Boone resigned three months later. Arn Thorn got a job in a TV series about a private detective in Malibu. Even if the papers burnt by Jane Doe were those referring to Cliff Boone's speculations at Scott Cosmetics, I could not see that it necessarily implicated Boone. Loren Hartt or Arn Thorn could have hired Jane Doe to kill Tammy Scott, and left that clue to point *to* Boone and *away* from them.

Sometime later I received a letter at my home in Lyons, with no return address on it. In English:

> Here's a bit of (misquoted) Elizabethan drama for you, cop:
>
> BARABAS: I must needs say that I have been a great embezzler.
> FRIAR BARNARDINE: Thou hast committed—
> BARABAS: *Contracted* for murder: but that was in another country; and besides, the wench is dead.
>
> L.C. (with apologies to C. Marlowe) B.

The Featherstone Plot

1.

Marta Camara found a vacant place in the parking lot at Jorge
Chavez International Airport and immediately drove her sky-blue
Honda in. Drained of energy by the exhausting drive from Lima,
she sat for a long, luxurious moment to refresh herself. The way
out on Avenida Elmer Faucett and Avenida Republica Argentina
from Lima Centro had been jammed with all kinds of Sunday
pleasure vehicles, and no matter how she drove—conserva-
tively, with moderation, or savagely—negotiating the traffic was
a losing battle in the war on everyday stress.

Black-haired, blue-eyed, and beautiful in a classic sense, Marta
eased the tension slowly from her system by taking steady long
breaths in the approved aerobics fashion. Classic though she
might be in appearance, she was modern in every other way.

Glancing at her digital wristwatch, she saw that she had at
least fifteen minutes before the scheduled arrival of the Los An-
geles-Miami-Lima jet. Conscientiously she picked up the manila
folder from the passenger seat beside her and opened it tentatively. It was utterly ridiculous, she knew, to work through that

maze of details again; she had spent the past three days absorbing all the facts she could muster about the archaeological team that was coming in from the United States.

It was the first dossier that intrigued her, as it had the first time she had seen it. Stapled to the top left-hand corner of the typed sheet was a black-and-white photograph of a face that was at once craggy and honest and crafty and dishonest, a face difficult to categorize or ignore. ABNER FEATHERSTONE, the dossier was labeled.

Since she had joined the Museum of the Nation in Lima the name Abner Featherstone had surfaced numerous times. He was one of the foremost archaeological experts of the 1990s. And yet, and yet . . .

"Mixed up in a very involved negotiation in Athens recently— some trouble with a dig on the island of Crete," Daniel Alvaraz had told her the Thursday before. Alvaraz, her immediate superior, was curator of the museum.

"Trouble?" Marta did not like the sound of the word. She wanted reassurance that Alvaraz was exaggerating in his usual fashion.

"Oh, it was all negotiated away," he told her with a smile. "But at least three items from Crete turned up later in the hands of unscrupulous dealers in the States. And God knows how many now reside in the secret little locked rooms of the very rich. *How* they got there is still a puzzlement. But it's pretty common knowledge that Featherstone *helped them along."*

That was specific enough. "Why don't they bar him from Peru?" Marta wondered.

"Innocent till proved guilty!" Alvaraz taunted. "Besides, with all that activity in the Upper Huallaga River Valley—the new U.S. antidrug base—we *have* to play nicey-nicey with the Yankees." A shadow passed behind Alvaraz's eyes. "Don't ask me why."

"Obviously you're telling me to keep my eye on him," Marta murmured.

"You could say that, love."

Further study of the dossier on Abner Featherstone proved

that what Alvaraz had hinted was quite probably the truth. Featherstone had been detained for at least a month in Athens during an investigation into how certain artifacts had been smuggled out to the U.S. black market in art. The U.S. embassy then became involved, trying to extricate him from the toils of Greek customs. In the end, someone had apparently pulled strings in Washington, and the incident became history. Very murky history.

All of which proved one thing—Abner Featherstone did not enter the fray entirely alone; he had a friend in some very high place indeed.

"The Morales estate," Alvaraz said a moment later, emerging from a kind of dreamworld. "That's where we'll billet them."

Lucky Featherstone team, thought Marta. The Morales estate was one of the choicest of the grand old homes located in the wealthy suburb of Barranco along the Costa Verde just southeast of Lima Centro. Many of these marvelous old *mansións* were complete with beautiful gardens and wooded landscapes.

"There are at least twelve team members," Marta said, leafing through the same folder she was now studying in her sky-blue Honda.

"Plenty of room. And we can keep an eye on them there. The director—" Alvaraz was referring to Peru's director of antiquities, the man in charge of all Peruvian archaeological projects— "doesn't want them setting up camp around the specific area they have indicated. They'll commute. Or not come at all."

"And we'll commute, too." Marta nodded.

"Seguro." But Alvaraz wasn't through yet. "Marta, there's another thing. I don't know if you're going to *like* the job, but—"

Marta bit her lip. If even Alvaraz thought she might object, she was certain to. And yet, since it was part of her job there, she knew she would have to comply.

She listened to what he was saying, a sense of disbelief and horror creeping through her as he outlined her actions . . .

A tiny item in Lima's *El Expresso* the day after that, to the effect that Abner Featherstone and a team of archaeological experts would be working in the desert area some fifty miles north of Lima in the windswept littoral, initiated a spate of telephone calls from indignant Lima citizens. Marta spent half the day trying to defuse the excitement.

"Too many Yanquis!" snapped one irate caller. "They're taking over the Upper Huallaga Valley! Keep them out of Lima!"

And so on. Even worse, a ragtag group of students from San Marcos University, leavened by a more or less civilized academic or two, showed up outside the museum that same afternoon, formed a picketing circle in front of the wide steps, and began shouting slogans into the evening air.

"*Abajo* Featherstone!" "Go home, Yanquis!" "Down with Yankee *huaqueros!*"

Both Marta and Alvaraz stood at the big window watching the group walk around in its clockwise circle in front of the steps. Hardly anyone was deterred from coming into the museum, but that was beside the point. Not many people visited the museum, anyway. It was ridiculous to become so exercised over something most people in Lima knew nothing about and were even less interested in.

Now, in the airport parking lot, Marta's eye was caught by a flurry of movement to her left. A number of young people—Limeños, mestizos, and cholos—were jumping down off the back of a small flatbed truck that had pulled up in the aisle nearby. They were carrying banners and signposts. Again, their numbers were bolstered by a handful of academics.

"Oh no!" moaned Marta. These were certainly the same demonstrators she had seen in front of the museum on Friday afternoon. Somehow they must have deduced that the American archaeological team would be arriving today and were prepared to stage a street theater protest in front of the airport's entrance.

Marta took a last glance at Abner Featherstone's formidable photographic face—the honest but somewhat deceitful combination conflicted over the determined and self-assured bone structure beneath—and folded up the files to thrust them in her shoulder bag.

Within seconds she was out in the sunshine and striding toward the side entrance to the airport. The students, if they saw her, did not apparently recognize her.

As it was her job to do, she walked around to the entrance to Jorge Chavez International Airport where Stefano Gomez had parked the bus that was to transport the Featherstone team south through Lima to the Morales estate. She beckoned him—a lean, leathery man with a stance that showed he was able to jockey a horse as well as a bus—and he came out to her.

"Meet me by the carousel. Ten minutes."

"Yes, ma'am."

She went into the airport just as the public address system announced in its booming way the impending arrival of Flight 22, originating in Los Angeles, California. Of course the announcement proved to be premature by at least a half hour, during which time Marta simply stood about at the carousel where all passengers would have to recognize and assemble their baggage.

It was ironic that less than four years ago she had been a student at San Marcos University herself, working her way through the minefields of upper division studies, trying to earn her degree—which she had earned with honors, including, especially, a commendation for her English language minor. Yet from that moment, she had plunged into the real world and had more or less donned an attitude of superiority over and disdain for the trivialities of education as opposed to the realities of life.

Demonstrations were exercises in futility, she now thought. She had participated in many of them herself, assuming them to have had much more validity and worth than they really did have.

Of course, in most of the street conflicts she was one of the hated ones—a part of the ruling class of Peru—and the rest of them were the newly arrived mestizos (Indians of mixed blood) and cholos (dark-skinned Peruvians from the Andes). Francisco Pizarro had set the battle lines when he had founded Lima in 1535, dividing Peru into European Lima and peasant-Indian eastern Peru. The conflict in ethnic backgrounds was the source of most of Peru's present troubles.

Mestizos and cholos—the "outs"—ran the coca export business, surviving from the money gained from the sale of coca paste for consumption in the United States; the "in" Limeños in Marta's class held the reins of political and financial power. It was a bad scene—inflation eating away at everything one tried to do; hundreds of thousands of mestizos and cholos living in tin and wood shacks along the Pan American Highway—*barriados* or *pueblos jovenes* in the local tongue.

Suddenly the disembarking passengers began appearing at the carousel, and almost immediately Marta identified the first face. Her excellent memory precluded any need for reference to the manila folder and the dossiers it contained. She counted the new-comers through six—mostly students in their late teens and early twenties. Some seemed older, and she was curious about their backgrounds. Earlier consultation with Alvaraz over the submitted photographs had elicited only a raised eyebrow and the quizzical questions: "CIA, you think?" "FBI?" "Drug En-forcement Agency?" "Antiquities Division of Customs?"

She had no idea if he was teasing her or not.

She saw a man in his middle fifties—his dossier said he was fifty-five—and she recognized him instantly. This was Alec Loo-mis, an important man in the Featherstone team. In fact, he was an extremely rich man who had inherited his family's extensive publishing chain in the Midwest, along with a thriving group of television stations and theaters. He supplied the money that brought the team to Peru.

Loomis was trim and youthful-looking, dressed in fine-cut tropical clothes, cool even though he was wearing shirt and tie. Marta could imagine him ordering his tailor to produce for him exactly what he was now wearing. He moved easily; he was meticulous and almost self-effacing. But she could sense that he expected to be obeyed immediately and without question. He was not a large man, but he was well balanced and well put together.

With him was a small woman with black hair and brown eyes. She had a very pretty oval face. She was slim and svelte, sport-ing the paradigmatic body of the modern-day model. The dossier of Lotte Loomis said that she had once been a professional model. She had learned the secret of carrying herself well during that training—and she now continued to do so from sheer force of habit. Her red dress was simple, stylish, and expensive. According to the dossier, she was in her late twenties.

As she moved forward to the carousel, her eyes kept going over the crowd, as if she might be seeking someone out. Marta moved toward Alec Loomis to introduce herself and ask if there was anything she could do for him.

But as she came near him, she saw him turn. Abner Featherstone had appeared in the entryway, was raising his arm and hailing Loomis.

The word *flamboyant* would barely suffice to describe Abner Featherstone's dress. He was decked out in a pair of toreador-type pants, with tight-fitting hips, tapered at the ankles and buckled there, a bright white shirt with ruffles down the front, a string tie, and an outlandish wide-brimmed sombrero that was more Texican than Mexican. He was a huge man, very tall, but slim enough to appear lean in proportion to his height. He seemed to be a concentration of intense motion—restless and ungovernable. Even now he was waving his arms about in agitation.

"Christ, it's hot!" he groaned. "Amigo, I think I left my glasses case on the damned plane. I've sent Bill Bonney back for it. Where the hell's our gear?"

"Oh, shut up, Rocky!" snarled Lotte Loomis, as her eyes darted about at the crowd around them. *"We* know you're a boor. You don't have to alert all of Peru, do you?"

In a quiet voice Alec Loomis explained to Featherstone that the bags had not yet appeared on the carousel and that they would simply have to wait. But Featherstone was neither shamed into silence by Lotte nor assuaged from irritation by Alec.

"Where the hell's the Welcome Wagon? I understood they'd have an army of people here to greet us. I don't see zip!"

"Somebody sneaked a character sketch of you to the Antiquities staff," snapped Lotte. "All amenities are off!"

Marta Camara decided it was time for her to defuse the incipient explosion. Striding toward Featherstone, she thrust out her hand.

"I'm Marta Camara, Mr. Featherstone. Peruvian Antiquities. Welcome to Lima!"

If Featherstone was surprised at Marta's command of English, he did not let on a whit. His eyes narrowed. He reared back a bit and stared down the wings of his nose at her. His eyes did a slow prowl of her body. She could *feel* them and they made her flesh crawl. He was interested—*very* interested. He continued to ogle her from her neck, her chest, her waist, her thighs, and down to her ankles.

"Well, *mucho buena,* or however the hell that goes!" brayed Featherstone. "I'm gonna like this country!" He took her hand in his two huge ones like a five-finger sandwich and held it close to his chest. The pull he exerted on her body drew her breast close to his arm—which proved to be the purpose of his grappling movement.

With a sigh, Lotte Loomis turned her back on the scene and began exhaustive research on the bags sailing by on the carousel.

Marta glanced up as a newcomer entered the group. The dossier on William Bonney was deep and crisp and even. Here was *the* whiz kid of the nineties—the brightest of the upcoming stars in the field of archaeology. Summa cum laude from Stanford University, Phi Beta Kappa, one of the most brilliant students of modern artifactiana.

It was bruited about that Featherstone was quite aware of his own slipping reputation, even though he pretended not to be, and that he had deliberately wooed and won William Bonney to bolster up his own sagging worth.

Looking at him closely, Marta realized that the photograph attached to the dossier had slighted the man. He was older than most of the other students, and seemed more maturely in command of himself. He was a great deal more rugged than handsome, and made up for any lack of beauty in the tasteful way he selected his outerwear. Even now he wore a silk shirt with bril-

liant purple scarf and sleek, hip-hugger slacks in golden brown.
His shoes were killer Reebok running shoes in off-white.

"Here's your sunglasses case, Mr. Featherstone," Bonney
said now, glancing aside at Marta with an appraising look.

"Like you to shake hands with one of the best kids there is in
the business, Señorita Camara! Meet William Bonney. He's the
best we've got in archaeology back in the States, ma'am. This-
here's Marta Camara. You be good to Billy, hear? He's my boyo!"

Bonney smiled faintly and shook hands with Marta. She felt his
hand strong against her palm and noted his eyes searching hers.
Something about the touch was electric, and she—

"And here's Dinah Foreman!" Featherstone went on. The man
talked in exclamation points. "She's older than the rest of the
kids, too. But she knows her rocks!"

"Howdy," said Dinah Foreman with a brief nod. Marta could
not read the truth in her eyes; everything inside the woman was
carefully veiled. She wondered what was being hidden. Certainly
it was something important. Dinah Foreman did not want to appear open at all. She wanted distance.

"How do you do?" Marta said, sinking to the noncommittal
phrase from her grammar books. She glanced around. The group
seemed to have coalesced around a pile of bags. It was time to
move on. She raised her voice: "I've provided a bus for all of
you. You'll be staying at the Morales estate outside Lima, not at
the dig. It's in a suburb of Lima called Barranco."

"Yeah, yeah," Featherstone said. "I read all that itinerary crap
on the plane. And you? You're going to be there?"

"Not tonight, sir," said Marta. "I have work to do. But I'll be
on hand to supervise transportation to and from the site of the
dig tomorrow."

"Hey, great!" He turned to Loomis. "Ain't she something
else? Speak-a da English, too. How 'bout that?"

"You stupid racist," Lotte Loomis cried out. "What are you
trying to do? Get us all targeted by the death squad?"

"Huh?" growled Featherstone, turning to Lotte with honest
puzzlement.

"Go soak your head!" she snapped and turned away from him again.

Alec Loomis smiled. "I'm Alec Loomis," he told Marta, reaching out and shaking her hand. He did it in the European fashion, once up, once down, and then a clasp for a moment. "And this is my wife Lotte. Honey?"

"Hello," said Lotte softly. "Are apologies necessary?" She tossed her head in Featherstone's direction.

"Not really," said Marta with an understanding half smile.

Luckily some of the archaeological team students who were pulling their baggage off the carousel engulfed Featherstone so that he was spirited away from Marta. She signaled to Stefano, who appeared at her side.

Gathering the straggling group into a semblance of order, Marta began leading them out toward the front entrance of the airport. It was at that moment that the university students suddenly made their appearance in front of Marta, holding to a tight circle, waving banners and chanting.

"Hey, look at that!" brayed Featherstone. "We got us a welcoming committee!"

"Afraid not," said Loomis with a smile. "It's a drop-dead committee, Rocky."

Featherstone stared at the group. His face turned nasty. "Shit."

"Go on, beat them up!" Lotte prodded in a sarcastic voice. "After all, they're just gooks and subhuman androids. Right, Rocky?"

Featherstone frowned and stared at Lotte in some surprise. "What's gotten into you?"

"Ignore them," said Marta decisively. She stepped out in front of the team from Los Angeles and led them around the demonstrators.

They were almost at the entryway when a sudden movement surged through the group of agitators. A yell went up. There was the sound of a scuffle, although Marta was unable to see who exactly was involved.

"Hey, for Christ's sake—" That was Featherstone.

His cry might have been a signal.

At that moment there was a loud concussion from inside the group of students. Featherstone's Texican sombrero seemed to take on a life of its own and flew off his head, to land upside down on the polished floor ten feet behind him.

"Who shot at me? Hey! I been hit?" It was a question, not a statement.

The demonstrators broke up quite abruptly, fleeing in all directions. The shot had come from within them, and yet it was not apparent who the actual shooter had been. Within thirty seconds, the floor was clear of them. Only a few banners lay about to attest to the fact that they had been there at all.

Featherstone was examining himself for any wounds that might prove mortal. There were none. Loomis and his wife stared in some concern at the archaeologist.

"Hell! They missed! I'm all right!"

"Pity," murmured Lotte. Alec said nothing.

Marta Camara stood to the side of the action for just a moment. She was extremely upset. This was the first time she had ever seen an actual attempt on a human being's life. And it was the first time she had ever seen a group of college demonstrators fire a gun—or even *own* one.

She was stunned.

Quickly gathering her wits about her, she rushed forward, herding the group out to the bus that awaited them in the sunlight, and she tried to keep her mind from overworking itself. The truth of the matter was she was frightened. Frightened and shocked.

Was it Shining Path?

Was it the Tupac Amaru Revolutionary Movement?

How could she cope with the security that would be needed to protect the Featherstone team?

2.

Justin Birkby sat with the insouciant unflappability of the born-and-bred Parisian in the driver's seat of his fire-engine red Porsche double-parked imaginatively on the Rue de Louvre almost in front of the imposing building that housed the editorial and production functions of *Le Figaro,* the world-famous newspaper and magazine.

His mind was not on the dark looks of drivers as they carefully skirted the bumper and fender of his car, but on what must be going on upstairs in the building where Irene Manners was meeting with René Bourget, her immediate superior and art director of the organization.

Of course Justin was one step ahead of *Le Figaro*'s management, as was Irene. The business had to do with a special assignment that Interpol had dreamed up for Justin Birkby, with Irene Manners to accompany him as a deliberate cover for Justin. Of course she would be going as *Le Figaro*'s world-renowned sketch artist and caricaturist. And he . . . ?

The operation had been generated from the top, rather than,

as usual, from the bottom. Interpol to the Paris Sûreté. Paris Sûreté to the mayor. Mayor to newspaper/magazine management. Then down from management vertically—to René Bourget. With Irene in an even lower echelon, playing surprise at the strange assignment.

And so on and so on . . .

Upstairs, in the offices of the art department of *Le Figaro,* René Bourget leaned back in his swivel chair and let his disbelieving amusement burble up out of his throat in tiny bursts of stifled laughter. Finally he leaned forward, clasping his hands and lacing them together on the desk blotter. René was a self-confessed hopeless traditionalist. Who blotted ink anymore with a blotter? Even a typewriter seemed old-fashioned in the offices of *Le Figaro.* But when René had demanded a blotter, they had supplied him with one—God knew where they got it in this day and age of computers, biros, and ballpoint pens.

Opposite him Irene Manners sat in a kind of bemused silence, waiting for his explosion. When it came, it was more a resigned sigh of amazement at her unconcern than an emotional outburst.

"I don't know, Irene," he told her in his meticulous French. "Management sometimes comes up with the most astonishing story ideas." He sighed. "I can't *really* say that sketches of artifacts excavated in the desert somewhere in Peru—my God, it's November in Paris, but it's spring down there now, isn't it?—but oddly enough the powers that be want you there for us."

"It's a dream assignment, René," said Irene with that closed-over smile that always had a strange effect on him. He was married, happily, with children, and surrounded by all the comforts of home. But Irene was one woman with whom he could easily have led a life of his own on the side. He shook himself.

"One of your—special deals?" he asked, with a lifted eyebrow.

The fact that Irene's significant other was Justin Birkby, a retired inspector of Interpol, had certainly *something* to do with this sudden trip to Lima, Peru, René decided. Exactly what, he had no idea. He did know, however, that when Justin Birkby was working on a special case, he was usually able to channel all the information for a first-rate story to *Le Figaro,* thus providing the newspaper with what the Americans liked to call a full-fledged "scoop." (Dreadful word! thought René Bourget. No taste in language, the Americans!)

"A bit of pleasure, a bit of work," said Irene airily. "They simply have no idea when I'll be back, they told me. I'll do a piece on Peruvian haute couture, if you like. Perhaps something on the countryside. 'The ubiquitous llama'? Something like that? Anything you think of. Let me know."

Still chuckling, René rose from his ancient swivel chair and conducted Irene to the door. "Goodbye, Irene," he said to her, reaching over and giving her a friendly peck on the cheek.

What have I gotten myself into? wondered Irene as she walked to the elevator and pressed the DOWN button. Justin had been his usual tight-lipped self, letting her know very little of what was demanded of him. Not even a murder, she thought offhandedly, or she would have read about it. . . .

"Hurry up," Justin called to Irene. "There's a meter maid marking tires down the street. She gave me a murderous look."

Irene was laughing as she opened the door and sank down in the bucket seat next to him, settling herself seductively. "I suppose you gave her a look back."

"Not to concern yourself," snapped Justin, gunning the engine, and pulling out into the flow of traffic toward the Seine.

"It's all set," said Irene, using the French slang. *"C'est goupillé."*

"I knew I could depend on you." Justin made a wry face. It had nothing to do with *her* at all!

"Come on. What's it all about?" Irene asked.

He glanced aside. She was incredibly beautiful. She was so incredibly beautiful that Justin wondered why she put up with him. Certainly he had a good mind, and he wore his clothes well. But he was not the macho type most women catered to. He always wondered what about him had ever persuaded Irene Manners to declare herself for him.

That was one mystery Justin was not going to try to solve. In silence he drove over the Pont Neuf and turned downriver toward the Rue des Saints Peres.

Soon he pulled up in front of a discreet little hotel on the Left Bank not far from the Seine, parking mostly on the sidewalk under a spreading sycamore tree. He and Irene were in the habit of using the hotel in Paris, especially when they were flying out of the country from De Gaulle Airport.

Within minutes they were walking down the street to their favorite bistro, where they were lucky enough to find two seats that had just been vacated by a couple of students.

"The jet schedule to Lima is terrible," Justin told Irene. "We have to rise at the crack of dawn."

They ordered drinks and sat back contentedly. "The crime, Justin?"

"A possible hit."

"Aha! A contract hit? By a hit man?"

Justin nodded. "There you have it."

"I do not have 'it.' I have *nothing!* You're saying this hit man may be someone in Interpol's files? An international expert?"

Justin shrugged. "Who knows?"

"For what purpose, Justin? Politics? Sex? Revenge?"

"We don't know." Justin said nothing as the *garçon* set their drinks down in front of them and left the check. When he was gone Justin resumed. "The initial attempt occurred last Sunday. It took a work week for Lyons to become interested enough to pursue it."

"Pursue what, for God's sake? Justin!"

"Did you ever hear of the 'Sendero Luminoso'?"

"Good grief, no!"

"It's Spanish and it translates to 'Shining Path.' In French, it's 'Sentier Luisant.' "

"If this is to be an extended lesson in languages, I beg to be excused!"

Justin smiled broadly. "Obviously you haven't heard of Shining Path. There's a Marxist writer named Jose Carlos Mariategui in Peru."

"I'm unfortunately not partial to Marxist dialectic, or even Peruvian philosophers, and so—"

"Don't interrupt. Pay particular attention. You may be quizzed on this material later." Justin was smiling dreamily.

"Apologies, O Great One!"

"Mariategui's writing intrigued a Marxist professor of philosophy teaching at the University of Huamanga at Ayacucho in the early 1980s. His name was Abimael Guzman. Guzman took up the cause, assuming the nom de guerre of 'Presidente Gonzalo' and soon began calling himself the 'fourth sword of Marxism'— the four being Marx, Lenin, Mao Tse-tung, and Guzman."

"And so the fourth sword of Marxism worked with Mariategui and—"

"The thing about Peruvian philosophers—as opposed to French philosophers—is that in Peru philosophers take their thoughts most seriously. They ride into the hills and form little bands of guerrilla terrorists. Especially in the Huallaga River Valley in Peru."

"Justin—that all means just about nothing to me."

"It's because you're a bit short on geography. Peru is a strangely shaped country. The headwaters of the Amazon River rise in Peru."

"I'm not short on geography! How dare you? The Amazon flows eastward through Brazil, not through Peru. You're the one who is short on accuracy!"

"The Amazon does indeed empty into the Atlantic Ocean. More geography coming up. The knife edge of the Andes Mountains cuts Peru into two parts—two unequal parts. The western slopes of the Andes plunge almost directly downward and into the Pacific Ocean. The eastern slopes drain off into the Amazon River. Lima is on the western edge of the continent."

"What's geography got to do with assassination?"

"It's the geography that permits terrorists like the Shining

Path to operate almost with impunity in the *eastern* valleys of Peru, safely away from the arm of the justice operating out of Lima. There is also *another* band of terrorists, this one friendly to Cuban Marxism. It's called the Tupac Amaru Revolutionary Movement—named after Tupac Amaru, an eighteenth-century Peruvian Indian rebel. This group is known as MRTA. Any disruption by either of these bands of terrorists tends to break down Peruvian authority, making it easier for lawbreakers to thrive."

"I don't yet see the connection with artifacts."

"These terrorist movements protect the drug dealers who grow coca in the eastern section of Peru, shipping it up into Colombia, next door to Peru, you know, and thence on to the United States."

"But of course. The American presence there has been increased recently. I read an item in *Le Figaro.*"

"Battalions of Yank soldiers are going to work on the traffickers of coca. For ten years Shining Path and MRTA have fought the law, making the growing, harvesting, and the shipment of coca paste possible. They have been making life miserable for honest archaeologists who want to dig for ancient artifacts in the graves located along the western littoral of Peru. They *pretend* to protect the grave sites. We think they're actually *in* with the archaeologists, extracting protection money to allow the archaeologists to proceed."

"And you said there were some Americans there?"

"Yes. Abner Featherstone's team."

"I've heard about him! Wasn't he almost killed at the airport when he appeared in Lima last week?"

"There was a student demonstration. We think one of Shining Path's people or MRTA's managed to infiltrate it, probably disguised as an academic. The shot flung Featherstone's cowboy hat off his head, missing him entirely."

"And the Peruvians want help."

"Exactly. I have a full dossier already. One Lima detective squad questioned the students closely. Mixed in with the students were a number of academics. Three of them were absolute unknowns. Now of course, all three are history—'long gone,' as they say. Antiquities believes the terrorists are going to strike again. What's more, Antiquities believes that perhaps the terrorists have decided to deal directly with the big illicit market in the U.S., making a little revolutionary money on the side for themselves."

"Ah. The rich men with private black-market collections!"

"Exactly. You sense the strategy already. Keep the archaeologists a little off base, let them dig to their heart's content, and then rob them!" Justin leaned back, sipping his drink slowly and thoughtfully. "That's about it, Irene."

Justin's mind went back to his private conversation with Jean-Pierre Gilbert, Interpol's secretary general, the afternoon before. "There's a good chance Shining Path may be working directly with the archaeological team in stealing antiquities. Your main assignment is to gather information about their smuggling tactics. Names. Modus operandis. Contacts. Connections. We'll need bulging files to fight this type of terrorist activity."

He had not told Irene the most important thing of all—and he was not going to. The fact was, the war between the guerrilla terrorists and the Peruvian government was escalating month by month. In one year there had been at least three thousand or more deaths attributed to the open warfare between government and guerrillas.

John Webster had once written: "Of all deaths the violent death is best." Justin did not believe that any more than Webster did. And he certainly was *not* going to remind Irene Manners of it! Let Irene think the trip to Lima was a romp in the Peruvian sunshine.

3.

Quintín Ibarra was a big man, powerfully built, with a formidable presence and an aura of authority—most appropriate for the man in charge of the Antiquities Division of the Peruvian government. Of Spanish extraction, but with roots deep in Peruvian soil for at least three hundred years, Ibarra was well educated, well heeled, and well entrenched in his duties as head of all archaeological excavations in his country. Since artifacts and history were basic to the economy and well-being of Peru, he was probably the third most powerful man in the country, after the president and vice president.

There were only three people in the huge corner office of the massive Presidential Palace on the Plaza de Armas, which housed the Antiquities Division and other governmental units. And, since it was Sunday evening, there were no other offices open in the building, except for those of the security guards and the maintenance staff.

With Ibarra were Daniel Alvaraz and Justin Birkby. In an adjoining office Marta Camara and Irene Manners were quietly

talking. Justin had sensed the instant hostility aroused in Irene
when Ibarra had relegated her and Marta to the next room, but
he had been powerless to subvert the machismo that was definitely a part of Peruvian culture and that had led Ibarra predict-
ably to divide the movers and shakers from the support team.
Nor did Justin feel it would be seemly to interfere. He would
suffer Irene's recriminations later.

Ibarra's command of English was firm enough to establish
instant control over the conversation. He embarked first on a
short résumé of the activities at the Featherstone dig during the
team's first week in Peru.

"Featherstone's advance men"—it seemed to Justin that
Ibarra must have been reading a recent book on American politics—"were correct in selecting the site." The director leaned
over a small map he had drawn, pointing to an enclosed area just
off the Pan American Highway some thirty-five miles north of
Lima. With the point of the ballpoint pen he indicated a tiny
circle. "The dig is right here. It's an ancient tomb. Of a king,
likely. We've allowed the team to draw a boundary line of a
square mile around it. They're using their own security forces."

Justin was alarmed. "Armed?"

Ibarra frowned and chuckled. "Oh, no! That's simply not the
way we do it here in Peru! This is *not* the Wild West."

Alvaraz glanced nervously at Justin and lowered his eyes. It
was obvious he did not agree with his superior.

"We have Señorita Camara as our own watchdog," Ibarra intoned. "She notes carefully each find and draws a picture of it.
Your—" Ibarra gazed at Justin Birkby a moment in thought—
"wife has agreed to help her now that she is here."

"The artifacts are kept under surveillance at the dig?" Justin
wondered.

"The team has brought along a large mobile home, remodeled
into a workshop, to house the *huacos* when they are brought up.
There is a safe in the van." He frowned at the word. "Caravan?"

"I understand," said Justin. "The mobile workshop is always
at the dig?"

"No, sir. It is driven to the Morales estate each evening, and housed appropriately. Each morning it is driven out to the site."

"It is secure?"

"The artifacts are locked in a safe inside the workshop." Ibarra smiled faintly. "One would have to steal the entire workshop to remove the safe."

Alvaraz stirred uncomfortably and emitted what might have passed for a chuckle of amusement.

For a moment Justin Birkby leaned over Ibarra's shoulder and studied the penciled map. "Why is the van kept so far from the excavation itself within the perimeter of the dig?"

"To keep it secure," said Ibarra. "Only two people are authorized to unlock the van during working hours. Señors Featherstone and Loomis. After each find is studied, sketched, and catalogued, it is put into the safe."

"And at night? In Lima?"

"Actually Barranco, a suburb of Lima." Ibarra smiled. "There is an old barn at the rear of the Morales estate. It is locked and guarded."

Justin Birkby again studied the map with a frown. "Are you trying to set a trap for the terrorists?"

Ibarra reared back in astonishment, staring at Justin with disbelief. "A trap? Heavens, no!"

Justin glanced at Alvaraz, whose eyes, he noticed, were opaque and unreadable. "It would seem to me that this setup is an invitation to the terrorists. All one would have to do would be to seize the van and drive it away."

Ibarra shook his head. "You overestimate the terrorists. Who among them would be able to drive?" He smiled. "And even if one was able to do so, how would he get a key to the van?"

"How has the dig been going?"

"Excellently!" said Ibarra. "At least seven genuine artifacts—all from the Third Period—are in the safe already."

Alvaraz nodded. "The dig has been unbelievably successful, Señor Birkby. Apparently Señor Featherstone has the one thing no archaeologist can do without."

"And that is—?"

"A bit of luck."

Justin smiled. " 'Tis better to be fortunate than wise.' "

Ibarra lifted an eyebrow. "I beg your pardon?"

"A self-indulgence," Justin admitted shamefacedly. "A comment from an Elizabethan dramatist."

"Ah." Ibarra was forgiving.

Justin looked Ibarra in the eye. "I sensed in your original communiqué with Interpol that you were *wary* of Featherstone."

"Because of his past, Señor," said Ibarra smoothly.

"And you suspect he may be—" Justin paused—"up to no good?"

Ibarra pursed his lips and studied the far wall. "We would like you to keep an eye on him, please."

"You have doubts about Mr. Loomis?"

"None whatsoever," Ibarra responded. "Señor Loomis is exemplary."

"As for Featherstone," Justin said softly, "you think he's made some kind of deal with the terrorists?"

"He needs watching, Señor Birkby," said Ibarra. He straightened and rose from his chair with an air of dismissal. He put his hand out. "It is a pleasure to be working with you."

Justin shook hands. Was it, indeed?

The Morales estate in the older section of Barranco, a suburb to the south of Lima Centro, was enclosed by a very modern cyclone fence ten feet in height. Dominating the estate was the old-fashioned nineteenth-century *mansión,* bulky and inconvenient, but sturdy and maintained in good form even though it was too large to sustain a family accustomed to the modern life-style.

Inside it was furnished in an eclectic blend of Mediterranean Spanish and Peruvian Moderne. Weighted drapes covered the high rectangular windows, through which the outside terrain was visible in distortion as if viewed through an imperfect camera lens. The furniture was squat, heavy, and ugly, but in spite of its squalid appearance it had a serenity and an aloofness that went with the total lack of style evident throughout the habitation.

The estate surrounding the *mansión* was much more wooded than the average Lima homestead. There was a large garden just in back of the two-story *habitación,* running all the way back almost to the end of the property. Huge eucalyptus trees, introduced to Peru from Australia some years before, grew high and thick, affording shade and cover. Smaller shrubs grew near the fence so that the ugly steel network of wire was largely invisible.

The estate covered three acres. It faced a tree-lined *avenida* rarely frequented by much traffic. The neighborhood was quiet and usually deserted at night.

The members of the Featherstone team had finished their Sunday meal, served in the spacious dining room at the rear of the dwelling, and were simply passing the time of day before going to bed. In the dining room, lingering over their coffees, were Abner Featherstone, Alec Loomis, Lotte Loomis, William Bonney, and Dinah Foreman. All the rest—most of them students— were out in the study on the other side of the house.

When a limousine drove up outside and popped to a halt at the end of the long flagstone walk no one even glanced toward the foyer, visible through the open double doors of the dining room. It was as if the five of them had little or no curiosity, as if the heat and the torpor of the Peruvian littoral had seeped into them and sapped them of all mental inquisitiveness, leaving them for the most part moribund.

The heavy front door swung open, squealing like an ancient castle gate, and then, finally, the team members looked around. They had been chatting desultorily about artifacts, but no one had really been saying anything arresting. Now they could see Marta Camara, Justin Birkby, and Irene Manners standing in the foyer, about to enter to join them for dinner.

They put their coffee cups down as Marta Camara began introducing the two new arrivals.

Bonney grasped the extended hand of the well-formed, well-clothed, well-built man introduced to him as Justin Birkby. There was a Continental panache there, Bonney recognized. Not American. The man had a controlled self-assurance that was missing from most of Bonney's fellow Americans. British? Possibly, although the inherent English snobbery was definitely *not* there—that elevated curve of the brow, that slight lowering of the eyes as if looking downward, that twist of the upper lip.

The woman, Irene Manners, was stunning. An artist, of course. Yes. She was talking about making sketches of the artifacts.

Nevertheless, Bonney's eyes kept coming back to Justin Birkby. There was a great deal more to him than just a well-mannered man. He stood for something; Bonney could not tell what it was. He had that quality of leadership and authority that was hard to feign.

"William Bonney," Birkby was saying with an amused smile. "Billy the Kid, himself?"

"Well, I'm *not* from Brooklyn as the Kid was," Bonney said good-naturedly. He was always being hassled about his name.

"You're one of the team?" Birkby was asking, his eyes assessing Bonney deliberately and thoroughly.

"Well, I'm Mr. Featherstone's right-hand man!"

"I'm here as an observer," Birkby said quietly. "It's Irene who is on assignment."

"And you're in—?"

"I beg your pardon?" Birkby was honestly puzzled. "Oh, you mean, what's my—my *line?*"

Bonney chuckled. "Sorry."

"That's quite all right. I'm retired, that's all."

"Ah. Retired from what—line of business?"

"I'm a one-time chief inspector of Interpol," said Birkby without missing a beat.

Bonney looked impressed. "I see!"

"I gave it up when I found that identifying criminals isn't really the be-all or the end-all. It's bringing them to justice!" Birkby laughed to take the sting out of the words.

"Let's hope you find none here."

"I'm on vacation," said Birkby, shrugging his shoulders in an almost Gallic way. He would have to be half French, of course, Bonney decided. After all, Interpol was geographically French.

"Yes, well, it's a nice vacation place, all right."

"Let's hope it stays nice," Birkby said softly.

Abner Featherstone was uncharacteristically silent, Bonney noticed. He shook hands with Birkby, gave Irene Manners his usual head-to-toe study, and retired to the background without saying much of anything. Unusual, Bonney thought, frowning. Now what—?

If Featherstone was out of character, so was Lotte Loomis. She simply shook hands with Birkby as if he were a visiting politician, and turned to Irene Manners. The two women sized one another up, said a few cordial words that meant nothing, and went their own ways.

It was Alec Loomis who seemed the most congenial.

"I've read about you," he told Justin Birkby. "A *New York Times Magazine* piece, I believe. About the Perigord kidnapping. Your biggest case."

Justin Birkby nodded deferentially.

"I had no idea you were interested in archaeology," Loomis went on.

Birkby spread his hands, palms up. "I'm not. It's Irene who is."

Loomis laughed. "Then it's Irene I should be talking to."

Justin Birkby backed away and selected a seat at the table. In a moment everyone was seated and the food was being brought in for the newcomers.

Odd, thought Justin Birkby. He had experienced a strange feeling of déjà vu when he had been introduced to the five people in the room. As with most déjà vus he could not quite focus on it. And as with some déjà vus, he could not even pinpoint any one of the five people as responsible for the feeling. Odd, indeed.

His eyes moved curiously to Dinah Foreman, but she was a sealed-off person who did not respond to others spontaneously.

When he took in Abner Featherstone, he felt sure he would have remembered the man if he had ever seen him before; he was a startling person with a high recognition factor. William Bonney? he wondered. Alec Loomis? It could certainly be Alec Loomis— but where had he seen the man? And under what circumstances? He looked into Lotte Loomis's eyes and found her watching him with a bold, appraising stare. She exuded sex. He should certainly have remembered *her* without any help.

He shrugged. It was a mystery. Irene never forgot a face. Nor did he, usually. But this time . . .

The night glasses helped very little as he focused them on the window and looked in at the people inside the dining room. Looking into a brightly lighted area actually decreased any night vision he might have gained. The man standing behind the eucalyptus trunk in the garden of the Morales estate lowered the night-vision glasses with a frown. If only he'd brought his Zeiss six-powers with him! Then he might be able to make out the new-comers. Of course, the grainy glass in the windows had a very high distortion factor. Enough to make any true assessment questionable.

A man moved into his line of vision. With his naked eye, the man in the garden could see the features plainly. And behind him—

He froze in shock. That Interpol inspector! Justice? Justin? That was it—Justin Burke. No—Birkby.

Instinctively he moved behind the trunk of the eucalyptus, trying to make himself scarce. Then he reassessed his panic.

What was the point of going all mushy inside? After all, it wasn't in the scenario for him to *appear,* was it? Absolutely not!

Besides, even if Justin Birkby saw him, he might not recognize him.

Still, it was a warning. He must not be too complacent. He must pay strict attention to business. He must keep out of sight.

Now he knew who the newcomers were. He didn't like it one bit, but that was the way it was. Slowly he packed the night-vision glasses into their case and hung it over his shoulder. In a moment he was moving swiftly through the grass and into the shrubbery bordering the estate. He vanished from sight and soon there was nothing but the soft sound of vibrating cyclone fence, a quick twang, and then the sound of someone or something hitting the weed-choked earth. And then there was only silence.

4.

Early on Monday morning Justin Birkby was standing at the front window of the Morales *mansión* as the Featherstone team's Land Rover revved up in the long driveway at the side of the house. Soon he saw the vehicle move out onto the roadway to head north in the direction of Chancay.

At the wheel was Alec Loomis.

Justin was curious about this man, whom Ibarra had labeled as "exemplary." He wondered, in fact, why Loomis was trying to beat almost everyone else out to the dig. As Justin sat down to breakfast with Irene, he was still pondering over this very well-to-do man. Perhaps it was Loomis, not Featherstone, who was involved in sweet dreams of thievery and hanky-panky.

Still that feeling of déjà vu haunted him. He was thinking now about Dinah Foreman, the inscrutable one. He did not mention his curious puzzlement to Irene, however, and soon he forgot about it himself. . . .

Meanwhile, Alec Loomis was driving out along the Pan American Highway northward to the site of the dig near Chancay. He himself had seen the mobile workshop start out from the Morales estate a half hour earlier, while he was gulping down a hurried breakfast. And he knew it would be in place on the site by the time he arrived there. He had a great deal of work to do. And—ever since the discovery he had made that very morning—a great deal of thinking to do, too.

He was, admittedly, frightened to death. He had been unnerved by that incident some months before in Los Angeles, but he had finally decided that it was simply an anomaly—a meaningless something that had occurred haphazardly in the concatenation of events that made up his life. He felt now however that it had been no anomaly, but the first link in a chain of events designed to destroy him. And now . . .

He shook his head to rid his brain of its debilitating thoughts, and he concentrated on the road ahead.

Sometime later he drove the Land Rover off the highway onto the site of the dig. He could see the mobile workshop parked where it always was, in the lower southwestern quadrant of the area. It was painted in gay red, white, and blue colors, with big letters screaming out FEATHERSTONE TEAM—RAH! RAH! Corny and cute, Loomis thought. Typical of Featherstone. The man simply had no taste.

Loomis opened the door of the workshop with his key and entered, snapped on the blue lamp that overhung a felt-topped workbench that ran along one wall of the caravan, and opened the safe, twirling the dial rapidly and accurately. The door opened and Loomis removed a box of pottery from its interior, placing the artifacts on the felt workbench in front of him. The light cast a bluish luminescence over the area, and soon he was hard at work, studying the ceramics under a huge magnifying glass that was almost a parody of a Sherlock Holmes burning glass.

Today was actually the eighth day of the formal dig, although a cadre had been working even before the arrival of the team from

Los Angeles a week before. In that time at least seven excellent treasures had been discovered; Loomis wanted to look over the collection once again. He could not get it out of his mind that Featherstone was up to something demoralizingly underhanded.

What Loomis was now looking at was a true *huaco* from the so-called Third Period of South American Archaeological History —a ceramic piece made sometime between A.D. 400 and 1000. And, according to photographs in the books he had seen, it was a genuine artifact of the Mochicas, who inhabited the littoral at that period. No one ever knew what the "Mochicas" really called themselves; they were given the name from a temple in the Moche Valley called Huaca del Sol (Holy Place of the Sun)—an enormous structure made of one hundred thirty million adobe bricks.

The pottery piece was typical of the period—a stirrup-type vase depicting the head of a man in extremely realistic fashion. The *huacos* from this period were mostly all funerary products, fashioned to accompany the corpse into the ground in its search for eternal rest. The "stirrup" was an arc of pipe that entered the head in two places, with a length of pipe sticking straight up from the middle of the arc—like the shape of a stirrup.

It was through the pipe that fluids were entered into and drained out of the pot. The dead person then might easily find solace and nutriment from the fluids that were with him on his underground journey.

Loomis was elated, although his characteristic unemotional expression might belie his interest. Within the space of two hours the team had unearthed several more items—including two that were in the shape of a "parallel spouts" vase. In the latter, two short pipes entered the top of the head, or the body of the vase, with a connecting pipe across the top.

All from the Third Period, Loomis knew. Featherstone would be preening of course; he had certainly lucked out on selecting this winning excavation site here. Loomis knew it and knew that Featherstone knew it.

There was a sound at the door of the van. Featherstone? he

wondered. To be completely safe, he moved all the ceramic pieces from the workbench into the large safe that stood against the wall next to the workbench. Security was absolutely sacred at a dig like this. Teams had been known to have their permits lifted for letting valuable artifacts be stolen from the site where they were found.

He twirled the dial of the safe and crossed to the door. He undid the lock and opened up. The heat of the desert blasted in on him like a tidal wave. William Bonney was looking up at him, his forehead gleaming with perspiration. He was grinning in exultation.

"Look at this!" he cried out, waving a ceramic piece in front of Loomis's eyes.

"Come on in!" Loomis told him. "Quick! Don't let the good air out!"

Bonney climbed into the van and the door slammed shut behind him.

With pride, Bonney set the new piece down on the felt covering of the workbench. The two of them sat there looking at it. The piece was a "parallel spouts" vase, across a double-image pot. It was an action form in the shape of a boxing match. One protagonist was hitting the other over the head with a balled-up fist. The expression on the loser was exaggerated and ludicrous. It was a marvelously comic artistic rendition of a fight.

"Absolutely fantastic!" Loomis exclaimed. "Let me clean it up and we'll take another look at it. This is just amazing!"

Bonney grinned. "You're going to get rich from this expedition, Mr. Loomis!"

Loomis shook his head. "I don't *need* the money. It's the prestige of digging up some of these treasures!"

"Hey, I could use the money." Bonney chuckled.

With that he turned and went out of the van. Loomis stood looking after him. The kid was a straight-arrow, all right. A kind of yuppie, really—or what had come to be *called* a yuppie.

He turned. Someone else was scratching at the door. He

opened it and saw to his surprise that it was Dinah Foreman. He smiled broadly, stepped aside, and gathered her to him as she came up the last of the steps. He shut the door behind her.

"Have you seen the new piece?" Dinah asked breathlessly. "Isn't it a triumph?"

He allowed a grin to break through. It was not often he let himself show such genuine feeling. He seized her by the shoulders and kissed her on the mouth in an overt show of fondness that surprised even him. Immediately he thrust her back and stood looking at her in a kind of mock ecstasy.

"It is really a triumph," he told her.

"And all genuine Third Period?" she wondered.

"Definitely," said Loomis.

"Well," she said softly, "I'd just as soon they were Fourth or Fifth."

He chuckled. She meant she would rather have found gold and silver artifacts than the ceramic pieces that were typical of the first three historical periods.

"Is Lotte out there with you?" he asked uneasily.

"She didn't come in the bus. I think she's in Lima shopping."

He frowned wryly. "I wonder."

"What's the matter, Alec?"

"Nothing," Loomis said. "Well." He seemed to make up his mind and reached into the breast pocket of his bush jacket for a slip of paper.

"What is it?" Dinah was concerned.

He changed his mind, thrust it back into his pocket. "No. It simply doesn't make sense." Loomis moved over to one of the windows and looked out. He could see the sand stretching away in the distance, the blue sky towering above the sand all the way to the sun, and the heat waves transforming the air into a kind of smoky incense ascending to the heavens. This was in the fog belt, but it was obvious that today would not be a fog day.

"I'm right, Dinah," he said finally. "She's—she's going to kill me."

Dinah Foreman moved quickly toward him, standing so she could see into his eyes. "You're not serious?"

"Never more so," snapped Loomis. "I *told* you what I thought."

Two months before the expedition, on his way back from a board of directors meeting in downtown Los Angeles, Alec Loomis had been mugged on Hill Street near Seventh—not a normal place for a mugging. The circumstances had been so strange that he had begun to think about it. At just about the same time, he had been alerted by one of his Swiss banking contacts in Geneva that his wife Lotte had opened an account on her own with her own money and her own number.

Further examination by his accountants had revealed that Lotte had been investing in various companies using money obtained by selling off certain securities in her own name—securities that Loomis had put in her name for business reasons. The two incidents had occurred so close together that Loomis had jumped to the obvious conclusion.

Lotte Loomis was preparing a safe haven for the future; did she have something to do with those out-of-place muggers? In other words . . .

"You mean you think she really did hire those men?" Dinah asked in a hoarse voice.

He nodded. Then he reached into his pocket and pulled out the slip of note paper. "Look at this."

Dinah took the note and studied it. It was written in square capital letters in pencil. It was brief but specific:

CHARLIE:
I HAVE THE PASSPORTS JUST IN CASE. YOU'D BE AMUSED AT THE NAMES I'VE INVENTED. I'M SAVING THAT AS A SURPRISE. HA HA.
ARE YOU ALL SET FOR FRIDAY MORNING AS PLANNED? IF SO, IT'S *ON*. IF THERE IS A CHANGE, WE COMMUNICATE AS ARRANGED.

ONCE I KILL HIM, WE PLAY IT BY EAR.
PLAN A OR PLAN B.
LOVE YOU.

L.

"Where did you find it?" Dinah asked, her face ashen.

"It was peculiar," Loomis said. "Usually she's the one empty-
ing my pockets for the trip to the cleaners. But this time it was
the other way around. We were in a hurry changing for dinner
last night. She's usually very neat—hangs up everything she
takes off, or places it in the laundry. She was in the shower.
Heaps of our clothes were piled on the bed together. I started to
sort things out. I was about to put her slacks aside when I
noticed a slip of paper just coming out of the pocket."

"Go on," Dinah said as Loomis hesitated.

"It's embarrassing. I *never* read people's mail. I read this. I've
been *sure*—" Loomis stopped talking and frowned. "Anyway. I
put it back. But I copied it before. These are my block capitals."

Dinah read it again, her eyes narrowing. "Good God! There's
no question about who 'him' is. It's you, Alec!"

"I was right, you see," he said morosely, taking the note back
from her.

"I believe you now." Dinah sighed. She lifted her head. "The
police! You've *got* to see them! You've got to stop her. And who's
this Charlie?"

"Come on, Di. If I knew, I'd have the law on him in five
minutes."

"Still—" Dinah said.

"Look. I'm more worried right now about Featherstone."

"What has he done?" Dinah asked apprehensively.

"Nothing yet. But we've had monumentally good luck so far—
wouldn't you say?"

"Absolutely!"

"He's going to steal this stuff. I don't know how, but I certainly do know he will."

Dinah Foreman walked over to a chair and sat down. *"I'd* go to

Justin Birkby and tell him about that note you've got. It's from Lotte to a person named Charlie. That should be proof enough something is in the works. Get him to help you."

"But *you're* my bodyguard!"

"I can guard you from muggings of the softer kind. But I can't save you from a lethal attack!"

Loomis stared at Dinah. It was strange. She looked exactly like a naïve twenty-year-old woman—but in reality she was twenty-eight, and trained in the martial arts, black belt in karate, and other types of physical encounter. After he had begun to suspect his wife Lotte of premeditating murder, Loomis had gone to great effort to find himself the proper bodyguard. Hiring a man would be too obvious; it would be an invitation to Lotte to hire a hit man to go up against the muscle.

This alternate plan seemed best. And then, almost immediately, after two weeks, he had realized he was involved in something much deeper than a simple case of security. He had fallen in love with the woman!

And, he was flattered to think, she, too, had fallen in love with him.

All the more reason now for Lotte to want to kill him. She had laid the fire, and to fight it he had thrown on more fuel instead of starving it.

Loomis had picked up the *huaco* of the boxing match and was holding it loosely in his left hand when he was aware of movement along his wrist. He glanced from Dinah to his arm—and froze in quick panic.

A large scorpion, its black feelers quizzing the atmosphere about its head, was making its way sedately and fearlessly up the sleeve of Loomis's bush jacket. It had obviously crawled out of the hollow tube of the artifact.

"My God!" squawled Loomis, feeling an absolute ass. He could not stifle his voice. His heart seemingly had ceased to function.

Dinah Foreman was on her feet instantly. In a split second she was facing Loomis, her flat hand sweeping across his wrist, hurtling the live scorpion onto the floor of the mobile workshop. Almost simultaneously her running shoes were grinding the remains of the deadly insect to pieces on the flooring.

"Jesus," whispered Loomis.

Dinah smiled. "You're as white as a sheet."

"I'm a gutless wonder, Di," he sighed. "Always been deathly afraid of scorpions."

"Only a fool isn't," snapped Dinah, dismissing Loomis's panic brusquely.

As she spoke she glanced out the window of the mobile van, looking past the closed curtain. "Speak of the devil!"

Quickly Loomis joined her, peering over her shoulder. Approaching the mobile workshop was Justin Birkby.

"You get out of here, Di," Loomis said quickly. "Let me take care of this."

"All right." She turned, lifted her chin, and kissed him affectionately. Then she opened the door.

Although Justin Birkby knew that Abner Featherstone was the keystone of the Featherstone Antiquities Team, he was astute enough to be aware that the financial backing came from one source—the fortune of Alec Loomis. Loomis interested him not only because he was financing the expedition, but also because of what seemed to be his rather diffident relationship with his wife Lotte.

Before dozing off the night before, he had determined to discuss the team situation with Loomis. It might be that Loomis knew something about Featherstone's operations that Birkby should know. With this in mind, Justin left Irene with the rest of the busload out from Lima and approached the mobile workshop.

He was just about to ascend the aluminum steps when the door opened and Dinah Foreman appeared. "Mr. Birkby!" she said musically.

"Good morning, Ms. Foreman," Justin said softly. He smiled. Dinah was a beautiful young woman, low-key, calming, and seemingly all of a piece. Yet Justin sensed something a bit ruthless and a bit too self-assured in her psyche. He did not quite know what to make of her. For the present, he would simply not try.

"Just leaving!" she told him, passing him by and turning to waggle her fingers at him. The sun struck her light brown hair, flashing a golden sheen in the hot air. She was in excellent physical shape, he thought absently.

The money man was peering out the front door, beckoning him inside. "Quick! The air-conditioning rig is going into cardiac arrest."

Once inside, Justin took a seat in a canvas director's chair and exchanged prosaics with Loomis, who had removed several artifacts from the safe and was perched on a high stool in front of the workbench.

Finally he gestured at the ceramic piece Loomis was inspecting. It was an interesting study of a reclining cat done in bright colors. The likeness of the cat was exceptional. Justin asked, "Third Period?"

Loomis chuckled. "You Interpol people *do* complete your homework, don't you? Yes. It is Third Period. Like it?"

Justin turned the piece over, studying it. There was a tiny bit of material lodged in a crevice where the pipes intersected the pot. It seemed to be a curl of silver less than an eighth of an inch in length. Justin dug it out with his fingernail.

As he handed back the *huaco* he slipped the metal into his pocket. Loomis was intent on another piece now, or was *pretending* intentness. Once the cat was back on the felt, he turned to Justin and looked him directly in the eye.

"Why actually are you here, Mr. Birkby?"

Justin looked out the window. The curtains acted as a scrim in front of a panoramic scene of sand and sky. In the distance vague shapes moved about like ants attacking a mountain of white sugar.

"It's the Featherstone incident, I'm afraid," Justin said, having made a decision to be straightforward with Loomis.

Loomis studied him. "The shooting at the airport?"

Justin nodded. "We're concerned it's the terrorists. The Shining Path. Or MRTA."

Loomis lifted one knee and clasped both hands around it, balancing precariously on the work stool. "I had thought about that, of course."

"But you feel differently now?" Justin had noted the incomplete thought and had drawn his own conclusion.

After a long moment, Loomis reached inside the breast pocket of his bush jacket and removed a slip of paper. As Justin read the note carefully, Loomis told him briefly about the incident of the mugging in Los Angeles.

A thought occurred to Justin as he listened, but he did not voice it. "Woman to man / Is either a god or a wolf." He made certain he would remember that line to quote to Irene later on. Right now it would be downright rude to mention it to this distraught man.

Thoughtfully Justin handed back the letter, its contents indelibly ingrained on his memory.

"Am I to assume that your relationship with your wife is as precarious as what you are suggesting? That is, that you feel she may be trying to kill you?"

"Isn't it obvious?" Loomis burst out.

Justin considered. "Is she capable of such mercurial psychological changes? Certainly you know her better than I, but I would put her down as a rational, normally sensible human being."

Loomis smiled wearily. "Of course. That's her party personality. When you're alone with her . . ."

"You're suggesting the shooting in the airport was actually an attempt by your wife to kill you? An attempt that misfired and almost killed Featherstone?"

Loomis pursed his lips and frowned. "It does sound like a lot of nonsense—all *Sturm und Drang*—when you put it that way, Mr. Birkby."

Justin studied Loomis carefully. "You don't think too much of your antiquities leader, do you?"

Loomis was immediately defensive. "His reputation precedes him, Mr. Birkby. He *has* been involved in shady undertakings, as you no doubt know."

"Which would certainly be grounds for mounting an attack on him for his unwelcome presence in Peru. Right, Mr. Loomis?"

Loomis spread his hands in the international language of acquiescence under duress.

Justin stood. "We'll remain in touch. Please inform me or Irene Manners of anything that might pertain to your suspicions of your wife's activities."

They shook hands.

Irene Manners was at that moment standing at the top of the area of the dig with William Bonney. In fact, she was making a rapid sketch of him as he stood there examining a potsherd he had just unearthed.

The actual site of the dig extended somewhat to the right of them, sloping down eight or ten feet. The problem with digging in the littoral was that sand did not brace itself when undermined; it simply imploded on itself when any quantity was removed.

Every time a new artifact was brought up, support boards had to be placed above the spot, or the sand would fall right down into it.

"You like Mr. Featherstone?" Irene was asking as she sketched away.

"He's a very good entrepreneur," Bonney said.

Irene laughed. "How is he as an archaeologist?"

There was a hesitation. "One of the best."

"But not *the* best?" Irene asked, quirking an eyebrow.

"Without Mr. Featherstone, there would be no dig here."

"And without Mr. Loomis—?"

Bonney nodded. "Touché. There would be no dig here."

"The two are an inseparable pair, then?"

Bonney shrugged. "If Mr. Featherstone's weakness is his technical ability to identify artifacts, it is more than made up for in his understanding of public relations and the value of showmanship."

Irene nodded. "And if quoted, you will deny you ever said that."

"Exactly!" Bonney was amused. She knew he was flattered by her attention to him. She lifted her eyes to say something to him and to her shock, discovered that he was gone. Vanished!

She looked around quickly, startled and frightened. What—?

Then the superb irony of it hit her. She threw back her head and laughed. The most common of occurrences at a dig in the sand was the sudden collapse of an area into itself. The ground on which William Bonney had stood had collapsed under him, dropping him down some ten feet into the earth.

He was in the dig even now, pulling himself up out of the sand, spluttering and brushing himself off in a frenzied, embarrassed way.

"It's not funny!" he snapped, lifting his head toward Irene.

"I'd say so, myself. I'd say it's bloody dangerous!"

As Bonney clambered awkwardly up a slope some ten yards away, Irene glanced past him to see Abner Featherstone looking over at the two of them, an unreadable expression on his face. When Featherstone saw that Irene was watching him, he turned completely away and bent over to retrieve something he had left in the sand.

It was hot and humid as it usually was in the Peruvian littoral. But Irene could feel just a tiny frisson of panic chilling her backbone.

5.

It was Irene Manners who established actual contact with Lotte Loomis and subjected her to a low-key and subtle interrogation in the famed Justin Birkby manner. She did it on Tuesday, the day after Justin's conversation with Alec Loomis.

At breakfast Lotte announced to everyone present that she was forsaking the dig—as she had on Monday, too—for a necessary trip into Lima Centro, Old Lima. She had trinkets to buy for relatives and friends, she explained.

"I'll join you," said Irene Manners with a smile. "If you don't mind?"

Lotte turned quickly to study Irene's face. "Well, all right," she said. Then with a faint smile she turned slowly, gazing at everyone present. "Anyone else for Old Lima today?"

No one responded.

"Then, Mrs. Birkby, it's you and me."

"Irene," Irene corrected her.

"We'll do Lima Centro from Plaza de Armas down to Plaza San

Martin along Jiron de la Union. That's Old Lima's main shopping drag. Okay?"

"Of course."

Lotte turned to her rapidly cooling coffee and drank. "Nine o'clock then? I've already arranged for transportation."

"I'll be there," Irene promised.

Everyone went back to eating as Lotte rose and left the dining room.

When the two finally met in the foyer of the *mansión,* Lotte was dressed in a style that was just a bit off from comfortably tasteful. She was in ankle-buttoned toreador slacks, with a white ruffled bodice, and dark jacket to match the pants. Her hair was covered by a sunshade she had apparently picked up in Lima the day before.

It was her makeup that made Irene shudder inwardly. She had mascaraed her lashes so thickly that the effect was of an older woman trying to hide her age. Nothing could be further from the truth, of course. Lotte also used a preponderance of lipstick— bright red, thickly applied, crimson-sheened. She even used too much eyeliner along with the overdose of mascara.

In spite of her appearance, Lotte Loomis was a very aware and observant person. Irene saw that immediately. The hard part of her quest was in gaining some kind of rapport with the woman. For a long time in the backseat of the Cadillac for hire she maintained a silence, but finally spoke.

"I didn't mean to make you look stupid at breakfast," Irene said, "but my name is Manners, not Birkby."

"I simply didn't know," Lotte answered, glancing aside. Her eyes were intelligent and aware, not what Irene would have guessed from the way her makeup was applied.

"You've been married to Mr. Loomis for how long?"

"Seems like a lifetime," Lotte remarked offhandedly. She realized she was being rude. "Three years."

"Justin Birkby and I have been together for five."

"He's a cop, huh?" Lotte asked, flat out.

Irene smiled. "An inspector."

"Yeah, well—"

"He's *not* a policeman. He's involved in the gathering of intelligence."

"Nevertheless, he's got quite a reputation."

Irene accepted that. "I guess he has."

"So have you." Lotte turned and gazed directly at Irene.

"I've been lucky. A lot of mileage on a tiny bit of talent."

"Modest, too," said Lotte, her eyes narrowing. "You're very stylish, you know that?" Lotte leaned back and giggled. "I'm not. I just get myself up the brassiest I can." Her face froze. "That's what you do when you come up from *nada.*"

"I see," Irene attested softly.

"No, you don't. I was born out of wedlock. Hell, it's the custom now. I have no idea who my old man was. Neither does my mom. Maybe he was a sailor. Maybe he was a millionaire. Maybe he was a bum." She grinned and turned her head slightly. "I *had* to get somebody like Alec Loomis, didn't I?"

"You love him?"

Lotte made a face. "What's love? Endurance? Strength of character? Fear of reprisal? Sure. I love him. I'm even faithful to him. In my fashion."

Irene blinked. Where had this obviously uneducated but streetwise woman come up with *that* telling phrase? It was too obviously literate to be an accident. Irene recognized it as a line from one of Justin's favorite poems: "Non Sum Qualis Eram Bonae Sub Regno Cynarae." Ernest Dowson, a Victorian poet, ended each stanza with the famous line: "I have been faithful to thee, Cynara! in my fashion."

But Lotte was moving on quickly. "You can't get at him, you know. That's what's great about the rich. They don't have to put up with you. Just shut the door and you're outside, banging on the panels to get in."

"He cuts you out?"

"Oh, hell yes. Cuts me out. Cuts everybody out. He's a real exclusive guy." Her tone was bitter. "Oh, not that it *means* anything. I've got my ways to cut him out, too."

"A little something on the side?" Irene asked, cringing as she forced herself to utilize the only phrase she knew that Lotte would understand instantly.

"Nothing crass, you know, sweetie."

Irene sensed that Lotte was *deliberately* subjecting her to an out-of-key version of lower-class vernacular. Why?

"He seems quite decent to me," Irene admitted, determined to get Lotte off this coarse tack she was now taking.

"What else? That's what he's trained to be, you see. Decent." She turned to Irene with a slight frown. "There's nothing wrong with him in bed, you know. Don't get that idea in your head."

"I—I didn't 'get that idea,' " Irene said, repeating the words carefully.

"He's a wimp. Hell, aren't all men wimps, really?" Lotte burst out into flat vibrating laughter. "Don't they want one thing only, and when they get it, roll over and start snoring?"

"No," Irene responded stoutly.

"Your guy isn't that type?"

"He's not my—guy!" snapped Irene, suddenly irritated and wondering why she had embarked on this interrogation for Justin. "He's—" She snapped her mouth shut.

"You're priceless!" Lotte crowed, laughing delightedly. "Come on. He's your live-in. You've been sleeping with him for five years and haven't quite got around to signing any papers to that effect. Am I right?"

Irene nodded in stony silence.

"So what's the problem of talking about it?"

"There *is* no problem." Irene's voice was icy.

"The only difference is that I've signed the papers and lied through my teeth to the minister—and I'm admitting it! I've even done the prenuptial-agreement bit. Very popular stuff, today, you know! And what a lot of garbage *that* is! How much you get if *you* get the divorce. How much you get if *he* gets the divorce. How much you get if he predeceases you. What an ungodly mess *that* all is. Just something to make the legal eagles rich. I tell you! You're a lot smarter than I am by just paying all that no mind."

Irene was gazing elsewhere, her face stiff and unrelenting. She was not pleased to be the target of this woman's obvious hostility toward her for *not* having indulged in all the legal complications that she had been engaged in. Lotte looked at her a moment in silence, and then went right on.

"The upshot of all this ridiculous folderol is, I sleep with him and I talk to him in the morning and whenever he wants to hear talk. And I run around with him when he wants to show off the fact that he's man enough to handle a good-looking woman."

Irene stared at Lotte now, about to speak.

Lotte caught the look. She had the decency to flush. "Yeah. You've got it now, Irene. I'm a first-class floozie today. Just to get his goat. Shit. You know what he's doing? He's banging that damned Dinah Foreman broad. Wouldn't that rip the frosting right off your cake?"

"But she's just a student—"

"Oh, no. That's where you're wrong! She's a goddamn bodyguard!"

"Bodyguard?"

"She's a black belt in karate and all that aerobics jazz. Strong as an ox."

"Why does he need a bodyguard?"

"He thinks somebody wants to kill him," Lotte said.

"Who?"

"Me!" Lotte shrieked, and then burst out laughing. "Can you *imagine?* My dumb husband is convinced I'm trying to kill him!"

She choked on her laughter and there was a long, pregnant silence.

"Are you?" Irene wondered.

There was an instant of communication between the two women as Lotte stared at her. It flashed through Irene's mind that indeed Lotte *was* intent on killing her husband. For something to *do,* if for no other reason. Irene wished she had never started this expedition into the mind of Lotte Loomis. There were things lurking in the corners that she did not want to see too clearly.

"You've got to be kidding!" yelped Lotte, with a breathless laugh. "Hey, here we are in the Plaza de Armas! You game?"

It was over. There would be no more intimacies. They were two women now, insulated from one another by the vagaries of modern life—observing, pricing, sampling, and questioning.

"I'm game." Irene smiled.

The two of them climbed out of the Cadillac, and Lotte instructed the driver to park it and meet them later at the Plaza San Martin directly in front of the American Express Building.

They were back at the *mansión* by three and Irene excused herself to take a shower and a siesta. Lotte Loomis took herself off to the telephone that was in the study. She locked herself in and did not emerge for fifteen minutes. When she came out she was surprised to find Dinah Foreman just coming into the foyer from outside.

"Where's the professor?" Lotte asked in a grating tone.

"You mean Mr. Featherstone?" Dinah asked, standing straight and bristling under the onslaught of Lotte's piercing gaze.

"I mean Alec, you stupid cow. My husband!"

"He's still at the dig."

Lotte snarled at her, mimicking her tone and accent. " 'He's still at the dig.' 'He's still at the dig.' What's he *doing* out there?"

Dinah blinked. "I suppose he's examining the *huacos.*"

"At least he seems to have finished examining you."

"What is *that* supposed to mean?" Dinah asked, straightening and forcing her face into an expression of neutrality.

"Take it any way you want, dearie!"

"I'll take it the way you mean it, or not take it!" snapped Dinah.

"All right. I'll tell you how I mean it. I mean it this way. Have you finished with each other for the day? Has he had his way with you?"

Dinah's face was white with rage. "If you want to make something of this, I'll be only too happy to oblige."

"I won't get into a hair-pulling contest with you. You're better at it than I am. I wouldn't have a chance."

"You're right," snapped Dinah. "So leave me alone."

"Is that a threat?"

"Take it any way you like."

"I'll maybe leave you alone—but not because of your threats!"

"And leave him alone, too," said Dinah as an afterthought.

"I haven't touched him for weeks!" Lotte exclaimed loftily.

"I don't mean sex," said Dinah. "I mean—"

A long silence stretched out. "Say it, love!"

Dinah turned away violently. She spoke in a low voice, not facing Lotte. "I mean the letter."

Lotte's eyes widened. "What—what letter?"

Dinah moved quickly away from Lotte, beginning to ascend the winding marble stairs to the second floor.

Lotte came right after her, grabbing at her shoulder. "What letter, you silly bitch?"

Dinah pursed her lips, realizing she had said too much. She began running, now trying to outdistance the enraged Lotte.

At the top of the stairs Lotte caught up with her, grabbing her by both shoulders and beginning to shake her.

"Let me go!" snapped Dinah.

"What letter?"

Dinah wheeled away, flexed her hands, and struck Lotte a karate chop in the neck. Lotte went down like a stone.

Dinah stood above her, her face flooded crimson. "My God!" she whispered. "My God!" She leaned down over her to touch her throat to explore for signs of life.

Lotte came alive abruptly, reached up, and clawed at Dinah's face. In a moment they were wrestling on the floor, pummeling one another mindlessly.

It was Abner Featherstone who came into the *mansión* at that moment and hastened up the stairs to pull them apart.

"Here, here!" he said. "What's going on?" All his boorishness seemed to have vanished. He was a desperate male trying to pull apart two lethal-minded females.

"Oh, go soak your head!" snapped Dinah Foreman in a very unladylike tone.

Featherstone was stunned. "But—"

"Bug off!" screeched Lotte.

She headed for her room. Dinah went down the other corridor.

Featherstone stood there looking in one direction and then the other, utterly confused. "What did I do now?" he wondered.

There was no answer.

Justin Birkby came in and lay down just before dinner. By now Irene Manners had rested and was bubbling over with information.

Once she had imparted everything she knew about Lotte Loomis to him, Justin asked, "What do you think of her?"

"About the possibility of murder?"

Justin nodded.

"I don't know. I think she could. But you've got to stop her."

"Of course." There was a pause. "How?"

"I don't know!" wailed Irene.

"I'm more worried about Featherstone," Justin said. "He's up to something. I don't want my interest in Lotte Loomis jeopardizing my inquiry into Featherstone's activities."

"Why do you think Featherstone was the target of that first attempt at the airport?"

"Was he *really* the target? Or did the shooter *miss* Alec Loomis?"

She shook her head. "It's all such a mess."

" 'Times must have their changes, sorrow makes men wise; / The sun itself must set as well as rise.' "

"That's a new one." Irene frowned.

"John Ford," Justin said softly.

"Come on! He was Hollywood Westerns—not Elizabethan dramas!"

Justin chuckled.

6.

That night Abner Featherstone sat on the shabby bed and stared at the rather plump woman who was beginning to disrobe in front of him. She was probably mulatto, Featherstone thought. One-fourth? A quadroon? One-eighth? An octoroon? It really didn't matter. He reached into the pocket of his bolero jacket and pulled out a wadded-up wallet, from which he quickly extracted a roll of Peruvian banknotes. With inflation the way it was in Peru, he was handling quite probably a million intis—in the current basic unit of Peruvian coinage.

"I'm tired tonight," he told the woman. *"Fatigado.* You *comprendo?"*

The woman grinned. She had a gold tooth on each side of her mouth. Featherstone assumed that she understood what he had said.

"Just keep quiet about me, huh? *Silencio?* You stay here— *quedarse,* you *comprendo?*—when I go. You see? You wait till *dos horas.* Okay? Then you can *ando* on the *camino* again."

"Sí, sí." The woman grinned.

Featherstone rose and opened the door to the hallway, glancing up and down quickly. No one was in sight. He closed the door softly behind him and walked rapidly along the corridor to the back of the hotel. There was a rear stairway and he took it. Soon he was in a darkened alleyway.

He glanced at his watch, reading the numbers from the shaded light that was mounted just above the back door of the hotel. Eleven thirty. He had seen the man who was shadowing him in the lobby of the hotel when he had come in. Sure. He would be in the pay of that Interpol guy, that Brit, maybe. Or the Peruvian beauty, Marta Something. And he would be tailing Featherstone, keeping a record of where he went. Not fucking likely! Not a smart operator like Featherstone, who knew the advantage of keeping one jump ahead of the bad guys.

Emerging quickly from the shadows of the *callejuela,* Featherstone moved quickly to a cab stand down the street from the shabby little hotel and climbed in the first cab.

"Hey, where you go, meester?" asked the cabbie, happily certain that Featherstone was a *Yanqui fabulosamente rico.*

"Comprendo Morales Estate?"

"Ah, *sí. Morada de Morales. Sí!"*

Featherstone slammed the door shut and leaned back so that his face was invisible from the sidewalk. Just in case. It was already late. Not many people were in sight. He cursed Justin Birkby. The arrival of the Interpol man had made things so damned complicated. Not, of course, that they were uncomplicated to begin with. But Featherstone had a natural aversion to policemen. As the cab gained speed, he leaned back to relax.

Almost on instinct he turned around and glanced out the back window. He had found himself increasingly jumpy ever since arriving in Lima two Sundays ago. Of course, that first adventure at the airport had, frankly, unnerved him. He wondered again if someone had deliberately targeted him for a hit. He simply could not believe it. What would anyone gain by killing him? If it was a member of Shining Path, he could imagine the shot might have been taken to gain points. Those terrorists were that way, of course. In it for the prestige. A better place in heaven.

On top of that, there was the unexpected arrival of that Interpol man. Somebody must have tipped the international police organization off to the manipulations of the terrorist leaders. *They* were the ones Interpol really wanted. After all, they *killed.*

"Alto ahi, would you?" he asked the cabdriver, indicating the corner of the square in which the Morales *mansión* was located. The cab rocked to a halt. Featherstone fished a roll out of his slacks and handed the driver the fare and a big tip. *"Gracias, amigo."*

With that the cab drove off.

Featherstone stood there getting his bearings. The Morales estate took up almost a full block. When he had arranged for the workshop trailer to be secured each night in the ancient barn at the rear of the *mansión,* he had done so because he was well aware of a break in the cyclone fence inside a thickly shrubbed area at the rear of the property.

Now he moved through the darkness and entered the thick growth, pushing his way through the tightly interlocking bushes that were clumped by the obscured barrier. Within minutes he found the cyclone fence and felt his way along it until he came to the break.

Now came the crucial test. He counted five paces beyond the break and stopped. Leaning down, he let his hand seek out whatever it might find. Excellent! There it was, just as he had ordered it! A black satchel about the size of a doctor's bag—loaded with . . .

Featherstone lifted the satchel and felt its bulk. Exactly as ordered. A good man, Rafael. Well worth the intis spent on him. The perfect forger. Quickly Featherstone carried the satchel with him to the break in the chain-link netting and began prying the strands apart.

Once inside, he moved cautiously toward the barn. He had left the window at the rear open, and within seconds he was inside the barn and opening the converted mobile home with his own key. Before entering it he paused in the dark, listening intently. There was no one in the immediate area. The security team had been instructed to keep the barn under constant surveillance, but from a distance, where other avenues of approach could be covered. No one had yet heard him.

He moved into the mobile workshop, closed the door behind him, locked it, and then proceeded to pull down all the shades. Once they were secure, he reached into his pocket and brought out a tiny pen-sized flashlight. On the way, his hand encountered the .38 Colt he had begun carrying. He had never packed a weapon before, not on a dig, but he had never been shot at before, either. There was a first time for everything.

The artifacts were in a box in the safe. Quickly Featherstone opened the safe and removed them. With the flash he examined them and then laid them all out on the felt-topped workbench. With that he reached down and brought up the satchel he had picked up at the cyclone fence and opened it.

He drew out the objects within, which resembled those already on the workbench. Carefully studying the numbers applied to the objects from the satchel, he put each duplicate next to its original and leaned back to observe them with increasing appreciation for the man who had made them so quickly and so handsomely *identical.*

Then from a drawer in the workbench he removed a number of soft silken drawstring bags and carefully put the original artifacts into them. Then he removed the pasted labels from the duplicates and put the counterfeits into the safe, which he closed quickly. He took up the empty satchel and the silken bags and turned off the flash.

The back window of the barn was still open, and he was over the sill easily and quickly. He moved toward the break in the fence and stashed the empty satchel where he had picked it up—Rafael would take care of that tomorrow—and made his way in through the break once again. This time he moved through the grass away from the barn to an area he had mentally marked out before.

When he had come to the preselected spot, he reached down into the grass and removed a large flat stone—a broken flagstone that had been removed from the pathway in front of the *mansión*. He pushed the treasures down into the deep hole underneath and covered it again with the flagstone.

Then he stood and was moving toward the *mansión* when the air around him exploded into a brilliant flash of light.

"Tente! (Hold it!)" snapped a Peruvian voice. *"No move!"*

Featherstone froze. His hand slid toward his slacks pocket and the weapon he carried. By God, if he went, he wouldn't go alone!

He saw the beam of light move along his upper body down to his slacks. His hand froze in place.

"Oh," said the voice suddenly. *"Está usted,* Señor Featherstone."

Featherstone nodded with a smile, hoping the perspiration on his forehead did not gleam in the light. He began very consciously moving *away* from the flagstone he had just replaced in the grassy ground.

"I wanted to see how good the security was." He chuckled. "Never know when somebody'll try to best you!"

"Yes, sir," said the guard. Featherstone could see him now. He was the one called Pancho. By now Featherstone was safely out of the area of the flagstone and the stash.

"Did you see me come out of the house?" Featherstone asked sharply.

"No, sir," said the guard, abashed.

"I did, you know. Came right out here and ducked behind the barn."

"Yes, sir," said the guard.

"You should be more careful," said Featherstone, and then he laughed to crack the tension. "You've done fine, you know. If you'll just escort me up to the house, I'll go inside again."

In a moment Featherstone was inside the *mansión.* He was shaking. For a long moment he stood in the foyer, glancing up the curving staircase at the upper floor. Being caught by the security man had been unnerving. But no one had seen him bury the artifacts.

He was conscious of being scrutinized soberly.

Justin Birkby was standing in the somewhat darkened lounge that opened off the foyer.

Justin smiled and nodded. "I saw the drawings Irene made of the *huacos* today. That *el doble*—the double-image—is a master-piece!"

"Valuable, too!" echoed Featherstone. "Say, the Peruvian government is going to make big money once these things are arranged for exhibit." Featherstone seemed to be beaming with pride.

"I'm sure they are."

"We may be on the verge of an important breakthrough, too. I hope to have some brand-new items before we're through tomorrow or Thursday. Stuff that has never been seen before in our time."

"I hope you're continuing to check security," Justin said mildly.

Featherstone patted the weapon in his pocket. "Already done just that," he said with a big grin. "Looks like it's working fine."

Justin turned as Alec Loomis and his wife Lotte walked out of the study, headed toward them.

"Thought you were in town tonight," Loomis said to Featherstone.

"Changed my mind," Featherstone admitted.

Lotte walked over to him and grinned officiously. "You're worse than an old woman!" she told him.

He burst into bellowing laughter.

Lotte sighed. "It's not that funny, Rocky!" She turned to her husband. "Time for bed, Alec." She took his hand and the two of them began the long circling walk up to the second floor.

Featherstone watched them as they ascended the stairs. He glanced at Justin and the two of them smiled faintly at one another. "Never did figure out what she saw in him," Featherstone opined.

Justin nodded. " 'In faith, you see, women are like burrs; / Where their affection throws them, they'll stick.' "

Featherstone thought about that a moment, and then he frowned. "Huh?"

"An early example of Elizabethan machismo," Justin said with a smile.

"Oh," said Featherstone doubtfully. "Sure." Then he brightened up. "Maybe she just saw a good meal ticket in him. You know?"

Justin nodded, defeated. Featherstone chose that moment to start up the curving stairs, following the other two into the upper corridor. Strange, Justin thought as he watched the archaeologist move from tread to tread. There was grass and mud all over his shoes. Checking security shouldn't have been *that* demanding a chore. There was even a gob of mud on the cuff of his slacks.

He made a mental note of it: something else to check into.

And that brought his mind once again to the odd feeling of déjà vu he had sensed that first night. He had been unable to isolate the face, figure, or element that had caused it.

Had he seen Featherstone somewhere before? Lotte Loomis? The present images of the five people involved—Featherstone, Loomis, Lotte, Bonney, and Dinah—were not sufficient to trip his memory. Something about *one* of them certainly had begun his obsessive need to *understand* the connection. It was almost as if one of them were in a different guise now—looking out from a new face, laughing at him. Laughing!

He shrugged and repeated his earlier thought: something else to check into.

7.

Not much happened on Wednesday out at the dig, but that night . . .

The place had the flavor of all international boîtes these days, William Bonney decided—loud disco music, plenty of action on the dime-size dance floor, and fast-moving stroboscopic colors flashing about. The blasting music was typical. The atmosphere of steamy high pressure adhered to the norm of such places the world over.

The slim, dangerous-looking, macho male waiter in his early twenties sported a golden earring in his left ear and a highly visible nick in his earlobe from a knife fight.

Bonney addressed the man in a low voice: "I want Paco."

"No comprendo," said the waiter, his lip curling slightly, his bad teeth showing. Bullshit, Bonney decided. Still, he thought, the man did have a *presence.*

"Yes, you do," snapped Bonney. "Tell him Israfel wants him."

"I don't fool around with no stuff like that," said the waiter in English that had only a slight accent.

"And bring me a pisco sour."

The waiter faded into the crowd.

There was a shift in the music as the disc jockey changed pace, and in the sudden silence Bonney found himself looking at the patrons along the walls. He had not seen Alec Loomis at first when he came in, but he saw him now. And, of course, he was not with his wife, but with Dinah Foreman. Interesting, thought Bonney. Certainly Loomis did not look like a typical womanizer. Alec and Dinah seemed engaged now in deep conversation as they occasionally sipped at their drinks. Odd. Somehow the pairing did not figure in the dynamics of the antiquities team.

But then, nothing about the Featherstone expedition seemed right anyway—placid enough on the surface, but creepy-crawly beneath. Was this pairing Loomis's choice? Was it because of a vacuum in his own sex life? That thought bore some examination.

Featherstone himself was always playing around. But in the week they had been working on the Peruvian littoral, Featherstone had not yet seemed to settle on any one woman. He was playing the field, perhaps.

"Amigo," a voice murmured in his ear.

Bonney stiffened, turned, and leaned around. A newcomer had slid into a chair beside him. Paco?

"Call me Israfel," Bonney said in a low voice.

"I got that already," said the newcomer. He wore a neatly trimmed spade beard. He was of medium size, but muscular and self-assured. He had startlingly blue eyes under a thick head of black, well-trimmed hair.

"You're Paco?"

"I'm Paco. I'm Arturo. I'm Stefano. I'm anything you want me to be, amigo." A smile. The eyes were not in it. The eyes were moving about the interior of the boîte.

Bonney reached into his jacket pocket and removed a small three-by-five photograph. He had snapped it a week before when he had first come to Lima. He palmed it and showed it to Paco-

Arturo-Stefano under the table's edge. It was a very good likeness of Alec Loomis.

"Him," said Bonney.

"So what I do?" Paco reached into his shirt pocket and pulled out a package of Winstons. He lit up, waving out the match on the table in front of them. Smoke trailed up between them.

"Follow him." Follow that cab. Bonney shook his head, almost overpowered by the parodic intensity of the conversation.

"Where I find him?"

Bonney glanced across the room at Loomis and Dinah's table. To his surprise, he saw that they had left. Bonney observed the man with many names. "I was told you, of all people, never *needed* information like that."

The lips pulled back and shark teeth appeared. "You funny man."

Then, without another word, he vanished into the darkness and obscurity beyond the table. He had not told him where to post his reports, Bonney realized. Yet, somehow, he thought it was not a thing to worry about. Bonney had been told this man was definitely one of the best in Lima.

He leaned back and indulged in a moment of amusement at himself and at the ways of the world. He had joined the Featherstone expedition because it was by far the most prestigious in operation. And yet, the more he learned about Featherstone, the more he realized the man was a fraud. Oh, he knew his archaeology, all right. But a genius at identification he was *not*. He had the world press by the short hairs, sure. But he did not have the academic fraternity—and sorority, now, of course—behind him at all.

And who was this Alec Loomis? A gifted amateur archaeologist. With plenty of money. And some kind of wife! Bonney suspected more than hanky-panky there, especially with that Foreman woman. Tough broad. He wanted to find out all he could about Loomis and the reason he had decided to back this expedition. Something was going on. Was he one of those wacko collectors who had secret stashes of expensive art and artifacts stolen from all over the world?

The really mysterious one was the Peruvian woman—Marta Camara. From the beginning Bonney had been suspicious about the group of so-called agitators at the airport. Had they been rounded up and masterminded by Marta Camara to provide warning to the Americans? Was she working for Shining Path? Was she, in effect, working against the expedition—trying to cause trouble for it and put it down? In short, was she trying to break them?

And there was the Englishman—the Englishman who was French, of all things! What was *he* after?

A slight pressure on his left wrist caused him to turn in surprise. He was looking into the deep, dark, marvelously liquid eyes of Marta Camara. "I didn't suspect you might be interested in studying the nightlife in Lima, Mr. Bonney," she said with a liquid, fluid, and distinctive Peruvian accent.

With fascination, he found himself watching her lips as she formed the words. She was a beautiful woman, beautiful and intelligent and worldly. Yes, she worked with Peruvian Antiquities—but what, Bonney wondered, was her real game?

"You have me at a disadvantage," Bonney said with a smile. "I thought you'd be up in your office, poring over old rocks and silver trinkets."

"But that's exactly what I thought *you* might be doing, Mr. Bonney. Slavering over infinite riches in a little room."

"Will, please."

"Will. And I'm Marta."

"Aha. Short for Margarita."

"No. Spanish for Martha."

"There was a song sometime in the past. 'Marta.' 'Rambling rose of the wildwood,' I believe the lyrics had it."

"What is a wildwood?" she asked, leaning a little more closely to him.

"It's a wood that is—well—wild."

"*Bosque,* we call that."

"You're an incredibly beautiful woman." The words just slipped out. Bonney felt himself flushing. Like a high-school sophomore, he thought ruefully.

She turned her head away from him. The noise pulsated about them—some kind of salsa/reggae medley. Booming.

"I've offended you," he burst out. He had always talked too much at the wrong time.

Her eyes were stricken as she turned the full force of her beauty on him. "Oh, no! No! You could never offend me. Or any woman, for that matter."

"Then why do you turn away from me?" He could feel the warmth of her body near him, was enveloped by the essence of her even in the reeking atmosphere of the pressure-cooker room.

"Because—because I feel I shouldn't have bothered you."

"Bothered me!" He was stunned. "Marta! When you joined me, it was as if a whole new world had opened up to me." Again his big mouth was taking over and ruining everything.

She smiled, this time saying nothing.

One hand closed on his shoulder as she rose. "I must go."

"Go? Why must you go?" He stared up at her, at the contours of her face, at the elegant high cheekbones, at the marvelous liquid eyes, at the tilt of her chin, at the clean lines of her nose, at her slender neck and throat.

"I must."

She moved away. He reached out without conscious thought and seized her hand in his. "Don't go!"

She did not fight him. Instead she turned and gazed down into his face. "Mr. Bonney," she said, "I have accosted you under false pretenses."

"Indeed?"

"Do not ask my reasons." She turned her head away.

He pulled her toward him, turning her so she must face him. "If I promise not to, will you come with me where we can talk?"

Her eyes brightened with amusement. "And where would that place be, Mr. Bonney?"

"Where it is quiet, Miss Camara."

"That would be elsewhere, then."

"Sí."

He stood up, still holding her hand, and guided her through the throngs of sweating bodies and gyrating arms and legs, through the flickering torrent of brilliant lights, and out past the checkroom to the entrance of the nightclub.

"Please," she said, looking down at her hand in his.

He seemed to notice it for the first time. "Oh. I apologize." And he let her go.

"I know a place," she said, and she turned from him, beckoning him to follow her.

He came up beside her and they were soon striding down the sidewalk in companionable silence.

The place she selected was so absolutely in contrast to the place they had left that he found himself almost laughing out loud at the difference. It was a quiet little café that resembled the kind of tea room you might see in London. Yet it was a saloon. Soon they were drinking glasses of beer that Bonney had never tasted before, but which, as Marta had promised him, was excellent.

"Cuzqueña," she said. "Cuzco beer."

The conversation itself lacked the spontaneity of the conversation in the boîte—but it was fated to be that way. Bonney had exhausted all his reserves of emotion. There was little he could say to her that would not be repetitious. And as for her, she had admitted her interest in a way that she had obviously never intended to.

And the words waned as they continued to enjoy their Cuzqueñas—and the presence of each other in a physical and psychic sense.

The talk drifted to archaeology. To Señor Loomis. To Señora Loomis. To Señor Featherstone.

Bonney hid a smile. "He's a clever man."

"Who?" Marta asked, as if she had forgotten whom they were discussing.

"Featherstone."

"The rather *loud* man."

Bonney chuckled. "He's a boor, you know."

"I'm very good at English," she told him challengingly. "I know what a boor is."

"Boor he is," laughed Bonney.

"They tell me he has been in trouble with the law."

"The law of Greece, for one country," Bonney said. "The law of Iran for another."

"Huacos."

Bonney nodded. "You're in Antiquities. You know all this."

A tiny flood of pink suffused her neck and cheeks. "I warned you I had bothered you under false pretenses."

"How does Featherstone do it?" Bonney burst out. "I don't know!"

Her face froze. She lifted her eyes to his. She was trembling, like a fawn frightened by the smell of smoke.

"I've offended you again?" Bonney asked flatly.

"I do not presume on our friendship that much," she said stiffly. "I am not engaging in a professional conversation. In fact, if you think I am doing so, I find your attitude outrageous." She stiffened in her chair and looked across at him almost with belligerence.

"I'm sorry," he said contritely.

"That isn't quite enough," she snapped. "If you feel that I am trying to ingratiate myself with you in order to find out things I should not know—"

His hand rested on hers. She snatched hers away.

"Please." Bonney was desperate.

"I'm so embarrassed."

"Why?" he cried.

Silence. A long silence. "Because—"

He waited.

"Because you think I was pushing myself at you. I—" Her eyes were liquid again, this time filling with tears.

"Stop!" Bonney begged in agitation.

She drew herself up finally, finished her glass of Cuzqueña, and turned to him. "I really must go. Thank you for the—for the companionship."

And she was gone.

Bonney was desolated. He waved the waitress over and ordered another beer. She knew, of course. She had seen him with Paco. She had seen him taint himself with a lowlife. That was the reason she had come on to him. To sniff him out. A slick little trick, wasn't she? Bonney could kick himself. Why hadn't he played it more smoothly, pretended things, glossed over the inconsistencies—and done what he wanted to do.

Make love to her, by God. Romantically. Psychologically. Physically. . . .

8.

Thursday evening Justin Birkby and Irene Manners spent their dinner hour at an intriguing tourist trap called Rosa Nautica on the Costa Verde. Built out over the Pacific Ocean on a cantilevered wharflike platform, Rosa's afforded its clients a spectacular view of night surfing alongside the restaurant's windows, with brilliant spotlights focused on the nocturnal surfers for dramatic effect. In spite of the artificial setting and the melodramatic backdrop, the atmosphere of the place was ambient, the décor tastefully executed, and the decibel level mercifully low.

As was customary with Justin and Irene, who above all else considered themselves civilized to the fullest extent possible, they enjoyed their food and drink with their usual gusto until they were well along into the dessert. Only then did they even allow themselves to turn their minds to mundane topics like artifacts, archaeological logistics, and the day-to-day working arrangements of the Featherstone dig.

Actually, once the first day had passed, there had been little activity of note. Justin had observed. Irene had sketched—not only artifacts, but diggers as well. Observed and cerebrated.

Irene brought up the first point of interest. "I've been meaning to ask you," she began. "Did you ever manage to check out that piece of silver shaving you said you found on that *huaco* your first day at the dig?"

"Yes. I did. And it turned out to be exactly what I thought it might be. Silversmiths frequently have to pare off pieces of silver when they work with it."

"All right. But what does *that* mean? How does that fit in with the Featherstone project?"

"It means that somewhere along the line, the newly found *huacos* have all made a surreptitious visit to a silversmith."

"But there are no silver and gold artifacts in Third Period ceramics."

"Exactly. But who works in silver?"

"Silversmiths. Artisans."

"Doing what?"

Irene blinked. "You're not playing Socrates on me, are you?"

"It's the only way to make you *think.*"

"All right. Oh. Making artifacts. Modern trinkets."

"Yes. But there's little money in that."

"Ah! Making fakes!"

"Yes. Making substitutes."

"Is there any point in that?"

Justin smiled. "A man makes counterfeits in some cases to substitute for something he is going to steal."

"Ahah! Then you mean that Featherstone—"

"—may be planning a bit of a fiddle."

"May be?"

"The point is, it may not *be* Featherstone who is on the take."

"How do you figure that?" Irene asked curiously.

"He isn't the only one who has a key to the mobile workshop and the combination to the safe. Loomis has them, too."

"Then your cop's mind is thinking that either Featherstone or

Loomis is planning to swindle the Peruvian government out of a number of valuable national treasures."

"It is your cop's mind that is putting thoughts into my cop's empty cranium, Irene."

"Pooh! You think there's dirty work afoot."

" 'Gold and the promise of promotion rarely / Fails in temptation.' "

"Really, Justin!"

"Sorry, my dear. I couldn't resist."

"Incidentally, have you ever figured out who Charlie is?"

"Charlie?" Justin blinked. "Oh. You mean have I ever figured out to whom the letter was addressed by Lotte. Or we *think* is Lotte."

"Exactly." Irene sat back and watched Justin with satisfaction —more at his discomfort than at his aplomb.

"Not really," he said cautiously.

"Well, *I've* got an idea!"

Justin looked up in surprise. "Go ahead."

"*L* stands for Lotte, but it also stands for Loomis."

"You mean *Loomis* wrote the letter?"

"Why not? We don't know much about Alec Loomis, do we? Suppose he's really a closet collector. I mean, he's got the money, hasn't he?"

"Hold it! You mean *he's* going to kill—"

"—Featherstone! Why not? Then he'll switch the real art treasures for the counterfeits, leave the fakes with Peruvian Antiquities, and be home free!"

"Why kill Featherstone?"

"Because Featherstone would know—wouldn't he?"

Justin thought a moment or two. "In which case, who's the third man—Charlie?"

Irene sighed. "I can only solve one part of your puzzle—not all of it, Justin. I think it would be cheating if I did the whole thing for you. Give me some credit for modesty!"

Justin shrugged, watching Irene laugh aloud at him.

"I have no idea who Charlie is," she went on airily. "I wouldn't even *pretend* to know who Charlie is."

Justin sat back as if chiseled in stone. His eyes widened. His face took on the configuration of a man struck by lightning.

"The Young Pretender."

Irene made a face. "The Young Pretender? Me?"

"Not you! Charlie! That's who Charlie is!" Justin stared goggle-eyed at Irene. "You're a genia, Irene!"

"What in hell's a genia?" Irene snorted.

"A female genius, you simpleton! You've done it! You've actually done it!"

"Me?"

"And, I must say, your timing is impeccable," Justin went on volubly. "Tomorrow is Friday, you know. And that's the day the killing is to take place. Congratulations!"

"What have I done?" Irene was dazed. "What *is* it, you twit?"

"You solved the goddamn puzzle, you nincompoop! All by yourself!" He was laughing gleefully now. Irene stared at him as if he were daft.

"Don't you see?" Justin was elated. His face was alive. People in the restaurant were turning to look at him. He fastened his eyes on Irene and started talking a mile a minute.

"It's the key to the letter, you idiot! It's a combination: upside down, *and* word association. Romeo sends a note to Juliet, but knows it may fall into enemy hands. And so he signs it Juliet, and addresses it to Romeo. If it's intercepted, it's misinterpreted!"

"But that isn't what happened!"

"I'm speculating! Okay, *L* is Lotte. She is receiving the letter. And she's getting it from Charlie. Charlie is Charlie. He's the one doing the killing. And *he's* the one I have to box in. Box in for good."

"And who *is* Charlie?"

"You said *pretend*. He's the Young Pretender. Charles Edward Stuart, 1720–1788. Also known as Bonnie Prince Charlie, you simp! Bonnie Prince Charlie! William Bonney! *He's* the potential killer. Just you wait and see!"

And with that he threw down his napkin and rose in triumph. "Let's get out of here."

They returned to the Morales *mansión* a half hour later, tired but pleasantly so. Justin was in a state of suppressed elation. He was quite sure now that he had the proper handle on all the myriad facts and details he had been dealing with.

Somehow the fates seemed to be cooperating with him. As he climbed the steps to the Morales *morada,* he glanced up to see William Bonney standing inside the front door in the foyer. Justin pulled the front door open. Bonney greeted Irene and him in that order.

"We found the most marvelous place to eat," said Irene, trying to cover her nervousness with idle chatter. "Oh, it's a tourist trap, no doubt about it, but we could watch night surfers ride the waves in! You should try it sometime!"

Bonney was smiling. "I'd love to! I'll get the details from you later."

Justin was studying Bonney with interest. The man seemed to have it all together, no matter how deep in this he was. The thing to do would be to probe just a bit—perhaps throw the man offstride a trifle.

But Bonney was faster than he was.

"Just had an interesting little conversation on the Morales grounds," Bonney said with a faint smile.

"Conversation?" Justin asked.

"Yes."

"With whom?"

"Oddly enough, another American. Here on a visit."

Justin took Bonney's arm and led him into the lounge where it was quiet and the lighting low. They sat down together. Irene took a seat on the couch and began leafing through the latest copy of *Mirabella.*

"Yes. I was getting a breath of fresh air outside the hacienda here—I ate in one of those restaurants in Lima Centro, noisy and stuffy—and I needed it. Anyway, suddenly there was a man coming toward me along the path by the side of the house. He seemed to be looking back over his shoulder. But then, when he turned around, he saw me."

"Would you recognize him again?"

"Oh, sure." Bonney cleared his throat. "Anyway, the two of us just stared at one another for a moment without saying anything. Then he said—"

"He spoke first?"

"Yes. He said something like this: 'I'm sorry—I seem to be lost, don't I?' "

"You're sure he was American? Not English? Not Spanish?"

"He *looked* American, you know. Well, I asked him who he was looking for. Actually, I think I put it another way. I must have said: 'Are you looking for someone?' "

"And was he?"

"He told me his name was Owen Lloyd. 'Just down here for the pleasure of it,' he said. 'Looking for my cousin's house. Carlos works in Lima, you see. Do you *live* here, old man?' "

"He actually used the words—'old man'?"

Bonney was nonplussed. "Yes, I believe he did. Rather odd, isn't it? More English than American."

"More music hall than either," snorted Justin. "Go on. What did you say?"

"I think I said I was just here temporarily. And then he said that he seemed to have lost his way. 'Isn't that just like a bumbling American?' "

Justin laughed. " 'Bumbling American'? Odd locution."

Bonney nodded. "Then he said he'd have to call a cab. I asked him if he'd like to use our phone inside. He shook his head at that."

Justin observed Bonney closely. "Was he at all flustered? I mean, was he nervous at your suggestion?"

"No," Bonney said, shaking his head. "He simply gave me to understand that he did not want to use the phone."

"I see."

"And he said something like: 'I'll just scamper down the street here. There'll be a cab along soon enough.' "

"Hardly the street to hail a cab," Justin muttered.

"I thought so myself," Bonney admitted. "He said he was sorry to inconvenience me."

"And that was all?"

Bonney frowned. "Then I think he kind of apologized for the encounter. 'Awfully clumsy of me, isn't it?' Yes! That's what he said."

"And you said—?"

"Nothing. I watched him go down the front walk and onto the street. When I couldn't see him any longer, I came back inside the *mansión.*"

There was a long silence. Justin turned to Bonney. "How did he look?"

"Oh, he was—well—rather plump."

"How old?"

"Middle-aged. You know. It's hard to tell."

"Ugly?"

"No, rather mediocre, actually. Not unhandsome."

" 'Not unhandsome.' " Justin sighed. "Well, we'll just call up all the I.D.s that say 'not unhandsome' on them."

Bonney shook his head. "I'm sorry, Mr. Birkby. I'm being honest about this. It's difficult to describe a person to someone else."

Justin smiled broadly. "Indeed it is. Anyone in my business learns that first thing."

That brought Bonney up short. "You—you think there's something significant about this man?" His eyes were wide.

Justin almost said what he thought: Significant only in that he does not exist. He's purely a figment of your imagination, Mr. Bonnie Prince Charlie! A counterfeit suspect, you might say!

Instead, he shrugged and said, "Next to nothing, really."

Five minutes later Justin Birkby tapped on one of the doors in the upstairs corridor and waited. There seemed to be no response.

"Miss Foreman," he called. "Miss—"

The door opened and he was facing her, his mouth open, his breath cut off suddenly by the unexpected movement.

She let her face relax and smiled. Justin noticed that she was one of the few people on the team who had complete control over herself—that is, her physiological functions. He had never seen her blanch, or blush, or turn angry, or do any of the million things most human beings do involuntarily.

Irene had told him that Dinah Foreman was in the business of physical security. That is, she was a professional bodyguard. Justin did not find it hard to believe.

"Could we speak?"

She shrugged and closed the door as Justin took a seat in one of the chairs.

"It's Alec Loomis I've come to talk about," he began.

"I see." Her face stiffened.

"No, no," Justin said. "I'm not here to give you a lecture in morality. He's your client. I'd like to make sure he's properly attended to from now on."

"You feel he hasn't been so far?" Her eyes were cold.

"I think I know who's working against him for his wife."

There was a long silence. "So you know about—*things.*"

"Enough."

"The letter?"

"I think his wife *is* working against him—with William Bonney."

Her mouth lifted in a quirky smile. "He's hardly the most dangerous—"

"I know he appears harmless. But don't forget. He was the one who brought that artifact of the boxers to Alec. The one the scorpion crawled out of."

"Of course you're right," Dinah said softly.

"Will you do it?"

"Oh, sure! I've got a lot of people pegged for the hit, though."
Her nose wrinkled up as she grinned at Justin. It was the first
really honest grin he had seen on her face.

"Who?"

"I'd vote for Featherstone, really. I don't like him at all. Too
phony."

"I wouldn't worry about him."

"And there are a number of the students I'm not so sure
about."

"Just make sure you keep an eye on Bonney, will you?"

She rose, led him to the door. "I'll take your advice. Although
I'm not sure why."

"Call it man's intuition."

"Why not?" she said with a laugh.

9.

On Friday morning at about nine thirty a jeep of American manufacture carrying four men dressed in U.S. Army camouflage fatigues drove down from Chancay and turned eastward off the Pan American Highway just before arriving at the site of the Featherstone dig. It pulled across the loose sand into a hollow out of sight of the archaeologists.

The driver, whose Shining Path sobriquet was El Lobo (The Wolf), climbed out over the closed door and walked slowly up the sandy incline to the top of the dune that overlooked the dig.

There he ducked down to a crawl, wriggling along on his elbows until he came to the top where he could see the activity below. He removed a pair of glasses from his neck and focused them on the members of the team who were busily working the excavation.

Slowly El Lobo scanned the terrain with the glasses. In the distance he made out the mobile van that contained the workshop. Then he moved the glasses slowly downward on the people working in the sandy pit. He could identify Featherstone. And he recognized Loomis. He knew some of the others, as well. He had been watching them for several days now.

He focused again on the mobile workshop. Loomis and Featherstone were the only two with keys. Obviously it was deserted. Good.

He wriggled back down the slope and rose to run across the sand back to the jeep. The three other men waited patiently. El Lobo climbed into the driver's seat and reached into his pocket for the paper map he had sketched the day before. On it were clearly marked the location of the mobile workshop, the Featherstone personnel bus, the digging site, and the access road from the Pan American Highway—which was delineated to the left of the large square marking out the claim.

The mobile unit was in the southwestern quadrant, the digging site in the northeastern quadrant. The access road split the claim square across the middle, and came straight to the center where it turned upward—north—and downward—south. Around the digging site El Lobo had marked three dots at the points of an equilateral triangle big enough to contain the dig. An arrow had been drawn from the workshop to the Pan American Highway; there it pointed northward.

The points of the triangle were marked **L** at the top, **C** at the western bottom, and **A** at the eastern bottom. The workshop was marked **B.**

"Charqui," said El Lobo, "you're here. You got that, man?" El Lobo was speaking the cholo dialect of the eastern slopes of the Andes. "You hold that position, you understand?"

"*Sí, comprendo,*" Charqui said. *Charqui* meant "jerked beef" in Spanish. It was the man's code name in Shining Path. His real name was something else entirely—not used in the brotherhood. Charqui was stout and his paunch was mostly muscle. He had bright little pig eyes.

"Abrojo," said El Lobo, "this is you." He pointed to the angle of the triangle lettered **A.** "You hold that point and you don't let nobody pass. You understand?"

"Oh, yeah," said Abrojo.

He was rail-thin with a mean face and a scrawny beard. His face was a mass of knife scars. He had malicious blue eyes—an accident of colliding genes somewhere in his remote past heritage. *Abrojo* meant "thorn."

"I got you," sneered the fourth man in the husky whisper he used for a voice before El Lobo could instruct him. His nickname was Bardo. *Bardo* meant "bard," "singer." A joke. He was a whistler, a wheezer, a breather. He had no real voice. It was gone away forever. "I get the van and I drive."

El Lobo nodded. He reached in his pocket and pulled out a key. "It's a dupe. You don't need no jump start. You understand?"

"Sí, comprendo," whispered Bardo.

"Get the gear," snapped El Lobo, looking across at the top of the dune. He was anxious to get started. He glanced at his wristwatch. One minute before 10 a.m. Good!

Quickly Abrojo distributed the ski masks and knit caps. Almost instantly the four men became anonymous figures as they slipped into the masks and caps. El Lobo snatched an AK-47 Kalishnikov for Abrojo, handed a second to Charqui, and took the Uzi assault rifle for himself.

Then El Lobo signaled them to move forward, and they ran across the sand to the top of the dune. El Lobo pointed eastward, then indicated Bardo. Bardo took off along the dune to begin a huge circle that would end up back at the mobile workshop.

El Lobo ran over the top of the dune and came to a halt with his two backups on the slope leading down to the dig.

"Hey, you!" shouted El Lobo in English. "No move! Stay where you are!" His English was clearly enunciated.

He could see the white faces of the archaeologists turn toward him in startled shock. No one dared move. Everyone seemed to take in the three men in a kind of numbed, defeated lethargy, as if they had been programmed to expect trouble of this kind.

El Lobo advanced, weapon at the ready. His two associates moved in with him, Charqui circling around to take his position to the west, and Abrojo moving in the opposite direction to take up his position to the east.

At the sign of movement below, El Lobo lifted the Uzi and got it almost into aiming position. "Hey, you!" he snapped. The mover was Abner Featherstone. "You don't move nowhere!"

Featherstone was smiling. "Hey, friend—"

"Just hold your position, *amigo,* and no funny business with that mouth of yours!"

"Shit," said Featherstone, looking around, somewhat abashed. "You'd think the guy *knew* me."

Marta Camara was one of the first to notice the three men as they came up over the dune to the north of the dig. She had been rather expecting something to happen, but of course she was not authorized to carry a handgun. She had her own way of defending herself.

The three hijackers had them cold. She knew that Featherstone had been right in not making a rush toward the man with the Uzi.

"Hey! The workshop!" someone shouted.

Marta turned. Lotte Loomis was pointing to the south of the claim. A fourth bandit, unarmed, had circled the dig and was approaching the van from the side. It was obvious that he was intent on getting into it. Marta felt helpless.

Featherstone was walking slowly up the slope toward the man with the Uzi. "Hey!" cried Alec Loomis. It was a warning. "Let it lay, Rocky!"

Featherstone turned slightly and paused. His eye caught sight of the running man in the distance and he put the glasses on him. The rest watched as the bandit climbed into the cab, settled himself, and started up the engine.

"Too fast for a jump start," muttered Featherstone.

"Yes," Marta said.

A spate of Spanish words erupted from Charqui, and the AK-47 began erupting. Marta turned quickly. Lotte Loomis was on her knees in the sand. She had apparently made some move the man with the Kalishnikov hadn't liked. He had fired over everybody's heads to warn them. Only Lotte had gone down to protect herself.

The van was moving now, starting for the Pan American Highway.

"Damn!" cried Alec Loomis. "They've got the *huacos!*"

Justin Birkby was parked alongside the Pan American Highway just south of the Featherstone claim when the first of the three gunmen suddenly appeared on the northern dune. Quickly he grabbed his Zeiss glasses and focused on the head man. Masked. Armed. Uzi. Justin quickly started the Land Rover.

He had been on surveillance for four mornings already. His own analysis of the security at the dig was that it was totally breachable. This attack proved him right. It also indicated to Justin that Featherstone might be working the same old street he had worked in Greece: in short, cut a deal with the local thieves and split the take.

But of course, it was only a supposition. And of course it was someone else's problem. What he had to do now was—

The Land Rover made a powerful start and soon Justin could see the people all contained inside a triangle by three armed men. Justin raced up the side of the highway, banging across the dry-gulch drainage ditch, and onto the shifting sand of the claim itself.

He could see that the driver of the mobile van was having trouble guiding it. It was bucking and jouncing around, throwing up sand and dust. The driver did not know the tracks that the team driver had sought out, and he was taking the shortest route to the Pan American Highway. There were hidden potholes and sinkholes everywhere.

Justin slammed the Land Rover across the sand at an angle that would intercept the mobile van. The Land Rover was far faster and more maneuverable than the workshop. Justin kept the throttle to the floor. He could see that the driver of the van was glancing out of the cab at him with an almost comically leery expression.

Now for tactics. The hijacker suddenly slammed on the brakes. The van rocked to a slower speed and almost slewed around in the shifting sand. Justin turned inward, toward the van. The driver realized his error, and he whipped the wheel to the right, gunning the engine once again. Now Justin had him. He turned right, too, keeping the circling van away from the highway, he in hot pursuit.

"No, no, no!" screamed El Lobo in a frenzy, waving his assault rifle in the air and cursing fluently in Spanish. Against all orders, Charqui had broken formation and begun to run across the sand toward the developing dogfight between the van and the Land Rover. Then, once again breaking all orders, Charqui stopped, knelt in the sand, and fired the AK-47 at the Land Rover, trying to intimidate its driver. The shots all went wild.

"You son of a bitch!" yelled El Lobo. "Don't do it, man! Stupid bastard!"

With the corner of the armed triangle broken, Marta Camara began to run after Charqui. This sent El Lobo into another outburst of rage.

"Stop! Stop, woman! I kill you—" El Lobo fired the Uzi on automatic and sprayed the air with unaimed rounds.

Marta paid no attention. She drew a slender knife from a hidden pouch at her belt and hurled it hard across the sand at the man now firing at the Land Rover.

The knife struck him in the back and quivered there. Charqui screamed and dropped the AK-47. In an instant Marta was on it, slapping it down with her foot, and then she raised it against him.

"Don't you dare make a move!" she snapped in Spanish.

"Shit," said El Lobo.

The windshield was holed, Justin noted; three rounds had blasted through the radiator. But he was still moving. By now the bandit had speeded up the van and was trying to make a wide left turn for freedom and the highway. Justin circled around, cutting him off. Finally the van driver screamed some obscenity and turned the van directly at the Land Rover.

Justin slammed on the brakes. The Land Rover bucked to a jarring stop. The van's front wheels suddenly sank at least two feet down into an invisible sandhole. There was a wrenching sound. The van crashed to a halt and the engine died.

Justin jumped out and made for the van. He opened the cab door and climbed in. Grabbing the driver from behind, he hauled him out of the seat, thrusting the hijacker's right arm behind his back, forcing him into a powerful armlock. Then he dragged him out of the cab.

"Move!" he snapped. And he pushed the hapless driver across the sand toward the sobbing and bleeding man whom Marta had knifed.

"Beautiful throw," Justin said to her. "You've got an instinct for English darts."

She flushed.

"God damn it to hell!" El Lobo screeched. "Get in the jeep!" he shouted in Spanish to Abrojo, who was the only one who had done anything right. He had done right because he had done nothing.

Abrojo needed no further prodding. He was over the hill and running. El Lobo was steaming mad. He stood there with the Uzi and sprayed it at the crowd of men and women at the dig. The hell with them! Let them all die! Damn it! *Uno proyecto perfecto*— all washed up!

Suddenly return fire erupted from the dig. El Lobo was startled. That damned woman had Charqui's AK-47 and was shooting at him! At *him!*

He zigzagged in a scrambling crablike run over the dune as the bullets sang through the air over his head. In a moment both he and Abrojo were in the jeep. He flicked on the ignition, ground the starter, and sloughed off through the sand. He had already mapped out his escape route. At least he had done something right. He was on solid ground now.

No one pursued.

"It's Mr. Featherstone!" someone shouted.

Marta saw a group of the team huddled around Abner Featherstone, who was down on the sand. She ran quickly up to him, Justin at her side. Irene was standing tall, looking down.

"He's been shot," she told Justin.

Featherstone looked up, gritting his teeth and angry as a bear. "Get me out of here! I'm losing blood!"

William Bonney was holding the hapless Charqui, and one of the students had the driver of the van.

"I'll get the Land Rover," Justin said, running back across the sand.

"A random shot." Featherstone waved it off grimly.

Marta Camara glanced briefly at Irene Manners, who had been looking across the dune at the marauders as they vanished from sight. She and Irene exchanged glances of doubt. Random shot?

"It was that gunman in the jeep," someone guessed.

A loud, wrenching scream rose like the wail of a banshee. "Oh, my God!" Everyone turned toward Lotte Loomis. She was kneeling down on the sand. At her feet was stretched the body of Alec Loomis.

William Bonney pushed forward and leaned down over Loomis. He shuddered and sucked in his breath. There was blood all over the sand below Loomis's head.

"Entry wound," said Featherstone mechanically, pointing to the blued mark on Loomis's forehead. He had hobbled over and was staring down at his financial backer. Bonney reached for the pulse in Alec Loomis's neck. After a moment he looked up at Featherstone.

"Man's dead," he whispered.

"Oh, no, no!" screamed Lotte Loomis.

Now Dinah Foreman was there, standing over the body of her client, staring at him with bulging eyes. Quickly she turned to

Lotte, on her knees in the sand, supporting herself by the forearms. Her position was vivid and melodramatic. How the hell, Dinah seemed to be asking Lotte, did you manage it with all these people around?

At that moment Justin drove up in the Land Rover.

Justin and Marta drove Featherstone down to the Clinica Anglo Americana in San Isidro, and there they telephoned the Lima police with a report of Loomis's death. William Bonney and Dinah Foreman took charge of the cholo driver and the wounded gunman. They were bundled into the team bus and driven in to Lima, one to the hospital and the other to the Morales estate.

10.

Within minutes, a Q & A team composed of Justin Birkby, Marta Camara, and Daniel Alvaraz discovered the code names of the four would-be hijackers of the Featherstone team's mobile workshop. The leader was a lower echelon *sargento,* code-named El Lobo. The three soldiers were Charqui, Abrojo, and Bardo. El Lobo and Abrojo, who had escaped, would be put on a police bulletin—but probably would never surface again.

Ballistics tests proved ineffective in discovering what caliber round had killed Alec Loomis. The round itself was still in the sand of the dig apparently; police were still searching for it. However, Featherstone had been hit by a stray bullet from El Lobo's Uzi. That much was known.

Arrangements were being made for Alec Loomis's body to be flown back to the United States on Saturday, accompanied by Lotte Loomis.

Justin Birkby met with Irene Manners in their room shortly after 2 p.m.

"You've got to tell me exactly what happened!" Justin told her. "I was off in the Land Rover!"

"There was *nothing* out of the way," Irene said. "I've told you that before. Nothing!"

"I can't believe a stray bullet killed Loomis—although I know it *could* have. Where was Bonney? I told that bodyguard to watch him. Dinah must have slipped up."

"Bonney wasn't in sight," said Irene wearily. "I didn't see him! And I didn't see *her*, either."

"Were they in it together?" Justin began to feel a chill rising from his stomach.

"I don't know!"

"I'm setting up a Q & A for our principals," Justin snapped. "I want Dinah Foreman, William Bonney, Lotte Loomis, and Abner Featherstone. We'll go down to the hospital to talk to him. Then we get to work on your sketches and see what we can make of this mess!"

NAME: DINAH FOREMAN. AGE: 28. BORN: PORT-LAND, OREGON. TAUGHT CLASS IN KARATE FOR WOMEN, SAN FRANCISCO. BODYGUARD FOR ROCK STAR ANTOINE POGUE.
RELATIONSHIP WITH VICTIM: WAS HIRED BY VIC-TIM AFTER MUGGING OF VICTIM IN L.A. RU-MORED TO HAVE HAD AFFAIR WITH VICTIM SINCE PROFESSIONAL RELATIONSHIP.
ACTIONS OF SUBJECT DURING RAID ON DIG: VERI-FIED.
WITNESS: WILLIAM BONNEY.

EXCERPT OF Q & A TRANSCRIPT:

JUSTIN: I've got to know just what happened at the dig when Loomis was killed.

DINAH: It was your fault he was killed! I was off on a

wild-goose chase watching the wrong man! Bonney had nothing to do with it!

JUSTIN: You stuck close to Bonney?

DINAH: Like glue. Following your ridiculous orders.

JUSTIN: I accept full responsibility. Go ahead.

DINAH: Go ahead with what? *I* feel responsible for my client's death! Let's see if I can get this all straight. It was very confusing.

JUSTIN: Take it from the moment when the man with the AK-47—code name Charqui—started firing at me in the Land Rover.

DINAH: Those were the first shots. I was watching Loomis, and when the shooting began, I turned immediately to cover Bonney. I thought it might be some kind of signal to him.

JUSTIN: You mean, he might be in with the raiders?

DINAH: Yeah. And when he began moving, I suspected that you might be right about him.

JUSTIN: What did he do?

DINAH: He went down into the dig.

JUSTIN: The excavation?

DINAH: Right.

JUSTIN: And you followed?

DINAH: Yes. He saw me coming after him. "It's safe down here," he assured me. And then he said a funny thing.

JUSTIN: Yes?

DINAH: "Hadn't you better look out for your boss?"

JUSTIN: What did you say?

DINAH: I didn't say anything. All hell broke loose up above. I couldn't see what was going on. There was shouting and shots from up on the dune. I stuck with Bonney. Unfortunately!

JUSTIN: Anybody else follow you down?

DINAH: No. But it's because I was down there that I couldn't help Alec!

JUSTIN: Do you have any idea who shot Alec?

DINAH: Sure do. His wife, Lotte.

JUSTIN: How? She was unarmed.

DINAH: Was she?

JUSTIN: There's nothing we can do about it now.

DINAH: I should have stayed with *her*.

JUSTIN: How long were you involved with Alec Loomis? I mean romantically.

DINAH: I don't have to answer that.

JUSTIN: Still, I'd like to know.

DINAH: It was no secret. Probably ever since I started working for him.

JUSTIN: Did the arrangement include money?

DINAH: He *was* paying me for my services as bodyguard!

JUSTIN: And that was the full extent of your financial involvement?

DINAH: Yes!

JUSTIN: Was Bonney armed?

DINAH: As a matter of fact, he was. That was the reason I stayed with him. I thought he was trying to decoy me with a feint and then get back to do in Alec.

JUSTIN: Then you weren't as sure I was wrong as you pretended to be just now?

DINAH: I wasn't sure about anything. I'm not sure now.

JUSTIN: Right. And you could be pretending now, too.

DINAH: Is that all?

JUSTIN: That's all.

NAME: WILLIAM BONNEY. AGE: 25. BORN: CHICAGO. EDUCATED: STANFORD UNIVERSITY. AMERICAN ARCHAEOLOGISTS PRIZE FOR PAPER ON DETERMINATION OF AGE OF ANTIQUITIES. TEACHER, ARCHAEOLOGY, UNIVERSITY OF SAN DIEGO.

RELATIONSHIP WITH VICTIM: MET VICTIM AT
ARCHAEOLOGICAL SEMINAR IN DALLAS.
ACTIONS OF SUBJECT DURING RAID ON DIG: VERI-
FIED. WITNESS: DINAH FOREMAN.

EXCERPT OF Q & A TRANSCRIPT:

JUSTIN: When did you meet Alec Loomis?

BONNEY: At the time I was assigned to the expedition by Abner Featherstone.

JUSTIN: Perhaps I should have asked you when you
met Featherstone.

BONNEY: I had done a paper on carbon tests for de-
termining the age of antiquities. I was awarded
a prize by AA. Featherstone saw the paper and
got in touch with me. He was interested in coming here to Peru. In spite of the Shining Path
troubles.

JUSTIN: You knew about Shining Path?

BONNEY: I can read, can't I? The papers were full of
it.

JUSTIN: You have ambitions in archaeology?

BONNEY: I'm good at it. Why not?

JUSTIN: Not much money in it.

BONNEY: There's not much money in being a cop, is
there?

JUSTIN: What do you think of Lotte Loomis?

BONNEY: Not much.

JUSTIN: I understand you ran down into the dig
when the shooting started today.

BONNEY: Seemed the most intelligent place to be at
the time.

JUSTIN: You were armed?

BONNEY: Well, yes. I do carry a Colt forty-five.

JUSTIN: Then why not stay aboveground and protect
the others?

BONNEY: I doubt that "protect" is the operative

word. What's one handgun against three assault rifles?

JUSTIN: Did you see Dinah Foreman during the
shooting?

BONNEY: She followed me down into the dig. I don't
know why.

JUSTIN: How long were the two of you down there?

BONNEY: Until the shooting stopped. See here, you
make it sound like we were having it on or
something.

JUSTIN: Were you?

BONNEY: Me? With Wonder Woman? No way!

JUSTIN: Rather it were Marta Camara, I imagine.

BONNEY: She's charming.

JUSTIN: Yes. But attraction is all in the eye of the
beholder. Why did you try to trace the movements of Alec Loomis and Dinah Foreman the
other night? You were seen, you know.

BONNEY: Since I've known him, I've become quite
friendly with Alec Loomis. I thought he was
getting a bit mushy with the help. I don't trust
her.

JUSTIN: And yet you spent the time during the raid
today in the dig with her.

BONNEY: I told you. She followed me.

JUSTIN: But you will vouch for the fact that she was
down there at the time Alec Loomis was shot?

BONNEY: If I could be sure of the time he was shot, I
might be able to say. Offhand, I'd guess yes.

JUSTIN: How poisonous is the bite of the scorpion?

BONNEY: Is this a trivia quiz?

JUSTIN: You don't wish to answer?

BONNEY: Oh, it's deadly all right. That what you
want to know?

JUSTIN: I was more interested in *your* opinion.

ASSESSMENT OF Q & A:

"This is a tough one." Justin sighed. "Here we've got the main suspect—William Bonney—under surveillance by Dinah Foreman, someone attached not only professionally but emotionally to the murder victim. And they're both alibiing each other!"

Irene sighed. "Nothing can be done about it. I thought his answer about why he tried to find out where Alec Loomis was last night was quite perceptive. He *is* suspicious of Dinah Foreman—particularly so since this morning."

"Did he really *like* Alec Loomis? It's hard to tell. Bonney is a kind of golden boy—a sort of delicious yuppie. Plays everything close to the chest. Very circumspect. Does everything right."

"What about Dinah?"

"She got in a dig or two at me," Justin said. "And she was right to. I did have it all wrong."

"Did you, really? I mean—maybe they're in this together now. Maybe he did shoot Loomis just at the end of the excitement."

"But how did he get Dinah Foreman to alibi him?"

"You've heard of money, my dear fellow? Or perhaps he's got something on her!"

NAME: LOTTE LOOMIS. NEE LESTRADE. AGE: 27. BORN: BROOKLYN, NEW YORK. FASHION MODEL AFTER DROPPING OUT OF HIGH SCHOOL. APPEARED IN MAGAZINE PIX. DID RAMP WORK AS WELL AS PHOTOGRAPHY. PARIS, LONDON, ROME, NEW YORK, LOS ANGELES.
RELATIONSHIP WITH VICTIM: MARRIED HIM 3 YEARS AGO.
ACTIONS DURING RAID ON DIG: VERIFIED. WITNESS: ABNER FEATHERSTONE.

EXCERPTS FROM Q & A TRANSCRIPT:

JUSTIN: Where did you meet Alec Loomis?

LOTTE: At a health spa.

JUSTIN: Where was this health spa?

LOTTE: In Arizona. He owns it.

JUSTIN: You were a client there?

LOTTE: No. I taught the aerobics class. I was a model before that.

JUSTIN: You played it smart. When did you marry the owner of the spa?

LOTTE: Three years ago.

JUSTIN: I understand there was a substantial pre-nuptial contract signed.

LOTTE: Yeah. Everybody was talking about prenuptial settlements in those days. I figured I should prepare myself for my old age.

JUSTIN: They say you did quite well.

LOTTE: I find this very tasteless in view of what's happened.

JUSTIN: I suppose it is. Nevertheless—

LOTTE: Yeah. It's iron-clad, too. I'm going to make out fine. You don't need to sob none for Lotte.

JUSTIN: I hadn't even considered it.

LOTTE: I'm sure not.

JUSTIN: Do you ever go back to the spa?

LOTTE: I work there off and on for a couple of months out of the year. I like to keep my figure.

JUSTIN: So I see. Do you recognize this?

LOTTE: It's a piece of paper. Never saw it before.

JUSTIN: Read it.

LOTTE: It makes no sense to me.

JUSTIN: It's signed *L*.

LOTTE: I see that. So?

JUSTIN: *L* could stand for Lotte.

LOTTE: Or "lettuce," or "lobotomy," or—

JUSTIN: Who's Charlie, Lotte? Do you know any Charlies?

LOTTE: Sure. Charlie McCarthy. Charlie "Bird" Parker.

JUSTIN: Funny, funny. You're in this very much up to your chin, honey. This letter was discovered in your possession.

LOTTE: Ah! Snoopy, snoopy!

JUSTIN: By your husband. Do you deny writing it?

LOTTE: Of course I deny writing it! I deny receiving it! I deny ever seeing it!

JUSTIN: Then, according to you, it doesn't even exist?

LOTTE: As something connected to me—and to Alec —of course it doesn't exist.

JUSTIN: "Once I kill him, we play it by ear." You didn't write that?

LOTTE: No. Besides, it's not even my handwriting.

JUSTIN: I'd like to know exactly what you saw when the shooting started this morning at the dig.

LOTTE: I was so scared I don't think I saw anything. Well, there was one guy with a big assault weapon. He ran down toward the van when it drove away. Then that woman threw a knife at him and stopped him cold.

JUSTIN: Where was William Bonney at that time?

LOTTE: I don't remember. I don't think I saw him at all—come to think of it.

JUSTIN: And Mr. Featherstone?

LOTTE: He was just standing there. I remember. Alec told him not to do *anything*. That's right. Rocky didn't move.

JUSTIN: Was anyone in the digging party armed?

LOTTE: Rocky carried a gun. But he didn't use it. And I think Bonney carried a gun. But he was —he wasn't there.

JUSTIN: You didn't see anyone take out a weapon of any kind?

LOTTE: No.

JUSTIN: Go ahead. Then what happened?

LOTTE: Suddenly the guy standing at the top of the

dune began yelling and screaming. Then he
flung up his assault weapon and fired right
down at us. And he hit Rocky. And killed Alec.
He killed Alec.

JUSTIN: Are you sure the man on the dune killed
Alec?

LOTTE: Had to be. I saw Alec go down. I was right
with him.

JUSTIN: When did you first meet William Bonney?

LOTTE: Huh? I suppose at the start of the flight
down. In Los Angeles International Airport. In
the lobby.

JUSTIN: Are you sure you never saw him before
that? Never knew him before that? At the
health spa maybe?

LOTTE: Bonney? The fat farm? Nah! I'd have remembered him!

JUSTIN: Perhaps during your career as a model?

LOTTE: The kid's younger than me. You think I'm his
long-lost mother or something?

JUSTIN: I'm just trying to find out the truth.

ASSESSMENT OF Q & A:

"At least she made no pretense at being the grieving widow,"
Irene said softly.

"On the other hand, she seemed pretty cool and collected for
someone who's just lost a husband."

"Cool and collected is the way you have to be today," Irene
murmured.

"You think she's connected with Bonney?"

"How can we ever be sure?"

"I'd like to know who 'Charlie' really is," Justin said.

NAME: ABNER FEATHERSTONE. AGE: 55. BORN: AT-
LANTA, GEORGIA. GREW UP IN HOUSTON, TEXAS.

EDUCATION: TEXAS CHRISTIAN UNIVERSITY.
SUBJECT: MINERALOGY. WORKED FOR OIL COM-
PANY; GOT INTO ARCHAEOLOGY AFTER MEETING
OIL MILLIONAIRE J. STERN WARE. MADE DOCU-
MENTARY FILM WITH ARCHAEOLOGIST DIEGO
TARN; IT WON CANNES AWARD. MARRIED AND DI-
VORCED ZENA ECKHART, BROADWAY SINGER.
RELATIONSHIP WITH VICTIM: SUBJECT WAS IN-
TRODUCED TO VICTIM BY MEMBER OF WHITE
HOUSE STAFF AFTER TROUBLE IN GREECE ON
DIG. VICTIM AGREED TO BACK NEW EXPEDITION
TO PERU.
ACTIONS DURING RAID: VERIFIED. IN FULL SIGHT
OF EVERYONE.

EXCERPTS OF Q & A TRANSCRIPT:

JUSTIN: Are you sure you're comfortable? I don't
want to subject you to any more grief than is
necessary.

FEATHERSTONE: I'm fine.

JUSTIN: I've gone over your background and am reasonably satisfied as to the accuracy of your
statements to us. I'd like to concentrate mostly
on your actions here in Lima.

FEATHERSTONE: Of course.

JUSTIN: With one exception. The incident in Greece.

FEATHERSTONE: Ah.

JUSTIN: It's all water under the bridge, you might
say, but—was your internment in Greece equi-
table? I mean, were they justified in keeping
you?

FEATHERSTONE: As you know, the government apologized after I was extradited to the States.

JUSTIN: I understand that.

FEATHERSTONE: All right. I'll be honest. Yes. They
were justified.

JUSTIN: We have reason to believe that you were re-

sponsible for having the Lima artifacts dupli-
cated—*counterfeited* would be a better word.

FEATHERSTONE: I'll be the first to admit *that*.

JUSTIN: So you could sell the real things on the black
market—and turn over the fakes to the Peruvian government?

FEATHERSTONE: Come on now, cop! That's ridiculous.
I've been burned before. As you so undiplomati-
cally reminded me. I wasn't about to let the
same thing happen to me again! You've got to
understand that Shining Path has operatives
everywhere. I guessed there was going to be a
raid on the dig. That's why I had the dupes
made. To protect myself!

JUSTIN: And you have the artifacts in a safe place?

FEATHERSTONE: I could take you there in a minute.

JUSTIN: There is another rumor floating about I'd
like to nail down.

FEATHERSTONE: Shoot.

JUSTIN: Have you ever had dealings with a Peruvian
named El Lobo?

FEATHERSTONE: Never.

JUSTIN: The rumor is that he led the raid this morning after making a deal with you. That is, what
he stole, he'd split with you.

FEATHERSTONE: But he stole nothing.

JUSTIN: He didn't know that when he initiated the
raid.

FEATHERSTONE: I had no deal with him. Besides, if I
had, he would have stolen worthless goods. You
think I'd want my head in a noose with *his*
band of cutthroats?

JUSTIN: You've been shot at twice since you've arrived in Lima.

FEATHERSTONE: Yeah, but this time it was with assault rifles! Wow!

JUSTIN: Was Alec Loomis standing near you when
you went down?

FEATHERSTONE: I think so. I've been going over it in my mind. I don't really remember where he was in relation to me. I know that he went down when I did. I thought he was just trying to duck down flat to get out of range of the bullets.

JUSTIN: Did you see anyone else around you who was armed?

FEATHERSTONE: No. Not that somebody couldn't have been packing. I don't know. I think Bonney had a gun. But I didn't see him at all.

JUSTIN: Where was Lotte Loomis?

FEATHERSTONE: Checking up on that rumor that she had a contract out on her husband, huh? She was right there all the time. I didn't see anything in her hand at all. She couldn't have shot him. I'm positive about that. Besides, don't think I wasn't curious about all that talk.

JUSTIN: Where are you going to get backing now?

FEATHERSTONE: This expedition's all paid for already. I don't know what I'm going to do next. I haven't exactly enhanced my image with this one, have I? Through no fault of my own.

JUSTIN: Score another for Shining Path, is that it?

FEATHERSTONE: Those bastards know how to hurt a guy, I'll say that for them!

ASSESSMENT OF Q & A:

"Seems all pretty straightforward to me," Justin said. "But just the same, the big man himself could be involved. Suppose he has been in it from the start with Lotte Loomis? Staged that near miss at the airport. Staged a near killing today for himself—with Loomis the real victim."

"Motive?"

"Money. Say he's got Lotte on the string. She's going to inherit plenty from Alec Loomis. He'll be in the catbird seat as Lotte's new husband!"

"But no one saw him shoot at all."

"Right. I'm trying to figure out some way he could have gotten the gun to Lotte herself—or someone else on the outskirts of the crowd." Justin sighed. "But I can't.

"I haven't even begun to try."

11.

Abner Featherstone was true to his word. As soon as Justin Birkby was ready to leave the hospital, he gave him detailed instructions on exactly where to find the *huacos* buried in the garden of the Morales estate. When Marta Camara examined the duplicates later, she found the secret mark on them that proclaimed them the work of none other than Rafael de Santos, one of the region's most talented forgers.

De Santos had worked for Peruvian Antiquities for years, authenticating various finds, but had gotten into trouble for making up a duplicate of an artifact for a collector he knew. What happened was that the model of the duplicate was later stolen and spirited out of Peru, with the counterfeit left in its place. Rafael de Santos, even though innocent of the deception, was dismissed from his job with Antiquities and, almost as a matter of revenge, went into the counterfeiting business.

Abner Featherstone's condition at the hospital was such that Justin and Irene were unable to see him until Saturday noon—the day after the raid. And so it was Saturday afternoon before they had a chance to sit down and try to figure out the truth about the murder of Alec Loomis, if indeed anybody could. By that time Marta Camara was at the Morales estate with them; they invited her to join them.

Irene went upstairs and brought down her art portfolio filled with drawings of the artifacts that had been excavated at the dig, along with portraits of the principals of the Featherstone team—Featherstone, Loomis, Bonney, Lotte, Dinah, Marta, and others.

Before they began, Justin halted Irene. He was staring thoughtfully at the likeness of Lotte Loomis on one of the sheets of sketch paper. *She* was the image that had awakened that feeling of déjà vu he had experienced when he had first come into the Morales *mansión* that Sunday night. He had been unsure of it up to now, but now he *knew*.

"Have you another picture of her?" he asked Irene. He kept his rush of excitement well concealed. "She doesn't always look the same, you know."

Irene glanced at Justin and then back at the sketch. She seemed to have intuited his excitement, but if she did, she kept it well veiled.

"She's a human chameleon," Irene admitted. She was sorting through the pile of sketches and finally came up with two more. "Try these." She handed them over to Justin.

He took them and stared at them carefully, comparing them to the first. But the more Justin studied Lotte's various likenesses, the more confused he became. He glanced up once, noting that Irene was staring interestedly at him.

In the end he handed the drawings back to her and shook his head.

"I'm dreaming. That's all. Dreaming. I thought I'd seen her somewhere before. Obviously I haven't."

Irene's eyes narrowed. "You're not usually wrong, dear. Where did you think you saw her?"

"I don't know!" snapped Justin irritably. "On a case?" He shook his head angrily. "I just don't remember!"

Then he took the drawings back, studying them one by one.

He glanced up into Irene's eyes. They were alive with expectation. "Do *you* remember her?"

Irene shrugged. She took back the drawings, and went through them, one by one. Then she sighed. "It's my business to size up faces and figures. I don't remember her. But that doesn't mean much of anything. I could be fooled, too. Disguise. Hairdos. Makeup."

Marta became interested now. "She uses a great deal of makeup. I've noticed that myself. And she *does* change her look from day to day."

"Almost as if it's deliberate," Irene murmured.

Justin flipped through the pictures once again. "I've broken enough disguises in my time. I should be able to break this one. But, you know, I simply can't. Sorry." He sighed. "Anyway. We know she didn't kill Alec Loomis herself. There were too many people around. And she had no access to a gun."

"At least that we know of," Irene corrected him.

"What's more," Marta put in, "she's flying to the States this afternoon—right now, I think—with the body of her husband. If she's the killer, she's out of reach now."

"Oh, we can always have her extradited," Justin pointed out.

"Yes, but—"

"It's clumsy." Justin smiled. "Indeed it is."

"Clumsy or not, the point is we don't really have anything on her," Marta reminded them.

"Touché," murmured Justin. He gave a wry moue. " ' 'Tis now too late to weep, let's have him home, / And with what speed we may, find out the murderer.' "

As Irene groaned, Justin smiled at Marta for the aptness of the John Ford quote.

"I'm beginning to get the proper feel for the case," Justin said finally. "I mean, I can look back on it and I can see the preliminary 'attack' on Abner Featherstone at the airport in Lima as deliberate misdirection. We were to think that Featherstone was a terrorist target. The killer of Alec Loomis used the shield of terrorism to obscure his primary target. Then, when Alec Loomis was finally shot to death, the killer's work was screened from view by the terrorist presence. In fact, that's what I thought first thing when we began to put together the pieces of the investigation."

Marta said, "Then you now feel that there *was* a plot all along to kill Loomis?"

"Oh yes," said Justin. "The attack on Featherstone was a feint. How the killer coordinated his work with the terrorists' actions is beyond me at this moment."

"If the killer was a Peruvian," Irene said, "it's not hard to believe that he was a member of Shining Path."

"But suppose he was an American hit man? A contract killer. *Then* how did he use the terrorist cover?"

Marta shook her head.

Justin began toying with some of Irene's sketches. "I'm not sure he was a Peruvian. I'm looking at that guy in the *jardin* Bonney met the other night." Justin made a face. "I certainly made a bonehead play when I instructed Alec Loomis's body-guard to stick to William Bonney."

"Which means that if Bonney is innocent, then the story he told you about meeting someone on the premises of the Morales estate may have been true," Irene said. "Perhaps, as you intimate, that man is the killer."

"One of our own in disguise?" Marta suggested.

Justin looked up. "Let's get Bonney in here. Meanwhile, I want another look at that damned letter!"

Marta had heard about "the Loomis letter," but she had not seen it. She studied it now.

"I don't really understand." She frowned. "You told me you had twigged to the name 'Bonney' through 'Bonnie Prince Charlie.' But Charlie is the receiver of the letter, not the sender! The *sender* would be the killer. He—or she—writes, 'Once I kill him . . .'"

"An upside-down," Justin said softly. "A head-to-tail inversion. The sender pretends to be the recipient; the recipient becomes the sender. Thus 'Charlie' is really the sender; L is really the recipient."

"I see," said Marta. "I think."

Justin frowned. There was something elusive at the back of his mind, teasing him, but he could not quite rein it in. Some vagrant idea . . .

William Bonney joined them. Once again Justin had him go over the conversation with the stranger in the night, word for word. Marta asked several questions, but gained no ground.

"How well did you *see* him?" Irene suddenly asked.

"Fairly well," Bonney admitted.

"Look. Can you guide me? I'll make a sketch of Mr. X and—"

"Be glad to!"

Irene got out her sketch pad and started in. Marta watched in fascination. So did Bonney.

It was during this prolonged sketching session—"eyebrows?" "mouth?" "ears?" "hairline?"—that Justin Birkby went into a kind of blue funk and sat staring out the window, frowning and trying to put together something in his mind. None of the rest noticed it, but at one point he went absolutely still. His mouth sagged open just the slightest. He held his breath, not moving a muscle.

Then, abruptly, he relaxed, and a big grin appeared on his face.

"Come on. We don't even need the composite now," he told Irene.

Bonney was flabbergasted. "You've thought of something important?"

"Oh, yes."

Marta Camara was exuberant. "You've finally found the smoking gun?"

"Not only that. I know who pulled the trigger."

BECAUSE THE MURDERER OF ALEC LOOMIS WAS NEVER BROUGHT TO JUSTICE, THE FACTS IN THE CASE HAVE NEVER BEEN MADE PUBLIC. IN THE FOLLOWING ACCOUNT, CHIEF INSPECTOR JUSTIN BIRKBY (RET) OF INTERPOL, HAS WRITTEN A DETAILED SOLUTION OF THE MURDER, COMPLETE WITH IDENTITIES, NAMES, AND CLUES THAT LED TO THE SOLUTION—WHERE APPLICABLE.

Who Killed Alec Loomis?
Written by Justin Birkby

The most difficult thing for me to unscramble was the simple fact that there were two possibilities in both of the main clues in the Featherstone plot. The main clues to the case were, of course, the letter found in Lotte Loomis's slacks and the conversation in the night between William Bonney and Owen Lloyd.

Taken at face value, the letter was a statement—a promise, if you will—by Lotte Loomis to kill her husband Alec and join "Charlie" after the killing. It seemed obvious that Lotte and Charlie would then walk off into the sunset to enjoy their ill-gotten gains (the Loomis fortune agreed to in the prenuptial marriage contract).

Taken other than at face value, the letter could mean several different things.

Frankly, the truth was right there staring me in the face from the beginning. But I did not *think* clearly enough to uncover it. I let surface distractions mislead me. It was all there in the letter, had I managed to *see* it.

Nor did I tumble to the truth even after my conversation with William Bonney about the stranger he had encountered in the night. Together with the truth in the letter, the words in that conversation itself should have led me immediately to the exclusive truth.

The irony was that immediately prior to my conversation with Bonney I had astonished myself with my own brilliance in ascertaining the fact that the "Charlie" referred to in the letter was "Bonnie Prince Charlie," and therefore William Bonney. So impressed was I by my own brilliance, that I wrote off the *real* facts that surfaced in the conversation between Bonney and "Owen Lloyd."

In fact, "Lloyd" did all he could to wave a red flag in front of my eyes. There, indeed, was the *L* we had been searching for!

By my own intellectual arrogance I doomed myself to total unenlightenment.

Let's look at the conversation between Bonney and Owen Lloyd, which, to the best of Bonney's memory, went like this:

> LLOYD: I'm—I'm so sorry—I—I seem to be lost, don't I?
>
> BONNEY: Are you looking for someone?
>
> LLOYD: Not really. Excuse me. I'm Owen Lloyd. Just down here for the pleasure of it. Looking for my cousin's house. Carlos works in Lima, you see. Do you *live* here, old man?
>
> BONNEY: Just temporarily.
>
> LLOYD: I seem to have lost my way. Isn't that just like a bumbling American?

I suddenly realized, on reviewing this exchange Saturday afternoon, that a number of important facts were concealed in it. But let's get back to the letter itself. It was an analysis of the letter, *combined* with an analysis of the Bonney-Lloyd conversation, that broke the case for me.

The name "Charlie" in that letter was a puzzlement to me from the beginning. There was no Charlie at all. That was the reason I was so tempted by the word association in the name "Bonnie Prince Charlie." Was why I fell for it, hook, line, and sinker. By Saturday afternoon, when I was looking at that letter again, I began playing with the name Charlie once more. Of course, the name Carlos had surfaced in the conversation Bonney had with Lloyd.

I was thinking of Charlie, and Carlos, and my mind continued to rove over possibilities. Charles in French is Charles—the English way. In Italian it's Carlo. In Spanish, Carlos. And more than that, Charles in the feminine is Charlotte, Carlotta, Carla, and so on.

And then I had it.

"Lotte!" Lotte could be a nickname for "Charlotte." Alec's wife.

If "Charlie" were actually short for "Charlotte," then the letter might have been *to* Lotte *from* someone else!

My original concept of the upside-down letter—*to* the person who sent it, *from* the person who received it—was right! I had suckered myself by getting the wrong association for the name Charlie!

The truth was, we *didn't* know if Lotte was the *sender* or the *recipient*. All we knew was that Alec found the letter in her slacks. Turning the whole thing upside down, I saw what this might mean. We had anticipated action on Lotte's part in killing her husband herself. If indeed it meant that someone outside was going to kill Alec, then it might well be whoever the letter was *from*. "L."

Note that the speaker in the night called himself "Owen Lloyd." Obviously a phony name. But he did use an *L*. What did *that* mean? Nothing? Something?

The very first attack at the Jorge Chavez International Airport in Lima was staged by Lotte (Charlie) and her accomplice (L), whoever he/she was. The plan was obviously to establish Featherstone as a prime target and kill Alec Loomis later. Then Lotte could remain complacent as the grieving widow in an accidental death and meet her accomplice later for whatever split or relationship they were considering.

Neat?

Now as for the who in the case. The hit man.

I have trained myself to study the way people speak. The flow of their words, the manner in which they express themselves, the intonation—all these things are important clues to their char-

acter. It was in reviewing the *actual words* William Bonney remembered that tipped me off to the identity of the killer.

It was a quirk of "Owen Lloyd's" to answer each of Bonney's
questions *with another question.*

On the *Shangri-la,* I remembered, I had been questioning one
of the suspects—he had a perfect alibi—in the matter of the
death of Tammy Scott. I noted this peculiarity and even mentioned it to him in my interrogation. I also remembered that he
had been especially nervous during the questioning—as if he
might have something to hide.

He was the principal suspect—Clifford Boone. I remembered
that on his dossier I had his full name down as "L. Clifford
Boone." You see? That's the *L* in the letter to Lotte Loomis
("Charlie"). (It later turned out that his name *was* Lloyd Clifford
Boone—just waiting for him to grab when unexpectedly met in
the dark outside the *mansión.*)

Then the bigger truth struck me. We had our obvious suspect
here—Lotte—and her accomplice. This was the exact opposite
of the earlier case. Our obvious suspect in the murder of Tammy
Scott was Cliff Boone. L. Cliff Boone.

The actual killer in the murder of Tammy Scott was the towel
girl, Jane Doe. She escaped. Boone disappeared. Now, if that girl
was really Lotte Loomis, we would have a pure case of mirror
opposites. After all, I *had* thought I'd seen her before. And she
did continue to change her appearance; to confuse *me?*

Thus we would have a classic murder ploy: the spectacle of
two would-be murderers *who switch victims* in order to establish
perfect alibis for themselves!

Exactly what they had done!

That is, Lotte Loomis, as the towel girl, would kill Tammy
Scott *for* Cliff Boone, who would be the logical suspect, but
would have a perfect, cast-iron alibi. Then in exchange, L. Cliff
Boone (Owen Lloyd) would kill Alec Loomis *for* Lotte Loomis,
who would be the logical suspect, but who would have a perfect,
cast-iron alibi.

The two cases were inexorably linked. They were Siamese

twins. Only by a quirk of fate had I been involved in both cases. I wondered what must have been in Lotte Loomis's mind, or in that of Cliff Boone, when either of them first saw me in Lima! And that was how I read Lotte Loomis—but only mistily and not clearly enough to identify her accurately and immediately as the suspected murderer of Tammy Scott.

Incidentally, I had forgotten another important fact. Cliff Boone was a bona fide marksman. It all came back when I made him for the hit man lurking in the Morales *jardin.* Made him for the hit man obviously operating in secret *outside* the terrorists on the raid but with one target in mind, Alec Loomis, whom he had shot in the center of the forehead! As any bona fide service marksman should have been able to do!

(We discovered later that Boone had seen the terrorists "casing the site" as soon as the Featherstone team had arrived at the dig. In exchange for inside information on the team, plus a copy of the van's key, Boone learned the timing and details of the raid, which he used as a cover for his own sniper's hit on Alec Loomis.)

I rushed to the telephone as soon as I had established the fact in my own mind that Boone and Lotte were in this thing together. The airport security agents were right on the ball. They rushed out to the California-bound AeroPeru jet that had not yet taken off, and they marched through the plane to notify Lotte Loomis that she was under arrest for questioning by the Lima police.

No Lotte Loomis.

The body of Alec Loomis was on the jet. The body of Lotte Loomis had vanished.

Off to meet Cliff Boone, of course.

I left the matter in the hands of the Lima authorities and flew back home with Irene on an Air France jet to Paris on the following Monday. A week later in Lyons I received a Lima newspaper clipping from Marta Camara in the mail.

"Two Killed in Car Explosion," the small headline read.

"Two people were killed in a fiery explosion just off the Loja-

Cuenca portion of the Pan American Highway in Ecuador Monday [two days after Lotte Loomis "vanished"] when their car crashed through protective fencing and plunged down a two hundred foot embankment.

"The victims were burned beyond recognition. However, detectives on the case traced the car to a rental agency in Lima, Peru, and it was ascertained that the vehicle had been rented to an American woman, Mrs. Charlotte Loomis, through a credit card.

"Nevertheless, according to Lima authorities, the case is still under investigation."

In her graceful handwriting, Marta had written across the clip: "I thought you might be interested."

Interested, yes. Triumphant, no. I have never liked open-ended cases. The authorities were unsatisfied, as I would have been, had I been in charge of the case. Who *were* the people in that burned car, anyway?

There were too many loose ends here to write *finis* to the case. I thought it appropriate to keep it open as well—at least in my own mind—until I heard otherwise.

The Philanthropist

1.

The Humboldt Building in Denver stood thirty-five stories high. The penthouse suite was an unforgettable combination of offices and recreational areas. A tennis court, a putting green, a hothouse area comprised of tropical trees and plants comingled in close harmony with boardrooms, individual offices on the grand scale, and smaller cubicles for heavy workers. It was here that Assistance Anonymous had its international corporate headquarters.

The penthouse was accessed by elevator number 1 of the Humboldt Building's express bank. Local floors below twenty were accessed in a separate elevator bank. The express bank contained eight elevators, one of which was used exclusively for the thirty-fifth floor. Although called an express, it could stop or be stopped at any floor on the building. This allowed the privileged penthouse inhabitant an opportunity to visit anyone in the building at will, without going to the main floor and up again.

Saul Brody stood in his chauffeur's uniform at the front of the Humboldt Building in the pickup area waiting for his employer to appear. He was leaning against the front left fender of the gray stretch limousine, reading the *Denver Post,* when his beeper sounded. He reached inside the Caddy and removed the cellular phone.

"Yeah?"

"He's getting in the elevator," a female voice told him.

"Thanks, Rosie."

Brody folded his paper, stashed it in the capacious dashboard compartment, and stood outside the car by the passenger door. From his position on the curb he could look directly in through the lobby to elevator number 1. There was a long row of light buttons on the panel to the left of it. He could see the light go on at the top, and then blink out, the second one blink on, and go out, and so on as his eye followed the elevator in its movement downward.

It took probably ninety seconds for the elevator to make it from top to bottom. Certain employees had complained of the lack of speed of number 1, but their complaints had fallen on deaf ears. If number 1 was changed to an automated express, cutting off the bottom thirty-four floors, the elevator would descend at a much faster rate. But since it was programmed to stop at any floor on demand, it acted much the way any local elevator would.

When number 1 reached the ground floor the light on the panel blinked off, and the white arrow at the top of the door glowed on. The doors slowly opened. Brody waited expectantly for his employer to step out through the opening, see him, wave, and hurry forward.

Instead no one stepped out. The doors remained open, with the elevator's interior revealed as empty. Brody frowned. He turned and reached into the limo for the cellular phone. He flicked on the talk button.

"Rosie."

There was a long pause. Finally a voice answered. "Yes?"

"It's me. What happened? Did he miss the elevator?"

"Who?"

"The boss!" snapped Brody. "You playing games with me?"

"He just went down. Hasn't he arrived?"

"No."

"He's in a hurry. Don't fool around, Saul!"

"He's not here. He wasn't in the elevator when it arrived."

"That's impossible!" Rosie said, then changed her mind. "Wait! Let me make sure."

He held the cellular handset and waited.

"I've looked all through the penthouse!" she said breathlessly. "He isn't here, Saul. I'm quite sure I *saw* him get in that elevator!"

"Maybe he stopped on the way down." Brody had calmed a bit now and realized that a number of possibilities could have occurred. "I'll check at the dispatcher's."

"Okay."

Brody had flicked off the TALK button and was hurrying across the lobby of the Humboldt Building. He stepped inside the empty elevator cage to make sure his employer was not standing behind one of the operator's panels out of sight. As he left, a passenger stepped inside number 1 and the doors closed on him. The cage shot upward for the thirty-fifth floor.

Saul Brody had a very good idea exactly what he would learn from the dispatcher. The elevator had *not* stopped on its way down, or even slowed. It had progressed in its usual downward direction without interruption. He knew it had; after all, he had *seen* the lights.

The dispatcher, a red-headed man named Gordon Maxwell, confirmed that elevator number 1 had made no stops on its way down. Nor had it made any stops on its way back up. It was now ending its ascent at the thirty-fifth floor. Maxwell showed Brody the lights on the miniature computer monitor in front of him. Sure enough, Brody could see the light at the top of the panel.

He hurried back through the lobby, looking about carefully, hoping that his eyes had deceived him and that the man he was waiting for would suddenly step out from the stationery store and greet him with a smile and a cheery hello.

At the Cadillac, Brody depressed the TALK button and got

through to the office once again. "I hate to repeat this, Rosie, but he never showed up."

"I don't believe it!" snapped Rosie, her impatience surfacing. "I *saw* him get in. At least, I glanced up and he was inside when the doors closed."

"You're sure?"

" 'Course I'm sure!"

"Well, Mr. McGuin never arrived at the lobby level." Brody thought a moment. "The boss was going home to Aspen. What had I better do?"

"I don't know!" wailed Rosie. "I guess you'd better call Mrs. McGuin, you know, and tell her."

"Uh huh," grunted Brody. "Tell her *what,* sweetie?"

"I don't believe this is happening!" shrieked Rosie. "Don't do anything until I talk to Mr. Allenby. I'll get right back to you."

Brett Allenby was Ray McGuin's treasurer and second in command at Assistance Anonymous. "Get back to me a.s.a.p.," snapped Brody. "I'll be arrested for loitering in the pickup area."

Rosie was true to her word. Within a minute, she was back on the cellular phone. "Mr. Allenby says to call Mrs. McGuin."

In a moment he was connected with Aspen and Mrs. McGuin.

"Mrs. McGuin, this is Saul Brody."

"Yes, Saul," she said immediately. Brody was familiar with the cool tone of her voice, with her precise intonation, with her Bryn Mawr accent that was so impeccably finishing school that it almost shattered the imprecise ear.

"I'm afraid I have some rather odd news."

"I'm prepared," Mrs. McGuin said. He could almost imagine her smile. Her first name was Abigail. She allowed none except her very close friends to call her Abby.

"Mr. McGuin seems to have vanished into thin air." Brody tried to make it sound like a joke, and, therefore—credible.

"I see," said Mrs. McGuin.

"He left the thirty-fifth floor of the Humboldt Building, but never got out at the main lobby," Brody pursued.

"Well, he's obviously *somewhere*. Wait there, Saul, and I'm sure he'll soon arrive."

Brody was not at all sure she was right. Raymond McGuin was in no way a man of indeterminate or unstable character. He did not play around with people. Not for him the practical joke or the out-of-line jest. For some very good reason he had *not* kept his appointment with Brody.

It was a stunned Brett Allenby who sat at his desk staring off into space at the time of Brody's conversation with Abigail McGuin. Of course, Ray McGuin certainly might be playing some sort of game—but it was so unlike him! He wondered again what had set Ray off.

He tried to recall the scene in detail. Allenby had been seated at his desk reading through some paperwork when the door to his office had burst open to admit Raymond McGuin in a state of towering rage. McGuin had even slammed the door shut behind him—a wholly uncharacteristic action.

The president of Assistance Anonymous had planted himself in front of Allenby's desk, hands flat on its top, leaning over toward him. The typical Jimmy Stewart appearance was absolutely missing from Ray McGuin's countenance. His face was flushed, his eyes flashing.

"What kind of nonsensical game are you playing with me, Brett?" snapped Ray McGuin, his voice low and hoarse. The vein at his temple was throbbing visibly.

Allenby blinked back his surprise and offered a conciliatory smile. "What are you talking about?"

"About that damned Steeley deal!"

Allenby swallowed hard. Sure, he'd been talking to Steeley about purchasing the company. But it was strictly exploratory. Nothing whatsoever in the way of a concrete offer. "What about it?"

"I never did like those Steeley brothers!" McGuin went on, enraged. "I go across town for lunch and the first thing I see on the way back is one of the Steeleys' goons keeping a close watch on me. They've used these strong-arm tactics before. Did you put them up to it?"

Allenby spread his hands. Obviously McGuin had every reason to be annoyed. "Honest, Ray. I know nothing about it!"

"This welterweight is standing watching me, Brett! Tall thin guy. Sharp profile. Especially the nose. Tiny ears. He's watching me cross the street and he's referring to a card in his hand. It's obvious he's been told to identify and tail me!"

"Not by me, he hasn't been," Allenby said seriously. "Calm down, Ray."

"It's psychological warfare, Brett!" snapped McGuin, calmed a bit, but still at a boil. "A lot of leaning. A lot of fear. To force us to sell! Never! Never, never, never!" To emphasize his words, McGuin pounded his right fist on Allenby's desk three times as he uttered the words.

Allenby put up his hands in a placating way. "Relax, Ray. You're imagining things. Sure I've talked to the Steeleys. But I've made no commitments."

"And you're not going to!" Now McGuin began shouting.

"Come on, Ray. Ease off. The staff will begin to talk." Allenby stood up and moved toward McGuin.

Quite suddenly Ray McGuin regained his normal cool. He was breathing heavily, but his face had returned to its natural color. And his voice was down a number of decibels.

"I'd swear I saw that same guy yesterday, Brett. Honestly! Following me." McGuin shivered. "Those Steeleys are bad people. I don't like this one bit."

"Sorry I opened talks with them," Allenby said as a concession.

McGuin was by now almost completely deflated. "Sorry I got so rough with you, but I'm not happy with this situation. I *feel* harried."

Allenby patted McGuin on the back. "Take it easy, Ray. Go on home and have a good weekend. There won't be any more trouble."

"I won't sell to those people!" Ray McGuin promised. "I won't sell to anybody! You can't force me, either."

The two men looked at one another. Allenby had the grace to back down. "Right, Ray. I know that. Business as usual?"

McGuin tried to smile. "I'm out of here now, Brett. See you Monday."

And he was gone.

In the open doorway to his office, Allenby watched McGuin go into his own next door, pick up his attaché case, and stride toward the reception area at the elevator. He could hear him exchange a few words with the receptionist, and then the elevator arrived. Allenby watched as McGuin entered, turned around, and faced outward. McGuin glanced slightly to his left, almost as if there might be someone there, but because of the angle, Allenby could not see anyone but McGuin.

The doors closed and Allenby crossed to his desk and sat down. He reached for the phone. In a moment he was talking to Jeremy Steeley.

"What kind of crap are you pulling on us?" Allenby said, knowing exactly how to deal with people like the Steeleys.

"Huh?"

"You put a tail on Ray McGuin, you dumb idiot! Don't you know he's got eyes?"

"What tail?" Steeley's voice lowered to a growl. "You said nothing was set. You said you could work it out."

"I can," said Allenby.

"So I don't do nothing!" Steeley said.

There was a pause. "You didn't put anyone on McGuin?"

"Hell no! For what purpose? We got nothing to settle yet!"

"Sorry, Jerry. I just thought—"

Steeley's voice came on as powerful and strong as a punch. "That's your trouble, Allenby. You *think!*"

The connection was broken by a loud slam.

Allenby held the handset and stared at it a moment before hanging up.

And now—a half hour later—Allenby sat at his desk, a thin sheen of perspiration suddenly making his flesh ice cold.

Had Steeley been lying?

Who had put the tail on Ray McGuin?

Allenby looked at the phone, thinking of Abigail McGuin. He decided not to bother her with a call. Everything would probably straighten itself out anyway. Why worry her?

Besides, deep down, Allenby knew he was afraid to talk to her now.

It was about eight o'clock. In the rear of a Burger King restaurant just outside Golden, Colorado, a Chrysler Impala with rental plates was pulled up in the weeds. The parking lot nearby was not full, and the Chrysler seemed somehow out of place.

Gene Bowman was twelve. He had been eating inside the Burger King with his parents and sister. Now he was headed for the men's restroom at the rear of the restaurant. The light that illuminated the walk to the restroom also fell on the car.

The twelve-year-old was startled as he walked by the Chrysler to see movement inside. Someone was sitting up near the rear window. Suddenly Gene Bowman saw a man's face looking out at him directly into the light. He could see the man's hair, the man's wide-open, frightened eyes, and his nose.

Below the nose there was a wide strip of adhesive tape, and it was the sight of the adhesive tape that frightened Gene Bowman. The face looked sort of like the taped-up head of the invisible man in the old black-and-white Claude Rains film they had on video cassette at home.

It was scary.

As Gene Bowman stared at the car, the man's eyes pleaded with him, seemed to be asking him to help him somehow.

What could Gene Bowman do?

He went into the men's room to try to think it out. He was scared, there was no question about it. But he'd talk to his father and discuss the matter. That was the idea. His father always wanted him to discuss things before acting.

But in the end Gene Bowman's decision came to nothing. When he walked out into the path the Chrysler had gone.

"I saw the invisible man," Gene Bowman told his sister when he got back inside.

"Ha, ha, ha," she said, turning up her nose and drinking her Diet Pepsi. She was older than he was, and she knew everything. "You can't *see* a man who's *invisible!*"

2.

When Justin Birkby walked into the living room of his cozy Lyons home to answer the telephone, he vowed once again to purchase a cordless extension so he could converse from the comfort of the garden where he had been sitting in the shade reading. He dismissed the thought irritably—the trouble with the modern world was that there were too many *easy* ways to do things. A man should face up to the difficult, should toughen up to life, as it were.

" 'Allo," he said in the prescribed French manner.

There was a short pause—a depth of silence, actually—and then a voice came on. Someone was talking from a great distance away. It was a woman's voice—speaking English, but with a strange American accent he had not yet encountered.

"I should like to speak to Chief Inspector Justin Birkby, please," said the voice.

"I'm Justin Birkby." Justin lapsed easily into Americanized English.

"Ah! I was told you spoke English. Excellent!"

"Who is this, please?" Justin asked politely. If she was peddling stocks and bonds, he'd get her off the line instantly. Marketing by telephone used everything against you except assault weapons. And those would be next.

"This is Abigail McGuin, Inspector Birkby." She was speaking slowly now, but with that very exotic accent. "I'm Raymond McGuin's wife."

By now Justin had it sorted out. Raymond McGuin was the well-known American philanthropist. Justin had met him briefly on the cruise to Malta celebrating the Loren Hartts' first anniversary of ownership of the *Shangri-la.* He recalled McGuin immediately—the look-alike for the younger Jimmy Stewart: the same drawl, the same languidity, the same midwestern casualness.

"I remember Mr. McGuin well."

"Actually, it's *about* Mr. McGuin," the voice continued in that steady graceful manner. "Have you a moment?"

"I have all the time in the world," Justin said graciously, deciding he could feast on that interesting accent forever.

"We live in Aspen, Colorado, Inspector Birkby. It's quite a distance from Denver, where my husband's office is located in the penthouse of the Humboldt Building. He usually leaves the office early on Friday afternoon to come home for the weekend. And he stays home until about noon on Monday, when he returns to the city."

"Does he drive back and forth, Mrs. McGuin?"

"Oh, it's much too far to drive! Almost two hundred miles. No. He uses the company Lear jet. We have a private chauffeur who is also a licensed pilot. He flew fighter jets in the service. He drives my husband to and from the airports and flies between Denver and Aspen."

"I understand."

"Raymond left the penthouse of the Humboldt Building last Friday afternoon with the chauffeur-pilot downstairs waiting. When the elevator stopped, it was empty."

Justin was puzzled. "Did he get off on the way down?" He was lapsing into the familiar old game of Q & A.

"He did *not.* Saul—that's the name of our chauffeur-pilot— was watching the lights on the elevator panel that traced his descent. The elevator did not stop en route. Yet when the doors opened in the lobby, Raymond was not there. Saul even stepped inside it to make sure."

She hesitated.

"I told Saul to wait around in case Raymond had made an unscheduled stop in the building, but he never did show up. Saul started for Aspen two hours later, alone." Her voice changed slightly, tightened, strained. "I never heard from Raymond during the weekend." She cleared her throat, took a deep breath. "There's more, Inspector."

"Yes?"

"Today I received a postcard in the mail. I cannot make it out. It's in some kind of code."

Justin's interest was piqued. "Code?"

"Numbers. Letters. Would you like me to—?"

"It would be too difficult to break a code over the phone," Justin said thoughtfully. "Let me ask you this. Is your husband in the habit of taking —shall we say?—*unannounced* breaks in his routine?"

She laughed in a low voice that raised Justin's profound interest in her to an even higher pitch. "Never, Inspector Birkby. He is simply not that type of person."

"You cannot envision any reason he might *vanish* the way he has done for a weekend?"

"No, sir."

"Even more important, Mrs. McGuin. Would there be any reason for any person or persons to want to sequester your husband privately? Even, perhaps, although I hesitate to mention it, to threaten him with bodily harm unless he followed their wishes?"

"He is a wealthy man, Inspector Birkby. Many people are envious of his success. However, I do not know of anyone who would—" There was a long pause. "I take your point. There are indeed serious efforts being made to force his company into a leveraged buyout." Her voice quickened. "Do you think these people might have—?"

"Speculation, pure and simple," Justin broke in. "But I don't understand 'leveraged buyout.' I thought your husband simply acted as nexus, putting together philanthropists with philanthropies."

"Which is exactly what he does. His corporation is called 'Assistance Anonymous.' "

Justin nodded. "I see. It is a fund-raising organization basically, but one involved with philanthropic allocations of large sums of money. Still, I do not *quite* see . . ."

The voice on the line turned thoughtful. "My husband has invested a great deal of the company's money in the Third World. Some of his debtors would do anything to have those debts written off, with the worldwide economy what it is today."

"Is there a problem with cash flow?"

"Perhaps. I do not know the details. But I trust you can now see the reason for my uneasiness over his disappearance."

Justin's subconscious had meanwhile been moving from one association to another, and almost as if by magic he suddenly realized what the disappearance of Ray McGuin in the elevator reminded him of. The Perigord case!

His mind went quickly to it, giving it instant replay. Emile Perigord, a Parisian banker, entered his limousine in front of his bank on the Champs Elysées one afternoon, headed for a conference in the Fifth Arrondissement. He was accompanied by a stranger the driver had never seen before. They sealed themselves off by activating the one-way glass panel behind the driver's seat for a private conversation. When the limo arrived at its destination, the driver was astounded to find *both* passengers gone—not a trace of them left in the limo!

And that was the beginning of a kidnapping case that lasted for weeks and caused the death of a policeman before it was done. The kidnapper, identified as Yves DuBois-Maison, remained at large. His file at Interpol was one of the thickest still active.

"Of course," Justin continued smoothly, "there is always the possibility of kidnapping. Perhaps by terrorists."

"Yes," Mrs. McGuin continued in a hushed voice. "I would not want *that* news bruited about in the media. The ability of the police to hush up the press is a joke in America, if I may put it that way."

Justin was thinking of Yves DuBois-Maison, and he was about to suggest Interpol's intervention, when Mrs. McGuin continued.

"I called you, Inspector Birkby, because I know of your reputation. Raymond was very much taken with you and Irene Manners during your short time together on the *Shangri-la*. You handled the matter of Tammy Scott's death so smoothly, Raymond told me."

"Unsuccessfully," Justin remarked ruefully. "I was just about to offer my help to you, on an unofficial basis, of course. I cannot represent Interpol, since I no longer work for them. Nor can I work with your police, unless asked. However, there are interesting aspects of the case. Therefore, I shall be happy to oversee your problem—at least until we determine what has happened to Mr. McGuin. If, indeed, anything *has.*"

"Excellent!"

"I'll arrange transportation to the U.S. and will phone you when I have the booking arranged. I'll need your number."

"Saul and I will meet you at Stapleton International Airport in Denver," Abigail McGuin promised. Her mood seemed lighter and much relieved. "Thank you, Inspector Birkby!"

Justin sat there after he had hung up, still enchanted by the sound of Abigail McGuin's voice. More than the accent attracted him. There was a personal *quality* that intrigued. She had a strength of character and a dignity that he had rarely encountered in an American woman. He was sure she would not measure up to the high marks he had set for her during his telephone conversation, but even in a lesser personification, she would be interesting to deal with.

He looked up to find Irene Manners in the doorway observing him with bemusement. "What was that all about?"

"Start packing, Irene," Justin told her. "We're going to Aspen."

Her eyes widened. "Oooh! The vacation spot of the rich and famous! That's—super!" She frowned. "What's the purpose?"

"I think it's a kidnapping. A lot of evidence points to it. But I can't be sure. It may even involve my old nemesis Yves DuBois-Maison—the kidnapper of Emile Perigord."

Irene sighed. "So it's just another job. I didn't really think it was a social invitation."

"In a way it is. Remember Raymond McGuin—the philanthropist on the *Shangri-la?*"

"Oh, yes! The Jimmy Stewart look-alike."

"His wife is putting us up."

"He's been—kidnapped?"

"Please, Irene! No more speculation. I simply don't know for sure!"

As she left the room, her face animated and her eyes dancing, Justin turned to the phone and dialed Jean-Pierre Gilbert, the secretary general of Interpol. Gilbert was the man at the top. His secretary put him on immediately.

"Studying the flowers that bloom in the spring?" Jean-Pierre asked sardonically.

"Something like that. I'm on a case."

"But of course!" But of course *not!* he meant.

"Let me tell you about this one." Briefly he outlined the disappearance of Ray McGuin.

"Yves DuBois-Maison!" snapped Jean-Pierre before Justin had even finished his sketch.

"Exactly. I'll need the files."

"They'll be at your door in—forty minutes. I want that man this time!" growled the secretary general, who was a man not usually given to growling or gnashing his teeth.

Justin understood and concurred. During the Perigord case, a police officer working for Justin Birkby had followed a trail laid down for him by the chief inspector and had indeed located the hiding place of Yves DuBois-Maison. There he had found the imprisoned Perigord, but had discovered to his dismay that the trail leading to the kidnap victim was a trap.

DuBois-Maison had shot the policeman to death on the spot, and had then dumped his body into the Seine at midnight. It was a definite blot on the work of the Paris Sûreté *and* Interpol. More than that, it was a personal defeat for Chief Inspector Birkby. To make matters worse, Justin had received a communication in the mail some days later with this rather jeering and sardonic three-word message:

SIC SEMPER INSPECTORIBUS!
[Thus always to Inspectors!]

In a later duel with DuBois-Maison, a terrorist-inspired kidnapping, Justin had been outwitted totally by the Frenchman—and had vowed to hunt him down to the ends of the earth. But since that time, DuBois-Maison had either kept his actions under deep cover, or he had involved himself in no lawless endeavors.

Now . . .

"This time we'll get him!" Justin promised grimly. "I guarantee it!" He meant it. The profile of Yves DuBois-Maison contained several earlier crimes involving cold-blooded murder. For the sake of Interpol as well as the record of Justin Birkby, he wanted this man as much as Jean-Pierre Gilbert did.

"You'll have your file in thirty minutes!" the secretary general promised, advancing the ETA by ten minutes, and hung up.

Justin stared out the window, his eyes narrowed, his metabolism on a high from the adrenaline so suddenly flowing through his system.

"Revenge is all the ambition I aspire," John Ford had written long ago. "To that I'll climb or fall; my blood's on fire."

"My blood's on fire," Justin whispered like a pledge.

3.

The body lay under a greasewood bush some twenty feet behind the fast-food kitchen at the rear of a Wendy's located within the city limits of the northwest section of Denver. It was an old man, Homicide Detective Sarita Giardino could see, dressed in worn-out, unwashed clothes. He was unshaven from what could be seen of his face—the part that had not been blown away by the gunshot he had taken in the left temple.

Homicide Detective Allan Dewars, Sarita's partner, made a sound in his throat. "What was he doing out here anyway?"

Sarita walked around the greasewood bush and reached down to separate the lower branches. Dewars could see an empty whiskey bottle lying in the grass.

"No night to be out in the cold," Dewars protested. "Even drinking."

"Somebody else thought the same thing," Sarita observed.

"Who found the body?"

She turned and beckoned a uniformed man. "I'm Detective Giardino. This is detective Dewars. Did you call this one in?"

"I did," said the uniformed man. "I'm Patterson. A woman found him early this morning. Seven thirty. On her way back from walking her dog. My partner's in the patrol car. We've been waiting for you."

"Any further information?"

"The M.E.'s already been here. Estimates he died about ten o'clock Saturday night," Patterson said, referring to his notebook.

"This is Monday. He's been lying here two whole nights?" Sarita asked.

"Looks like it."

The area was a secluded one—overgrown with wild brush and lying between a wooden fence and the rear wall of the fast-food establishment. It was no wonder the body had not been found till now.

Sarita stared down at the corpse again. She could see that whoever had shot the man had pushed him farther in under the tight branches of the greasewood, as far from sight as possible.

"Any I.D.?"

Patterson shook his head. "We turned out his pockets and couldn't find anything except a crumpled-up five-dollar bill." He held up a plastic bag containing a very ancient five-dollar bill.

"That's it?"

"That's it, Detective."

"Photographer's been here?" Sarita asked.

"Yes. He's all ready to go. Just waiting for you."

Dewars nodded. "Thanks."

Sarita glanced at Dewars. "Let's take a closer look before we bag him. If he was out here drinking, maybe he left something lying around. Or maybe his killer did."

Dewars grimaced. "Fat chance. It's fairly certain he wasn't fighting with another homeless drunk over whiskey or over money. Because he ended up with a five-dollar bill. That's a lot of money in *his* neighborhood. And his killer left it on him. How come?"

Sarita was down on one knee, bending over the body, reaching over it into the brush. The body had been pushed hard to work its way into the thick wiry lower branches. It was lying flat on its stomach, the head turned to one side. Flies were moving over the blood already clotted black on the skin. Sarita repressed a shudder at the aroma rising from the corpse already.

She moved her hands over the ground lightly. There was an old book match cover, a soggy aspirin or two dropped by someone, and a wadded-up Kleenex. As she finished her search, two men brought a gurney up alongside the rear of the Wendy's and began chatting with Patterson.

"We're ready," said Sarita, standing up. "Take him."

They brought the body bag out, elevated the gurney, and wrested the body from under the greasewood. It took the two of them to manhandle the body into the bag. When they had finished, they zipped it up and pushed the gurney along to the waiting ambulance.

Sarita pounced on a white square of paper lying in the flattened grass under the greasewood. It was two inches square, and contained dot-matrix letters and numbers. Dewars was peering curiously at it over her shoulder.

"What is it?"

"Don't know." She smiled slightly, then brightened. *"Do* know. It's a boarding pass. What you have to have to get on a jetliner."

Dewars shook his head. "It wasn't *his,* you can bet on that!"

"No," said Sarita. "For airline it says 'TW.' TWA? For flight it says 'TW25.' For date it says 'June 10.' That was Thursday. 'ORIG: CDG.' Origin: Charles De Gaulle Airport, Paris? 'DEST: DEN.' Destination: Stapleton International Airport, Denver? It's soiled there. But I think it's Destination Denver. 'NAME: DeVille D. SEAT: 29B.' A French traveler? Name sounds like it. Or a Denverite returning from a vacation?"

"Let's go," Dewars said, already in motion.

"Where?"

"Stapleton International."

"In a minute. First let's talk to the night man who was working Wendy's Saturday."

"We're taking too much time checking this one. I don't think the victim ate at Wendy's. I think he was *drinking.*"

"So do I. But what about D. DeVille, seat #29B?"

They found the night man in a rented room near Interstate 25. He was a handsome Hispanic named Hector Valdez. In his early twenties, Valdez had just gotten up and was reading the morning paper in his rented room. Coffee could be smelled brewing in a Mr. Coffee.

"Who gave you my address?" Valdez asked as he studied both police I.D.s carefully.

"The manager of Wendy's."

"So what can I do for you?" The words were precise, but slightly accented. Valdez kept staring at Sarita. Sarita did not mind. She was a good-looking woman; she knew that. Even if she was five ten, a bit tall for some of her male friends, she was well put together and in excellent physical condition.

"A man was killed in back of Wendy's Saturday night."

Valdez pursed his lips. "I did not know."

"Just discovered the body this morning."

"Ah. That cluttered-up backyard."

Sarita smiled. "You go out there much?"

"I didn't go out there Saturday night!" Valdez's black eyes were alert.

"Just wondered if you *noticed* any suspicious person Saturday night."

Valdez frowned. "I see a lot of people I think might be suspicious—but I don't pay much attention to them." The corner of his mouth quirked up slightly.

"Don't get wise with us," Dewars interceded. "A well-dressed person, maybe? Somebody who ate in Wendy's before going out to the car?"

"Man or woman?"

"Male," said Sarita positively. "You have trouble understanding anybody?"

"I speak good English!" snapped Valdez, his face darkening.

"This could be a Frenchman who might not be fluent in English."

Valdez relaxed. "I understand." His eyes narrowed. "Not really. Of course, there was one *hombre* who had trouble telling me his order."

"What did he buy?" Dewars interrupted.

"A deluxe hamburger. He ordered two, you know. With fries."

Sarita nodded. "What did he look like?"

"Thin guy. Pasty face. I mean, *pale.* Hung-over eyes. Bags under them. Very sharp nose. Pointy. Little ears. Straight haircut."

"What color were his eyes?" Sarita asked. She was taking notes now.

"Kind of gray," Valdez said after a moment. "I tell you, he was in shape. He walked like a big cat. Had jeans on. Too tight. You could see they kind of held him up off the floor."

"Crotch too tight?" Dewars asked easily.

Valdez winked and pointed his forefinger at Dewars. "Bingo."

"What else did he wear?"

"Nothing especial. Jeans. Shirt."

"Anything else about him?"

"I forget if he had boots on. But he was carrying a bag with him. A hold-all."

"Was he in a hurry? Nervous? Scared?"

"Very cool fellow. He waits right at the counter for the chef to bring his order. He pays. He goes."

"You didn't see what exit he took?"

"Sure. The east exit. The side away from the parking lot."

Dewars looked at Sarita. "I wonder why?"

"I got no idea," Valdez said. "Hey, I get some kind of reward you catch this guy?"

"Sorry," said Sarita.

"Me, too," said Valdez as he let them out the door.

They put it together as they drove over to Stapleton International Airport in Denver.

"He's a stranger. He comes in and buys the burgers. He pays for them. The cash register is near the east exit. I noticed that. He goes out that exit, but when he gets outside he realizes the parking lot is on the other side where, obviously, his car is. He doesn't want to come back in and pass through the restaurant. He doesn't want to come around the front. He's apparently trying to keep a low profile. He goes around the back to get to the car. There's a homeless drunk in the dark. He stumbles over him, maybe. The drunk wakes up. He's been kicked and he's mad."

Sarita picked it up. "Our traveler is unfamiliar with his surroundings. Besides, for some reason he's nervous. He thinks the homeless drunk is lying in wait for him. There's an argument. It turns nasty—the drunk has had a bit too much to drink. They quarrel. The traveler pulls a weapon out of his hold-all, and maybe the boarding pass with it. He kills the drunk, with the gun barrel close to the head to deaden the noise."

"Is our traveler an American on a return flight? Or is he a French citizen?"

"Either way, we're *assuming*. The rest of the scenario sounds accurate."

Dewars shrugged. "It's what we have now. Let's go with it."

"All we have," said the TWA agent at Stapleton International Airport, "is the name D. DeVille. Boarded the jet in Paris. Is there any problem?"

"No," said Sarita. "Just trying to check on his identification."

"Try U.S. customs. That was a direct flight from Paris. The passenger will have checked through there. If there was anything irregular—"

There had been nothing irregular. Mr. DeVille was indeed on the list of visitors to the U.S. His passport was in order. His effects were in order. He had been passed through without complication. The customs official who had passed him through showed the two detectives the alert list. There was no D. DeVille on it.

"He spoke a few words of English," said the customs agent. "Mostly we chatted in French."

"What did he have to say?" Dewars asked.

"On a visit. Vacation. Loved the Rocky Mountains. Said he was an amateur hunter and liked to go after game. Said he was an outdoorsman—liked to hike. He also rode a bit. Horseback. Nice fellow."

Sarita and her partner were chewing over that information as they left the customs section and headed back toward the parking lot exit through the baggage claim section. Suddenly Sarita thought she recognized someone she could not believe was in Denver—or, for that matter, would ever have cause to be in Denver.

Her mind immediately went back to an international conference on evidence she had attended in London three years before. There she had gone to a score of panel discussions, lectures, and consultations on the art of detection. One of them was memorable. A man from Interpol had given a fascinating talk on identification through mannerisms of body and characteristics of speech.

And so it was with considerable surprise that Detective Giardino recognized—using some of the little tricks she remembered from the talk—the retired Interpol chief inspector named Justin Birkby. There was no question about it in Sarita's mind. The man *was* Birkby. With a lovely-looking woman, he had just entered the area where the baggage carousel was about to begin its game of "last one to grab the bag loses."

She was so absorbed in trying to figure out what Inspector Birkby was doing in Denver that she barely heard her partner telling her he was going up to car rentals to see if "D. DeVille" had rented one.

When she realized what he was about, she immediately responded. "You go on, Dewey. I'll join you later."

She would go up to Birkby and introduce herself— Abruptly she broke off the thought. Too stupid. But the sudden coincidence of the arrival in the U.S. of a killer who might be French, and the subsequent arrival of retired Inspector Birkby of Interpol, located in France, was too much for her. As she tried to put together in her mind what might have happened, there was a sudden distraction. She watched a stylishly dressed woman in her forties move quickly across the baggage area. What was Abigail McGuin doing in Denver? She usually stuck close to the McGuin mansion in Aspen.

And Abigail's husband. Where was Ray? One rarely saw *her* without him—not in Denver, anyway. In Aspen, she had her own circle of friends. And they were tony, indeed. Raymond was obviously elsewhere. Back at the office? Sarita had talked to him during the Scanlon case in that aerie he inhabited, surrounded by that staff of self-indulgent, self-proclaimed "humanitarians." For Sarita, Ray McGuin was just a bit hard to take. Considered himself a kind of reincarnated Jimmy Stewart, she knew. The one from *It's a Wonderful Life*. To Sarita, Ray McGuin was not quite the untarnished idol most people perceived.

Now, to her astonishment, Sarita saw Abigail McGuin move straight up to Justin Birkby, reach out her blue-blooded hand, and shake the retired inspector's warmly, as if they were old friends.

Now, where *was* Ray? Sarita felt in her bones that almost immediately the lanky, slow-talking sage of the prairie would surface from somewhere—the men's room, possibly, zipping up his slacks and adjusting his pleats—to take charge of the group in his jaunty, low-key way.

He did not appear.

"We'll stay at the hotel tonight," Abigail McGuin was telling the Interpol man and his companion. "I do want to show you the office and introduce you to the staff."

Justin Birkby nodded.

Where *was* Ray McGuin?

"Ahah!" the Interpol man said, and ran over to the carousel to lift off a bag. Shortly after that, another bag came sailing by, and he grabbed at it, too. Soon four bags were standing at Justin Birkby's feet, and Abigail was waving in the distance.

Sarita backed off, too curious to leave the airport. Her gaze now searched the crowd and found another familiar face. It was the McGuins' chauffeur. Brody, his name was. Saul Brody. Half Irish, half Jewish. Nice guy. She had talked to him during the Scanlon thing. He was sharp. Straight-arrow. But not a nerd. Down-to-earth.

He came at Abigail's signal and picked up two of the bags. When Justin reached over to take the other two, he shook his head. "I'll take care of them."

Abigail waved the Interpol man off. Irene stood watching with amusement.

"To the Hilton," Abigail told Brody. "Then we'll go to the Humboldt Building."

Things were getting curiouser and curiouser. It was the Scanlon affair that had occupied Sarita for a long, frustrating period of time several years before. It was buried now, buried in the inactive files of Denver P.D. Was that why the Interpol man was in Denver? It made sense, all right. Raymond McGuin was an international figure. Perhaps somehow the Scanlon affair had become international in scope.

And in that case Inspector Birkby's appearance so soon after the arrival of a possible killer of a homeless man in back of a fast-food establishment was simply a coincidence.

Sarita saw Dewars hurrying over toward her, shaking his head.

"No luck. Come on, let's get out of here. We'll be getting the M.E.'s report at the bureau. I'd like to know where that 'traveler' got the weapon he used to kill our man."

Sarita opened her mouth to speak, but then closed it. After all, everything she had on her mind was speculation, pure and simple. Why burden her partner with it?

"What is it, Sary?" Dewars asked, noticing her expression.

"Nada, nada," said Sarita with a smile. She was afraid her partner would laugh at her. It was just one of those things.

Nonetheless, she was left wondering about the similarity of the French name "DeVille" to the English word "Devil." A killer with a sense of humor? she wondered. Or, again, just a bizarre coincidence?

4.

Abigail McGuin escorted Justin Birkby and Irene Manners into Raymond McGuin's special suite at the Denver Hilton. After Justin and Irene had showered and changed, Saul Brody drove all three of them to the Humboldt Building.

There Abigail introduced Justin and Irene to Donald Chilson, the building manager. He had a slight western drawl, nothing too obvious. A China doll kind of man he was, petite, blond, and blue-eyed, but nobody to be pushed around.

"Let's look at the elevator," Justin suggested.

Chilson nodded and summoned the elevator in question—number 1. Justin backed up and watched as the lights flashed on and off, floor by floor.

"It's not express?"

"No. It's a local that behaves like an express."

The lobby light glowed. The door opened. They all stepped inside.

Justin studied the buttons on the panel. They were numbered 1 to 35, with B-1 and B-2 added.

"Then there *is* a basement?"

"Yes." Chilson pushed the button labeled B-2. "Two underground levels. B-1 and B-2. Show you."

The elevator doors closed and the cage began to sink. At B-2 it stopped. The doors opened. Justin looked out into a crowded garage two floors below ground level. Chilson pushed the button labeled B-1. The doors closed and the elevator rose.

Justin gazed around at the four walls and the ceiling of the cage. It was a standard design, nothing special. Diffused lighting shone through a frosted glass ceiling.

The doors opened at B-1. Justin looked out at another crowded belowground garage level. Then Chilson punched the button for 35. The elevator began its long ascent.

At 35 the doors sprang open. They walked out into a spacious foyer where Ray McGuin's suite began. Justin could see that the receptionist could watch the elevator doors and at the same time see into several of the offices to one side of the reception area.

"What's above this?" Justin asked Chilson.

"The roof. I'll show you."

The building manager moved over to a door in a wall at right angles to the elevator doors, removed a set of keys from his pocket, selected one, and opened the door.

They went up a flight of concrete steps to a landing, then followed the continuation that reversed direction. At the top of the second flight there was another door—equipped with a panic bar, the kind used in movie theaters. Justin pushed on the panic bar and the door opened outward.

They were in bright sunlight.

"What a marvelous view!" cried Irene. She got out her sketchbook and before Justin could even smile, she was drawing the spectacular rise of the Rocky Mountains seen to the west of the building.

Justin was studying the structure they had just come out of. He walked around to its rear. There was another door there.

"Do you have a key for this?"

"Certainly," said Chilson. He unlocked it. "For the maintenance men."

Justin nodded. The closet was filled with equipment—buckets of tar, brooms, mops, rakes. There were grease buckets and oil containers and all kinds of tools: wrenches, pliers, hammers, cutting tools.

"Thank you," Justin said, and the two of them joined Irene and Abigail and went down into the penthouse.

Abigail McGuin gave her two guests the grand tour of the penthouse suite where Assistance Anonymous carried on its day-to-day functions. Everyone was circumspect and polite—behavior obviously adopted to give the impression there was nothing strange about the disappearance of the company's chief executive officer.

Once the tour was over, Rosemary Gaitenby proved to be the center of attention for the next ten minutes.

"I want you to tell me everything you can remember from the time Mr. McGuin came out to the reception area Friday afternoon until the elevator doors closed," Justin told Rosemary.

"Yes, sir," said Rosemary. "Well, he came out through the doorway there"—she pointed to the corridor that led off the reception area—"and nodded to me. I think he said, 'Have a good weekend, Rosie,' or something like that."

"How did he seem, Rosemary? Disturbed? In a hurry? Upset? Calm?"

"He seemed exactly the same way he always is, you know. He is a very quiet and unassuming man, Inspector Birkby."

Justin nodded. "Go on."

"Well, he said something about going fishing over the weekend, I believe, and then as we were chatting there, the elevator arrived."

"Let's back up, Rosemary. When Mr. McGuin came into the reception area, did he go over and press the elevator button to summon the elevator?"

"Oh, yes! I forgot. He did that!"

"So the elevator was definitely not *waiting* for him when he came out to talk to you."

"No, sir."

"Go on."

"The elevator arrived and the doors opened. Mr. McGuin nodded to me, waved, and stepped inside. I was not watching him closely, you understand. I just sort of glanced up when the elevator came and the doors opened."

Justin walked over to Rosemary's work station and looked across at the elevator doors. "Your desk isn't situated directly in front of the elevator. It's off to one side." Justin turned to the building manager and said, "Can you get that elevator up here and keep it here, Mr. Chilson?"

Chilson nodded and pushed the button. The upward arrow lighted. Soon the elevator doors opened and the empty cage stood in front of them. Chilson walked inside and inserted his master key in the panel. Then he came out.

"It's all yours, Inspector."

Justin joined Rosemary Gaitenby once more at her work station. "Now you and I are both looking into the elevator from the side—our right-hand side. You can see anyone in the middle of the elevator or the left-hand side where the button panels are. As you know, there are button panels on the right side, too. My point is, you can *see* anyone who might be in the middle of the elevator, as Mr. McGuin was, *or* on your left-hand side. But you *can't* see anyone who might have been standing directly behind the right-hand panel."

Rosemary's eyes widened. "You think there was someone *waiting* in the elevator?"

"I don't mean *anything*, Rosemary. Irene, will you get into the elevator and stand in the front left-hand corner? I mean, our right-hand side."

"Yes." Irene moved into the elevator and vanished.

"Where was Mr. McGuin standing when the doors closed, Rosemary?"

"Right—right in the center." Rosemary was obviously discomfited by Justin's experiment.

"Mrs. McGuin," Justin went on, "would you please enter the elevator and stand in the middle, facing out?"

"Of course." Abigail walked into the elevator and turned around facing them.

"Was Mr. McGuin standing just about where Mrs. McGuin is?"

"He was a little bit to the left—our left."

"Mrs. McGuin, could you step just a bit to your—to your right?"

Abigail McGuin moved several inches to her right.

"There?"

"That's about it," said Rosemary.

"Actually, someone could have been standing in the corner of the elevator, couldn't he—or she?" Justin addressed the question to Rosemary at her desk.

"Y-yes, sir."

"Don't look so concerned! This is only an experiment. I'm not saying there *was* anyone there."

"But there could have been!" said Rosemary. "You know, I never thought of that! I just never—"

"It still doesn't mean there was someone in the elevator with Mr. McGuin." Justin straightened. "But it does mean that there could have been."

Rosemary nodded, chagrined.

"Now. Close your eyes, Rosemary. Think back. You say you just glanced up at Mr. McGuin as he took his stand in the elevator."

"Yes, sir."

"What did he do *exactly?* Did he simply stare ahead of him, the way Mrs. McGuin is doing? Or did he glance to his left—that is, into the invisible portion of the elevator cage?"

For a long time Rosemary kept her eyes closed. "You know," she said finally, "you know—now that I think of it, he simply *might* have glanced to the side."

"His left side?"

"His left side," she agreed. "I think he might just have done that."

Justin nodded.

Rosemary opened her eyes. "He just glanced there but then looked away immediately. It was just as if he were reassuring himself that—well, that he didn't know the person there at all. So he didn't have to say hello, or whatever." Rosemary blinked her eyes.

"Okay," said Justin. "Mrs. McGuin, Irene, come on out. Mr. Chilson, you can let that elevator go down if you wish. And I want to thank you very much for your demonstration of the roof area."

The building manager smiled. "Any time, sir. Good day, Mrs. McGuin."

Justin turned to Rosemary Gaitenby. "Rosemary," he said, "I want you to look at this picture. If there's anything familiar about it, tell me. If there isn't, tell me that, too." He handed her a reduced-size sketch of Yves DuBois-Maison from the Interpol dossier.

Rosemary studied it carefully. "Well, I really didn't see anyone, you know. Yet, it's odd, but the man here *does* seem familiar. I mean, I think I've *seen* him! The way his hair looks in the picture. The hair and the small ears in the profile. Oh, and the sharp nose."

"But you can't remember *where* you saw him?"

"That's right, Inspector."

Justin nodded. "I certainly won't hold you to it, Rosemary. The point is, people *do* see more than registers in their memories."

"And I've got a terrible memory!" Rosemary burst out. "You should have heard my teachers at school!"

Justin smiled. "I'm not going to grade you on your answers, Rosemary."

She smiled tremulously. "What—what do you think happened to Mr. McGuin?" she asked.

Justin smiled faintly. "We simply don't know." He leaned down over her again. "Who's Mr. McGuin's secretary, Rosemary?"

"He doesn't really have one. I do his letters and arrange his appointments."

"Then you're his right hand."

"His Gal Friday, he called me once," Rosemary said with a smile.

"Was he booked up with appointments today?"

Rosemary turned to the computer desk at the side of her work station and punched a few keys. A list of names appeared on the monitor. "He had four appointments today, you see."

Justin stared at the monitor. "Diebold, ten a.m. Janisak, eleven a.m. Satherwaite, twelve-thirty, lunch. Amberly, two p.m." Justin wrote the names down. "Tomorrow?"

She scrolled down. "Three more."

"Riley, eleven a.m. Cookney, two p.m. Harlowe, three p.m." Justin held up his hand. "That's enough. We know he wasn't *planning* any of this. Thank you, Rosemary."

"You're welcome, sir," said Rosemary.

Justin was assessing the woman. She was tall, well-built, with a face that was architecturally satisfying, if not exactly pretty or beautiful. She had an erect stance, an excellent figure, and her skin was glowing with health. She seemed an extremely well-coordinated person, one without psychoses or psychological quirks.

"You've known Mr. McGuin how long, Rosemary?"

Justin was stunned to see a pink glow rise slowly from her neck into her face. She quickly turned toward Mrs. McGuin and then back to Justin. Her eyes looked frightened. She immediately averted her gaze from him as she made a note on a pad in front of her. Justin's glance confirmed a frantic doodle.

"I used to work for the National Insurance Company across town," she said in a low voice. "Mr. McGuin used to have lunch occasionally with Mrs. Gordon over there. She was their treasurer, you see."

"Then you actually knew Mr. McGuin before you took a job here," Justin said.

Now Irene and Abigail McGuin were chatting together, waiting for Justin to pack it in and join them. Rosemary straightened. Justin noticed that the pink suffusion had vanished and she was completely at her ease once again.

"In fact," she said boldly, "he telephoned me one day and said that he had just lost his receptionist, and would I like to take the job."

"I see," Justin said.

Oh, yes. He certainly *did* see. He wondered if the liaison between McGuin and Rosemary had continued long after she had taken her position as receptionist. It really didn't matter, at all. It was, if anything, a key to an element in Ray McGuin's character that Justin had not uncovered in any of his prior conversations.

He filed the information in his memory for future use.

Justin joined Abigail and Irene.

"I want you to meet Brett Allenby, the second-in-command here at Assistance Anonymous," Abigail McGuin said. "Actually, Ray and Brett and I are the officers of the corporation. I'm third in line. The three of us own the corporation." She smiled conspiratorially. "Background, Inspector Birkby. Background."

Justin nodded.

The door next to Ray McGuin's deserted office was labeled TREASURER. Just under the title was the name BRETT ALLENBY.

Abigail knocked on the door and it was opened almost immediately by a man who was probably as much up-front as McGuin was laid back. In build Allenby was somewhat like McGuin's yin-yang opposite: big-boned, wide, muscular, hard. He had a granite-rock face. One had the impression of a person who was not uncomfortable with the feel of iron weights and support bars.

He spoke in a machine-gun staccato that was the opposite of McGuin's soft Midwest drawl. He was cool in personality—as cool as McGuin was warm. And Allenby had the appearance of being as ruthless as McGuin was clement and compassionate.

Once the introductions had been made Justin felt himself being scrutinized from head to toe by a professional assessor. "Abby McGuin has a collector's instinct for only the greatest objets d'art in the world. She tells me you're the *best* detective that lives."

Justin bowed, for the moment rendered speechless. He could see Abigail McGuin's eyes snapping in rage. Why Allenby had chosen to attack her through him, Justin did not know. The best way to react was in silence.

"My esteemed associate is miffed at me, Inspector Birkby, because *he* wanted the local police in on Raymond's disappearance! *I* did not." Abigail's voice was sharp and edged as a new-honed razor.

"Don't mind Abby," said Allenby with a grin. "She's mad at me because I assumed naturally that Ray was just up to something on the q.t. You know." He winked almost obscenely at Justin. "That was, of course, until the unexpected arrival of that postcard yesterday. Now Abby feels this is most certainly a true ransom note. I haven't seen it myself at all. That's for you as the expert to work on."

Justin still said nothing.

Abigail picked up the conversation, which seemed to have dropped in tatters all about them, by saying: "Irene and I are going to look over the gardens." She announced to Allenby, her voice on the rise, "I want you to talk to Inspector Birkby. I want you to give him a full picture of Assistance Anonymous. I want you to tell him *everything!*"

Justin was studying Allenby carefully. Allenby was watching Abigail now, his green eyes sardonically amused. He was interested in her ruffled attitude, but he was not of a forgiving nature. Abigail in turn was absolutely outraged, almost beyond control, but she was trying to govern herself now, playing it as casual as she could.

The flow between these two was not exactly what it *seemed*. It was not intrinsically hostile. It was intimately interconnected. There was something sexual—in both a positive and negative sense—and something physical likewise in the air.

Abigail threw Allenby a look of baleful annoyance and sailed out of the office with Irene in tow, giving Justin a fleeting and sweet smile as she passed by.

Justin pulled up a chair opposite Allenby's desk and sank into it. Between the two men lay a desktop as sparse and bare as a no-nonsense statistician could maintain. A crystal bowl full of piñon nuts sat in the middle of it. Allenby took a handful. He shoved the bowl forward, as if suddenly recollecting his manners. "Pine nuts?" he asked Justin in a flat eastern tang.

Justin shook his head: no thank you.

"Mind if I—?" Allenby did not finish the sentence, apparently assuming it was complete without further verbiage. Allenby chewed and ruminated. "You're familiar with our setup?" Allenby's bright green eyes glinted at Justin.

"I believe so. Your firm specializes in fund-raising. Your clients are sometimes companies, sometimes charities. I don't know what you charge; that's your business. But I understand that you also put needy charities in touch with well-to-do philanthropists who want their money to go to the right places."

"Sure. And in some cases we even ask wealthy individuals with names and reputations to bequeath amounts of money directly to us in their wills. We call them bequest pledges. Then we take care of the allocation of the funds."

"I see," said Justin. "And you do the soliciting?"

"Naw. Ray does that. He's got that easygoing charm, you know. I come on too hard. No. He's the go-getter that comes on like a cat. Low key. Subtle. Very good with the really tough prospects." He grinned.

Justin could see that McGuin had all the proper moves down pat.

Allenby tilted his head in what was for him an enthusiastic signal of approbation. "Ray and I go back a long way. Philadelphia. Direct-mail solicitations for clients of all kinds. Books. Leather goods. Athletic equipment. Ess-Em accessories. You name it. Ray had the genius for conning people as clients. I did the books."

Allenby reached for more piñon nuts.

"Elected a U.S. president, you know. Raised millions for him. Got him in office. Turned against us, the bastard. Didn't matter much. Because we'd done the impossible, people got the message. Moved to Denver where we signed on with Onward Christians. From Onward Christians, it wasn't far to the Forward Way. Long time before Tammy Bakker and Jim did the whole cause in."

Allenby sighed.

"We raised a fortune for those emerging nations, too. Got them on their feet. Then, once they had the money, they hired their own P.R. firms. And worked up big foreign-aid packages from Congress." Allenby snorted.

"The money was always coming in, coming in. We began investing it. I was in charge of investing it. We had a lot extra, and it went into things that made us look good. The 'look good' was Ray's idea. Yeah. We invested in the Third World. *Invested* in it!"

There was a long pause.

"Listen. It wasn't long in coming. Some of those Third World countries were as corrupt as I always suspected them to be. We got our loans paid up one way or another for quite some time. But about a year, year and a half ago, the Third World began to come apart. We were *short* money. Can't run a fund-raising organization without operating capital. No cash flow excuses for us."

"What did you do about it?"

"Worked harder, that's what!" Allenby stopped chewing on the piñon nuts and stared at Justin.

Justin looked into Allenby's eyes. They were green and unwavering. Justin was still trying to take the measure of the man. Allenby was elusive. Elusive and mercurial.

"Did Ray McGuin ever—disappear—this way before?" Justin asked.

The piñon nuts vanished into the maw. Short silence. "Well, yeah. We were working for this direct-mail company in Philly together when he disappeared for a holiday weekend. Moved in with some broad he had met at a cocktail party. Don't let that dumb midwestern act put you off. He's as much into foreplay as he is into byplay."

"So you're really not worried about a kidnapping?" Justin asked matter-of-factly.

Allenby looked at the handful of piñon nuts and slowly returned them to the crystal bowl. "Hell yes, I'm worried. Where'd you get the impression I wasn't?" Allenby took a deep breath, almost as if he had made up his mind about something, and half turned toward Justin. He did not, however, look directly into his eyes.

"Didn't want to alarm Abigail," he said softly, "but there *was* something unusual Friday. Ray came back from lunch huffing and puffing. Said he'd *seen* someone following him. I mean, a regular tail—looked at a picture of him in his hand, and kept following him. That kind of thing."

"And you never told her?" Justin asked, his eyes wide in disbelief.

"She gets nervous. Besides, I checked it out."

"How did you check it out?" snapped Justin.

"Ray and I both figured it was the Steeleys."

"Who are the Steeleys?"

"The Steeleys run a firm like ours—a fund-raising organization. They're big in the working-class area. Union members. Union pension funds. You know. But they run their organization like a Mafia cell. Pressure. Part of the pressure, Ray felt, was this tail following him. But when I called Jeremy Steeley, he told me they hadn't put one on Ray. I figured Ray was imagining it."

"Come on!" snapped Justin. "You *knew* he wasn't imagining it. You did check the Steeleys, didn't you?"

Allenby was writhing now. His green eyes were darting everywhere but into Justin's eyes. "I could have made a mistake. I probably should have believed him. Because it was only about a half hour after that that he left—and vanished!"

"How did Mr. McGuin describe the man who had him under surveillance?"

Allenby frowned. "Let's see. Thin, I think. Sharp nose. Little ears. That's about all I caught. I should have questioned him more." Allenby sighed. Even so, when he finally looked at Justin, there was a kind of suppressed joviality in his green eyes, a kind of held-in humor, an amusement that was not entirely larded with *simpatico.*

Justin handed the small drawing of Yves DuBois-Maison to Allenby. Allenby took it, looked at it, did a double-take, and then stared in dismay at the profile of the French terrorist-kidnapper-assassin.

"My God!" he breathed as he handed it back. "You mean—you think—*he* took Ray?"

Justin stared at Allenby. "It's only supposition—but a pretty strong one."

"Jesus," said Allenby. His handshake, when Justin left, was tentative, and his smile was fixed and unreal. It was obvious he did not know how to take Justin now. He had considered him at best a simp—too cool, too remote, too *superior,* of course. Hello, jerk, his attitude had been at first. Now he didn't seem to know how to act with him.

Justin was silent as he, Abigail, and Irene entered the elevator and pushed the button for the lobby. In fact, Justin found himself studying the operating panel where the buttons were located. He eyed the heads of the screws that held the panel in place. They were not ordinary screws with flat-across slots for a screw-driver, or even Allen cross-slots. Each had an odd-shaped hole requiring a special tool to remove the panel.

Justin stared at the basement buttons and his eye went to the floor of the elevator. It was carpeted wall-to-wall with man-made fiber matting. Something caught his eye and he bent down to pick it up. It was a tiny broken piece of glass, the kind of splinter that might have come from the corner of a woman's rectangular mirror in a compact.

Justin put it into a small envelope and patted it in place in his pocket.

Once back in their suite at the Denver Hilton after dinner that night—"We'll dine tonight at Mario's," Abigail had said. "You must get used to our western steaks, you know!"—Justin settled down by the phone as Irene sat working on sketches she had made of Brett Allenby, Saul Brody, Rosemary Gaitenby, and Abigail McGuin. Justin put in a call to Interpol Headquarters in Lyons, France. Jean-Pierre was of course not on duty—it was 11 p.m. in Denver, and 7 a.m. in Lyons *tomorrow.*

Justin finally spoke to the night duty officer, whom he knew by sight. "I'd like background on the following people," he told the night man, as he watched Irene work. "Saul Brody; current address, Aspen, Colorado. Rosemary Gaitenby; current address, Aurora, Colorado. Mrs. Abigail McGuin; current address, Aspen, Colorado. Brett Allenby; current address, Colorado Springs, Colorado. Also Raymond McGuin; current address, Aspen, Colorado."

"I thought Interpol kept records only on criminals?" Irene said with a frown.

Justin turned to her. "Who said any one of these people might *not* be one?"

She made a face. "Have it your way."

"I'm in a preliminary phase," Justin explained to the night man. "Later I may be able to work with the Denver Police Department. But as yet I have not made my presence known. Let's go through channels and see what's on record."

"Yes, sir," said the night man. "Where can you be reached by phone?"

Justin gave the number at the McGuin residence in Aspen. "You might also check the Interpol files for any current information on the known activities of Yves DuBois-Maison."

"Yes, sir."

Justin hung up and stared into space for a few minutes. Then he said, "Cyril Tourneur wrote in *The Revenger's Tragedy:* 'The world's divided into knaves and fools.' Let's see if Interpol can separate them out!"

5.

Aspen, Colorado, was a surprise to Justin Birkby. Somehow he had thought of it as a year-round mecca for the rich and famous, an all-year stamping ground for Jack Nicholson, Arnold Schwarzenegger, Chris Evert, Cher, Michael Douglas, Don Johnson, and anybody else who *was* anybody.

Yet here he was on a hillside overlooking the town itself, and it resembled a village time-warped out of the nineteenth century. Sound asleep. Out cold.

"It's dead and doesn't know it," he told Irene, not bothering to conceal the mild censure in his voice.

"It comes *alive* on Christmas and New Year," Irene Manners told him, "because that's when the slopes boom. And *only* then!" She shook her head at him. "You don't pay *attention*, you know. Not where it matters."

They were standing at the window of their comfortable room in the Raymond McGuin mansion built on the hillside overlooking the quiet village below. Of course, there was a rather large airport—large at least for a town the size of Aspen—built to accommodate the winter guests who descended so dramatically from the skies onto the small concentration of expensive real estate to celebrate the winter holidays.

They had checked out of the Denver Hilton late in the morning and had arrived in Aspen in the afternoon. Abigail McGuin had promised Justin the run of Ray McGuin's "office" in the mansion after a light and tasty snack.

And, sure enough, right after they had eaten, she had taken her guests to a room on the main floor, a room that was furnished in the manner of an "office in the home"—in the immortal words of the IRS—spare and utilitarian and uncluttered.

There were very few papers lying around—some clippings of stories about Raymond McGuin in the Denver paper, a Xerox of a *Time* magazine story, another article in the *Wall Street Journal,* and a mention in *Forbes.*

But it was the mysterious postcard that had precipitated the whole business of Raymond McGuin's disappearance that became the center of attraction once Abigail McGuin had brought it in and laid it down in front of Justin and Irene—like the centerpiece of the crown jewels.

"My goodness!" said Irene in rapt perplexity as she stared at the picture on the postcard.

Justin picked it up. It was a photograph of a ghost town named Jimson City. He turned it over. The postcard was addressed to Raymond Standish McGuin, with the address of the Aspen mansion scrawled beneath it.

Other than the address, there was nothing on the message half of the card—no salutation, no comment, no signature.

The picture itself was a black-and-white photograph of a typical ghost town—a line of wooden shacks with a broken wooden sidewalk alongside it and splintered timbers lying about in what used to be the main street of a long dead western town.

"Where is this place?" Justin asked Abigail.

"Jimson City? Oh, it's about seventy miles as the crow flies. You go up through Dowd and Loveland Pass to get there. It's near Silver Plume."

"Is there anything significant about Jimson City?" Justin wondered.

"No. It's just one of the many ghost towns in Colorado. They used to mine silver here, you know—in the nineteenth century. Raymond and I have visited a number of them. Jimson City is quite lovely. It's built, as you can see, on the edge of a beautiful meadow, right along the edge of a rocky slope. If you look carefully you can see some mine openings still remaining in the hill in back of the street. There's a marvelous little creek running through the meadow, dotted with stands of aspens and poplars."

She shook herself, as if her reminiscence was in bad taste, what with her husband's disappearance.

"The ghost towns are all closed up now. I doubt there are even squatters around Jimson City. Ghost towns are tourist traps, you see. Easterners like to walk around pretending they've discovered something pretty marvelous—Americana from the nineteenth century."

"What's the meaning of the name Jimson?" Irene wondered.

Abigail thought a moment. "It's a poisonous plant—something in the deadly nightshade family. There are big trumpet-shaped flowers, either white or violet. They smell bad. I don't know. Cattle used to go crazy after eating it. Or was that a legend?" She frowned. "Jimson. I know. That's an eastern name. It's a shortened version of 'Jamestown'—the first colony in Virginia. I don't know *how* it got attached to that poisonous plant—or to the ghost town!"

Justin had been studying the address side of the card and now gave a sudden "Huh!" Abigail smiled.

"Look," said Justin, handing the card to Irene. "Along the left-hand side of the message space. Running up and down, along the border. You see those numbers?"

Irene nodded. "I see them."

"The code," Justin said. He took the card back and studied the numbers carefully. This was the sequence of the numbers, running from left to right, from the bottom to the top, of the left-hand border of the card:

6   18   2200   50M   3.4   2.8

"I don't know yet what it means," confessed Abigail. "And if it's a ransom note, as we now expect, how are we supposed to read it?"

"Six could mean June," Justin said slowly. "Eighteen could mean the day of the month. That's this Friday. Twenty-two hundred is European time—ten p.m., at night. 50M?" He looked at Irene.

"If it was 50K, I'd know it was fifty thousand," Irene said. "Dollars, obviously. But I don't know 50M."

"Yes, you do," said Justin. "The letter K stands for 'kilo' — which means 'thousand' in Greek. The letter M stands for 'mille' in Latin. M is also the Roman numeral designation for a thousand. It's fifty thousand, all right. Don't forget, you're not reading the want ads now, Irene. You're reading a life-or-death communication."

"But what about the 3.4 and 2.8?" Abigail wondered.

Justin had been turning these over in his mind. "Coordinates," he said suddenly. "In inches—and tenths of an inch. It refers to, I would bet, three and four-tenths inches from the—say—left side of the postcard picture and two and eight-tenths inches down from the top of the postcard picture. Where they cross is the coordinate. And, I'd suspect, that's where we're to leave the money."

"Let's work it out," Irene said, her excitement beginning to bubble up.

In a moment Justin had it. They stared in puzzlement at the picture. According to the coordinates, they would be expected to leave the money in the weed-choked ground that formed the street of the abandoned town. It made no sense.

"Maybe the coordinates are backward. That is, maybe the three and four-tenths inch measurement is from the right side—" Then Justin paused. It wasn't right to left or left to right that was wrong. It was the entire combination.

"I'm stupid," he said with a *mea culpa* shake of the head. "I should have known! Just follow the rules of navigation. First measure latitude—the distance from the equator to the north pole (in the northern hemisphere, anyway)—*then* measure longitude—the distance from right to left (west of Greenwich mean time). So much north latitude, so much west longitude. So. Two and eight-tenths inches from the bottom of the postcard, and three and four-tenths inches from the right-hand border!"

He put in the markings accordingly.

A cross appeared exactly in the middle of the gaping hole that had once been a window of the third shack from the right in the picture.

"There it is! Pitch the ransom in the window there!"

Irene was frowning. "Fifty thousand isn't much for a ransom," she said. "Not after all the trouble the kidnapper went to in grabbing Ray McGuin in that complicated elevator trick. Plus the danger of capture."

"No. But we have to assume it's a ransom note. I have one problem. If it *is* a ransom note, why is it addressed *to* Raymond McGuin? It seems it should be addressed to the people who would be paying the ransom."

Abigail had been thinking, and now she spoke up. "A ghost town seems a very likely place to leave ransom money for Raymond, you know."

Justin was puzzled. "Why?"

"I don't remember Jimson City especially, but Raymond and I have been to a number of the Colorado ghost towns. Quartzville. Breckenridge. Alma. Salida. St. Elmo." She smiled. "Raymond always made it a point to send a postcard home. As a kind of souvenir."

Justin was sharply attentive. "He sent cards to himself?"

"Yes." Abigail's eyes widened, as she understood the odd parallel. "He'd just write his address on them—no note at all."

"Could *he* have mailed this card? Or gotten someone else to mail it? Is this a note smuggled out to us to tell where he's being held?"

Abigail picked up the card. "I don't know. It's not his writing."

Irene took the card and looked at it carefully. "I'd say it's a woman's hand, although I've been fooled before. I'm no holographic expert. Of course, it could be a man's writing—if a man is neat, precise, and well-organized. But I'd say, woman. Look. She makes her *M*s in a strange way. Each *M* is exactly like a *W* upside down. I mean, the outside stems are splayed, not vertical."

Justin took the card and stared at it. "Right. And her numbers are quite well articulated. Look at that three. Most people make a three with two reverse *C* s atop one another. She starts at the top with a right horizontal, then follows it with a left diagonal, to end with a reverse *C*."

Irene added, "That four is drawn with care, too. Most people leave the crossbar's extension open. She makes a perfect triangle, and extends the altitude and the base."

"My father was an architect," Abigail said suddenly. "He made his fours that way."

"We're not getting anywhere sitting around staring at postcards," Irene said. "I would suggest that you authorize Justin to go through your husband's records to see if he can spot any clues as to who might have done this thing to him."

"Yes, you're right. Inspector?"

"Irene has a habit of reading my mind," he told her. "I need to know more about your husband and who his friends are."

Abigail stood up and waved her hands at the workroom. "It's all here. If you can unlock the secret."

Five minutes later Justin was deeply involved in sorting through the papers and records of Raymond McGuin. What he had found after a very few moments of searching was that there was very little about that could give him any idea as to what Ray McGuin was really like.

After a short and casual examination of the papers on top the desk, he found McGuin's personal bankbooks neatly filed in the bottom drawer of the desk. It was quite likely that some item might be hidden in the money records.

Cyril Tourneur, the Elizabethan playwright, had written about it long ago: "All the purposes / Of man aim but at one of these two ends— / Pleasure or profit."

Money was behind this disappearance—money or sex. Or, perhaps, a combination of both! Of the two, Justin was most certain of money.

He scanned the checks for names that might prove enlightening. And in fact he did come across several individuals who were not familiar to him. They were: Avery Jones. Samuel Reisling. Mitchell Fixx. Obviously the payments to these persons were for services of one kind or another.

Fixx, for example, had received one payment during the summer, and then another in the fall. Two months later, a third. These sums were in low four figures. Fixx was apparently doing something for McGuin on a regular basis. Jones and Reisling were also represented by similar payments, but usually in middle three figures.

Justin wrote the three names down in his notebook and was just about to get up to leave when he noticed the top of a sheet buried in the mass of papers.

"BEQUEST PLEDGES," the typed notation said in capital letters.

Justin pulled the sheet out and studied it. There was nothing on it but a list of names of people who were quite familiar to him. For example, the name Lee Iacocca, Jr., was there. So was the name of Robert Redford, with an X after it. And so was Calvin Klein. And—wonder of wonders!—there was Tammy Scott X!

Justin smiled in reminiscence. He and Irene had witnessed that amusing exchange between McGuin and Tammy Scott in the Sirkorsky helicopter about to set out for the *Shangri-la*—"I gave at the office," was the way Tammy Scott had greeted McGuin.

Oprah Winfrey. Phil Donahue. Frank Sinatra X. Ted Turner. Loren Hartt X. Swifty Lazar. Alec Loomis X.

There were no other names that particularly piqued Justin's curiosity, and he laid the page aside and went out. On the way to the garden in the rear where he had heard Irene and Abigail talking, he came across the mansion's library. It was in fact located very near McGuin's "office in the home."

Like most libraries today, McGuin's had a whole section of wall space devoted to video cassettes. The McGuins were obviously not renters of movies, but owners of scores of motion pictures—some old classics, and some very new blockbusters.

Justin investigated some of the titles. The Hitchcocks were all together. There was *Rear Window,* starring Jimmy Stewart and Grace Kelly, made from a short story by Cornell Woolrich. Justin wondered if McGuin might not show it in order to practice his Jimmy Stewart personality from time to time—and immediately chastised himself for being frivolous. There was *Rebecca,* from Daphne du Maurier's novel. There was also *Strangers on a Train,* from the novel by Patricia Highsmith, starring Farley Granger and Robert Walker. And more.

"I see you go in for Hitchcock," Justin remarked to Abigail as the three of them sat out in the garden later on.

She looked blank, but then seemed to understand what Justin was talking about. "Oh, yes, the videos. Raymond loves to watch films ever so much."

"Has he special favorites? Hitchcock perhaps? John Ford?"

She shrugged. "I hadn't really noticed."

Justin gave Irene a warning glance, and then turned back to face Abigail in a relaxed and casual manner. Irene drew back and waited for Justin's words, curious as to his intent.

"Who's Samuel Reisling?" he asked her.

"Sam's our family lawyer." She glanced up, puzzled. "Why do you ask?"

"And who's Avery Jones?"

"Our groundskeeper," said Abigail.

"And Saul Brody is your chauffeur. Who's Mitchell Fixx?"

Abigail hesitated. "Who?"

"Fixx. With two *X* 's."

"I'm sorry—" Abigail was honestly puzzled.

"It's of little matter," said Justin airily. "Just something I'm going to investigate." He glanced down at his wristwatch from force of habit. "This is Tuesday. We have three days to get the money ready." Justin looked at Abigail. "Will that be a difficulty?"

"Money is always a difficulty. But the company always seems to be able to come up with it when Raymond needs it." She frowned. "I'll talk to Brett Allenby."

Abigail's immediate response in turning to Allenby for help was not lost on Justin Birkby—nor, from the expression Justin saw on Irene's face, was it lost on her. Yet neither spoke a word. Abigail was thinking her own thoughts.

Justin smiled easily to take the sting out of what he was about to say.

"Mr. Allenby will undoubtedly advise you to call in the police," he told Abigail.

"I'm sure he will!" she snapped. "It's just that I don't intend to!" Her eyes came up to Justin's as she leaned toward him, almost as if she were trying to force her decisiveness onto him. "The publicity will hurt Ray. Hurt the organization. Cut off support. Don't you see?"

"Perhaps," Justin admitted. "Yet if you'd like my advice—?"

Abigail stood and faced him valiantly. "Which is?"

"Do not pay the money and let the police handle it!"

"I'd rather pay the ransom and trust you to get him back safely, Inspector." She let her eyes linger on him, then turned abruptly and left the room.

6.

It was Wednesday and Abigail McGuin always lunched with a group of close friends in Aspen. The Wednesday Club generally moved from home to home among the members of the luncheon group, and this week it was the turn of the George Amberlys to entertain. Justin Birkby and Irene Manners opted to eat a late lunch that day at Guido's Swiss Inn in Aspen, one of the more famous restaurants of the area.

They had been seated by the head waitress and were working on their cocktails at a table near the window when they were interrupted by the approach of a tall young woman dressed in skirt and blouse and wearing a loose outer jacket. She appeared to be in her late twenties. It was not difficult for Justin to categorize her immediately as someone he had once met. He searched his memory for her name.

"I'm Detective Sarita Giardino of the Denver P.D.," she said with an affable smile.

Justin nodded, his face brightening. "Of course. I thought I had seen you before when I spotted you Monday at Denver Airport. And it's true. London, wasn't it?"

"Yes. The General Assembly session of Interpol. Three years ago. You spoke on identification procedures."

By now Justin had noted the folder she carried with her and immediately stood. "Join us, won't you? I take it from the file you're carrying that this isn't just an incidental meeting of old friends."

"You're absolutely right," said Sarita, and she drew up a chair from the empty adjoining table. "And thank you."

Justin introduced her to Irene and frowned. "Isn't Aspen a little out of your jurisdiction?"

Sarita flushed. "Indeed it is. I took a day off to fly up here to meet you. I must say that this is *not* in the line of duty."

"But the file you have in your hand *is*." Justin smiled faintly.

"It was seeing you with the McGuins that piqued my interest."

"Seeing me with *Mrs.* McGuin," Justin corrected her, watching her carefully.

"Of course. I assume Mr. McGuin is out of town?" Sarita's brown eyes were studying Justin.

Justin ignored the pointed question. He indicated the file. "You wanted to discuss a specific case?"

"Yes, sir." Sarita was reverting to her training. She sensed Justin was probing for details she might not wish to impart.

"Has the case to do with Raymond McGuin?" Justin asked kindly. There was no use pushing this woman against the wall. She had been open with him. She was visiting him unofficially. She wanted to talk about a case she was interested in. That she was trying to find out what had happened to Ray McGuin was obvious, but Justin felt he could handle that.

Sarita nodded. "Three years ago a man named Dusty Scanlon was killed in a midnight fall from the Humboldt Building in Denver."

"Who was Mr. Scanlon?"

"He was, properly, Michael Rhodes Scanlon. They called him

'Dusty' because of the obvious word association between 'Dusty' and 'Rhodes.' He was a bookkeeper for Assistance Anonymous."

Justin kept his features expressionless. "I see. He was, in effect, working under Mr. Brett Allenby's supervision."

Sarita's eyes had widened just a bit at Justin's knowledge of the structure of Assistance Anonymous. That fact seemed to encourage Sarita's pursuit of information from Justin.

"That's right. After the body was discovered in the loading zone at the rear of the Humboldt Building, he was identified by building security. A search of the penthouse suite revealed that he had fallen or jumped from the balcony outside his office."

"Was there a suicide note?"

"None was found."

"Was he despondent in any way?" Justin asked.

"Far from it. Deidre Scanlon, Mr. Scanlon's estranged wife, told me that prior to his death he had assured her he was coming into a large sum of money."

Justin frowned. "How large?"

"Six figures."

"When the penthouse suite was searched, was anyone found in it at the time?"

"No one."

Irene broke in. She had been sketching Sarita Giardino in a leisurely fashion as the woman detective was speaking. "That doesn't actually mean no one was there with the man. Any top officer of the firm would have had keys and thus free access to the suite. Also free egress. Isn't that what you call it, dear?" She turned to Justin.

Sarita sighed. "No one was present in the suite. No suicide note was found. Yet the coroner's jury came up with a verdict of death either by misadventure, or by his own hand. Even so, Denver P.D. carried on an investigation for some months."

"With what result?"

"The case was closed. Nevertheless, I for one do not feel a man about to come into a large sum of money would end his life the way Dusty Scanlon did."

"Could Mrs. Scanlon have been lying?" Irene asked.

"Oh, certainly. In fact that was the position Brett Allenby took. He was Scanlon's immediate superior in the company."

"Do you suspect Mr. McGuin of involvement in the case?" Justin asked.

There was a pause. Sarita looked hesitant. "He *is* president of the company."

"Yes, but Mr. Allenby is the treasurer," Justin noted. "Scanlon was *his* concern."

Sarita considered. Finally she made up her mind. "I went over the history of the company, Inspector Birkby. I learned that Allenby and McGuin had started it together. I also learned that historically the two always had differences of opinion on the way to run things."

"There are always alternate approaches to any business situation," Justin pointed out equably.

"True. But these were basic differences in philosophy. Mr. Allenby was of the opinion that Assistance Anonymous should be sold while in good financial health. Mr. McGuin didn't want to sell it at all."

"You felt this conflict might have had something to do with Mr. Scanlon's death?"

Sarita looked discomfited. "Hypothetically, if the company were to come on hard times, it would be much more vulnerable to a leveraged buyout by some aggressive conglomerate."

"Perhaps someone in the company was manipulating funds to endanger its financial health?"

"It *is* just a theory," Sarita admitted thoughtfully.

"Dusty Scanlon discovered something he shouldn't have found out and got pushed from his balcony for his pains?"

There was a long silence.

"Well, Detective?" Justin pursued.

"I think it quite possible, inasmuch as there was the hint of a large sum of money promised the man—perhaps to keep quiet about something he knew."

"Highly imaginative," said Justin. "But are there any facts to support your theory?"

She shook her head. "That is the reason the files have been closed on the case."

"I'd like to read that file anyway, Detective Giardino."

Her face lighted up. "That's what I was hoping."

"He reads *anything*," Irene said with a light laugh. "Absolutely no *feel* for literary style."

"When I saw you at Denver Airport I did not notice Raymond McGuin."

"Oh, he wasn't there," said Justin, picking up the file and leafing through it.

"Where is he?" Sarita leaned forward, watching Justin's face intently.

"I believe he's out of town," Justin said blandly, gazing at the typed pages.

"Before flying out here this morning, Inspector Birkby, I telephoned Mr. McGuin at his office. I was told he was not in. I telephoned Mr. Allenby, and he gave me some humbug reason about Mr. McGuin being on a trip out of town. I got the impression he was lying. Where is your host?"

Justin closed the file he had been using as a distraction and laid it on the table. "The fact of the matter is that I cannot tell you where Mr. McGuin is—even if I knew. I have pledged myself to silence on the matter."

Sarita nodded slowly. "I understand. But I think I could make a good guess."

"I adjure you not to try."

"I like that: 'adjure.'" Sarita smiled charmingly.

"We'll be in touch," said Justin, standing and putting out his hand to shake hers as she prepared to leave.

The George Amberlys liked to entertain daytime guests in their marvelous rock garden. A Far East buff, Gertrude Amberly had imported a number of Japanese bonsai specimens and had set them out in a kind of stylized Japanese rock garden, complete with small lake, curved bridge, and interesting paths through the rock groupings.

The Wednesday Club was composed of four couples and Abigail McGuin. Her excuse for Raymond's weekly non-appearance was not needed at all. Everyone in the group knew that he lived in Denver during the week and spent his weekends and Monday morning in Aspen. Most, in fact, saw him on the weekends the McGuins chose to entertain.

Louis and Tricia Benson were long-time Aspen residents. Tricia was the local doyen of artistic endeavor. The Bensons owned a local art gallery, which, while not the most exclusive in Aspen, was right up there with the best. The Bensons spent six months in Aspen and six months in Paris every year.

Brian and Lynn Eckhart had joined the Wednesday Club six months before, when they had first arrived in Aspen and bought a Western oil landscape from the Benson Gallery for their posh little apartment. The story was that Brian Eckhart had been big in international stocks. He had retired after a number of conglomerate deals had made him a very rich man. He and Lynn had spent the previous weekend in Las Vegas at the gaming tables.

The Jordans were the last pair—and the most stable of the group. They had been in Aspen longer than anyone else; their roots were there. Jabez Jordan had come from a ranching family that had settled in Aspen after making a fortune in cattle at the turn of the century. Allison Jordan had been born in Aspen, and worked in a diner, where Jabez had met her.

When Abigail McGuin arrived, she found to her dismay that she was the last one in.

"Now we can *begin,*" said Trudy Amberly with a wide smile. "Abby is here."

"Good thing you got here when you did," Jabez Jordan remarked with a big grin. "We were just about to start dissecting you."

"I'm sorry!" said Abigail. "I guess my wristwatch was slow."

"Pfui," said Louis Benson. He was a mystery buff and had read all of Rex Stout's books at least twice. He pronounced *phooey* the way Nero Wolfe did in the Stout books. "You've got a good sense of the dramatic, Abby. You know how to make an entrance."

Abigail blushed.

"It's those attractive guests you've got," Tricia Benson said, waving an errant hornet away from her drink. "Where did you dig them up?"

Abigail shrugged. "They're just friends," she said vaguely.

"What does *he* do?" Tricia continued at steamroller pace. "I just happened to be passing by when you all got out of the Lear jet Saul Brody flies. He looks *interesting!*"

"He's retired," Abigail said with a smile. "I think he was in some kind of research." That wasn't too big a lie to describe an Interpol job, she decided.

Brian Eckhart had been following the conversation in silence. Now he joined in. "I don't like to seem so out of it, Abby, but I'm afraid Lynn and I haven't *seen* your guests at all. What's their name?"

"Actually *his* name is Justin Birkby," Abigail said, as if she had not wanted to mention him at all.

Eckhart glanced at Lynn, his face unreadable. She was inspecting the hors d'euvres with a kind of counterfeit aplomb. As if on cue she glanced over at Abigail. "Are they joining us for luncheon?" she asked in a voice that seemed just a bit hoarse.

"No," Abigail said airily. "They have their own things to do."

Eckhart seemed to relax. "Birkby, Birkby," he murmured. "Isn't he the guy that—?"

"You know *everybody!*" snapped Lynn Eckhart with a kind of long-suffering tolerance. Meaning: Shut up and drink!

"Research reminds me of old books and papers," Tricia commented, getting back to the subject at hand. "Your guest— Birkby?—doesn't seem dry as dust to me!"

"*She's* an artist," Abigail observed, rather deliberately getting off the subject of Justin Birkby. "She's very well known all over the Continent."

"Ah!" said George Amberly, his eyes lighting up. "Nude studies and that kind of thing? Any kinky stuff? Neo-art?"

There was laughter.

"No. She's a sketch artist. She works for one of those big Paris publications."

"What's her name?"

"Irene Manners," said Abigail, on safer ground now. "She's so quick! So fast! And what she draws looks just like you!"

Louis Benson looked at his wife. "Tricia, isn't that the woman who works on *France-Soir*?"

"I think it is, Lou!" Tricia gushed.

Lynn Eckhart set down her cocktail glass. *"Le Figaro,"* she corrected.

Brian Eckhart chuckled. "My wife knows a little bit about a lot of things," he said. "We were in Paris last year for a couple of weeks, weren't we, dear?"

Abigail watched as Eckhart seemed to telegraph some unreadable message to Lynn. He was smiling, but his manner was not one of amusement. When Lynn glanced at him, her eyes were ice-cold and she shrugged her shoulders.

"We did South America last year, too," she remarked casually, almost as if daring him.

Brian Eckhart subsided.

Abigail's eyes lingered on Lynn. Of all the fairly regular Saturday night dinner guests of the McGuins, Lynn Eckhart seemed to be the most appreciated by Raymond. At one time Abigail had even suspected something was going on between them, but Ray was simply not the type and she had abandoned her suspicions. And yet . . .

"Do you travel a lot?" Jabez Jordan was asking Brian Eckhart.

"Enough," said Eckhart. "I think we'll be staying around here for a long time, though. I like it here—don't you?"

"Oh, sure."

"It's a place where all your dreams come true," said Lynn with a bemused smile.

"All it takes to enjoy Aspen is big bucks!" laughed George Amberly.

The mention of money seemed to stimulate the group, and soon everybody was chattering with everybody else, leaving Abigail alone with her own worries.

Saul Brody drove down to Aspen to pick up Justin and Irene in the late afternoon, and when they entered the McGuin mansion, the two of them could hear Abigail McGuin on the telephone in the alcove just off the stairs. Her words came to them clearly.

"I don't know *how* they're taking it, dear! It's quite a strain. I expect them back at any moment. If you want to talk, you'd better choose your time better. Now, I *have* to go, Brett. This thing is obviously very complicated. I don't want to make any mistakes! It could mean—"

There was a short silence.

"That's *quite* enough! Good-bye!"

And she hung up.

Justin cleared his throat and struck up a loud conversation sparkling with trivialities to cover the fact that they had clearly overheard Abigail McGuin's confidential words on the phone.

" 'Dames maritorious ne'er were meritorious,' " Justin said to Irene, quoting George Chapman, the Elizabethan playwright, in a dramatic manner. "Maritorious," he explained, meant "excessively fond of one's husband." The jest was not particularly appreciated by Irene, but she smiled dutifully—in no sense a "maritorious" nuclear-age woman herself at all.

Abigail came around the corner in an excited and somehow agitated manner.

"Where have you been?"

"In Aspen."

"How was Aspen?"

"Shaking," said Irene, and she laughed. She seemed to think it was a much better joke than George Chapman's.

"I got a telephone call!" Abigail told them, wringing her hands

—or making a disturbed motion of some kind that reminded Justin of "wringing one's hands."

"Did you tape it?"

"Of course!"

She took them into the study and played the tape. It was very brief and very specific.

"Hello?" they heard Abigail say tentatively.

The voice came on the other end, speaking in a husky, scratchy tone. Justin knew what was causing the voice distortion. The caller was speaking into a filter—an electronic device that altered his (or her) normal tones into something that resembled the speech pattern of a robot or mechanical voice box. The caller obviously did not want a voice pattern on record.

The conversation was mercifully short. "There's been a change in numbers," the voice said. "Listen carefully. Six. Eighteen. Twenty-four hundred. One thousand em. Three point four. Two point eight. And look in your mailbox."

Then there was a decisive click.

Justin was uneasy. "That's a considerable escalation in the amount of payment. Fifty thousand to one million. I'm also puzzled about the change in the time of the ransom delivery." Now Justin suddenly looked foolish. He sighed and shook his head. "My *mind* is sluggish. Here I've been waiting and waiting for some positive indication that the kidnapper is indeed Yves Du-Bois-Maison. Certainly the change in time is proof positive!"

"I don't quite see that," Irene said quickly.

"Nor, I confess, do I," Abigail added boldly.

"You wouldn't, of course, without knowing the details of Yves DuBois-Maison's modus operandi. Without burdening you, I have to say that the man is a consummate magician. Part of his M.O. is the *timing* of the exchange and the *timing* of his escape. Some detail we aren't aware of has obviously dictated his sudden change in time. In order not to confuse us, he has made the change on the telephone, communicating in person, with your acquiescence in person."

"What possible reason could he have to change the time?"

Justin smiled. "I have no idea."

"Why not *pretend* we never received the change?" Abigail suggested.

"And only deliver fifty thousand dollars?" Justin asked, frowning.

Abigail made a face. "It wouldn't work, would it?"

"We might be placing your husband in grave danger by not following the orders," Justin said softly, watching Abigail intently to make sure she understood him.

"I see," she said with a smile. Then suddenly she thought of something. "The taped conversation isn't all!" She leaped to her feet and hastened into the next room, returning with a small envelope in her hand. "The voice told me to check the mailbox. Look at this!"

Justin took the envelope and withdrew a small photograph. It was a Polaroid snapshot taken with a flash in some dark interior that was fairly indistinguishable beyond the point of illumination. What was most distinguishable was the figure directly in front of the camera. Without any question, the man seated on the ground with his back propped up against some kind of rocky surface was Raymond McGuin.

He was holding the front page of the *Denver Post* in front of him, with the headlines plainly visible. He was bound with ropes, his ankles tied together in plain view. His hands were looped together at the wrists. He was staring into the camera with a pleading look in his eyes.

"It's him all right," said Justin.

"Oh yes!"

"And, I presume, that's yesterday's *Denver Post*?"

"I already checked. Yes."

"But how did the mail come so quickly?" Irene asked.

"The envelope was stuck in the mailbox."

"Somebody hand-delivered it!" said Justin. "Aha!"

"But you haven't seen anything yet." Abigail McGuin seized the envelope, plunged her fingers inside, and drew out a card. It was a playing card—from a Tarot deck. It was the Hanged Man card.

Justin winced. "It's a warning. Just in case you're thinking of *not* paying up. Definitely a warning." He turned to Abigail. "Can the new amount be arranged?"

Abigail had been staring out the window, her face transformed. Now she turned back and frowned at Justin as if she were trying to remember who he was. "It won't be easy."

"Who actually will put together such a sum?" Justin asked.

"Mr. Allenby," Abigail said without hesitation. "It's just too much for me to handle."

"Understandably," said Justin. "I'm going to go in to Denver tomorrow to see him anyway. First thing. I'll discuss this latest development with him."

"Would you like me along?" Abigail asked.

"It's not necessary," Justin said with a smile.

Just what kind of game were these two people playing? he wondered. Or was it three—with Saul Brody the third point of the triangle?

While Irene and Abigail McGuin engaged in conversation in the study as they both watched a news program on a Denver station, Justin moved into the "office" and stopped to check the telephone where he had attached the tape recorder. He made sure the connections were secure and in good working order. Just in case. He had had tapes go out on him in the past—nothing messier, nothing more disturbing, nothing more frustrating. They were getting close to the climax of this affair, and he wanted all the mechanical contrivances in full working order.

As he turned to move away he knocked a pencil off the pad near the phone, and he bent down to retrieve it. It had rolled perversely under the chair in front of the phone stand, and he had to move his fingers around to search for it.

In his groping he touched the wall, and it was there, out of sight and out of reach of anyone seated at the phone, that he discovered an object that he had not really anticipated. It was a limpet-secured device about an inch square and a half inch deep. A bug—typical of the kind of listening device most surveillance agencies now used.

Agencies and private individuals.

Who was plugged into the McGuin line? Why?

Thoughtfully Justin retrieved the pencil and laid it on the pad next to the phone. The thoughts that immediately raced through his mind were upsetting indeed.

How secure was the McGuin mansion? How had someone been able to get inside? The cook only dropped in every day. Saul Brody, on the other hand, had an almost free run of the place.

His thoughts kept returning to Abigail McGuin.

The nearest telephone extension was in Raymond McGuin's office. Justin moved quickly inside, closed the door behind him, and turned on the desk lamp very low. In a moment he had traced the wire to the wall, and in behind a small occasional table he found another of the limpet-secured devices. Two out of two for telephone extensions.

Justin moved into the dining room. Just behind the ornate and lovely credenza where Abigail kept her best plates and servers he found another. The place had been thoroughly and professionally bugged. By an expert. And most extensively. Every word spoken in the McGuin household was now on record for history to study.

His earlier supposition that the tap was an inside job was somewhat suspect now. Why, Justin asked himself, would anyone on the inside want to know so much about everyone else on the inside? Things were indeed taking a murky turn.

Exactly seven minutes after Justin had rejoined Abigail and Irene he was summoned to the telephone for a call from Lyons.

"I have some information for you, Inspector," said the man he had talked to Monday night in the Denver Hilton.

"I'll call you back in ten minutes," said Justin. "I am not secure."

"Yes, sir. I'll be here."

Justin excused himself from his hostess and Irene and walked back to the garage apartment where Saul Brody lived. He told Brody he wanted to drive into Aspen. Brody got into his windbreaker and cap and backed the Range Rover out of the garage.

At the telephone office in Aspen, Justin put the call through to Interpol in Lyons and located the night man.

The report was interesting. Justin took rapid notes as the night man read out several files that had been collected during the day in response to Justin's request. After eleven minutes, Justin was through. He folded his notes, tucked them into his jacket pocket, and patted his jacket possessively. As he sat there in the Range Rover next to Saul Brody he glanced aside once and thought how deceptive appearances could be.

John Webster had played with the idea a bit when he wrote in *The Atheist's Revenge:* "What end was this disguise intended for?"

To Brody, Justin said: "Irene and I have chores in Denver tomorrow. I'm going to ask Mrs. McGuin for your flying services in the morning."

"Yes, sir."

7.

Saul Brody was the picture of relaxation. He sat in the driver's seat of the McGuin Range Rover, head back against the rest, cap tilted over his eyes, feigning deep sleep. Justin Birkby could tell by his breathing that he was not asleep at all, but simply resting and striking the pose of sleep.

It was still early morning, and Brody had driven them down to the Aspen airfield for the flight in to Denver in McGuin's Lear jet. However, some rich Aspenite's private chopper had broken down with a flat tire on the main landing strip and was being tended to by mechanics. They would have to wait until they secured clearance from the tower.

Irene Manners had taken out her sketch book and was drawing the spectacular mountain scenery and the naked ski slopes visible against the clear blue sky. Saul Brody had gone to the Range Rover for a catnap. Justin had bought a cup of cardboard coffee from the coffee shop. He now strolled over toward the McGuin's chauffeur-pilot and stood by the vehicle finishing off his coffee.

Brody opened one eye and looked up at Justin. Then he rolled down the window. "Couple more minutes."

Justin smiled. "No problem." He cleared his throat. "You don't do much talking."

"Part of the job description," Brody responded.

"Were you around here when McGuin's bookkeeper fell off the Humboldt Building?"

"I was here."

Justin let the silence build up. "Talk was that he might have been pushed."

Brody sat up a little straighter. "By Mr. McGuin?"

"Tell me about it."

"Scanlon was cooking the books, way I heard it, taking something on the side, got caught, and went bye-bye."

"Then there was no black cloud hanging over Ray McGuin's head?"

"Such as?"

"Business problems? A disappearance engineered to enable a leveraged buyout of his company?"

Brody stared at Justin a long moment and then settled back. "Difficult for a man like me to get onto hot news like that." Brody was playing the role of humble family retainer.

"Which is exactly what leads me to believe you *do* know something you aren't talking about."

"And which is exactly what leads me to continue keeping my mouth shut."

Justin took a deep breath and plunged in. He didn't like extorting information from people—but he *needed* Brody's input. "That Santa Barbara episode of yours was touch and go, wasn't it?"

Brody froze. After a long moment his right thumb came up and tipped his cap off his eyes. He turned slowly toward Justin. "That's all over, you know. All settled up."

"But it wouldn't be the kind of thing you'd like Abigail McGuin to know about—would it? Or—worse—Mr. McGuin?"

"You're a devious bastard, aren't you?"

"Just a detective doing his job." Justin eyed Brody.

"Is that a threat? You'd spread that around about me?"

"Not unless forced to."

"Forced?"

"I mean if you didn't come up with some good data about your employer's private life. His women, maybe. His other activities."

"Silence would force you to—?"

"—to mention some details of your past. That bored wife. That betrayed screenwriter. That Santa Barbara stand-off."

Brody slid down again and closed his eyes. "There have been women," he admitted in a whisper. "Mrs. McGuin knows some of the details. But not all."

"I'm listening."

Brody shrugged. "There are rumors. A young son. Fathered by McGuin." Justin straightened. "Nothing more than a *rumor,*" Brody protested. "Mrs. McGuin can't have children. Some obstruction. This is all whispered about, Inspector. It's just speculation."

"I sense something going on in that company. Some conflict that hasn't been resolved."

"Rumors. Very recent rumors. Another fund-raising operation wants to buy Assistance Anonymous for big bucks. McGuin doesn't want to sell. Allenby does. Mrs. McGuin? She's as tight-mouthed as the Sphinx. I don't know where she stands. McGuin disappears." Brody paused. His eyes were still closed. "If Allenby and Mrs. McGuin sign without McGuin on scene, the company's history."

"Details?"

"None. Rumors, Inspector."

Justin gripped Brody's shoulder. "You find out names and numbers for me, and you're off the hook."

"I can but try," Brody said softly.

Justin turned around as a young man approached the Range Rover and signaled Brody. "Runway's cleared. We'll be moving again in five minutes."

Brody nodded. "That's it! We're on our way."

The ubiquitous crystal bowl was still there on Brett Allenby's desktop, but the piñon nuts had undergone a miraculous metamorphosis. They were now pistachio nuts dyed a brilliant purple.

"Abby has kept me in the picture," Allenby said as Justin took a seat.

"What about the money? Can you come up with a million in cash by tomorrow night?"

"Doing my best," Allenby said blandly. His eyes were hooded and seemed to be watching Justin with a kind of wary hostility.

Justin's face tightened. He suddenly reverted to his Scotland Yard days, pulling off the velvet gloves. "You've been lying to me from the beginning. Why?"

Allenby blinked. His green-eyed gaze retreated further. "For instance?"

"For instance that 'all is sweetness and light' story you gave me about you and Raymond McGuin. Total bullshit."

"I may have gilded the lily a bit," Allenby admitted with the ghost of a smirk.

"It's a known fact that both you and he disagree fundamentally on many financial issues!"

"Hell, that's business, Inspector!" Allenby's green eyes glinted.

"Isn't it just possible that you *favor* a leveraged buyout right now to convert your share of the business into cash?" Justin snapped. "And isn't it just possible that the kidnapping and unavailability of Ray McGuin might give *you*—and Mrs. McGuin!—the opportunity to sell the company?"

Allenby's face was flushed. He began perspiring. "Who asked you to meddle in this?"

"Here's another 'for instance,' " growled Justin, his anger now simmering just beneath the surface. "The Dusty Scanlon case."

Allenby himself was fuming now. "Hell, that's just a simple case of cooking the books. We caught Dusty dead to rights. He could see we had him by the short hairs. And he went off the balcony."

Justin looked directly into Allenby's eyes. They were venom-
ous. In his own rage he just *might* be telling the truth. Scanlon's
death might have been the result of his own peculations and not
the result of discovering too much about the internal finances at
Assistance Anonymous.

Quis custodiet ipsos custodes? Who will oversee the overseers?
How could anyone check the facts when they were buried in
mountains of paper?

"Do you have proof of Scanlon's peccadilloes?"

"Not really," said Allenby morosely. "It was Ray who located
the cover-up in the books. Had to do with some special rainy-day
fund he had set up. That little bastard Scanlon went in with both
hands, clawed out the money, and wrote it off as some kind of
phony cost."

Justin maintained his silence by staring at Allenby.

"Hey, it got so complicated I even hired an investigator to get
onto this little jerk. But Fixx couldn't find out a thing about the
money, or where it went. There was no trace of it. Scanlon was a
genius at hiding the stuff. It's probably in some unnumbered
Swiss bank account now, just rotting away!"

Justin had caught the name and now could not resist repeating
it. *"Mitchell* Fixx?"

Allenby nodded. "A private eye. Kind of on the fringes, but he
knew his stuff. Used to be a cop on the Denver police force. Ray
got quite taken with him. They had a big fight in the middle of
Fixx's work on Scanlon, but Ray was always having trouble with
guys who worked both sides of the thin white line. Once he got
onto Fixx's wavelength, and Fixx onto his, they became friends.
Well, acquaintances."

Justin smiled.

"Anyway, like I was saying, even Fixx couldn't get a thing on
Scanlon. And then, right when the thing turned into a Mexican
standoff, Scanlon had the gall to dive off his balcony into the
loading zone!"

Justin waited.

"The police thought *we* were cooking the books, *we* killed

Scanlon to shut him up. Us. Me. Ray. Even Abigail, for God's sake!"

"Well, did you? Did you help him over that balcony?"

"Hell no, we didn't push him. We put the pressure on him, sure—he was a thief. First thing you do when you're caught, you blame the guy that caught you. Standard operational procedure. He blamed us. Little prick! Ray was too soft on him. Almost agreed to pay him a hundred g's to buy the books he'd cooked! *I* put a stop to that, you can bet your ass!"

"What was the actual outcome of the Scanlon case?"

Allenby frowned, shook his head. "Actually, nothing's been the same since then. Ray began to run into financial troubles. Something personal. Hell, poor Abigail hasn't got a cent of her own, you see. I don't know what was causing the trouble, but Ray started borrowing from me. Then he borrowed from the company. It got worse and worse."

Justin could feel his ears prick up. "Something personal? Something personal—*and* financial?"

"You can't get any more out of me, Inspector. I'm not that damned close to Ray, you know. Never really was."

Carefully Brett Allenby picked up a handful of pistachio nuts and began inspecting them in the palm of his hand. One by one he broke the shells and lifted the meat into his mouth and chewed slowly. He was performing deliberately against the grain of his quick-take character, and it made Justin aware of his vulnerability.

"Look, even if I might favor conversion of my stake in this lash-up into cold cash instead of fighting off a leveraged buyout, it'd be hard to start up all over again. A buyout would ruin everybody here—all the guys I've worked with. Most of all, Ray. I'm not a hundred percent *for* a takeover, you know. No matter what you've heard. I've even talked to the Steeleys, confidential-like, and called them off for good."

"The point is, whoever kidnapped Ray McGuin might be orchestrating a takeover," Justin said. "Any others besides the Steeleys who might want to exert leverage?"

Allenby shook his head. He stared stonily at Justin. "What's your *honest* advice—as a policeman?" Allenby asked him suddenly. "About the ransom?"

"I wouldn't pay it."

Allenby shrugged, as if Justin had answered a question Allenby already knew the answer to. "Well, I would! But don't forget, I'm his friend."

"By paying the ransom, you're putting the company into deeper financial distress," Justin reminded him.

"I suppose, but—"

"Thus leading to a possible leveraged turnover."

Allenby picked up a pistachio. "I'm damned if I do, and damned if I don't."

No, Justin silently corrected Allenby. Either way it goes, you can't possibly lose. If you're in this thing the way I think you are, you win if you pay out the ransom. And if you don't, then you win if you bring about a leveraged buyout. You're a two-time winner, no matter how you look at it!

But he said nothing aloud. Instead he simply walked out of the office, while Allenby munched dreamily on a pistachio.

Mitchell Fixx was easy to find. He had a small ad in the yellow pages of the Denver telephone book. "Private investigative research," the ad said. Justin telephoned ahead of time, introduced himself, and spoke about Ray McGuin. The private investigator invited him over.

While the office Fixx inhabited wasn't exactly shabby, it was by no means posh. In fact, it was not even normally middle-class. It was simply what one would expect of the office of a "private eye."

"Consultant for the family," said Justin Birkby, after introducing himself by name and settling into the broken upholstered chair facing Fixx's scarred and cluttered desk. "The McGuin family."

Fixx was cursed with small stature—not quite midget, but approaching midget. He had a pumpkin-shaped head, with red hair on top, amber eyes, and freckles even at forty-nine. He had a grin he could turn on and off like a flashlight. In fact, when he turned it on too quickly he resembled a hollowed-out jack-o-lantern with a lit candle inside. Gap teeth and everything.

"What's Mr. McGuin done now?" Fixx asked with a token grin —as opposed to the full-powered one he was capable of. He spoke in a loud, clear voice—almost as if he might be learning how to project it.

"We could play games for half an hour," Justin said sadly, "but I'm really in a hurry."

"Long way back to Aspen," Fixx agreed.

"Mr. McGuin is busy on one of his fund-raising ventures," Justin explained comfortably. "He asked me to act as liaison between the two of you."

Fixx grinned. "Liaison in what particular area of his life? Business? Pleasure? Other?"

"The usual area in which you deal with him."

"Perhaps I am being dense, but I fail to follow."

"You have had some dealings with him in the past year?" Justin asked cautiously.

"It would be ridiculous to deny it," Fixx said. He glanced at his desk calendar. "Yes. The timing would seem about right. And Mr. McGuin finds it difficult to attend to things himself?"

"He finds it—inconvenient," Justin observed. His mind was working swiftly. The payments to Mitchell Fixx had not been on any specific schedule, but obviously the work Fixx did for McGuin *was*. A schedule flagged one specific operation in which a private detective could be used to good effect. That operation was the payment of blackmail money. Blackmail! Justin thought, with a whole new range of leads open to him. Over what issue? His mind began preparing a laundry list.

"What are the specifics?" Fixx asked, leaning back with his hands laced over his stomach.

Justin smiled faintly. Fixx's posture was relaxed, but his voice was still overexercised. Justin's eyes moved to the rear of Fixx's office, where a door led to—what? Another room? A closet? A bathroom?

"A sum of money," said Justin.

"How much?"

"Enough," Justin responded with a smile.

Fixx nodded. "Place of delivery?"

"A ghost town."

"Of course. Which one?"

"Jimson City. An interesting choice. It appears odd to me that Mr. McGuin would find it—inconvenient."

Justin shrugged. The less he said in a conversation like this the better. In this case, the first person to open his mouth—lost the game.

"When?"

"Tomorrow night," Justin said, without naming the hour of midnight.

Fixx leaned forward and made a mark on his very clean desk calendar. "I'll be there."

"Because of Mr. McGuin's hurried departure, he failed to give me specific details," Justin said, winging it now, waiting for data to fall from the tree like ripened fruit. "How would you like the product packaged?"

Fixx smiled broadly. "Any carry-on will do. The usual fifty?"

"A thousand," said Justin gently. He saw Fixx's eyes glaze over slightly and his mouth drop open. The private detective was obviously translating the "thousand" into 2 million dollars.

"I'll expect you when?"

"The usual time."

"Good day, then," said Justin, rising and moving toward the door. His hand on the knob, he turned, now quite sure of himself. "Were you ever successful in penetrating the identity of the payee?"

"Not really." Fixx's eyes narrowed. "Mr. McGuin can be very tight-lipped."

"Was there any indication of the reason for the payments?"

"Never found out."

"Do you think Mr. McGuin knows whom he was dealing with?"

"Oh, yeah. At least I think so."

"You mean there is a possibility that Mr. McGuin paid off blind to someone he *didn't* know?" Justin did not have to assume a playacting role to project true incredulity.

"Somebody had something real good on him." Fixx grinned.

Justin realized they had not agreed on a meeting place to turn over the money to Fixx. "Tomorrow night?"

Fixx nodded.

Justin prodded. "At the McGuin residence?" Fixx gave him a startled look. Justin dipped his head. "I wasn't apprised of the details of the exchange between you and Mr. McGuin."

"Let's keep it the way it was. Mr. McGuin's suite at the Denver Hilton."

Justin nodded. He opened the door and this time departed.

The rear door to Mitchell Fixx's office opened a few moments after Justin's departure, and a woman came into the little office. She was short and billowy and walked with a pronounced, forty-ish roll. She was followed by a lean, surly red-headed man of indeterminate middle years. He carried the remnants of pimples from an obviously troubled adolescence. His blue eyes were slightly crossed—enough to give him a rakish piratical squint.

The man lit a cigarette while the woman leaned over Fixx's desk, propping herself up on her outsplayed hands. Fixx looked up.

"You were right, you know," he said. "There *is* something going on."

"Yeah." Deidre Scanlon walked over to the window and looked out into the busy street. Harry Scanlon leaned against the back wall and gazed at Fixx with a squint-eyed leer.

"So what's happened to McGuin?" Harry asked.

Deidre turned from the window and studied her brother-in-law. "You think he's gone?"

"Probably out of town on some philanthropic roll-over," Fixx suggested with a grin.

"Something's cooking at the Aspen place," Harry said in his gravelly voice. "I been watching."

"Who *is* this guy?" Deidre gestured toward the door, indicating the imagined afterimage of the departed Justin Birkby.

"No idea." That was Harry. He turned to Fixx. "How much do you think this joker *knows* about Dusty and McGuin?"

"Not much," Fixx said.

Harry sneered. " 'Not much,' he says." He turned to Deidre. "Some detective you've got here!"

"Truth!" snapped Fixx. "He's just poking around. You heard the way he kind of backed into every one of my statements."

"I want to know what's coming off!" snapped Harry. "If they nail the son of a bitch for my brother's death, I want part of the action!"

"Oh, shut up, Harry," snapped Deidre. "McGuin's the only one to pay off for that. If, for Christ's sake, he did it. We don't know the truth. Never will, probably."

Fixx looked up at Harry with anger surfacing in his eyes. "Stay out of sight," he told Scanlon. "Keep real low to the ground until this joker leaves town."

"*If* he leaves town."

"He'll leave," said Fixx confidently. "I think he's a go-between this time around. I think McGuin's hired him to pay off the current fee."

"But a million!"

Fixx frowned. "I know."

"You think we'll ever collect?" Deidre asked Fixx.

"How do I know?" He stared at her. "You stay away from that female cop in the Detective Division. She was snooping around here yesterday. Did you send her?"

"No way."

"Maybe she's got onto something," Harry said, coughing and dragging deeply on his cigarette to stop the retching.

"Wouldn't that be something!" snarled Deidre.

"What do you think she knows?" Harry asked in a hoarse voice.

"I wish she knew something!" Fixx said.

"I still think he killed Dusty," snapped Deidre, folding her arms across her ample chest.

Harry laughed harshly. "I think he talked Dusty into doing himself in. My dumb shit brother!"

"Beat it," Fixx told them both. "I got a business to run."

"Some business," said Deidre as she opened the door. "Unless you can figure out a way to keep that million." She grinned obscenely at him.

Justin Birkby was drinking a cup of very sloshy coffee in a diner across the street from Mitchell Fixx's office when Deidre and Harry Scanlon walked out the front door of the building and started up the sidewalk to the parking lot.

He flipped through a small envelope of mug shots reduced to playing-card size and found "Deidre Scanlon." He nodded to himself and kept on flipping. Finally he found the second one and noted the name "Harold Scanlon" on it. Dusty Scanlon's brother. He had picked them up from the Scanlon file Detective Sarita Giardino had given him Wednesday.

It was quite a marvelous coincidence that the two Scanlons should be visiting Mitchell Fixx at exactly the moment Justin Birkby came to see him. And one thing Justin Birkby did not believe in was coincidence. The blackmail schedule was apparently firmly established. Obviously the two of them were as aware of it as Mitchell Fixx was.

Or, possibly, it might be that all three of them were working together. Perhaps the blackmail of McGuin was a Scanlon enterprise—based on facts known privately to them. Facts that proved McGuin a murderer. . . .

If Deidre Scanlon and Harry Scanlon actually *were* the blackmailers, and Fixx was in it with them, what did they really have on Raymond McGuin? Or were they running a bluff on him—a bluff that was soon going to pay off in a million dollars?

It was a weird situation. A blackmail scam that suddenly escalated into a kidnapping. What could have caused the metamorphosis? His eyes widened. Of course! The unexpected balking of Ray McGuin against payment of the blackmail. And the subsequent inspiration of the blackmailer to hire Yves DuBois-Maison to grab McGuin and hold him for a suitable ransom that would wrap up the entire episode with a million-dollar payoff.

He looked up. Irene was smiling down at him. He had telephoned her to meet him at the diner, to be picked up by Saul Brody for the flight back to Aspen.

"What's new?"

"Interesting developments," Justin said with a smile. He would tell her what he had learned on the way back to Aspen.

But before that:

" 'Man may his fate foresee, but not prevent,' " he told her, out of *The White Devil* by John Webster.

She thought about that one. "I like it," she said. "It tells it like it is."

Justin shuddered at her fractured English, but he knew exactly what she meant.

8.

On arrival at the McGuin mansion, Justin and Irene were met by an excited, breathless Abigail McGuin. Her appearance, so at odds with the cool and composed demeanor she normally affected, startled Justin, who had been looking forward to a contemplative evening.

"It's the picture!" she kept saying over and over as she led them into the house toward her husband's "office." On the desk Justin saw the Polaroid photograph of Raymond McGuin with a large magnifying glass lying on top of it.

Abigail sat down, her face flushed, her eyes sparkling. "I've been studying this picture," she said. "And I think I know where it was taken!"

Justin moved quickly toward her. "Where?"

"It's another ghost town, not Jimson City. But this one's not far from here at all. It's called Lucky Strike, named after a mine that opened there." She glanced around. "Where's Saul? He'd know. He's been there with Raymond."

"I think I saw him driving around the back to put the car away," Irene said.

"I'll call him." Abigail moved quickly out of the office toward the kitchen.

In a moment she was back. "He's on his way."

Justin was looking at the Polaroid through the glasses under the bright light. He could see that indeed there were possible objects and a detailed background behind the figure of Raymond McGuin, but everything seemed so blurred it was difficult to make out the scene. He wondered why DuBois-Maison should be keeping Raymond McGuin sequestered so close to home. After all, he had gone to a great deal of trouble to effect the actual kidnapping in Denver. Why then bring the prisoner back so close to Aspen for holding?

Saul Brody entered the room without a shade of expression on his face. Justin, glancing up at him, wondered at his masked appearance. Then he decided it might possibly be because Brody always exhibited the mask of inferior servant when he was in the presence of Abigail McGuin. Why? Justin wondered. To hide the way he really felt about his job? Or was it simply a precautionary method of self-preservation in the oddly anachronistic role of servant?

Briefly Abigail explained her discovery to Saul, who took up the picture and looked at it closely and then put the glass to it and studied it some more.

He glanced up once, eying Justin Birkby, and then turned to Abigail. "You're talking about that hint of the steel rail in the background?"

"Yes!" said Abigail excitedly. "Don't you think it's the narrow gauge they built at Lucky Strike?"

Saul took a deep breath and sat down in the chair, looking at the photograph again through the magnifying glass. He put the glass down, squinted at the picture, and shook his head. "It's so blurred." His mouth tightened. "But I'll be damned if it doesn't look like that narrow gauge at Lucky Strike."

Abigail was so excited she reached her arms around him and

hugged her chauffeur from behind. He looked at her, startled. Glancing quickly and apologetically at Justin and Irene, Saul Brody stood up and laid the magnifying glass down on the Polaroid.

"What do you want me to do about it?" Brody asked Abigail.

Abigail McGuin appeared drained of energy. She stared at Justin Birkby, her eyes suddenly hollow.

"Well, I don't really know. I thought by finding out where Raymond was, we were going to be one up on the kidnapper!"

Justin stared down at the desk top. "We definitely are one up on him, if the picture was taken where you say it was."

"What do we do now?" Saul Brody asked.

"We go to the cops," said Justin flatly. He turned to Abigail McGuin.

"No!" snapped Abigail, adamant. "No cops!"

"But we now know where they are holding your husband!" Justin said pleadingly. "Let's turn it over to the professionals and let them handle it!"

"I don't want it that way," said Abigail McGuin. She smoothed down the blouse she was wearing and tucked it more firmly into her gray skirt. "I can imagine it now. They go in there, guns blazing, and he ends up a corpse."

"This isn't the Wild West, Mrs. McGuin!" Irene protested.

"Isn't it?" She turned and stared down Irene. "Please! Inspector, I brought you into this thing so I could keep Raymond out of the hands of the authorities! I don't trust the police. Not at all! If you turn this over to them, you're quite definitely betraying my faith in you!" She stared willfully at Justin. Her hands moved onto her hips and she suddenly resembled a housewife in a nineteenth-century painting, arms akimbo, staring down a recalcitrant child.

What was she afraid of? wondered Justin. Obviously *something.* Irene was about to launch an attack, but Justin silenced her with a motion of the hand.

"Where is this place?" he asked Saul Brody.

"Six miles or so."

"Close!" Justin's brows rose.

"Yes."

"The narrow-gauge railway was supposed to connect Aspen with the mines in the area," Abigail said. "They were blasting a tunnel through the mountain when the vein of ore pinched out. There was no more need for the Lucky Strike. And so the unfinished railroad was simply left as it was. A landslide caved in the front about ten years ago. Obviously there must be some other way in."

Justin listened in silence. Then he said, "You know a lot about that railway, don't you, Mrs. McGuin?"

"Enough. I said Ray and I did used to go to ghost towns as a kind of recreational activity."

"I'm thinking simply of reconnoitering the area," Justin said quickly.

"I can show you exactly how to get there," Abigail offered immediately.

"Not you, Mrs. McGuin," Justin said sternly. "Saul Brody and I."

"Oh, no!" snapped Irene. "If Justin goes, I go!"

"Before we get into a big argument here," Justin said softly, "think about the situation. We *must* have someone here to answer the phone, if it does ring. And, I'm afraid, that leaves you, Mrs. McGuin. Besides, I don't like to endanger you in any fashion. If these people feel enough animosity toward your husband to kidnap him, perhaps they feel some hostility toward you as well. You *are* married to him."

Abigail McGuin appeared subdued. She slowly nodded her head.

Justin turned to the chauffeur. "I do not like to walk about armed, but neither do I like to reconnoiter without sufficient protection."

Saul Brody grinned. "I'll get you a weapon, Inspector. And Ms. Manners?"

Irene shook her head. "If Justin is armed, I'll be all right."

The last mile of the dirt road to Lucky Strike was rough but passable. Justin and Saul Brody had agreed to travel it with the lights out. Once Saul had accustomed himself to the darkness, he was able to execute the turns and switchbacks with a minimum of anxiety.

"We're about a half mile out now," Saul whispered to Justin.

"Stop the car and park it."

Saul nodded.

The three of them got out of the Range Rover and proceeded on their way along the empty roadway as it wound along a steep slope and turned into a protected box canyon. Once they were in sight of the box canyon, Saul stopped them. They stood there, listening, looking to the left and right for any sign of light.

There was none.

Following Saul's direction, Justin and Irene moved slowly up the steep road into the canyon. It was then that Justin was able to make out a huge rock slide that had sheared off the front of a steep cliff.

"Is that it?" he whispered to Saul.

"Yes."

"How do we get in?" Justin wondered.

Saul merely lifted a finger and waved the two of them forward. The roadway ended and Saul led them to the left of the slide, where there was a more gradual approach upward. As they struggled up the slope toward the top of the slide, Justin drew Saul aside. Holding his mouth close to Saul's ear, he breathed: "If there's anyone in there, wouldn't there be some sign of life?"

Saul shrugged. "They've got to be guarding him somehow! You can't leave a prisoner alone for long. He'll get away!"

"I don't think *anybody's* in this place," scoffed Justin.

"Let's find out."

They moved upward and finally stood at the top of the slide. Justin could see that there was a tiny hole at the top, which led back into the rock.

"That's it," Saul told Justin.

Justin moved forward and crouched down over the opening in the rock. He thrust his head down and listened. No sound.

Irene crawled beside him. "I can get down in there, you know."

"Not yet you don't." Justin was gazing around at the rocky slope. Then he crawled back to Saul. "I'm going in," he said.

Saul snorted. "You're either dumb, crazy, or both!"

Justin smiled. "I think it's an empty hole."

"Be my guest," Saul said.

Justin returned to the top of the slide and was horrified to find that Irene was gone. "Irene!" he started to call out, then broke off the sound. The damned little fool! he thought. She had crawled in through the hole while he was talking to Saul Brody.

Justin turned, waved to Saul, and plunged into the hole after her. He could smell the dust rising in her wake, and he was appalled at the darkness that suddenly seized down all around him. He finally reached her and grabbed her leg. She felt back and touched him, cautioning him not to make any noise.

Almost immediately the hole through which they had entered widened out into an obvious tunnel. They found themselves standing up now in its strange, fetid warmth. Justin listened again, putting his ear to the surface of the rock wall. There was absolutely no sound at all, nor any vibration.

He reached into his pocket, removed a flashlight, and switched it on.

They were standing on a rocky surface that had been hollowed out of the mountain. The narrow-gauge railroad that Abigail had mentioned was at their feet. The ties that held the tracks firm were hewed out of old logs. The sides of the tunnel were jagged and unfinished, as if the work had only been begun.

"Justin!" cried Irene.

"Yes!"

"Someone's been here! Look!" She bent over and held a paper in front of the flashlight for Justin's examination. It was the developing paper from the back of a Polaroid print. Proof that indeed Raymond McGuin had been in this tunnel—even if he was here no longer.

"What's that?" Justin cried, turning his head.

"That" was the sound of two shots from outside the entrance of the tunnel.

Justin began running back for the entrance. "It's a trap! It's—"

The ground under their feet shuddered as a tremendous blow struck and a landslide covered the tunnel entrance. Justin pulled back, grabbing Irene's arm and holding her. Dust flew up in front of them. What had happened was fairly obvious. More rocks had fallen down into the entrance.

After about forty seconds, the noise ceased. Dust roiled up. Justin shone the flashlight ahead of him. The entrance that had appeared at the top of the rock wall was no longer there. They were sealed in.

Saul Brody was astounded to see Justin Birkby, a man he considered normally intelligent, suddenly vanish into the hole at the top of the slide. Then he realized that Irene Manners had vanished, too, presumably into the entrance ahead of Justin.

Brody ran up the slope, drawing his weapon. It was an instinctive gesture. He had no idea what was going to happen. He knew that it was foolish to explore a site in which a dangerous criminal was holding a prisoner. Yet at the same time, there were peculiar vibrations in this affair that he did not understand; he did not know from one minute to the next who was on whose side. Even if he had known, it would not have eased his anxiety any.

He peered into the hole and glanced around.

Quite suddenly he thought he heard the sharp click of a rock knocking against another rock somewhere uphill from where he stood.

Instantly he crouched, pulling himself down into the rocks about him, making himself as small as he could. Someone was up there, waiting.

He picked up a rock shard and pitched it as far as he could to the right of the slide. It ticked as it landed. Instantly there was a loud explosion of a handgun. Brody could see the flame up above him on the hill.

He fired at the point of light.

"Merde alors!" came the sound down the slope. At least that was what it sounded like to Brody. He had never studied much French, except in high school, but he knew what it sounded like. Jesus, he thought. The Frenchman was up there, ready to cut down all three of them.

And then, shaking the mountainside as it came, a new slide pounded down on him from above. Right from the spot the voice had sounded.

Saul Brody ran back the way he had come, pulling behind a sturdy pine tree. The slide thundered for a half minute, and then stopped. The French son of a bitch had sealed the two of them inside!

Brody could hear a click somewhere in the distance, a click and a voiced curse, a rock falling down the cliff, a footstep, and then finally silence.

He waited ten minutes. There was no further sound.

Brody studied the slide. Too much had fallen down. He'd have to get help to unseal the two of them. A trap. That's what it was. And the three of them had walked right into it! Could Brody free them before they ran out of oxygen?

The air was stifling inside the tunnel. With the dust flowing down on them, it was almost impossible to breathe. Justin was coughing and sneezing, and Irene was vainly trying to clear her throat.

"Back farther!" Justin wheezed out. "Away from the dust."

They moved along the narrow-gauge tracks, Justin's flash showing them the way.

"Were those shots?" Irene asked.

"We've been set up," Justin said, not even bothering to answer her. "It's a very neat trap. Just the kind of thing Yves DuBois-Maison is famous for!"

"You think it's him!"

"I haven't the slightest doubt."

"We've got to get out of here!"

Justin laughed mirthlessly. "Indeed we do."

The dust was less cloying in the rear of the tunnel. They sat down to rest. Justin could feel the heaviness of the stale air about them, air that had not circulated for months and perhaps years. The two of them were perspiring freely now. Justin realized his heart was beating fast—not only from the high altitude that he was not used to, but also from the lack of fresh oxygen in the sealed tunnel.

They simply could not last long here.

At least Justin had been right in his analysis of the Lucky Strike. He had said that they would not find Ray McGuin there. If it was any consolation, he had been right about that. They had not found Ray McGuin; instead they had found a neat little trap, ready to snap shut on them.

"Keep alert!" whispered Justin to Irene. "Don't let yourself doze off. You'll never wake up!"

Ever so suddenly Justin was aware of a strange phenomenon. His neck was cold. His neck was wet with perspiration, and yet it was cold. What had changed the atmosphere? It was no longer fetid. It was—

"On your feet!" snapped Justin. "Stand up!"

Justin gripped the weapon he carried, lifted it, and pointed at the rear of the tunnel. There was someone there, someone approaching in the darkness, menacingly, threateningly. Yves Du-Bois-Maison? Obviously—to finish off Justin Birkby once and for all.

As soon as he could see him, Justin would fire. . . .

9.

"For you, Sarita," said Detective Sarita Giardino's partner, Detective Allan Dewars, holding the phone out to her across the desk in the detective bureau.

"Hello?"

"Detective Giardino?" a woman's voice asked hesitantly.

"This is she."

"Thank you. I am Mrs. Raymond McGuin." The voice was stronger now, and Sarita could hear the pure Bryn Mawr accents coming across loud and clear. She tried to hide her surprise. "Yes, ma'am?" she said awkwardly, and she could have kicked herself for reverting to preliberation diction and inadvertently assuming, even if she did not feel it, the fawning attitude of a member of the servant class.

"We have a serious problem," Mrs. McGuin ventured. "I had hesitated to inform the police, but now I feel I must. We need your help."

"In what way?" Sarita asked, holding the phone close to her ear and grabbing up a pencil. About time! she thought. It was pretty obvious that *something* had happened to Ray McGuin. Now she'd know.

"I'm afraid my husband—Raymond McGuin—has vanished."

"Vanished?"

"I mean he disappeared Friday afternoon late and I haven't heard from him since. We have received what we think is a ransom note, however—and a threat."

Sarita hesitated. "Mrs. McGuin. You're in Aspen. I'm afraid Denver P.D. has no jurisdiction over crimes that take place in Aspen."

"You don't understand," Abigail McGuin said quickly. "Mr. McGuin was last seen in the Humboldt Building late Friday afternoon. Am I not right in assuming that you do have jurisdiction over his disappearance, inasmuch as it seems he was kidnapped there in Denver, not here in Aspen?"

Sarita agreed and asked for the details, at least as Mrs. McGuin knew them. She scribbled down the facts as her caller outlined them briefly—the postcard, the Polaroid, the Tarot card, the million-dollar ransom, the site of Jimson City, Friday night.

"Why weren't we informed earlier?" Sarita asked, her tone stiff and unyielding. "It's terribly difficult to come in so late on a case! Here it is Friday already!"

"My fault," Mrs. McGuin admitted softly. "I was afraid there might be adverse publicity—"

"Publicity is not the business we are in here at Denver P.D.," Sarita said, trying to keep her voice neutral.

"I'm sorry. I realize that. It was what happened last night that decided me."

"And what was that?" Sarita asked, her pencil poised.

As Mrs. McGuin spoke on, Sarita's eyes widened and she began scribbling rapidly.

At the McGuin mansion in Aspen, Abigail hung up the phone and stared across the breakfast table at Saul Brody. "She thinks

I've forgotten all about the way they bothered Ray during the Scanlon investigation. I haven't." Abigail's eyes were hard.

"What's the next move?" Brody asked, his eyes hooded and observant.

"She'll be out here this morning later."

"Are you sure that's a good idea?" Brody wondered. "I told you she met with Inspector Birkby in downtown Aspen. I've got a feeling she knows a lot more than we think she knows."

"I don't believe Inspector Birkby would tell her anything that wasn't absolutely necessary."

Brody shrugged.

"Now! We must get ourselves together here and be ready to receive the police when they come."

"The two of them still asleep?" Brody nodded his head toward the guest suite.

"Possibly. I thought I heard a shower five minutes ago."

Brody leaned back and gave a huge sigh. "It was touch and go there last night," he said nervously. "I tell you, I thought they were goners—and I even thought I was!"

"You shouldn't have gone!" snapped Abigail. "It was a foolhardy expedition!"

"Not necessarily so," Brody said. "If we'd *found* Raymond—"

"But you didn't. You only found where he *had* been!" Abigail's eyes were angry. "And you're no closer to finding out who has kidnapped Raymond than you were before!"

"Don't point at me," Brody said with a smile.

"Well, the inspector," said Abigail.

"No. But we do know *part* of the cast. The man who shot at me spoke French. And Inspector Birkby is positive that man is a terrorist agent known to Interpol and an old enemy of the inspector's."

Abigail pursed her lips grimly. "I don't like any of this! I'm looking at everybody I know as a suspect. I mean, trying to figure out who hired this terrorist to kidnap Raymond!"

Brody's eyes narrowed. "Maybe you *should* be looking at everybody slantwise."

"That's a crude way of putting it!"

"It's a crude world out there, Mrs. McGuin."

"You don't have to play the boor to impress me, Saul!"

"Sorry."

"I don't mean to attack you!" Abigail said softly, reaching over and gripping his wrist. "If it hadn't been for you last night—"

Brody lifted his shoulders. "Look. That was one of the first ghost towns Mr. McGuin and I explored. None of the town is even left. It's just that railroad tunnel. I shouldn't have agreed to take the inspector there."

"Forget the *mea culpas*," Abigail sighed. "They never get you anywhere."

"Lucky I read that book out of the Aspen library," Brody said. "I mean, I never would have known about the air hole the workers put in after the two blasters died of methane gas."

Abigail shivered. "It was smart of you to find the vent and remove the rocks that covered it. But I begin to shake when I think how close you came to—"

"The inspector's no amateur with a gun," Brody said softly. "He didn't shoot when he heard me coming. I don't know but what I might have, in his place. He held his fire until I was visible to him." Brody stared at Abigail. "That's what differentiates the amateur from the professional."

"Well, you got them out. I'm only sorry they had to go through that ordeal. It wasn't even necessary."

"I disagree," Brody said. "It *was* necessary. It made you see the need of telling the police what's going on."

Abigail ran her fingers distractedly through her hair. "I do hope you're right. All I want is Raymond back safe and sound."

"I think you've a better chance now than before."

"Perhaps."

Brody turned toward the door. It opened and Justin and Irene came in. "Do I smell coffee?"

Abigail smiled in relief. "You bet you do. Sit down! We'll join you in a second cup."

Refreshed by a tasty ranch breakfast prepared by Abigail's skilled drop-in cook, Justin and Irene excused themselves for a short sojourn in the garden.

"We want to compare notes," Justin told Abigail. "We're approaching the climax of the case. With the police visiting us, I want to be sure my thinking is in the clear."

"What he really means," Irene countered, "is that this is the time he loves to point out how illogical my own logic is. I go through this every time we work together!"

Justin reached into his pocket and removed a pack of three-by-five cards, checking to see that he had them all. Then he nodded and he and Irene walked out into the garden.

"You've told me about the blackmail scam Raymond McGuin was involved in. I don't quite see how *that* ties in with his kidnapping," Irene said as they sat down to talk.

"A normal evolution, I guess," Justin suggested with a half smile.

"How so? Here's a successful blackmail operation in the works. Why should the blackmailer suddenly decide to go in for kidnapping? I mean, why should the blackmailer kill the goose that lays the golden egg? Figuratively speaking, of course."

"It's a very good point." Justin frowned. "I really don't know. I simply accepted it at face value, once I heard from Fixx that McGuin was paying off regularly."

"If there was an escalation from blackmail to kidnapping, something must have forced the change," Irene observed.

Justin sat up straight. "I simply haven't been thinking clearly. We *know* it's DuBois-Maison we're dueling with. If the blackmailing operation was still going on without opposition from Raymond McGuin, I have a feeling we wouldn't be dealing with a kidnapping right now. I'd guess McGuin must have balked at the blackmail routine. So, to follow a possible scenario, let's suppose that he indicates in no uncertain terms he *won't* pay any more money. The blackmailer immediately senses that his cushy scam has run its course. The blackmailer wants out, but with a bang, not a whimper. And so the blackmailer hires Yves DuBois-Maison, ups the ante astronomically, and effects, with the French terrorist's help, the interception of Ray McGuin."

"You feel the kidnapper *is* the blackmailer."

"The *hirer* of the kidnapper, if we assume the kidnapper to be DuBois-Maison, is the blackmailer."

"That brings up the hard question. Who hired Yves DuBois-Maison?"

"You've definitely dropped the idea that DuBois-Maison is in this on his own?"

"I never thought that," Justin explained quietly. "An outsider like DuBois-Maison would never have taken up a kidnapping in a foreign locale—all on his own. No. He's definitely working *for* someone—someone who is directing him in the drama. Ghost towns! DuBois-Maison probably never *heard* of a ghost town until he got mixed up in this."

"So? Who hired him?" Irene was smiling indulgently.

Justin turned quickly on her. "I want your input, first."

"I'd select Abigail McGuin. She admits she's penniless without McGuin's money. Judging from her attitude, she wants out of a rather dull and boring marriage. Plus which, I'll bet she's carrying on with Brett Allenby."

"But what's the purpose of the kidnapping? If McGuin's company gets up the money, she pockets it—but for what? I mean, what doesn't she have already?"

"It gives her a stake to work out whatever she wants to with her husband. A separation. A divorce."

Justin shrugged. "I read it almost the same way as you, with a slightly different twist. I see the key person as Brett Allenby. I see him as the one who hired DuBois-Maison. I see him as the one extracting the ransom money from the company and putting it eventually in his own pocket. I see him orchestrating a leveraged buyout of Assistance Anonymous to accumulate a great deal *more* money. I see him then walking into the sunset arm in arm with Abigail McGuin."

"With Ray McGuin watching at the picture window?"

Justin smiled diabolically. "You have forgotten the one active ingredient that makes my theory superior to yours. You have forgotten the fact that Yves DuBois-Maison is not at all above bloodshed. I foresee an intricate ransom sequence—with a so-called accident at the last moment. Some lethal misunderstanding. The victim? None other than Ray McGuin. Leaving Abigail completely free for Brett Allenby—and getting all his money in addition!"

"My God!" Irene had turned pale. "What a dreadful scenario!"

"Yes. A little bloodshed mixed in with the magic. What do you think?" He was challenging her now.

She took a deep breath. "How did DuBois-Maison actually kidnap McGuin? I don't understand that 'disappearance' on the elevator."

Justin shrugged. "There are many ways in which he could have done it."

"We have only the word of Saul Brody and Rosemary Gaitenby that the actual kidnapping occurred in the elevator. I'm wondering if the two of them—Brody and Rosie—might not be in this thing together. Don't forget, *they* could be blackmailing Ray McGuin."

"I see what you mean. With only Rosie as witness, DuBois-Maison puts a gun to McGuin's head as he rings for the elevator and takes him? With the details of the elevator disappearance—dependent on the testimony of Rosie and Brody—made up out of whole cloth?"

Irene sank back and closed her eyes. Then she sat up straight. "Let's see those cards you made up. Do you have one for Brett Allenby?"

"It just so happens I have." Justin handed over a three-by-five card.

NAME: BRETT ALLENBY. AGE: 55. BORN: PHILADELPHIA, PENNSYLVANIA. GRADUATE, PENN STATE. OPENED DIRECT MAIL BUSI-

NESS WITH RAY McGUIN DEALING IN INEX-
PENSIVE MERCHANDISING BY POST. COM-
PANY EVENTUALLY BECAME "ASSISTANCE
ANONYMOUS," A FUND-RAISING ORGANIZA-
TION. WAS FIRST TREASURER, AND THEN FI-
NALLY BECAME AN EQUAL PARTNER WITH
RAY McGUIN.

"Not married?" Irene asked.

"No record of it." Justin hesitated. "That doesn't mean he
wasn't married somewhere along the line. But it's not recorded."

"No rap sheet of any kind?"

"None."

"What about Mrs. McGuin?"

Justin flipped through those in his hand and pulled out one.
"I've been busy, as you can see."

NAME: ABIGAIL ASTOR McGUIN. AGE: 48.
BORN: SAN FRANCISCO. GRADUATED, BRYN
MAWR. MASTER OF ARTS: MILLS COLLEGE.
WROTE COPY IN ADVERTISING AGENCY IN
SAN FRANCISCO. WAS WORKING ON CAM-
PAIGN TO PROMOTE ASPEN, COLORADO,
WHEN SHE MET RAYMOND McGUIN. MAR-
RIED TO HIM FIVE YEARS AGO.

"Astor," said Irene. "Is she one of the *real* Astors?"

"I guess all Astors are real," said Justin.

"*You* know what I mean."

"All right. I do. In answer to your question, I have no idea."

"Got a master's at Mills," mused Irene. "I've heard of Mills.
Very high-toned women's college."

Justin was watching her with amusement.

"I wonder how she managed Bryn Mawr, coming from the
West Coast and all," Irene said.

"Have to ask her."

"I'm not going to!" snapped Irene. "I thought you might know."

Justin shrugged.

"What about Rosie the receptionist?"

Justin sifted through his deck and handed over another card.

NAME: ROSEMARY LYNCH GAITENBY. AGE: 32. BORN: DENVER, COLORADO. SECRETARIAL SCHOOL. RECEPTIONIST AT VARIOUS FIRMS. HIRED BY ASSISTANCE ANONYMOUS AS RECEPTIONIST. MARRIED TO AND DIVORCED FROM AN ELECTRICAL ENGINEER LIVING IN AURORA. HAS ONE CHILD.

"Not much there," said Irene. "Except, of course, she's a single parent. That means she might be interested in latching on to a husband."

"You can't always count on that," Justin said. "Suppose she felt she was burned by marriage. Suppose she's off men for good."

"How did she strike you?"

Justin considered. "Fairly normal."

"Then she's in the market," Irene said quickly.

Justin laughed. "We'll base your judgment on intuition rather than hard evidence."

"If you insist," Irene said frostily. "What about the chauffeur?"

NAME: SAUL BRODY. AGE: 39. BORN: KANSAS CITY, MISSOURI. GRADUATE KANSAS STATE, AT MANHATTAN. CAPTAIN OF TENNIS TEAM. TENNIS PRO IN LOS ANGELES, SANTA BARBARA. CHAUFFEUR TO PROFESSIONAL FILM WRITER IN SANTA BARBARA. AFTER TANGLE WITH WRITER OVER HIS WIFE, MOVED TO ASPEN, COLORADO, AND GOT JOB WORKING FOR THE McGUINS.

"A little hanky-panky with a film writer's wife?" Irene said with a smile. "He sounds interesting." She blinked. "Actually, he *looks* interesting. There's something there that's just kind of— you know—waiting. He's in pretty good shape for thirty-nine, too!"

Justin shook his head with resignation. "What do you want to do next? Check out his sex life?"

Irene giggled. "Don't be so smart! Still, he does have a past with surprising nuances in it. I wouldn't put it past him to involve himself with someone like her—not so much for what she is, but for *where* she is. He could be feathering his nest on the inside and the outside at the same time!"

"Irene!" Justin sighed, quirking an eyebrow. "You certainly do have an active imagination about the human animal!"

"Come on, now! Chauffeurs, tennis bums, pilots, and bored wives have become a cliché in fictional romance. Don't you think liaisons occur frequently? And what about Brody and Abigail? Don't you think they'd make a fitting pair?"

"I'm not saying it couldn't happen," Justin protested. "But somehow I feel Abigail is just a cut above your average bored Lady Chatterley."

Irene glowered at him. "You've been fascinated by that accent from the moment you heard this woman on a transatlantic telephone. Admit it, darling!"

Justin shrugged.

"Let me see that private detective. Mitchell Fixx."

NAME: MITCHELL FIXX. AGE: 49. BORN: BOULDER CITY, COLORADO. WORKED IN DENVER POLICE DEPARTMENT FOR FIFTEEN YEARS, BEFORE RETIRING TO BECOME A PRIVATE INVESTIGATOR. WAS INDICTED ON A CHARGE OF BRIBERY, BUT WAS NOT RELIEVED OF HIS LICENSE. WAS SHOT ONCE IN AN EXCHANGE WITH A DRUG MERCHANT IN AURORA. NO OTHER ARRESTS.

"A gem in the rough," said Irene with raised eyebrows.

"Very streetwise," Justin said noncommittally.

"You're using him to deliver the ransom money to Jimson City?"

Justin nodded.

"What do you think of him?"

"I don't know quite what to think. I do know he was well aware of my own shortcomings. I had to hint at things, and he was quick to take up the hint. He knows I *don't* know as much as he knows."

"How did you play him?"

"As obscure as I could. He knows I'm a foreigner. I didn't hide anything. I can only guess what he might think I am. Probably he's not far off the mark."

"But he's willing to cooperate?"

"Oh, sure."

Justin pulled out another card. "Denver P.D. gave me the background on her. As well as on Fixx. It was in the file on the Scanlon case." Irene took the card and read it with interest.

NAME: DEIDRE FINLEY SCANLON. AGE: 46. BORN: DENVER, COLORADO. WORKED AS FILE CLERK AT SEVERAL COMPANIES IN DENVER. MARRIED DUSTY SCANLON TEN YEARS AGO. NO CHILDREN. IS FIRMLY CONVINCED THAT RAY McGUIN KILLED HER HUSBAND IN THE FALL FROM THE HUMBOLDT BUILDING.

"Have you talked to her at length?"

"No. I have never met her face to face. She was waiting in the other room when I talked to Mitchell Fixx."

"How do you know?"

"I simply got the feeling that Fixx was speaking a little louder than ordinary. I felt it might be for the benefit of someone else. I had noticed the second door the first thing I entered his office. Later, I saw Deidre Scanlon leave the building with a man."

"What man?"

"This man," said Justin, handing over another card.

NAME: HAROLD SCANLON. AGE: 51. BORN: DENVER, COLORADO. HIGH-SCHOOL DROP- OUT. JOINED WORK GANG—HEAVY CON- STRUCTION. LATER BECAME FOREMAN OF WORK CREW ON HIGHWAY MAINTENANCE GANG. JAILED SEVERAL TIMES FOR DRUNK AND DISORDERLY. MARRIED, DIVORCED, THREE KIDS. HANGS OUT WITH CONSTRUC- TION-CREW TYPES, DRINKING AND CAROUS- ING.

"So this is Dusty Scanlon's brother," Irene observed.

"Right. Rough and ready."

"He sounds so."

Justin smiled. "I think he and Deidre get along fine."

"Hanky-panky?"

"No, no. I mean, I think they're both getting as much mileage as possible out of Dusty Scanlon's death. If you know what I mean."

"I do." Irene looked up at Justin for a long moment. "Could *they* be the blackmailers?"

Justin put the three cards back into the pack he carried and inserted them into his jacket pocket. "They most certainly could be. I haven't been able to verify their bank accounts. They live in the opposite of luxury. But you never know how shrewd some people can be—at hiding money, I mean."

Irene nodded. "I didn't need these three added suspects any more than you did, you know."

Justin shrugged philosophically. "John Webster said it, not me."

Irene flinched, but smiled gamely. "What?"

" 'So who knows policy and her true aspect / Shall find her ways winding and indirect.' He might be working on the same case we are." Justin smiled faintly.

10.

Shortly after eleven a cab from the Aspen Cab Company drew up in front of the McGuin mansion and two people got out, paid their fare, and approached the entryway. Justin Birkby recognized one as Detective Sarita Giardino. Her companion he had never seen before. He was a huge man with a round smiling face and brown hair cut only slightly long. At least six feet four, he made his companion's height of five feet ten appear almost minuscule.

Detective Giardino introduced herself to Abigail McGuin, and then her partner as Detective Allan Dewars to Justin, Irene, and Abigail.

"My superior, Sergeant Ron Volare, has given us the case," said Sarita to Justin as soon as the group had moved into Raymond McGuin's "office."

"If you'll all excuse me," said Abigail suddenly, "I'd just as soon have nothing to do with any of this planning. I feel that the less I know about this the better."

Justin stared at her.

"If you need any information from me," she hastened on, flustered now, "just call me. I'll be within reach."

Detectives Dewars and Giardino exchanged glances, and Sarita nodded. "All right, Mrs. McGuin. I understand."

The four of them set themselves up in the chairs available and Justin presided behind McGuin's desk, which had been cleared for the occasion. He reached down and removed two folders from an attaché case leaning against the right-hand front leg of the desk.

He laid them in front of him in the center of the desk and patted them possessively. There was a very thick file on the bottom, and a fairly thin one lying on top. Justin removed the thin file and riffled through it.

"Profile on Yves DuBois-Maison," he said in explanation.

Sarita frowned. "And who is he?"

Justin smiled, ignoring her question, patting the thick file that lay on the desktop. "File of the Emile Perigord case."

Sarita understood. "Your most famous case." Then she tumbled. "Aha! It was Yves DuBois-Maison who kidnapped Emile Perigord! Was he ever apprehended?"

Justin shook his head. "That's what I'm here for."

Stewart's brown eyes were intent on Justin. "You think the kidnapper is this Yves DuBois-Maison?"

"Indeed I do."

"But why?"

"His modus operandi. And other evidence."

"But why would a Frenchman be involved in a kidnapping here in the United States?" Dewars asked.

"Because the case may have international ramifications," Justin said, sounding a bit lofty and pretentious even in his own ears.

"Has this anything to do with the Scanlon case?" Sarita asked quickly.

"It's my impression that the Scanlon suicide may have been exactly what Denver P.D. thought it might be—murder. Or at least to all intents and purposes, no matter how Scanlon's death was accomplished."

Sarita was looking over the thin file. Dewars was still staring at Justin.

"Interpol, through me, has asked for the assistance of Denver P.D.," Justin went on smoothly. "You tell me that your superior, Sergeant Volare, has given you carte blanche—at least within reason. Mrs. McGuin has decided that she needs help in wrapping up this case of unlawful detention of the person."

"The person being Raymond McGuin."

"Exactly. The kidnapping of Raymond McGuin."

Dewars picked up the thick file and hefted it without looking inside. "And this is the Emile Perigord kidnapping file?" he asked. "With information on this Yves DuBois-Maison's M. O.?"

Justin nodded. "I want you two to read through that file on the Perigord case. It's a classic of its kind. But DuBois-Maison's M. O. is the most important part of it. There's no need to go into all the details. You'll see them in the file. The man is a natural-born conjurer. He makes things appear to be something other than they are. He deals in distractions to shield actions."

"How can we help at this point?" Sarita wondered.

"By setting a trap for the kidnapper. Interpol has a red notice out on him. That means he's to be picked up immediately on sight."

"If we are not present at the exchange of the ransom and the kidnapper, how can we—?"

Justin tapped the thick file that Dewars had laid down. "The two most important elements of Yves DuBois-Maison's modus operandi are the opening gambit and the endgame—if I may put it that way."

"You may," said Sarita. "I'm a certified chess buff."

"DuBois-Maison has adhered to his profile in the opening gambit. The kidnapping of Ray McGuin is a classic magician's trick. I have to infer that he will stick to his profile in the endgame. That is, his getaway will parallel his previous getaways."

Sarita flipped open the huge file and looked helplessly at

Dewars and then Justin. "What is it particularly about the get-away?"

"It is not necessarily the manner in which it occurs, but the *time* at which it occurs."

Dewars raised an eyebrow.

"The Perigord case is a good example. The payoff—the exchange of money for the kidnap victim—occurred in Paris. Specifically, it occurred at an indicated area in the Bois de Boulogne —a woods to the west of the city."

"I've heard of it," said Sarita.

"But"—Justin held up his forefinger—"the kidnapper's getaway occurred at the Gare du Nord, the rail terminal in the Tenth Arrondissement in the city."

"And?"

"The payoff took place at five in the morning. *And* the getaway at exactly the same time! Five a.m.!"

"But how—?"

"—did the kidnapper get the ransom money? He sent an accomplice to the Bois de Boulogne to pick up the money at the appointed hour. While all attention was concentrated on the woods, the kidnapper calmly bought a ticket for Brussels at the Gare du Nord—in another part of Paris miles away. Using a physician's beeper, the accomplice signaled the kidnapper that he had picked up the ransom; the kidnapper then boarded the early morning train unnoticed. Too late to put up roadblocks, you see."

"Was Mr. Perigord released before the kidnapper went to the railway station?" Sarita asked.

"No. He was allowed to work his way free following the kidnapper's departure from the hiding place—less than a block and a half from the Gare du Nord. By the time the kidnapped man made himself known, the kidnapper was well on his way to Belgium."

Dewars nodded.

"The ingeniousness of the kidnapper is evident in the misdirection he applied. While attention was focused on the *collection* point, he was making a smooth getaway in another part of town!"

"And you think he's going to follow the same pattern this time."

"Why should I doubt it?" Justin asked with a smile. "Denver is the obvious getaway point. From Denver one can go in any direction one pleases. By air. By train. By bus."

"By car?" Sarita suggested.

"Roadblocks could hinder a car," Justin protested. "And, unless it's stolen, a car can be traced by credit card rental and license plate."

Dewars was working this out in his mind. "Your guess is that he'd go by public transportation?"

Justin nodded. "Until he's out of the danger zone."

"And the time to cover?" Sarita wondered. "I mean, when is the time of the exchange?"

"Midnight tonight."

Sarita riffled through the pages of the thick report. "You think Yves DuBois-Maison has engineered this whole kidnapping?"

"I am fairly certain of it. Enough to put my reputation on the line," Justin said slowly. "Besides that, I was able to ascertain last night that we seem to be dealing with someone who speaks French—like a native."

Dewars and Sarita exchanged glances and both stared at Justin.

"Now as to exactly how you can both help me."

Dewars said, "Shoot."

"As in the Perigord case, I intend to cover two disparate sites —the escape site and the exchange site."

"And the exchange site is—?" Dewars asked.

"Jimson City. The ghost town."

"I see!" Dewars grinned.

"He's the best mountain man on the force," Sarita said. "You couldn't have a better man."

"Detective Dewars, if you'd volunteer—"

"I'd love to! It's perfect!"

"You're on. Jimson City. I'll need you to observe Jimson City for two individual purposes. One. I want you to oversee the delivery of the ransom money."

"You're not going to have me deliver it?"

"I have already arranged for an associate of Raymond McGuin's to handle that. He's a private investigator named Mitchell Fixx."

Sarita and Dewars looked at each other. "We know him," Sarita said.

"He was on the force here, you know," Dewars said.

Justin shook his head. "Yes, as a matter of fact, I did." Justin frowned. "Well, since we're this close to the end, I suppose it won't hurt to explain a bit more. Mitchell Fixx has been acting as go-between for Mr. McGuin for almost a year."

"Go-between?" Dewars repeated.

"Blackmail, Detective Dewars," said Justin. "Blackmail which has escalated into kidnapping."

"You said there were two assignments for me," Dewars reminded Justin.

"Right. Two. I want to insert a direction finder in the ransom bag. You'll be out of sight at the delivery of the ransom money. And you'll be out of sight when DuBois-Maison's accomplice picks it up. After he leaves, you'll follow him back to where Raymond McGuin is being held."

"The ransom money. You want me to check it once it's been delivered?" Dewars asked.

"Yes. It's not that I don't trust Fixx, but—"

"Standard operational procedure," Dewars interrupted.

Sarita smiled.

"Meanwhile, I'll need other operatives to cover all the main exits from Denver. Railroad station. Airport. Bus station. You understand?"

Sarita Giardino nodded. "I'll handle one. I'd say the railroad station is too predictable. Chicago and New York would be the obvious targets. And then transfer to the East Coast for a flight to France. Once on the train, it would be easy for us to phone ahead and get out an all-points bulletin to arrest him. So he wouldn't want to risk that."

"Good point. Airport?"

"Possible. And yet I rather like the bus depot. Because it's a little less likely somehow. But I understand the problem. We'll cover them all."

"Remember," Justin said. "This man is a slippery character indeed. He could appear as a soldier, a marine, an air force officer, a policeman, even. You have to remember that he could be *anything*—even a woman."

Sarita smiled.

"Mrs. McGuin will remain here in Aspen. Irene and I will be going to the Denver Hilton. We'll be staying in the Raymond McGuin suite there. If anything comes up and you need to get in touch with me, I'll be there."

"What about the ransom?" Sarita asked.

"That will also be dispatched from the Hilton." Justin turned to Detective Dewars. "Have you ever operated a direction finder?"

"Yes. In a car. But this is going to be interesting. I think I may be on foot this time." He grinned. "That's a new one!"

Justin nodded. He hoped Dewars would be smiling as broadly in the early hours of the following morning.

"Oh, one other thing," Justin said slowly. "Don't take any chances with Yves DuBois-Maison. He's a wily man. He's a tricky one. He's quick and he's smart. But the main thing he is is dirty. He's a killer, has killed a number of times. Take absolutely no chances. Don't be a hero. Heroine." Justin paused. "Understand?"

"Yes, sir," they said in chorus.

Sarita swept up the files and rose from her chair. On the desk under the files lay a line drawing of Yves DuBois-Maison that had come out of the folder. Justin saw by Sarita Giardino's face that she was too stunned even to speak.

"Detective Giardino?" he prompted her.

But Detective Dewars had also come to life. "The Wendy's killer!" he cried.

"Exactly!" Sarita gasped, picking up the Interpol drawing and studying it more closely. She read the description below it, checked the color of the eyes, the build, and the accessory data.

Rapidly she outlined the details of the murder of the homeless man behind the Wendy's in northwest Denver—a murder which apparently had occurred late Saturday night. As she continued, Justin's eyes widened, and he made rapid notes on his pad.

"What'll we do now?" Dewars wondered.

"Simply follow the scenario we've agreed on!" Justin said promptly. "We'll get him!"

The two Denver detectives stared at him, wondering if he had lost his mind. How could he be so *sure?*

At precisely five o'clock an armed guard brought the million dollars to the McGuin suite at the Denver Hilton, and minutes later Justin and Irene were laboriously counting it out. It was all there—every dollar.

Detective Dewars appeared at six and spent some time planting the miniature transmitter in the underside of the valise, checked it for function, and pronounced it satisfactory. He then disappeared.

Later, at ten o'clock, Mitchell Fixx showed up to collect the money for delivery. He was dressed in rough-and-ready wear, and Justin discerned a bulge at his waist where a gunbelt might be buckled on.

After being introduced to Irene Manners, Fixx politely remained silent as Justin showed him the valise and the money.

"It's all there?"

"Every penny of it! We'll hold you fully responsible."

Fixx grinned, his pumpkin face beginning to glow. "It's a snatch, ain't it?"

Justin said nothing.

"I mean, this isn't just another blackmail delivery!"

"You're right. It's a kidnapping."

Fixx patted his waist. "Thought so. I'm prepared."

"You're not to precipitate trouble," snapped Justin. "Just carry out the orders. Deliver that money where it's supposed to go."

"Gotcha."

"No heroics."

Fixx lifted his hands, palms out toward Justin. "Just one of us chickens, boss!"

"Good." Justin stood up and shook hands with the private detective. "Good luck."

Fixx picked up the valise and moved toward the door.

"Oh," said Justin. "You'll be watched, of course."

Fixx turned and eyed him slyly. "Figures. A million bucks—that ain't hay. Right?"

"Right," said Irene.

Fixx glanced at her with a hard stare and then he was gone.

11.

At ten thirty a sleek lime-green Alfa Romeo bounced along the winding roadway that led to what had once been the main street of Jimson City. At the wheel was a woman and at her side a man. They were both quietly surveying the scene of the ghost town as they had been surveying the roadway all the way up from Silver Plume. Both had been to Jimson City before, acquainting themselves intimately with the terrain and its man-made artifacts.

The woman now drove the Alfa Romeo into a clump of trees off to one side of the meadow that led up to the ghost town. She pulled the car into the brush and parked it where it was obscured from view. For a moment she sat there with it idling and then switched off the lights and the engine.

Together the two listened to the deep silence.

All the night sounds that had died with the arrival of the automobile and its two occupants gradually resumed. The man and the woman continued their sharp surveillance of the meadow and the ramshackle silhouettes of the buildings on the slope.

"I'll cover you," said the man, turning to the woman.

She nodded. "Here I go."

Once out of the sports car she closed the door as quietly as she could, and she stood with her hand on top of it. Then she gestured in farewell to the man and started moving out of the cover of the brush.

It was dark, of course, but in the clear night air the stars glinted dangerously bright. The immense hulking shadow of Gray's Peak loomed high before the millions of stars brilliant in the sky against the emptiness of the universe. The night animals continued to make their cries heard, until the woman came near them, at which point they refrained from their noisemaking, only to resume after she had passed by.

She was moving jauntily now, swinging her arms, feeling perky, almost unreasonably jubilant, full of herself. It was working still, she thought, working well against all odds. Who would have thought that Raymond McGuin would deliver so carefully, so completely, so guilelessly?

In the middle of the vale she turned once, looking back at the clump of trees behind which the Alfa Romeo and the man with her were hidden. It was a necessary precaution. She had once thought of driving right up to the main street of the town, climbing out, grabbing the bag, stowing it in the trunk of the car—then driving off as easily as greased lightning.

Nevertheless, there was always the possibility of—

Whatever, she thought, and stopped thinking.

She could see the dim outlines of the buildings, now, recognizing instantly the target—the one with the big gaping window hole in it. She was humming under her breath in a kind of euphoric ebullience as she crossed the weed-choked street and made for the front of the structure.

The broken sidewalk creaked and strained as she stepped onto it. She put her hands on the broken siding and leaned over the edge, looking down at the floor of the shack. She reached in, groping. Where was the carry-on? Where was the money?

She straightened. Christ! She fumbled for her tiny flash and snapped it on. It was like a lightning bolt. Everything for miles around seemed to go brilliant white. She poked the beam down into the interior of the ancient building.

The carry-on was not in place. Had the damned fool mixed up the signals? What in hell——?

She strode down to the next building, flashed the light inside it. Nothing. Leaning against the ancient siding, she looked over toward the clump of trees.

"It's not here!" she hollered.

"It's got to be!" the man's voice sailed across the night.

"I'm telling you——"

Out of the blackened silhouette of the trees came the sound of crashing brush. Then quite suddenly a figure emerged. The woman could see the man striding decisively across the meadow —now in plain sight.

She did not hear a sound, but she was stunned to see him fall flat on his face, uttering as he did so a sharp cry of pain.

"I been hit!" he yelled in agony.

"What in hell?" the woman cried, moving quickly across the main street, hurrying toward the man.

But he had his handgun out now. She could see the bright line of flame as he fired into the night—at the side of the slope behind the ghost town, actually. And then, almost instantly, he cried out again. She thought she saw his body jump from the ground and settle back, this time limply.

"Keep down!" he shouted. "Keep down!"

She was running now, disregarding his warning, running toward him. And her leg caught fire.

"Jesus!" she screamed.

She pitched onto the ground. She had not heard the sound of riflefire, but she had felt its result. And she was close enough to the man now to crawl over toward him.

"God, it hurts!" she gasped. "It *hurts!*"

"I'll get him!" cried the man, lifting his weapon again and firing twice somewhere into the darkness.

And then she could hear the sound of something harsh and dull smacking into him. He went back, his face arched up, staring at the stars in the sky.

Then he lay still.

She reached out for the gun he had dropped. Another sliver of light lashed out from the darkness of the hillside. She saw it and she aimed at it and fired the man's gun again and again. And as she fired she felt the hammer of the rounds as they entered her chest and shoulder and head—

But by then she could feel nothing, could sense nothing, could only fall forward on her face in her own blood and lie there without motion.

A shadow detached itself from the silhouettes of the ramshackle huts that were Jimson City. The shadow was that of a man; he carried a rifle, from which he removed a long silencer as he walked. The barrel was warm in his hands as he hefted it in perfect balance at the point where the trigger guard was mounted.

He strolled over to the meadow where the two bodies lay. There was enough starlight to see them clearly now. He looked first at the man, prodded at the body. It rolled over, lifeless. The woman seemed to be breathing, but that was only illusion. She, too, was quite dead.

The man with the rifle looked across at the clump of trees. He had seen the Alfa Romeo drive in there some minutes before from where he was holed up on the hillside waiting.

Now the rifleman laid down the weapon he carried and leaned over the woman's body. Quite effortlessly he lifted her from the ground, hoisted her into a fireman's carry, and walked carefully over to the line of shacks ahead of him. Moving cautiously, he passed between the walls of two shacks and came out behind them on a rising slope of ground.

Within thirty yards he had come to an open hole in the ground, the entrance to a long-abandoned silver-mine shaft. The shaft was inclined gradually, but within ten feet it plunged downward in an almost vertical direction.

The rifleman gently laid the woman's body on the steep incline and gave it a push. The body started to roll, hesitated, and then finally plunged over the rim of the shaft and vanished from sight. He listened as rocks and gravel rained down in the distance.

In ten minutes he had the man's body in the abandoned mine as well. He had a harder time persuading the body to roll, but he succeeded finally, and listened as it plummeted down into the darkness of the mine shaft.

Then all was still.

The rifleman walked off across the slope to the main street of the ghost town, strolled into the field, and picked up his rifle. He turned and moved off in a northerly direction. He moved fast and straight.

Mitchell Fixx glanced at his wristwatch and allowed a pumpkin-eater's smile to appear on his face. It was five to midnight. He had almost perfectly timed the difficult drive up the winding road to Jimson City. He could see the shacks in the distance where the headlamps of his Chevy pickup limned them in the night.

He turned to glance at the carry-on in the passenger's seat next to him and patted it affectionately. A million bucks! It was the nearest he would ever come to that much cash—in this life, at least.

The Brit was all business, he thought somewhat erratically, as he maneuvered the jeep in the meadow, and turned it around so he could get a good start over the bumpy road after he had delivered the money.

He reached for the carry-on. A mill, he thought covetously. So close, and yet so far! He hoisted it clear of the gearshift and bounced it across the driver's seat into his arms, and began the walk toward the main street of the crumbling ghost town.

Something was wrong.

He could *feel* the wrongness in the night. He laid the carry-on down on the ground. He had a small pocket flash and snapped it on. The line of shacks appeared in the distance, exactly as they had appeared in the picture on the postcard Justin Birkby had shown him. He could see the building he was supposed to leave the money in.

Yet something was definitely wrong!

He picked up the carry-on again and started across the field toward the street itself. He thought he heard a sound in the distance—behind the row of shacks—but after a moment he was sure he had imagined it. And he kept on, headed for the open window space that identified the building where he would leave the carry-on.

He stepped over the broken wood that had once formed the ghost town's sidewalk and turned on the flash again. Everything was disreputable and dried out, as most ghost towns were. He put the carry-on down and leaned through the window space. Then he reached out and lifted the carry-on, which he set down on the flooring below the window.

Funny. He thought—

With the beams of the flashlight he explored the interior of the shack, but saw nothing amiss. Finally he turned and started off across the field toward the car. As he walked, he suddenly began to speed his pace. Something was telling him to get out of there —and he was paying attention to that small voice.

He had never before felt so unnerved, and he had done this job at least ten times. Why the unease? he wondered.

He was sweating by the time he reached the car. With trembling hands he opened the door and climbed in, putting the flash in the dashboard compartment. Then he flicked on the ignition. The dash lights came on.

The engine turned over perfectly.

Fixx remained frozen, staring fearfully at the floor of the car.

The dash lights outlined his right shoe brightly. It was not the shoes, but the cuff of his slacks that caught his attention. Something damp. Dew? Hell, there was no dew up this high in the Rockies—not at this time of the year! Moisture . . .

He reached down and touched his cuff, bringing his finger fearfully up toward his face to identify the source of the moisture.

Reddish brown. My God—

Blood?

Fixx stifled a scream. He switched off the motor, opened the door, and almost fell out of the car. He was absolutely frozen with terror. Blood! Where had he gotten blood on him? He had only walked to the shack and—

Good Lord! he thought. Blood. Death. It could be that there had *already* been bloodshed here, even before he had arrived. He remembered the British chief inspector's mention that he would be "watched." Had the kidnapper come early and killed the watcher in order to ensure his escape with the million dollars? Had the watcher double-crossed the Brit and killed the kidnapper or maybe even McGuin for the million dollars?

Anything could have happened! The thing for him to do was to play it as cool as he could. And yet there was no sense being a nerd about this. He had risked his life to bring a million dollars in blood money to this very spot. Wouldn't it be marvelous if he could end up with the money? If the scam had wound up like the last act of *Hamlet* and everybody else was dead, he might be able . . .

No. He saw suddenly what *might* have happened. Two animals could have gotten into a fight in nature's continual struggle for survival of the fittest. Fixx had brushed by the carcasses on his way across the field. That was all there was to it. And that meant that everything about the ransom was A.O.K.!

Immediately came relief. But he was still trembling from the aftermath of his terror.

Taking deep breaths to keep from hyperventilating, Fixx climbed back into the Chevy pickup and turned on the ignition. In a moment he was out of there.

As he rambled down the roadway, he wondered why he had suddenly panicked tonight. He had done this job before, with no consequences whatsoever. Why was he so undone tonight?

He grinned. Odd. That was all. Odd.

He called the Denver Hilton at a pay phone.

"Mission accomplished," he told Justin Birkby.

"Anything to report?"

Blood on my cuff, damn you! thought Fixx.

He said nothing. Merely chuckled. "Nothing out of the ordinary."

"Good," said Birkby.

Fixx detected a note of puzzlement in the Brit's tone. Did *he* know something Fixx didn't know? he wondered.

What in hell was going on here anyway?

Fixx got back in his Chevy pickup and considered. He had done his job. He could go back home. He'd be paid what the Brit had promised him for services rendered. And he could curl up and go to sleep happy in the knowledge that he had made an honest buck for a change.

Or he could shake the dice he held in his hand and see how it came up. Craps? Boxcars? Or a lucky seven-eleven?

By the time the engine had caught, Fixx knew what he was going to do. After all, he didn't want to live the life of a loser all his years, did he? Better a dead winner than a live loser.

Somehow, that didn't seem to make much sense, did it?

Fixx grinned and made a U-turn in the highway.

12.

In the Denver bus terminal at 19th and Arapahoe streets, Detective Sarita Giardino picked up her soft hold-all and moved leisurely from the magazine stand where she had spent the last five minutes looking over the current crop of periodicals. She walked by the line of people purchasing bus tickets and scanned each one carefully.

It was ten thirty-five now. So far she had not seen anyone resembling the face and physical measurements supplied in the Interpol profile Justin Birkby had given her. And yet, somehow, she felt that soon enough her own logic would justify the selection she had made in posting herself at the point where the action would take place.

Of course, she could be dead wrong.

As she passed the line she hesitated, frowned, as if she had just thought of something, and turned to retrace her steps across the length of the terminal. Then she found a place on one of the benches, slung her hold-all to the polished floor, and sat down again.

These were crucial hours—just before midnight—and the lines had to be monitored carefully. If, of course, Justin Birkby's deductions were on the nose and not a wide-ranging miss. She rather thought he was on target.

She had studied the profile of Yves DuBois-Maison in the thin folder Justin Birkby had given her very carefully, memorizing the salient physical features of the man in question. And then she had gone through the extensive file on the Perigord kidnapping case.

In the end, she came to the very same conclusions that Justin Birkby had come to: that the kidnapper would indeed make his getaway at precisely the moment the exchange would be taking place. And that escape site would be Denver—either Stapleton International Airport, Union Station at 17th and Wynkoop streets, or the bus terminal—all of which were now covered by detectives from Denver P.D.

She had studied DuBois-Maison's picture for hours, until she had memorized all the main features of the man's face. She remembered Justin Birkby's advice: "He could be a soldier, a marine, an air force officer, a policeman, even. You have to remember that he could be *anything*—even a woman."

She considered that latter possibility carefully. He was not a bulky man, but he was tall and slender. He could certainly be dressed as a woman—and could pass for one.

The tension became unbelievable. By quarter to twelve Sarita was the next thing to a basket case. She rushed into the ladies' room and checked her holster and .38 Colt automatic. Everything was working fine. The rounds were ready; the mechanism was well oiled. She stared at herself in the mirror, wriggling her shoulders a bit to settle the shoulder holster. She still managed to look as if she had broken all her ribs and was bandaged from the waist up in a body stocking.

At five of twelve she was pacing back and forth, studying each person who entered the terminal.

And then she saw him.

He did not actually resemble the picture she had in the file, but the features of the tall slender rancher *seemed* close enough to justify a match. Trying to keep her eyes hooded, she looked at him again more carefully. He had blue eyes—and that was in line with the description. He had graying hair that had been brown. DuBois-Maison was black-haired—but that could be browned easily.

He had made himself up to resemble the typical rancher familiar to the Denver area. String tie, a neat little southern touch. He had on a soft white ten-gallon hat, with a brown band around it. In the band were stuck some fishing flies. He had a fancy belt with a huge silver buckle and a lot of Indian ornaments—beadwork, metal, and tooled leather—holding up his jeans. And cowboy boots, too—well-worn and scuffed.

"Ticket to Chicago," he was telling the woman selling tickets.

Sarita held her breath. The man had certainly boned up on his accents. He sounded absolutely authentic—there was no French accent there at all. There was *nothing* out of the way. Sarita would swear he was native-born and native-bred.

"When's the next bus to Chi?" the man asked.

The ticket seller told him something.

He grinned and sauntered out into the terminal.

Sarita was right behind him. Yves DuBois-Maison. Denver Police. You're under arrest! She had those words in her mind and was about to speak them when—

The priest who had just purchased a ticket at the window behind the rancher turned around. His eyes met Sarita's. They were gray. His face was relaxed, without makeup, half-smiling.

That was Yves DuBois-Maison! *He* fitted the description even more than the rancher!

Sarita was stunned.

She looked at the ticket he was holding. His eyes took note of her interest. Quickly he turned, so that she could not see his expression. The ticket she saw as he wheeled around was to Salt Lake City, Utah.

What the hell would a priest be going to Salt Lake City for? Of course, there were Catholic missions there—but they were few and far between. Even Protestants not of the Mormon faith found it difficult to flourish in Utah.

She turned. The rancher had sauntered over to the magazine rack and was fingering the girlie magazines. The priest was moving unconcerned toward the men's room.

"Police!" Sarita shouted, pulling out her .38 and holding it in her hands, pointing it directly at the priest's back. "Don't make any sudden moves! You're under arrest! Turn around—slowly—and—"

The priest hesitated, turned slightly, and then smiled at Sarita Giardino. "I don't understand," he said slowly. "Are you speaking to me?"

"You bet your life I am! Keep your hands in sight!"

"Certainly." He *did* have an accent! she thought with relief. "You're under arrest!" she snapped.

"But I am only a simple priest," said the man, smiling blandly.

"Sure you are," said Sarita Giardino sardonically.

"Father Esteban De Nieve," the priest went on.

"Anything you say may be held against you," she said, forgetting the wording of the Miranda warning, and then thinking: What the hell, *he* doesn't know it word for word either!

She had the cuffs on him in seconds.

Then she was on the phone.

"Who hired you?" she asked the priest as the two of them sat in the waiting room, the man's wrists cuffed. "Or was this your own bright idea about how to pick up a little extra cash?"

"Pardon?" He smiled again. "I think you make a big mistake. I am Father Esteban De Nieve."

"Oh, sure. And I'm the Madonna with Child."

He shrugged. Oh, he was French all right, Sarita thought. Nobody but a Frenchman could put such a feeling of tragedy and defeat into a tiny, ordinary gesture.

TRANSCRIPT OF TELEPHONE CONVERSATION MONITORED 2 A.M. SATURDAY, JUNE 19, BETWEEN DETECTIVE ALLAN DEWARS AND CHIEF INSPECTOR JUSTIN BIRKBY:

DEWARS: The package has not been picked up. Repeat. Not been picked up.

JUSTIN: It's intact?

DEWARS: Exactly as delivered close to midnight.

JUSTIN: Any sign of trouble?

DEWARS: I knew you expected action after midnight. When it did not occur, I walked down to check the package again. It had not been moved. On my way across the field I noticed two areas where the weed grass had been flattened. *Two.* I made a wider circuit of the area and discovered to my surprise that someone had driven a car in and hidden it in a cluster of trees across the field.

JUSTIN: What make?

DEWARS: Forget makes. It's a rental. I looked inside.

JUSTIN: Who rented it?

DEWARS: Who do you think? "Bert Jones"!

JUSTIN: Where *is* the driver?

DEWARS: Missing. I used my light and began to search the grass more closely—especially where the indentations were made. I found blood.

JUSTIN: Blood!

DEWARS: Dried blood. As near as I could make out, two people were apparently shot or knifed in those spots. I began a more intensive search and found occasional drops of blood on the grass, indicating that one of the victims at least had been carried—or had moved on his own— through the ghost town and up the hill behind.

JUSTIN: You're sure?

DEWARS: Yes. Unless someone is playing games with us. Let me finish. I traced the path of blood up the hillside to an old abandoned mine shaft. It's a dangerous hole. It goes into the hill on a slight downslant, but then rapidly turns vertical. I found blood inside the shaft, too. If the victims—I'm assuming there are at least two— were dumped there, it'll take a lot of work to get the bodies up out of the bottomless pit.

JUSTIN: If there *are* two.

DEWARS: I think one's a man, and the other's a woman. I found a tissue with lipstick on it on the car floor. Also a pair of dark glasses in the dashboard compartment. They're a man's— cheap convenience-store stuff, probably untraceable. Oh, and there's a bunch of unstained cigarette butts in the slide-in ashtray. I'd guess a man and a woman are the victims.

JUSTIN: I'll telephone your superior.

DEWARS: Never mind. I've contacted him already. A crew's on its way.

JUSTIN: You're reasonably certain this isn't just a blind trail?

DEWARS: What can I say? Somebody could have caught a jack rabbit and dropped blood all over the grass for me to find. Honestly, I don't know.

JUSTIN: Go back to the ransom bag.

DEWARS: Yes, sir?

JUSTIN: Check it for content.

DEWARS: My God, you mean—

JUSTIN: Do as I say. Quickly.

DEWARS: The money's gone. The transmitter's there.

JUSTIN: I see.

DEWARS: I was conned by that blood! It's only a blind—

JUSTIN: Perhaps not. Remain in place until your associates arrive.

DEWARS: I was suckered!

JUSTIN: We all were.

Statement Made by Raymond Standish McGuin, June 19:

I, Raymond Standish McGuin, declare under oath that this is the true and accurate account, from inception to completion, of my imprisonment for ransom by a person unknown, from June 11 to June 19.

On June 11, a Friday afternoon, I entered the elevator in my penthouse suite in the Humboldt Building in Denver. There was a man in the elevator, and when it began to descend, he squirted a tiny spray gun at me. I recognized him instantly as a man I had seen following me around town. I lost consciousness immediately. I have no idea what kind of nerve gas he used, but it was very effective. When I awoke I was as sick as a dog from the drug and was trussed up in the back seat of a car. I struggled upright and looked out the rear window. A small boy was out there in the dark. I tried to scream, but I realized my mouth was taped shut. I think the sight of me frightened him.

When my captor returned, I slumped back, pretending to be asleep, and he drove on. I lost consciousness again and when I came to, I was inside an abandoned silver mine I recognized instantly by the narrow-gauge railroad in it as the Lucky Strike. I was tied hand and foot and propped up against a rock wall. My mouth was still taped.

The man from the elevator was there with me. He was middle-aged, and spoke with a decided accent, which I believe was French. He was gray-eyed, black-haired, with little ears, and a sharp nose. He was rather debonair looking. He treated me with respect. He told me he had nothing against me, that he had been hired to kidnap me, and that it was not personal at all, but just business. He refused to explain further. He went out once a day to procure food for us. He said he used fast-food places so he would be lost in the crowds.

He eventually took off the tape so I could talk. He told me a man and a woman had hired him to kidnap me. I knew who they were. They had been systematically blackmailing me for a year now. They wanted him to arrange a kidnapping so they could get enough ransom to start new lives in another country.

I am ashamed to say I had been lured into an affair with the woman—a sordid liaison. Once I tried to break it off, she was infuriated and threatened to expose me. I was terrified the truth might get out. I agreed to pay her ten thousand dollars. She upped the ante to fifty. I paid it.

And I *continued* to pay it! Month after month.

She would send me a postcard of a ghost town each time, with a code message on it, instructing me where and when to leave the money. I followed her instructions faithfully, using a hired investigator, Mitchell Fixx, as go-between. The payoffs went on for about a year.

I suppose she felt she was not squeezing me hard enough. She and her accomplice apparently hired the Frenchman to kidnap me for a final payoff of a million dollars. I assume the woman or the man got the Frenchman's name through the international underworld.

On Tuesday, I believe it was, the woman came to the railroad tunnel and took a Polaroid snapshot of me holding the morning's *Denver Post.* I assume it was delivered to poor Abigail.

I think it was Thursday night when the woman arrived in a panic, had a spirited conversation with the Frenchman out of earshot, and then vanished. Without a word to me the Frenchman sprayed me with the nerve gas again, and when I came to, hours later, I discovered I was in another abandoned mine shaft —one I didn't recognize. The Frenchman admitted that the Polaroid had identified the Lucky Strike mine to Mrs. McGuin and that I had to be moved immediately to prevent discovery. The Frenchman had tried to seal the mine, but apparently had failed.

Nor was all going well between the blackmailers and the kidnapper. Early on Friday morning the Frenchman came storming back into the mine with something to eat for us, raving in French about a "double cross," as close as I could figure it. When he could calm himself enough to translate into English, he told me his employers had cut his payment in half. Expenses were mounting up.

He said he had threatened them with exposure, but they simply counterthreatened him—they knew he was on American soil with a false passport, etc., and they would blow the whistle on him.

My hope was that this "falling out among thieves" might cause them to relax their guard on me and enable me to escape. But it was not to be.

On Friday night the Frenchman told me that as soon as the ransom money was delivered and he got his cut he would return and set me free. Then he drove off in the car.

He never came back.

I managed to work my wrists free and finally got out. It was almost dawn when I walked out of the mine and found myself on a hillside in the wilds, having no idea where I was.

I started down the slope, and found myself on familiar ground —the ghost town of St. Elmo. I had visited it many years before. There was a store there. I immediately telephoned home. Within an hour I was in police custody.

I have given this statement of my own free will.

[signed] Raymond Standish McGuin

Further the deponent sayeth not.

As Justin Birkby and Irene Manners watched the early dawn break to the east of Denver they ordered breakfast from room service. Nothing had gone right. There were surprises galore, some that seemed beyond credibility. How had Justin managed to be so far from the truth?

There were two corpses, apparently, at the bottom of a mine shaft in back of Jimson City. Who were the victims? How did they get there? Who killed them?

As they slowly began to eat their breakfasts, Justin and Irene began to talk it out. It was Irene who started to assess the situation.

"It was *not* your fault, Justin, that two people were killed at Jimson City. I don't know why you have such a guilt complex about it."

"I should have *known* about them. Besides, I still have no idea who they are!"

"The blackmailers! The blackmailers who hired Yves DuBois-Maison to kidnap Ray McGuin! You've got that in McGuin's statement. Don't you see? It was the Frenchman who double-crossed them and took the entire ransom—instead of settling for a flat payment."

"Where *is* Yves DuBois-Maison?" Justin asked after a long moment of silence. "The person picked up in the bus terminal claims he's only a simple priest—Father Esteban De Nieve."

"He may well be," said Irene. "Isn't it within the French ter-rorist's bag of tricks to be *not* where you figured he would be making his escape from Denver, but perhaps back at the ghost town picking up the ransom and making off with it? Misdirection, you call it."

Justin flipped through the written statement Ray McGuin had made to the authorities on his escape. "At least Ray McGuin came out of it without a scratch. Of them all, he was the lucky one!"

"The problem now is to determine who actually *hired* DuBois-Maison. I think it's the blackmailer. Or blackmailers, as we now know them to be. Who do you think they are?"

Justin shook his head. "I have absolutely no idea." He reached over and pulled the thin file on Yves DuBois-Maison toward him and leafed desultorily through it. It was a gesture of defeat, a marking of time, an avoidance of thought. He saw the file number at the top of the packet. "DM-143." It was typed on a slip of paper and inserted into a plastic tab. For a long time Justin re-mained transfixed. Something was jogging his memory. Some-thing buried in his subconscious was stirring to be let out.

Then he had it.

"Of course!" he said as he leaned back with satisfaction. "When you look at it *that* way, there's only one possible solution that fits all the facts!"

"You know who kidnapped Ray McGuin?" Irene asked, her eyes wide.

"More than that. I know *why* he was kidnapped!"